## Chapter One

# FAREWELL TO ISTANBUL

Prince Ibrahim Ibn Sa'd leaned back on the raised cushions in his boat as its four oarsmen propelled it down the Bosphorus towards the Golden Horn. From time to time he let his hand trail idly in the water as he reflected on the letter he had received earlier that day from his uncle, King Muhammed XI, more customarily known as Boabdil of the dynasty of the Nasrids, King of Granada, the last remnant of an Iberian empire that had once stretched to the Pyrenees, and even well beyond. How different a saga from that all around him, where Islam was so triumphantly in the ascendant and where only some thirty years before, in 1453, it had seized the erstwhile capital of the Eastern Roman Empire, the city of Byzantium, the former Constantinople, from the enfeebled hands of the last of the Byzantine Emperors. Here, Sultan Bayazet II, the Sword of Islam, Avenger of the Faithful, ruled over one of the mightiest states of his time, one that glittered fabulously in a constellation of states where the great cities of Italy, the Christian Papacy, the newly united Iberian kingdoms of Castile and Aragon, Portugal, and the nascent nation states of England and France, pulsated alternately with internecine conflicts, corruption and vaulting ambition.

It was more than five years since he had first arrived in Istanbul, sent by his uncle as Envoy Extraordinary to the Sublime Porte, the Sultan Bayazet, the most powerful monarch in the known world. Prince Ibrahim had then been only twenty-two years old, but his selection was only partially due to the privilege of birth and his close blood relationship with the king. His own parents had died while he was still in very early childhood: his mother in giving birth to his sister, Ayala, three years younger than himself; his father killed campaigning against the Castilians in one of the unending desultory wars between the Moslem kingdom of Granada and the powerful neighbouring kingdom of

1

Castile, now linked dynastically to that of Aragon, and bent of the reconquest of the entire Iberian peninsula. The occasional truces between them were little regarded, and Granada lived uneasily in the shadow of the permanent menace from the north. As a result of the death of both his parents, he had been attached to the Alhambra school, immediately adjacent to the royal palace, famed throughout the Islamic world for its teaching, but where he had also received, on his uncle's direct instructions, a rigorously martial and military upbringing. As he grew older, he had found the royal will concerning himself ever more difficult to comprehend. King Boabdil was a man of considerable culture, but of nonchalant, libertine disposition, little given to arduous exercise and seldom known to have held a weapon in his hands, save only on purely ceremonial occasions. The only explanation that seemed to make any sense was that the King believed it to be his duty in memory of his dead sister, Ibrahim's mother, and her husband, who had been an outstandingly successful soldier as well as a scholar of some distinction. But if this was indeed the case, he never spoke of it to his nephew and, indeed, saw him but seldom. And then, suddenly, he had dispatched him, as if on the spur of the moment, with no particular diplomatic instruction or message, as envoy to the great Sultan in Istanbul. He had arrived there, bearing gifts of rather a modest nature, chosen by King Boabdil in person, on an Egyptian trading-ship. The Sultan, a massively built, hawk-eyed and heavily-bearded man, in his prime, admired by the entire Islamic world, a conquering hero to all his followers, had received him kindly. The modesty of Granada's gifts did not appear to have offended him.

He could see the landing-stage now, at the bottom of a sharp incline that led up to the wide plateau with the great mosque, the former Christian basilica of Saint Sophia, built by the Emperor Justinian, and reputed to have been in its time the grandest of all Christian churches. Close to it they were building the slim minarets pointing skywards in a mason's tracery of elegance and grace that would mark the spot of the Bayazet mosque, still under construction, but already hailed as one of the wonders of the age and a glowing symbol of the overwhelming, irresistible onrush of the Green Banner of Islam. Soon he would have to leave it all behind him: the glory, the power, the deep sense of triumphs past and triumphs to come that pervaded Istanbul.

Prince Ibrahim had adopted the style and mode of dress of the conquerors of Byzantium, the Ottoman Turks, with their passion for vivid colours and the grandiose. Confidence seemed to pulsate through their veins and sparkle in their eyes. The letter he had received from his uncle or, to be more precisely accurate, from his uncle's Grand Vizier, had been cast in a very different mould. Drawing the letter from one of the deep pockets in his golden kaftan, he reread it once more. There, the message was one of grim foreboding and of the imminence of war against huge odds. It had long been known that Their Majesties of Castile and Aragon had sworn on the altar of their Christian God, on the day of their wedding, to drive the infidel out of all the Spains, and to re-conquer the kingdom of Granada, the last surviving remnant of the once great Moslem Iberian peninsula. His uncle had written to tell him that the efforts being made by the Christians to bring to an end the struggle between King Ferdinand and Queen Isabella and Isabella's half sister, the Princess Juana, supported by some as the rival and more legitimate claimant to the throne of Castile, and assisted, if obliquely, by the King of Portugal, seemed to be close to success. If confirmed, this would mean that Ferdinand and Isabella would be free to concentrate all their forces for an assault on Granada. The border forays would turn into a full-scale war, with as its aim the outright annexation of Granada by the Spanish sovereigns and the forced expulsion of all its Moslem inhabitants. King Boabdil had ordered his immediate return to Granada, before proceeding to the court of the Spanish kings, where he was to lead a Granadan delegation with, as its mission, the avoidance of war and the preservation of an independent Granada. Prince Ibrahim shook his head in silent dismay; it was hard for him to see what he could contribute to, or achieve in, such a mission. While he spoke Castilian with reasonable fluency, he had had little or no contact with the kingdoms of Spain or Portugal; and while he felt that he had undoubtedly matured and learned a great deal during his years at the Ottoman court, this was a very different world from that of the Frankish West.

He had yet to inform the Sultan of his recall, who was in any case unlikely to be much concerned. Once or twice, admittedly, the Sultan had, in a half-musing tone, spoken of a campaign in the West, a return to the old concept of a westwards thrust against Christendom, with Morocco as a base and crossing over from there into the kingdoms of Spain and so on into France to avenge, finally, the defeat of Islam at the hands of the Frankish king, Charles Martel, some six centuries before. But latterly these musings had not been repeated and it had become evident that the Sultan had in mind objectives and designs nearer to home that aimed rather at the conquest of southern Greece, Hungary and even Vienna, the prestigious capital of the Hapsburgs and the Imperial House of Austria. There were occasional rumours of movements of men and of plans to devastate the Balkan lands and to repopulate them with

Anatolian peasants, thus simultaneously resolving the problems of overcrowding in Anatolia and securing a loyal and dependable population in that part of the European landmass that the Sultan coveted in order to ensure the safety of Istanbul against any surprise attack from the West. Although regretting the Sultan's lack of interest in a Western front, Prince Ibrahim approved his strategy. Austria was a formidable foe, and there could be little doubt but that, faced with a growing Ottoman threat, other European powers would be tempted to march to Austria's assistance. The Sultan would be ill-advised to divide his forces and so dissipate his strength; but the immediate and stark corollary was that the little kingdom of Granada would have to look to itself, and itself alone, for its salvation.

The boat was approaching the landing quay. Prince Ibrahim stuffed his uncle's letter back into the recesses of his kaftan and waited as they drew up alongside. On the quayside all was bustle and activity. Hawkers were selling fish, huge water melons, sweet cakes and sherbets in a sweltering riot of bodies, close together, sweating, and swaying to and fro as if in a breeze that did not, however, exist. There were piles too of pistachios, of figs and dried prunes, of spices in a kaleidoscope of colour. One fat woman was loudly smacking her lips, cackling words of gross obscenity as she peddled her rich store of aphrodisiacs. A little way further along were snake charmers and water carriers in bright red tunics, carrying goatskin bags full of water that they sold by the cupful to the passers-by. Sometimes a holy man, naked except for a white loincloth, with glazed eyes and an unsteady gait, would shout out unintelligible words, before falling to his knees to praise Allah and call on all those around him to follow his example. Quite a large number did so, leading to muttered curses from the throng of massed humanity as they tried to struggle past them.

Price Ibrahim leapt ashore and thrust his way through the crowds. The heat was intense and the pungent smell of the huge mass of humanity around him singularly unpleasant. He would have to seek an audience of the Sultan to inform him of his uncle's instructions and to beg his permission to leave Istanbul. He did not think it would be difficult to find a passage; if absolutely necessary he might even charter a vessel, although the coffers of the Granadan embassy in Istanbul had not been replenished for close on two years and were running perilously low. Granada's gold, he had been informed, was needed for more dire and immediate purposes than fitting out the embassy to the Sublime Porte. But perhaps the Sultan might be prepared to help.

Turning aside from the thronged quayside, Prince Ibrahim clambered up the steep incline, clutching occasionally at some of the dense spiky shrubs to steady his balance. Superbly fit, it did not take him long to reach the top.

Leaving the great mosque to his left, he walked quickly to his own residence, a small former Byzantine palace near the quarter of the main foreign embassies and graciously placed at his disposal by the Sultan. He nodded nonchalantly at the guard at the entrance and shouted to Samuel, his head servant, to come to him as he entered the palace.

The palace, like the majority of old Byzantine buildings that had been preserved, had a high perimeter wall, with a massive metal door that was generally kept shut. When opened, it revealed a narrow and short, but brightly lit, corridor that led to a first inner courtyard with two fountains and four oleander trees in brilliant blossom and giving off a fine scent. Taking a glass from a small marble table that stood to one side, Prince Ibrahim drank slowly, savouring the refreshing coolness of the water.

Samuel appeared, silently as always. Of Jewish origin, he had come to Granada with his father, a trader in oil, when he was only six years old. The family had stayed but his father soon fell into debt; he had been imprisoned and his son sold as a slave. Prince Ibrahim had liked his appearance: strong, bold and outwardly unemotional, and had purchased him on the spot and later brought him in his personal train to Istanbul. Now some forty years of age, he had proved to be a faithful servant and Prince Ibrahim looked upon him in many ways as his closest confidante.

Prince Ibrahim sat down slowly on one of the long low couches, covered in yellow silk, that in daytime in spring, summer and early autumn were scattered around the courtyard, except in the hottest periods, when they were brought inside at night-time.

Prince Ibrahim, although rigorously enforcing obedience and the observation of proper rules of address by his servants, could, on occasion, adopt a gentler and more personal approach. He had done this quite frequently with Samuel and, this time too, motioned to him to come and sit close by him. Samuel bowed low before taking his place.

'I will give you a letter to take to the Grand Vizier without delay,' he said quietly. 'I have been instructed to return to Granada and we shall leave as soon as I have the Sultan's permission to do so. You will of course accompany me. Will you be glad, Samuel, to go back to Granada?'

'I will of course be with you, my lord,' he answered, with only the lightest stress on the first four words. 'Where you go, I will follow, That is my fate. It cannot be otherwise.'

'But you will be pleased to return to Granada, to see your father and the rest of your family? These have been good years here in Istanbul – for me certainly, and I believe for you also?'

Samuel gave a fixed smile. 'I have known peace, my lord. Comfort too, of course, in this beautiful palace and this city of countless enchantments. Here one can believe in the magic of the thousand and one nights, in the tales of Scheherezade, in a return to the days of the Abbasid Caliphate, in djinns and spellbinders. But above all, I have known peace. It is strange, my lord, is it not, that it is a place where Islam has reached its highest pinnacle that I have been able to be a Jew without fear and without shame?'

'But that is true in Granada also, Samuel. Granada allows all its inhabitants freedom of worship and religion.'

'That is true, my lord, in Granada. But the distance is small from there to the neighbouring kingdom of Castile and there a great menace is lurking for all of my race. I, too, have followed the news from Spain. It is not difficult to predict what will happen once the internal struggles in the Spains and Portugal will have come to an end.' And Samuel drew his right hand quickly across his throat.

'I think sometimes, Samuel, that you read my thoughts before I have begun to open my mouth. Like you, I fear that dark days lie ahead for us, for Moslems as well as Jews, for if Granada falls there will be no room for either of us. My uncle wishes me to go to the Spanish court, as ambassador, to delay, if at all possible, the inevitable. May Allah be my guide.'

'I do not believe, my lord, that you have met Their Majesties of Aragon and Castile,' said Samuel in an affirmative rather than a questioning tone. 'I have some contacts with my father's merchant friends of old in the Spains, men who outwardly have adopted the trappings of their Christian overlords. Some of them have met both Queen Isabella of Castile and King Ferdinand of Aragon – Their Catholic Majesties as they would wish to be called. I understand that among the merchants there are few who hold out much hope for the survival of an independent Granada.'

'And on what do they base this view?'

'On their direct and indirect knowledge of the aims, intentions and, above all, the religious convictions of both sovereigns, but of Queen Isabella in particular. Do not forget, my lord, that the kingdom of Aragon faces north. Its preoccupations have been, and still may be, protecting its domain from encroachments by the French. France is, and I think has always been, greedy for land, gold and the acquisition of might. It is insatiable and has the ability with its manpower and wealth of natural resources to sustain a policy of virtually permanent external aggression. Aragon has already suffered at the hands of the French and King Ferdinand will not, my friends believe, readily or easily forget this. But Queen Isabella has a far greater vision, of almost epic proportions.'

'Epic,' repeated Prince Ibrahim incredulously. 'How do you know these things, Samuel? Are you so privy to the secrets of Their Majesties?'

'Not I, my lord, but my father still has many contacts, even now. You should not forget that he was once a very highly reputed merchant and extremely well connected. I do not need to tell you that all Jews are men of business, of trade and commerce. Business can only flourish if it is served by good intelligence. Now many of his friends write to me.'

'And what do your informants tell you that we do not know? Queen Isabella has made no secret of her ambitions.'

'It is one thing, my lord, to know your enemy's ambitions; it is another thing altogether to know the extent of his determination, of his capacity for war and of his willingness, if so forced by circumstance, to compromise.'

'And your informants, Samuel, have told you all these things,' said Prince Ibrahim in surprise, but no longer as incredulous as before.

'I do not lay claim to miracles of knowledge, my lord, but I can assure you that our network of communication and information has no rivals among us Jews or, indeed, in their Christian world. We have, you see,' Samuel added with a sudden bitter twist to his voice, 'needed it so much more. But we have special reason to study Their Majesties of Spain. Their bridal oath was not just for the re-conquest of all the Spains, their *Reconquista*, but also for the cleansing of Spain of all infidels and non-believers. It began with a requirement that all Jews should abandon their faith and embrace Christianity. The alternative was banishment, exile and the despoliation of all their land and property. Most Jews took the easier route and recanted, accepting Christianity, outwardly at least. Inwardly, I am happy to say, they remained in almost all cases true to the faith of their fathers. Latterly, however, Queen Isabella, at first half tolerant of the *conversos*, has become hardened towards them. They are now depicted as depraved, cowardly, despicable wretches, having neither the blessed purity of the Christians nor the courage of their infidel faith. As such, they are not worthy to be allowed to stay in Spain. To help separate the pretenders from the true converts, Queen Isabella has restored the Holy Office of the Inquisition, with at its head Fra Tomas de Torquemada, formerly Prior of the Dominican monastery of Santa Cruz at Segovia. It seems he has wasted no time in getting down to his task. Those whose conversion is regarded as genuine are left in peace and, indeed, there are many highly-placed *conversos* in both Castile and Aragon. But for those who fail the test, and most often the names of their accusers or of those who testify in secret against them are not revealed, pay an awful penalty. I cannot tell you how many *auto-da-fe* there have been so far, but my informants have told me of at least four. At the last, at the *quemadero* in Seville, not far from the borders of your own kingdom of Granada, my lord, nearly thirty people perished in the flames.'

'I am sorry for your people, Samuel,' said Prince Ibrahim quietly, 'but this is a matter between Christians and Jews.'

'Indeed it is,' said Samuel equally quietly, 'and I do not tell you this to seek your sympathy for my people, but to show you the implacability of your future enemy. Queen Isabella is a remarkable person, a woman of high intelligence and with a powerful will. It was she who determined that she would marry Ferdinand of Aragon. That she lusted after him physically is no doubt true; he is an exceptionally handsome man of great courage and considerable intellect. But it is Queen Isabella who is the visionary. It is she who by her determination united the Spanish crowns. It is she above all who is bent upon Granada, and it is she who will try to give reality to the Spanish dream that seeks at its supreme moment to attain to the re-conquest of Jerusalem and the unfurling of her royal banner over the church of the Holy Sepulchre. She, my lord, is indeed a formidable foe. Your embassy to her court will not be easy, for nothing short of the unconditional surrender of Granada will satisfy her.'

Prince Ibrahim sat in silence. He knew from past experience that Samuel was no idle dreamer or teller of tales. He had often been surprised at his servant's range and depth of knowledge, but this was the first time that Samuel had spoken so openly of the source of much of his intelligence. That the odds were stacked heavily against him, and against the survival of Granada, Prince Ibrahim knew only too well. But he had hoped, and still hoped, that the bait of gold, combined with intrigue, might win time. It was Granada's only card. Who could tell what might not come to redeem the situation? A renewal of the internal conflicts within Spain or between Spain and Portugal? A new threat of a French invasion or renewed incursions into Aragonese Rosellon? Or even the consequences of the victorious onrush of Islam from the East as Sultan Bayazet moved towards Vienna? Prince Ibrahim did not doubt the accuracy of his servant's analytical portrait of Queen Isabella, but he would not, *must* not, share in his predisposition to defeat. He thrust the notion from him. Defeat was the hallmark of Samuel's people. Their history and their diaspora had conditioned them to it. But for those of his own religion defeat was unacceptable and should be unthinkable. Much once-Moslem-held territory in Spain had admittedly been lost, but there was a triumphant counterweight in the East.

'We will talk of this again, Samuel,' he said at last. 'I value your information and will not forget what you have told me. You will, I hope, be able to accompany me to the court of Their Majesties of Spain. They will scarcely dare to instruct Granada on the acceptability of members of its embassy. Wait for me here and I will come and give you my letter to the Grand Vizier. I will ask him, if at all possible, to let you have an immediate answer to my request for an audience of the Sultan.'

Prince Ibrahim rose quickly from his silken couch and went from the first into the second large courtyard; here again there was an elegant fountain with boxes full of flowers in a riot of colours, but mostly red, yellow, orange and crimson. At the end of this second courtyard a wide sweeping stairway led up to his personal apartments in the palace. Here, too, the original Byzantine decor had been retained, with thick Anatolian carpets and furniture of oak that an earlier Byzantine prince had had imported from Germany or England.

Seating himself at his customary writing-desk, Prince Ibrahim picked up his quill and began to write his letter of farewell to the Sultan, explaining the reasons for his departure, asking his permission to leave, and seeking his blessing for the enterprise of Granada. Signing the letter with a flourish he took it down in person to the first courtyard where Samuel was still sitting, his eyes closed, as if waiting for a sign. Prince Ibrahim shook him gently by the shoulder and handed him the letter. Samuel nodded obediently, rose and, after respectfully saluting his master, walked quickly towards the palace stables.

Prince Ibrahim returned to his apartments. The day was drawing slowly on. Looking through an open casement he could see the blue waters of the Bosphorus below him, sparkling still in the mid-afternoon sun. He would miss this glorious city enormously. It was, for him, the hub of the Mediterranean world and it belonged now to the people of his own faith. True, the same could be said of Granada, but unquestionably beautiful though his native city was, it was beset by fear, by searching nervously for compromise, and by uncertainty about the morrow. Somewhere, somehow, a spirit of resolution would have to be found or generated which could then be infused into all Granadans. As he looked, a squadron of six big galleys came slowly into view. He recalled hearing that a large fleet was being assembled to prepare for an expedition against the Knights Hospitallers of the fighting Order of St John in their island fortress of Rhodes. It was reputed to be virtually impregnable and there was no plan for a major assault upon it for the present. But the Sultan was intent upon giving the knights a taste of their own medicine and the expedition's aim was to ravage the island and, where possible, engage and destroy the Order's fearsome galleys, known, feared and respected as the finest warships of the age. The six galleys had only just been launched and were the largest warships in the Ottoman fleet. Prince Ibrahim watched them with pride as they glided past, their oars rising and falling in a slow motion tempo.

He was still gazing through the open casement, the six galleys long since lost to view, when Samuel returned. The Sultan, Samuel announced, had graciously consented to receive Prince Ibrahim that same evening, and would be pleased if he would stay for an evening's entertainment in the Sultan's private quarters in the Topkapi palace.

Prince Ibrahim felt his body suddenly glow with the news. Istanbul, he knew, had been an interlude in his life; agreeable, invigorating, inspiring even, but his audience with the Sultan would mark the end of all that. The next stage would be infinitely more exacting.

He chose his dress with care for the audience. The Sultan, a man of magnificent physique, had a passionate fondness for fine clothes and liked those around him to be equally well-attired. Silk, in particular, was much prized by the Ottomans and through the keen-eyed trafficking of Samuel, exhibiting in the process yet another of his seemingly innumerable talents, Prince Ibrahim had become the owner of a deep gold-coloured silken tunic with long wide sleeves slashed with emerald and sparkling with tiny jewels; it caught every light and sent the rays of the sun cascading round the room like streaks of lightning. A turban of a similar colour and long slender boots completed his attire.

Travelling in one of the palanquins placed at his disposal by the Sultan, Prince Ibrahim had himself borne quickly to the Topkapi palace. Although still far from being completed, it had already become the Sultan's favourite residence and it was here that he chose to spend most of his time when actually in Istanbul. Sultan Bayazet believed in action and in a strategy of rapid response. It was, consequently, a common occurrence for him with his personal escort of five hundred picked Janissaries to set out, with virtually no notice or advance warning, to various Anatolian cities or even, if persuaded of the need, as far afield as Antioch in Syria or to the Caucasian mountains.

At the gates that marked the entrance to the Topkapi palace, Prince Ibrahim was waved through by a junior Janissary commander, but only after he had alighted from his palanquin so as to go the rest of the distance on foot, as Ottoman court etiquette required.

The first area beyond the massive archway that marked the entrance to the palace had been laid out as a garden with shrubs and flowers of countless different scents and hues. A number of trees had been planted to provide shade from the sun, but these were still recent plantations so that the trees were still low in height and not yet fully able to protect the flowers from the blistering midsummer sun. To the far right there stretched the kitchens, while to the left, heavily screened and guarded by a platoon of magnificently accoutred Turkish guards, was the Sultan's harem, the home of his four legal wives and some twenty concubines. Prince Ibrahim paid no attention. Women had played little part in his life. Unlike the Sultan, or his uncle, he had up till then found little pleasure or assuagement in sexual indulgence. In this respect he took after his father for whom sexual and amorous adventures had held little attraction. When he thought about it, Prince Ibrahim dreamed of a girl who would be beautiful and gentle, able instinctively to understand his own longings and search for a meaning in his existence. So far, or so it had seemed to him, such girls were as rare as the lions of the Alhambra. His sister, Ayala, as he remembered her, was of that kind. It had been one of the few hardships of his stay in Istanbul to have been separated from her for so long. They had exchanged letters frequently, but many had been lost in transit for the sea-passage through the central Mediterranean was perilous.

The entrance to the second courtyard of the Topkapi palace was guarded by two platoons of Janissaries. Their commander, with whom Prince Ibrahim had occasionally crossed buttoned foils in one of the fencing-schools in the city, recognised him at once and waved him through without any of the customary and often tiresome formalities.

The principal audience chamber of the Sultan, on which some final decorative work was still in progress, was located in the fourth courtyard, the furthest from the entrance to the palace and on the edge of the plateau that overlooked both the Bosphorus and the Golden Horn. For less formal occasions the Sultan preferred to use various rooms that gave onto the third courtyard and it was to one of these that Prince Ibrahim was directed.

He found the Sultan leaning over a large square-shaped table pouring over a large-scale map of the kingdom of Hungary that lay immediately next and north to the confines of the Ottoman Empire. On either side of the Sultan were two giant mastiffs, while behind him, standing erect and with an air of absolute deference, stood some half dozen court officials. As Prince Ibrahim bowed low before him, the Sultan took him by the hand and pointed to the map in front of him.

'So, my lord Prince,' he said with a faint smile, 'you will not be coming with me to Vienna and are bent on returning to Granada. It is a pity. I venture to hope that our campaign will go well and that we shall be able to make these Hapsburgs in Vienna quake behind their walls.'

'Great Lord, there is nothing I would like more on this earth than to march under your Green Banner for the glory and triumph of Islam. Are you not the Avenger of the Faithful, the Sword of Islam, destined to smite all unbelievers and bring retribution to the Franks? But I am not free, Great Lord, to do as I would choose. As I have written to you, my uncle the King bids me return to Granada. There, Great Lord, Islam in under great threat and Their Majesties of Spain have grown very powerful and ever more ambitious.'

The smile had gone from the Sultan's face and a touch of restlessness had come into his eyes.

'I know,' he said abruptly. 'I am well informed about developments in Spain. I would send men to Granada if I could, but I shall need all my strength for the war against Austria. I cannot help Granada, Prince Ibrahim. You will have to bear that unwelcome message to your uncle. Later, perhaps, the situation may change. But I fear that the war with Austria will not be a short one.'

Prince Ibrahim remained silent. The Sultan's words had come as no surprise. He had not in any case really solicited any assistance. Even so, it was a heavy blow. As long as those words had been left unspoken, there had been at least a small vestige of hope that a final desperate cry for help from Granada might have found a favourable echo in the Sultan's heart.

'So,' continued the Sultan, 'you will not be able to return to Granada as the bearer of good tidings. Does that grieve you, Ibrahim?'

'I had always hoped, Great Lord, as I still hope, that you may yet find some way of helping Granada.'

The Sultan shook his head. 'You are, I think, a man of realism, Ibrahim. If war comes, then Granada's position in untenable. The Spain of Ferdinand and Isabella is a great power; one day it could well become the most formidable state in Christendom. Granada's sole hope lies in securing time, in prevarication. Who knows what time may not bring?'

Prince Ibrahim reflected that the Sultan's words were almost a repeat of those of Samuel. No doubt it was all so very evident. But evident also to the Spaniards, who would see little merit in a policy of delay when they so clearly had the upper hand.

'If Granada does indeed fall,' Prince Ibrahim said slowly, 'if it does, what then? Will Their Majesties of Spain then be satisfied? Or will their appetite not be whetted and their ambitions grow? In which direction, Great Lord, might they then not turn?'

The Sultan nodded. 'For that knowledge I would be willing to pay handsomely, for it is a question that concerns me greatly. There have, I know, been contacts between Castile and Egypt. A certain Pedro Martir from Castile has been on a mission to Cairo and met there with al-Ashruf Qansuh al-Ghawri, Sultan of Babylon and Lord of Egypt, Syria and Palestine. All our Christian enemies dream of the recovery of Jerusalem. It is not so much, I believe, a matter of faith or religious obligation, but rather of the glory that would go with it. A triumphant Spain might well be tempted to seize the leadership of a new crusade. You, Ibrahim, will be the ears and eyes of Islam in the West, for I too will be eager to have your news when you reach the Spanish court. Will you do this for me?'

'I am yours to command, Great Lord,' Prince Ibrahim answered simply, 'in all matters that cannot harm Granada.'

'Well spoken. I too, you see, need time to complete my preparations against Austria. Strong though we are, we could not resist an alliance of all the Christian powers. Such a league could well be fatal to our cause. Reports have reached us of rivalry between the Kings of Spain and Portugal over possessions in Africa and islands off the African coast. Some chance of discord may perhaps be found there. There have been rumours also of a Genoese called Christofero Colombo who claims that it is possible to reach India and Cathay by sea by sailing across the Atlantic. Perhaps Spain's energies can be channelled in that direction. Diplomacy is a noble art, Ibrahim. Practise it well and you may, perchance, go far.'

The Sultan glanced back at his map of Hungary.

'Time,' he mused, as if momentarily oblivious of Prince Ibrahim's presence, 'I need time. May Allah grant me enough of it.' For a moment he remained silent before turning back towards Prince Ibrahim. 'But I will not let you leave Istanbul completely empty-handed. That would not befit the Sultan of the Ottomans, nor one about to brave the Spaniards in their den. As a farewell gift, I give you one of my new galleys. They are swift and powerful, and should be able to hold their own against most of our foes; only the Hospitallers have stronger ships. Take your galley back to Granada, Ibrahim, and may Allah be with you and with your good cause. I will dispense you,' he concluded kindly, 'from further attendance upon me this evening. I had thought that it might amuse or distract you a little, but already, I fear, your spirit – if not your body – has left Istanbul and you are thinking only of Granada. You have my dispensation, and you also have my blessing. May Allah be merciful to you always and smile upon your endeavours. Remember too, Ibrahim, that you will always be welcome at my court and in Istanbul.'

The Sultan gave Prince Ibrahim his hand to kiss as a signal that the audience was over. Prince Ibrahim bowed low three times before retiring from the audience chamber. He felt strangely drained, as though this signal of farewell had brought with it the loss of the intoxicating vigour of the Ottoman court and the pulsating city of Istanbul.

Nevertheless, the recollection of the Sultan's princely gift, and the thought of returning to Granada in some style as the commander of his own galley, quickly revived his spirits. Granada had virtually no war fleet and relied heavily upon the corsair ships of Tunis and Algiers to protect its sea-lanes in return for a substantial payment in gold. Prince Ibrahim had made a point of sailing frequently in ships of the Ottoman fleet and knew himself to be regarded as a notable seaman. The return journey to Granada promised to be much faster than his outward trip some five years before when the Egyptian trading vessel in which his passage had been booked had called at seven ports along the North African coast before finally crossing the Mediterranean and arriving at Istanbul.

Confirmation of the Sultan's gift came early the following morning when a high-ranking court official delivered a letter to be handed personally to the King of Granada, a scimitar of fine workmanship engraved with a verse from the Koran for Prince Ibrahim, and a written instruction authorising him to take on board all necessary provisions and to take command of one of the newest galleys of the Ottoman fleet, with a complement of forty fighting-men, one hundred and twenty oarsmen, six overseers and twenty-five ordinary crewmen for the everyday tasks of cooking, cleaning, repair work and other general management tasks of the ship. There was also a sailing master with two assistants for the relatively rare occasions when the ship's sails would be unfurled. The forty fighting-men, the overseers and ordinary crewmen were all from the Anatolian mainland; the men at the oars were slaves, most of them from the Balkans, although they also included some Venetians, Genoese and French captured by Tunisian pirates and sold in the slave markets of Istanbul where the price paid for slaves of prime physique was generally higher than in Tunis itself or in Algiers.

Prince Ibrahim lost no time in going to the arsenal a little way down the

Golden Horn to inspect his ship. He was not disappointed. He recognised it at once as being one of the six galleys he had seen through the casement of his personal apartments only the previous day. All six had only just been completed and were fully manned. He was met by the captain of the fighting-men, a dark-skinned, thickset Anatolian called Yakoub. He greeted Prince Ibrahim respectfully.

The galley was long and comparatively narrow, notwithstanding the parallel banks of oarsmen, seated three abreast on twenty benches on either side of a central gangway that led from the front to below the rearcastle of the ship. Above the galley-slaves, at a height of some five to six feet, was the massive wooden frame of the main poop with its single squat mast and furled sails that were used solely as a reserve source of motion. At the front of the galley, mounted on the forecastle, were two small guns capable of firing medium-sized cannonballs and canisters of Greek fire. All the slaves had manacles round their ankles that were kept firmly padlocked.

Prince Ibrahim walked slowly along the central gangway between the galley-slaves, accompanied by four of the overseers carrying vicious-looking whips of rawhide studded with small pieces of metal. Most of the slaves were sitting with their eyes cast down or sideways, but the occasional man stared back at him with varying looks of hope, curiosity or outright hatred. Prince Ibrahim did not speak as he moved slowly along the central gangway. Virtually all the slaves were in good physical condition, The Sultan had indeed made him a superb gift for such men were not cheaply bought.

As in most of the newer galleys in the Ottoman fleet, there was provision for a series of awnings that could be unrolled to give some protection to the galley-slaves against excessive heat or rain. It had been found that awnings of this kind extended the rowers' useful lifespans by several years. It was likely that few, if any, of the galley-slaves had come from wealthy families or they would, no doubt, long since have been ransomed. For those not so fortunate, there was little left in life to look forward to, except capture in combat with a Christian ship and release from captivity for those lucky enough to survive the fighting.

Prince Ibrahim's own cabin, as well as that of Yakoub, and the quarters of most of the forty fighting-men, were in the rearcastle. His cabin was spacious and fitted out comfortably, with small portholes that ran along its whole semi-circular length. Looking through them, he could see on one side the high walls of the arsenal and, on the other, two more galleys that lay close alongside, their oars shipped so as to reduce as much as possible the space between the vessels.

Now that he had come on board he was seized with impatience to go. Turning to Yakoub and his senior officers, Prince Ibrahim told them that he wished to be ready to leave in three days' time, and to have the ship fully victualled and provided with water by that time for a lengthy sea journey. They had, he knew, been told that they had been placed at his disposal and that their destination was Granada. Although none of them had ever been there, the prospect seemed to please them well enough.

Prince Ibrahim spent most of his last three days in Istanbul at the arsenal. His men appeared to work with a will. Even the galley-slaves, bent most of the time over their oars, seemed to feel a tingle of excitement. Prince Ibrahim gave instructions that small groups of six of them at a time should be released from their benches and be allowed to come ashore under close guard and loudly stated orders that any man who attempted to escape would be castrated on the spot. The terrible threat, and the proximity of the guards, proved enough to discourage any attempt to flee, and the slaves seemed grateful for their master's unusual act of kindness.

Prince Ibrahim was minded to make directly for Granada. There was little to be said for calling in at Tunis or Algiers on the way. He was ill-informed about recent developments and relations between Granada and the corsair states. It would be more prudent, therefore, weather and fate permitting, to return to Granada first. But this meant storing on board sufficient provisions and water for some five weeks in case of storms or prolonged periods of unfavourable and contrary weather. With one hundred and twenty oarsmen the galley would, in normal circumstances, be able to maintain a speed of six miles per hour that could be kept up for ten to twelve hours a day, with periodic breaks for the rowers to recuperate.

He spoke many times with Yakoub and the men under his command. Yakoub, he learned, was an experienced soldier and had fought since he was sixteen years of age, sometimes on land but more often at sea. He was a man of a cheerful disposition and asked many questions in return about the Spanish kingdoms. He had been born in Izmir and had been accustomed to boats since early childhood. Most of his men had also seen service at sea. Their enemies had included men from most of the states bordering onto the Mediterranean. They had respect for most of them, and greatly admired the skills and navigational prowess of the Genoese and the Venetians; but for sheer fighting strength and power there were none to equal, let alone surpass, the knights Hospitallers of the Order of St John, operating out of their island fortress of Rhodes. The knights of the White Cross were terrible warriors

16

and it was considered advisable to avoid battle with them wherever possible, except in cases of overwhelming superiority in numbers.

Prince Ibrahim spoke also with the sailing master, a thin tall man called Yusef from near Lake Van in the eastern Kurdish province. He was unenthusiastic about the likely performance of the galley under sail, with only one short mast and its two square-shaped sails. With a favourable wind it would enable the ship to advance, he estimated, at a speed of one mile, at best one mile and a half, per hour. Yusef deplored what he considered to be the grossly excessive reliance upon the muscle-power of galley-slaves. It was his opinion that sailing ships armed with batteries of guns were much more effective, but this view had not found favour with the admirals of the Ottoman court. They considered galleys to be more reliable and more readily manoeuvrable under the prevailing Mediterranean weather conditions than sailing ships.

The work on provisioning the galley made good progress and Prince Ibrahim was well pleased when in the mid-afternoon of the third day he was told by Yakoub that all was ready.

Prince Ibrahim knew that it was normal practice for men to be allowed to spend their last night ashore, to do as they wished, leaving only a small guard on board to watch over the manacled galley-slaves. It did not need Yakoub's questioning look to remind him of the custom. With a slight smile he gave permission for all those who so desired to go on shore, provided a secure guard was kept on the ship and that all should be ready to set sail two hours after daylight on the following morning.

He had instructed Samuel to bring his personal effects to the galley in the late afternoon and watched for a while as these were being stowed away. It was the first time that Samuel had been on board the galley and he inspected it with admiration.

'It is a fine ship, my lord. Would that Granada had a fleet of such galleys!'

Prince Ibrahim nodded. 'Yes. But I fear that all the gold of Granada would not be sufficient for even the smallest of squadrons. I do not know how long we shall be able to maintain even this single galley. The Sultan's generosity will more than provide for the first year's upkeep, but after that . . . who can tell? But we shall see. I wish you to stay on board, Samuel, for I am minded to take one last look at Istanbul. Your quarters are with the crew.'

He left the ship and walked through the arsenal which was a veritable hive of activity. At the Sultan's express direct command a building programme had been put in place that provided for the construction of two new galleys a month. Sultan Bayazet was fully aware of the importance of sea power and was intent upon the establishment of Ottoman naval supremacy in the eastern Mediterranean. To assist in this programme shipwrights had been recruited from the corsair lairs along the North African coastline, as well as renegade gunnery experts from a number of European countries. The pay being offered was extremely good and there appeared to be no shortage of men willing or volunteering to help in the building of the Sultan's fleet. The thud of huge metal hammers, the whistling of saws, and the loud din of hundreds of voices shouting orders or yelling for pieces of equipment built up to a volume of noise not unlike billowing waves that echoed and re-echoed from the towering external walls on the land side of the arsenal.

Once outside its walls, Prince Ibrahim was back in and among the familiar colours and smells of the city he had come to love so much. Street vendors jostled past him as they sang out their wares. Some bellowed more than they sang; others squawked from sheer fatigue or, more cruelly, as the result of tongues mutilated at birth. It was above all the riot of colour that stirred his imagination. The miniature mountains of spices in their extraordinarily bewitching variety of colours, the green henna, the bright yellow saffron, the plump purple figs, the yellowing rice, all provided a feast for the eyes of which he was never tired.

He climbed up one of the steeply curving roads that led back up to the plateau. It was not so much the palace of Topkapi that drew his steps as the one-time Christian church of Santa Sophia, with its history that went back to the time of the Emperor Justinian some seven hundred years before. Prince Ibrahim felt a momentary pang of jealousy. To be remembered one day as such a man had been: then one would not have lived in vain!

Removing his shoes he entered, almost reverently, into the converted mosque. On the thick carpets that now covered its floor several dozen of the faithful were on their knees, their hands touching the ground in front of them, praying to Allah. Prince Ibrahim joined them, his mind dizzy with anticipation of the future and the dread uncertainty that enveloped the fate of Granada.

It was beginning to grow dark as he left, the lights inside and out sparkling like miniature stars. For a while he wandered about without any particular goal, going past the great Roman-built cisterns that still provided the greater part of the city's water supplies, inhaling for one last time the scents and smells of Istanbul. Perhaps, one day, Allah would vouchsafe him a return visit. There were fewer people about now and the hawkers and vendors had largely disappeared. Istanbul under the Ottomans was a safe city for disorder and violence were savagely punished.

It was considerably later that Prince Ibrahim began to walk deliberately back in the direction of the arsenal. The darkness was by now fairly general, relieved only here and there by house lights or the occasional passers-by with rush flares that gave a faintly orange light. It was in the gloom that he suddenly stumbled and almost fell over a body crouched down so low as to be almost flat against the ground. His hand went immediately to the small dagger at his waist, but he relaxed as the figure in font of him, and which he could now see was that of a woman, rose slowly and, it seemed, painfully to her feet.

'Forgive me,' she said in a voice that was hardly audible.

Prince Ibrahim took her by the arm and led her forward some ten steps to where there was a small lantern over an open doorway. He saw now that the woman was in fact a young girl, attractive to look at, probably not more than fifteen or sixteen years of age. A prostitute, in all probability, he guessed. There were growing numbers of them in Istanbul, where they were readily tolerated by the Ottoman authorities.

He felt pity for her. For a moment her face, which was completely uncovered, reminded him of his sister. Besides, she looked pale and sad, with big eyes that seemed to brim with tears.

'Come with me,' he said, and, going through the open doorway, he came into a large room, dimly lit and with low couches set round small tables with red candles. Two men with long staves in their hands, although with smiling faces, came towards them. Prince Ibrahim felt the girl trembling by his side.

'You are thrice welcome here, lord,' said one of them. 'This is a house of good repute. But the girl does not belong here, not any more. She is rotten and can give no more pleasure. She has been contaminated. Our orders are to cast her out.'

'I do not seek to bring her back,' said Prince Ibrahim quietly. 'But the girl is exhausted. Allow her to rest a little.'

The two men did not stop smiling but moved a step nearer, raising their staves and uttering a short warning cry. Almost at once, four more men, similarly armed, seemed to emerge from the shadows.

'I told you, lord,' said the same man who had spoken before, 'this is a house of good repute. You may stay, if you wish, but the slut who is with you must leave, at once.' As he finished speaking he raised his staff with the clear objective of hitting the girl. She yelped with fear.

Without a word, Prince Ibrahim jumped forward and, hitting the man with his fist, grabbed the staff from him as he fell. Turning towards the other five, he again drew his dagger from its sheath.

'By Allah,' he shouted, 'I will not be treated in this way. Fetch me your master or I will have this place utterly destroyed.'

The five men hesitated, impressed by the tone of authority in Prince Ibrahim's voice and uncertain how to act, when a far door was flung open and a man of medium height, and holding a large whip in his hand, entered the room. Prince Ibrahim recognised him at once as a former captain of the Janissaries. The recognition was mutual for the newcomer at once dropped his whip and greeted Prince Ibrahim with effusion.

'My lord Prince, you are welcome indeed. You have but to command and I shall seek to give you pleasure.'

Prince Ibrahim returned the greeting without effusion. 'Thank you, commander, but all I want is some comfort for this poor creature.' He pointed to the girl cowering by his side. 'I stumbled across her in the street. She merits compassion.'

'You have a kind heart, my lord Prince,' answered the former Janissary. 'I will help you as far as I can, but it is beyond my power to allow her back in here. This house has high standards. The girl is of the royal blood of Aragon, fit for our finest houses. But now she is contaminated. She has the woman's disease. I cannot keep her.'

Prince Ibrahim turned to the girl by his side. 'Is this true? Are you of the royal blood of Aragon? Tell me who you are. Whomsoever you are, I will not harm you.'

'My name is Leonora de Antequera,' the girl murmured piteously. 'I am a cousin of the King of Aragon. Please help me. Please. Please.'

Prince Ibrahim stared at her in disbelief. A princess of Spain here, struck down with the curse of her profession. Perhaps the girl was mad. 'Say that again,' he snapped, speaking this time in Castilian.

'I am Leonora de Antequera, Princess of Aragon,' she whispered anew. 'Please, please help me.'

Prince Ibrahim turned back to the former Janissary now turned owner, or at least the man in overall charge of the establishment.

'Very well,' he said. 'I will not impose upon you. Give the girl some water and we will go.'

'You are indeed the kindest of men, my lord Prince,' said the master of the house, not seeking to hide his manifest relief at this issue. 'Give the girl some water,' he ordered the man whom Prince Ibrahim had thrown to the ground and who had chosen to remain there, his smile gone and his eyes sullen with bitterness.

The girl gulped down the water. She was no longer trembling so much and Prince Ibrahim took her by the hand and led her back outside into the dark street. She seemed to have no fear of him.

'I am returning to Granada tomorrow,' he said slowly. 'You had best come back with me and I will arrange for your repatriation. You had best dress as a man; it would be dangerous otherwise aboard my galley. Was that man speaking the truth? Are you sick?'

'I am, my lord,' she said simply.

'Poor child,' he murmured.

There was little more he felt he could say. Instead, he hurried his steps, still holding her by the arm and heading now back to the arsenal and his ship as by the most direct route. He noticed with some relief that two of the crew were keeping watch as they approached. He had covered the girl in his kaftan and was glad that the men on duty paid no particular attention to his companion. Once in his cabin he pulled out a pile of clothes.

'You had best cut you hair. Cut it very short. Choose whatever clothes you can find in this pile that more or less fit you. You will be my page and I shall call you Leonardo. You had best sleep here on the floor. We will keep your secret, never fear.'

The girl was still dressing when Samuel came in, bearing a tray with glasses and a tall jug of water. Prince Ibrahim smiled to himself. Samuel had not been in sight when he and Leonora had come on board. But sleeping or waking, he had clearly known at once that his master had returned, and had been accompanied. There was no possible course other than to take him into their confidence.

'This, Samuel, is the lady Leonora de Antequera. She will accompany us to Granada, as my page. She is very sick.'

Samuel's eyes spread wide with wonder.

'The lady Leonora de Antequera, travelling on your ship,' he repeated. 'But how? Was she a prisoner? Has she escaped? Will they not pursue her?'

Prince Ibrahim started in surprise. He had not given the possibility a moment's thought. But Samuel's question was quite pertinent. But it was the girl who, no doubt divining the meaning of the question, spoke first.

'No one will pursue me,' she said in a voice that was hoarse to the point of croaking. 'I am contaminated, my lord, contaminated,' she repeated in a cry that ended up as a wail. 'They threw me out, like a piece of filth, like a slut that is of no more use.'

The two men looked at each other with compassionate eyes. Turning towards his master, Samuel murmured, 'I have heard of doctors among my race who are able to treat and even cure such diseases. Perhaps for her too there may be hope.'

Prince Ibrahim nodded. 'We shall take you back to Granada. You perhaps understood what Samuel said. Whatever can be done for you, will be done. I promise you that. When we reach Granada you will be free, to stay with us or to return immediately to Aragon. It shall be as you wish.'

'I can never go back to Aragon,' the girl said despondently. 'I have suffered too great a degradation. You are generous, my lord, but why do you burden yourself with me? And why do you go to Granada?'

'This is Prince Ibrahim Ibn Sa'd, nephew of the King of Granada,' said Samuel in a smooth voice. 'We are returning to Granada after several years in Istanbul.'

'Prince Ibrahim Ibn Sa'd,' repeated the girl. 'Do you know then my cousin, King Ferdinand?'

'Not yet. But I am to go soon to the court of Their Catholic Majesties. You can no doubt accompany me there, if you wish it. But there will be time enough to think of all that. Now it is time to rest. Samuel will sleep with the crew. You, Leonardo, will perforce have to sleep here. As my page that will not cause any surprise. There are rugs enough and to spare in this cabin. For your personal needs . . .' he hesitated for a moment, 'I shall give you as much privacy as I can.'

Prince Ibrahim threw himself on the low couch in his cabin. Although physically tired he felt elated. Pleasant though the years in Istanbul had been, they had not been a time of achievement. Now, hopefully, a real task awaited him. It would be a stern and exacting time, but he felt himself to be ready to face it. Strange that fate should have chosen this particular moment to throw a dishonoured Spanish princess in his path. She, for her part, seemed to have fallen asleep and he could hear her breathing deeply.

She was still asleep when he awoke the following morning. The sun had just risen and gave promise of a brilliant summer's day. He washed and dressed quickly and went onto the main deck. Some of the fighting-men were standing in small clusters of three or four, looking, it seemed, none the worse for their last night on shore. Below them, the galley-slaves showed little sign of life. Prince Ibrahim had not been standing long on the forecastle before Samuel appeared with hot coffee, bread and dried fruits; he was followed almost at once by Yakoub and Yusef. Both reported a full complement, with no man missing. Prince Ibrahim nodded his contentment. There was no reason to delay before casting off and setting sail for Granada.

A slow and methodical drumbeat marked the moment of departure, the oars dipping gently into the water as the galley-slaves obediently followed the beat of the drum. They had come to life rather like a bunch of automatons, their faces wooden and their eyes staring without any life or expression. Three of the overseers stood menacingly on the central plankway, but they had had no cause so far to wield their whips.

Seen from the Bosphorus, the city of Istanbul looked more beautiful than ever, sparkling in the sunlight, its myriad cries travelling straight across the water. There was a slight following breeze and, with the galley-slaves rowing at a moderate pace, the galley was smartly moving forward.

'So, Samuel,' Prince Ibrahim said quietly, 'the time has come and we have left Istanbul behind us. Little did we think five years ago that we would be leaving in our own ship. May Allah grant us a favourable passage home.'

'I think, my lord,' said Yakoub, 'that we have no cause to fear. There are few enemy galleys that could hold their own with us.'

'It would be well, Yakoub, if we made quite sure of that. I want daily practice. Ensure that your men learn how to operate in small units of four or five. There will be daily exercises on the main poop. I wish to see us ready to go at full speed, both to attack and to escape. We must do the same with our two guns; and you, Yusef, must see to it that we have Greek fire ready to use at short notice. We shall start this afternoon.'

Yakoub and Yusef seemed well pleased with their instructions. Prince Ibrahim judged them to be thoroughly competent professionals. For an hour or two there was little for him to do. It would provide an opportunity to hear Leonora's story and to accustom the crew to see the sight of his page by his side. He instructed Samuel to go to her and bring her to him.

He was favourably struck by her appearance. Her slim figure looked boyish and, dressed as she was in a loose fitting dark blue blouse and black trousers, there was no particular reason to suspect her true sex. She had, he noticed, a long dagger strapped behind her back. Only her gait was slightly unnatural and too hesitant to be really convincing. But she appeared to have attracted no special attention so far.

'You will have to become accustomed to going about the ship, Leonardo,' he said in a perfectly normal tone of voice, 'but look, there you see Istanbul. We are leaving it behind us. You will be quite free of it.'

'Free? I shall never be free of it for what remains of my life.'

'You must not despair, Leonardo. Life is as Allah wills it. You may still be healed. You must not lose hope. Remember Samuel's words, help will be given you.'

'Why, my lord, do you do this for a whore?'

Prince Ibrahim could see the look of distrust in her eyes. He did not really know the answer to her question. Was it pity, opportunism or just an instinctive reaction, taken on the spur of the moment? 'I cannot tell you, Leonardo,' he said truthfully. 'Perhaps a little of your Spanish knight errantry to begin with. You see,' he added with a smile, 'we Moors have not lived in Spain for more than seven hundred years without acquiring some local customs. Then perhaps also the fact that you are a princess of the House of Aragon. I cannot simply ignore that fact, whatever your circumstances may be now, nor the fact that your country and mine are likely soon to be at war. But it is not our custom to make war on women. Be that as it may,' he added with a flourish, 'here you are on board. We shall decide later, jointly, what is to become of you.'

'We, my lord?'

'You and I, Leonardo,' Prince Ibrahim said gently. 'I tell you again, you will not be forced against your will. Now tell me what misfortune placed you in the hands of those men in Istanbul.'

'At the brothel,' she said bitterly, 'there is no need to play at words.'

'Very well,' he said, 'at the brothel.'

'It is not a long story,' she replied. 'We, a delegation from Aragon, were on our way by sea to Rome. It was an embassy to His Holiness the Pope. I was due to spend six months with the Marquesa de Vilhamosa, my aunt, to learn music and Italian. We were escorted by two armed galleys, but we lost our escorts in a sudden squall off the coast of Corsica. When it abated, we found ourselves close to three Tunisian corsairs. They attacked at once. I believe our men fought bravely, but I saw nothing of the battle. Only, when it was over, we saw the corsairs tossing bodies into the sea. Some twenty persons, mostly women, were taken to Tunis. We were well treated at first, as ladies of rank. Perhaps they expected large ransoms for us. But Aragon does not easily pay ransom money.'

She stopped for a moment, her face twisted as if by the pain of the memory. Prince Ibrahim did not attempt any words of consolation, but remained standing close by her side.

'When they tired of waiting for ransom money that did not come, they decided to sell us in the slave markets of Istanbul. They transported us like so many cattle, but prize cattle, so that we were amply fed. Some of the older women tried to console me and three other younger girls, but they were, I think, too terrified themselves to be very convincing. But the men in the ship that transported us did not touch us; no doubt their merchandise had to be unspoilt on arrival. It was not till we were exhibited in the slave market that our real Calvary began.' She stopped again, her face puckering as she fought back the tears.

'The younger women and I were stripped bare and made to stand with arms and legs akimbo. They had long thin rods which they could use to beat us with if we disobeyed them for even a moment. Then the buyers came to examine us. Some of the regulars felt our breasts, looked all over us as their hands travelled over our bodies. It was then that I vomited. They beat me for that and then sent me to fetch a pail of water to clean up my own vomit. One of the buyers, a tall ugly man, quite fat, watched it all, then said loudly that he wanted to buy me. He probably got me on the cheap. He bought one of the other girls too. He told us to dress and had us taken in a closed carriage to his house. It was the brothel outside of which you found me, my lord. I was placed in the hands of an old Turkish woman. She instructed me how to dress, what perfumes to use, and showed me very graphically how I should please the clients. Apparently I was well appreciated. Many men came back and had me again and again. The old woman even smiled at me. I saw the tall ugly man only twice, and even he smiled. I was given a room of my own and ornaments of turquoise and gold. I was cossetted, until at one of their regular morning inspections they found that I had contracted the disease. The same day they threw me out. They wanted no contaminated whores in their establishment. The rest of my story you know,' she ended lamely.

'Did you tell your master in Istanbul who you were?' Prince Ibrahim asked quietly.

'He was not interested. The corsairs must have told him that there was no possibility of a ransom. Besides, I was earning good money for him. They started me off at three ducats a time, but then it became five, and twenty for a whole night. I was nauseated, but it made little difference. I prayed for death. Perhaps it would have come by now if you had not taken me away. No doubt you expect me to be grateful, my lord. But how can I be grateful to you for a long life of hell. My life is finished. Finished. Finished.'

She did not cry this time, but gave her shoulders a vigorous twist, her face set hard out towards the sea. Perhaps indeed it would have been better, Prince Ibrahim reflected, to have left her to die on the streets of Istanbul.

'Do not imagine,' she said, turning back suddenly towards him, her eyes staring unwaveringly at him, 'that I shall be of any use to you. Aragon will disown the slut I have become. Nor would I want it any other way. You are a humane man, my lord, or so I would believe. But you are of the same faith as those who have made me vile and have destroyed my life. I have nowhere to turn. I wish only to die.'

'You must do as you think fit, Leonardo,' Prince Ibrahim said coolly. 'You will have time to reflect on the journey back to Spain. Go now and tell Samuel to come to me.'

He watched her go, square-shouldered and with apparent determination. Of course, it was, it was true, a cruel fate for one born a princess of a distinguished royal house, but his own fate and that of all Granada could well prove to be not dissimilar. It was a thought that left little room for pity. Given her state of mind, she was indeed likely to prove of little value to him. But when one was dealt a poor hand at cards, the littlest royal card should not be thrown away. With luck, it might even win a trick.

When Samuel appeared a few moments later, Prince Ibrahim gave him instructions to keep a discreet watch over Leonardo. The boy-girl was to be handled kindly, but also firmly. Samuel nodded a silent assent.

Walking over to the edge of the rear poop they looked down at the galley-slaves below. They were rowing at a slow to medium pace, propelling the galley forward at an easy moderate speed. The overseers were walking slowly up and down the length of the central gangway, disappearing every so often from their view as they passed beneath the poop. Already, Istanbul was beginning to fade away in the late afternoon haze. They could still see the occasional minaret, and sometimes a flash of light as a ray of the sun hit upon a large plate of gold or brass. Prince Ibrahim had left behind the centre of power of Islam. He wondered how much of its invigorating force he would still feel coursing through his veins when they reached their destination in Granada.

'Fetch me the chess game from my cabin, Samuel,' he cried suddenly, bringing his reverie to an abrupt end. 'It is time for a moment's relaxation before I see Yakoub about the battle-worthiness of this ship.'

Samuel bowed and went to do his bidding. He was well used by now to his master's frequent and, sometimes to him, bewildering changes of mind. Prince Ibrahim was, he reflected, a man of great attributes. There was a certain brilliance about him that was undeniable, but had he, he wondered, the dogged underlying stamina that was required for greatness? So far he had not been really tested.

They played their game of chess on the rearcastle. Prince Ibrahim's eyes were restless, roving incessantly from the galley-slaves below to the men on the fore and rearcastles, and then from them back to the chessboard. They were both talented players and their matches were nearly always hard-fought. It was Prince Ibrahim's normal practice to play a cautious, prudent game, leaving it to his opponent to attack while he preferred to counter and seize upon his opponent's unguarded flank. Samuel, he knew from experience, and after some initial surprise, was one for attacking and for a highly aggressive game. But on this occasion Prince Ibrahim threw aside his habitual caution and, playing white, launched an immediate attack. Samuel, somewhat disorientated, was soon in retreat but, castling neatly, was nevertheless able to fall back on a strong defensive position. A long game of attrition seemed in prospect. For a moment Prince Ibrahim considered a daring exchange of his queen for one of Samuel's castles with a possible but very uncertain opening for the checkmating of his opponent. It was tempting; but it was also reckless for, if it failed, his own defeat would be inevitable. He saw that there was a ghost of a smile on Samuel's face. Prince Ibrahim relaxed. It was to be attrition after all.

They stopped the game a few moves later, agreeing to a draw. Yakoub and Yusef were waiting and the game had already taken long enough.

'Thank you for the game, Samuel,' he said. 'Go now and see how Leonardo is faring and let me know. I suppose,' he continued with a smile, 'that you were prepared for my Queen's sacrifice?'

Samuel nodded. 'I was, my lord, but I knew also that it was against your nature. It would have been a dangerous move.'

It would have irked Prince Ibrahim greatly to have lost the game against Samuel. Defeat at any time was unwelcome, in any field. He turned instead to Yakoub.

'So, Yakoub, what have you come to tell me? When shall we be ready for battle?'

'You have a good command, my lord,' replied the Anatolian. 'All the fighting-men are hardened and experienced. The sailors know their business and the galley-slaves have been hand-picked. All they need is some hard drill and practice. With your permission, we can start on this immediately.'

'Do so,' said Prince Ibrahim. 'I hope to be able to reach Granada without a fight, but I will gladly accept whatever Allah wills and may send us. But we must be sufficiently well-prepared. But let it be for tonight, Yakoub, for it is growing late. You can start your preparations for battle practice in earnest tomorrow morning, as early as you wish.'

Yakoub gave a slight smile.

'Then we shall start soon after daybreak, as soon as these dogs,' he said, motioning contemptuously towards the galley-slaves, 'have swallowed their morning swill.'

Prince Ibrahim nodded. For a brief moment he considered a light reprimand. He had no wish to see some of his galley-slaves beaten until they were senseless and useless. They were expensive commodities and any losses could prove difficult to replace before they reached their destination. On the other hand, there needed to be a discipline of iron and a clear knowledge of the crew's abilities and capacities under pressure. That was Yakoub's domain and, for the present at least, he would leave it entirely to him.

The darkness was descending fast now. He ordered three lanterns to be lit, one at either end of the ship, and one on the rearcastle close to where he was standing. He could no longer distinguish the coastline and the galley was doing little more than keeping its position with only a small handful of the galley-slaves bent over their oars. He could see an occasional twinkle of light, far away in the distance, almost certainly somewhere on land. A watch had been set but there was little sound to be heard. Most of the men on board had bedded down for the night, their prayer mats rolled up by their sides.

Prince Ibrahim decided to follow their example. The sea was completely calm and the galley rocked very gently as small wavelets seemed to bounce against its hull. Samuel was lying wrapped in a rug just outside his cabin. He rose as Prince Ibrahim approached.

'All is quiet, lord. I went in to speak to Leonardo, but he refused to answer, only shaking his head. Are we really wise to take him with us?'

'Who can tell, Samuel? But let us give it a little more time. You can go and join the others now.'

Prince Ibrahim went into his cabin. There was a candle in a small jar that flickered hazily as he entered and it took him a few moments to adjust his eyes to the gloom. He could make out Leonora's form now, lying on the floor and using her arms as a pillow for her head. Her breathing was almost imperceptible.

Prince Ibrahim undressed in silence, folding his clothes on a chair that had been placed next to his couch. Two of the windows that ran round his cabin had been left slightly ajar, providing a little coolness. He wondered for a moment where to put his weapons. While he did not think that Leonora would be so foolish as to try and seize them and kill him, or herself, it seemed preferable not to take any risks. Reopening the door of his cabin he passed them, wordlessly, to Samuel who was still squatting there. It was only a few minutes later that he remembered that he had seen Leonora come out on deck with a knife stuck in her belt. He shrugged his shoulders. He would let the matter lie.

Pulling out his prayer mat Prince Ibrahim knelt down and prostrated himself towards the east, in the direction of Mecca. His fate would be what Allah had prescribed, but he prayed for the blessing of hope, hope for the future and hope for the survival of Granada. From prayer he passed to reverie, thinking back to the years that he had spent in Istanbul. There was a certain intoxication about the power and glory of Islam in the East. He saw again in his mind's eye the Sultan pouring over his maps. Already the Ottoman Empire, since its epoch-making victory over the Serbs at the battle of Kosovo some one hundred years before in 1388, had overwhelmed a vast tract of land comprising not only Serbia but also Bulgaria, Montenegro, Albania and much of Greece. Now it stood poised for further conquests. It was indeed a sad, bitter and ironic contrast to the end of splendour in the West.

He sensed more than felt a subtle change, although the ruffling of his hair by a small gust of wind gave him confirmation of his senses. A slight breeze had sprung up, portending perhaps a change of weather for the morrow. It was almost as if the wind were sighing, with the wooden boards of the vessel creaking, scraping and occasionally moaning. It was as if it too was lamenting their departure from Istanbul, chanting in its own way a last and plaintive farewell. It was, he mused, at once in part a dirge and in part rather like a gentle whiplash.

*Chapter Two*

# HOMEWARD BOUND

Prince Ibrahim had a fitful night, alternately dozing and waking, listening to the lapping of the water against the sides of the ship and the occasional sound of human voices that came to him clearly. Sometimes his eyes wandered over to where Leonora lay sleeping on the floor. In the darkness of the cabin it was as if she had been immobilised and her breathing made inaudible. But most of the time his thoughts were of Granada. The time for thinking back to Istanbul was over. He wondered how he would find his land and its people after his five years of absence, and what his own role would be. Could he, would he be listened to? The prospects for Granada were dark. Time, and allies, were the only obvious possibilities of salvation; or perhaps an accommodation with Their Spanish Majesties? Was there any likelihood whatsoever that Spain would accept Granadan vassalship? Such an option would mean Spain tolerating a continuing Moslem enclave; but that in itself would mean nothing radically new. The Normans in Sicily, and the Holy Roman Empire more recently, had permitted religious freedom, for Christians, Moslems and Jews, and as long as this tolerance had lasted, so also had Islam flourished. There, of course, lay the rub. Diplomacy, however skilful, could only avert the inevitable for a while. To survive, military strength was essential. But where to find it for Granada?

At daybreak he rose. There was enough light in the cabin now to wash and dress. Leonora's eyes were open and he noticed her watching him. She rose in her turn, shaking her head as if to clear it of dreams.

'Lord,' she said, 'what would you have me do?'

'Dress, Leonora, and then come and join me on the rear poop.'

She nodded silently. He opened the door and saw that Samuel was already there, waiting, holding his sword and dagger out to him. Prince Ibrahim buckled them on, then stepped back, almost involuntarily, into his cabin, impelled by a feeling of curiosity that at once irritated and amused him. He found Leonora on her knees, her hands uplifted as if in prayer. She started violently on his return. Then, her face expressionless, she rose and threw off the sheet that she had around her so that she stood completely naked in front of him.

'So,' she almost hissed, 'you are no different after all, my lord. But take heed. I warned you. I am contaminated.'

Prince Ibrahim stared back at her, equally expressionless. She had a beautiful body. Her breasts, medium-sized, were wonderfully rich and swelling, perfect in their roundness. Her thighs and legs were slim and inviting. Even as he looked at her, she walked quietly over to his couch and threw herself onto it, her legs and arms spreadeagled.

'Do not seek to ply your trade with me, woman,' he said icily in Castilian. 'But remember you have a choice to make. Either you act out your role as page, in male attire and eschewing all feminine ploys, or you die. This is a ship of war and I shall not refer to this matter again. Is that understood?'

She nodded and grabbed the nearest sheet to cover herself. Prince Ibrahim turned on his heel and went out of the cabin. Outside, the sky was a light grey colour and the faint breeze that he had felt on his hair on the previous night was blowing more strongly. The galley-slaves had resumed their rowing at a moderate rate and the ship was moving forward at a fair speed. Yakoub came up to him with a smile.

'We are ready, Lord, to start our manoeuvres. You have but to give the word.'

Prince Ibrahim nodded. 'Very well. You may commence.'

Yakoub took a small bugle that hung at his waist and blew three quick blasts. 'We shall start with faster rowing speeds, lord. Once we have reached our top ramming speed I shall give another signal for a simulated boarding attempt. The fighting-men will be divided into two equal groups, but the fighting will be with blunted weapons.' As Yakoub finished speaking the thunder of the drum that beat time for the galley-slaves, beaten by a massively-built Egyptian, grew rapidly deeper till it became like distant thunderclaps that followed upon each other ever more rapidly as the rhythm accelerated. Prince Ibrahim stared down at the galley-slaves. The muscles in their backs had taken on the appearance of knotted cords, the sweat poured down their faces and their backs as they panted and gasped as the ship cut through the water. All six overseers were standing on the middle gangway, their whips curled and at the ready. Prince Ibrahim noted with satisfaction that they appeared to be in no hurry to use them. The slaves were pulling well and there was nothing to be gained by gratuitous cruelty.

It was another ten minutes before Yakoub blew his bugle again. About twenty-five men had crouched low down on one side of the lower poop. Now with wild whooping cries they leapt up and rushed towards the other side of the poop where another slightly smaller party of some twenty men stood stock still, awaiting their assault. Prince Ibrahim watched them keenly. The battle, even if arranged as an exercise, gave every appearance of being fought in earnest. These were seasoned men and they fought with gusto. Most of them fought with scimitars, their sharp points covered with small wooden plugs, and small rounded shields, but he also noticed several who held Frankish-style swords, larger and heavier, although more tiring for the arm. He picked out three or four who appeared to be men of special skill with their weapons. Prince Ibrahim became so absorbed that he had almost forgotten the passage of time, until Yakoub blew his third set of blasts announcing the end of the exercise.

The sigh of relief from the galley-slaves sounded like a low wail, and some uttered half-muffled screams that seemed to forced their way through their parched throats before they collapsed upon their benches.

'Very good, Yakoub,' said Prince Ibrahim. 'Give all the galley-slaves a beaker of water and some bread and meat. They deserved it. Your fighting-men also; and when they have had a rest, I will have a bout with one or two of them. I mean to keep my hand in too,' he added, seeing Yakoub's look of surprise.

Prince Ibrahim walked on ahead down to the lower poop to join the fighting-men. Several among them had received some quite severe bruises but no bones had been broken and no one incapacitated. Prince Ibrahim went round the poop speaking to several of them. Turning to Yakoub, who had followed him, he said with a smile, 'Look for a volunteer, Yakoub, for a bout with his captain.'

Prince Ibrahim smiled at Yakoub's apparent discomfiture. Yakoub could clearly have no knowledge of his captain's skills, whether they were good, bad or indifferent. He could probably be relied upon to select his first volunteer with prudence. He was not mistaken. Yakoub's first choice, a Bulgarian renegade, was, he had noticed, more by way of a battering ram than a fencer.

At least the man had no inhibitions. Without a word he took up his scimitar, smiled briefly and rushed straight at his opponent, raining down his blows from on high. It was a way of fighting that could indeed be effective in a general mêlée, with little room to feint or move quickly to one side or another. But in an individual contest, against so lithe and agile an opponent as Prince

32

Ibrahim, the result was not long in coming. Twice Prince Ibrahim stepped lightly to one side and, on the second occasion, brought down his scimitar with such force on the junction of the Bulgarian's blade and pommel that it was wrenched out of his hand.

'Next man,' shouted Prince Ibrahim with a touch of excitement in his voice.

This time Yakoub did not give him so easy an opponent. Prince Ibrahim had noted his new adversary, a tall, athletic Anatolian called Khaled, during the exercise. This man fought with his head as well as with his arm and alternated quick feinting attacks with a sound defence. They fought and parried for several minutes as each sought to gauge the other's strengths and weaknesses. Satisfied at last that he had his man's measure, Prince Ibrahim launched a bewildering succession of cuts, feints and jabs that forced his opponent back against the side of the ship with Prince Ibrahim's scimitar at his throat. Prince Ibrahim jumped back and lowered his blade.

'My congratulations,' he said to the man. 'You fought well. We shall practice again.'

The Anatolian muttered a few unintelligible words, but their meaning was clear enough. Prince Ibrahim had established his credentials. Yakoub looked impressed. Returning his scimitar to the scabbard at his side, Prince Ibrahim went down to the central gangway on both sides of which the galley-slaves still sat slumped over their benches. Although exhausted, they looked to be a fine body of men. A few were holding up their beakers for more water. Prince Ibrahim nodded. 'Give more water to those who ask for it,' he said to Yakoub who had again followed him. 'It looks as though we can expect rain soon,' he went on. 'Put out buckets when it starts so that we can add to our supplies.'

The sky had indeed grown dark, from a light grey to a much darker grey, while the military exercise had been taking place. Even as he returned to the upper poop a few drops of rain began to fall. Samuel and Leonora were waiting for him, standing side by side. Samuel was smiling with contentment, but Leonora's eyes were expressionless.

'I have brought you more coffee, Lord,' said Samuel, proffering a cup. Prince Ibrahim accepted it gratefully, sipping as he watched the ship riding in the water. The galley-slaves deserved a longer break after their exertions. He turned to Leonora.

'Go, Leonardo, tell Yusef I want him to set his sails for an hour or two. Let him show us what his skills are.'

The ship advanced very slowly under sail. Prince Ibrahim watched with interest as the two sails stood out like shark fins raised high above the water.

Yusef's theories about the potential of sail sounded quite convincing to him; and there was, furthermore, the fact that the Portuguese and the Northern Spanish used no other means of naval propulsion, even in the Mediterranean where the oar-driven galley still ruled supreme. But he finally thrust the thought from his mind. He had no time for such niceties for the present.

That day set the pattern for the next four as their journey proceeded. The daily exercises were conducted with discipline and determination. The galley-slaves, too, rowed well and impressively. On the third day two of them collapsed through exhaustion. Prince Ibrahim, contrary to the normal usage, had them lifted off from their benches and brought up onto the rear poop where they were permitted to lie on canvas sheeting for the rest of the day. They were both young men and by evening had recovered sufficiently to be returned to their benches. Prince Ibrahim instructed Yakoub that they should be dispensed from high speed rowing for another day.

'Don't you think you are spoiling your slaves, Lord?' asked Yakoub, ill-pleased at what he could clearly perceive as a sign of indulgence or weakness on his captain's part.

'Possibly,' replied Prince Ibrahim, 'but I will take that risk. It could make a difference if ever we were to meet an enemy vessel.'

'I am no believer in indulgence,' said Yakoub shortly. 'These men are slaves. They should, in my view, be treated as such, at all times. Nor do they expect anything else. They would show us no pity if our roles were to be reversed.'

Prince Ibrahim did not reply. Was he, indeed, lacking in ruthlessness? Was that in any case necessarily the best way forward? He turned to look at the galley-slaves, pulling gently now at their oars. Their faces showed little by way of expression. It was probable that all of them, without exception, felt only deep hatred for him and for all their masters. If he, in turn, did not hate them, was it not because they were simply tools, his tools, to be used to his own best advantage? What Yakoub deplored as his indulgence towards them, he himself saw as nothing other than making the optimum use of his resources. He was neither afraid, nor would he be reluctant, to be ruthless when the time was right to be so.

It was, he went on to muse, the sixth day since they had left Istanbul. He estimated their position to be just beyond the southernmost tip of the Greek mainland. In a few more days they would be approaching the eastern coast of Sicily where they could expect to meet numerous other ships, traders mostly, using sail as well as oars, carrying wine, grain, cloth and pottery. Perhaps, too, some Genoese or Venetian war-galleys. They had sighted few ships so far and then only on the far horizon. Prince Ibrahim was keen to avoid any kind of engagement, although quite determined to fight if attacked or special circumstances were to warrant it.

It was in fact in the afternoon of that same day that one of the lookouts reported a ship low down in the water on the starboard side. Nodding in response to Yakoub's question, Prince Ibrahim ordered the galley to make for what could now be clearly seen to be a sinking vessel.

'It is an old Ottoman galley, my Lord,' said Yakoub tersely. 'I recognise the ship.'

Prince Ibrahim stiffened. The Ottoman Empire was not officially at war with any Christian powers. There were few who would have dared to attack an Ottoman galley at a time of peace.

They had come near enough to the wreck now to be able to see that a number of bodies were lying on the deck. Most of the vessel's oars had been smashed, but there were still enough left to slow down the sinking of the ship. Although there was no sign of life, Prince Ibrahim instructed a small party of his men to board the stricken vessel lying well below them in the water. Samuel and Leonora joined him on the rearcastle as they watched the boarding party go round the bodies, There was a sudden short cry of excitement as they found one man who was still alive. Lifting him with care they carried him to the side of the ship before laying him flat on a stretcher that had been lowered down to them with ropes. Prince Ibrahim was one of the first to reach the man's side as the stretcher was lowered gently onto the deck. The man's hair was matted with blood and there were deep sword cuts on both sides of his face, but his eyes were open.

'Can you hear me? Can you speak?' asked Prince Ibrahim.

The man closed his eyes, then re-opened them as if to bring the questioner into better focus. 'Some water,' he murmured, 'water.'

It was Leonora who, with great care, lifted up his head and held a cup to his lips. The man gulped noisily.

'We shall dress your wounds,' Prince Ibrahim resumed, 'and find you a place to rest and sleep, for as long as you wish; but can you tell us who attacked you?'

'It was the Order,' murmured the man. 'The Hospitallers, they took us by surprise. It was all over very quickly; many were killed, others they took prisoner. I was left for dead.' The man motioned for more water and then lay panting like a dog after a great exertion.

'How long ago was it?' asked Yakoub.

The man closed his eyes again before replying. 'Four, five hours, maybe six,' he said, 'but they lost a lot of their oars as they attempted to sheer off to one side. They will have lost speed.'

'Then they will probably be heading back towards Rhodes,' said Prince Ibrahim, turning to Yakoub as he spoke. 'We can probably catch up with them.'

'Catch up!' repeated Yakoub. 'Lord, would you risk a battle with a galley of the Order? Alone? Unaided? It would be folly.'

'Not if they are handicapped. Have courage, Yakoub, I shall be prudence itself. But it would be poor recognition of the Sultan's generosity if we did not make even the slightest attempt to avenge the wanton destruction of one of his galleys. Row steadily and not too fast. Our slaves must not be exhausted when we catch up with them.'

'If, Lord, they really are making for Rhodes.'

'That, Yakoub, is a chance we must take. But it seems a very likely course for them to have taken. We will give it a day or two, at least, even if it does take us out of our way.'

While outwardly calm and striving hard to appear totally unmoved, Prince Ibrahim felt his limbs tingling with excitement. Perhaps it was the scent of a quarry, or the inebriation of the chase, or the sheer bravado of pursuing a galley of the most feared fleet in the whole of the eastern or central Mediterranean. He could not help but break into pacing, albeit slowly, up and down the short length of the rearcastle. Leonora and Samuel had stayed near to him, while Yakoub had gone to talk to the overseers to determine their rowing schedule for the next twenty-four hours. Prince Ibrahim could see a look of near consternation on Samuel's face, while Leonora seemed almost relieved at the imminent prospect of danger.

The hours passed slowly at first. They continued to row after dark, but at a greatly reduced speed. On Yakoub's instructions, the galley slaves took it in turns, by alternate rows, to rest for two hours at a time. Water and double rations of bread and meat had been given to them and they had been promised the same for their morning meal.

The sea was relatively calm and the galley made quite good progress in the darkness, seeming to glide over the water, with only a small sliver of a first quarter moon high above them in the sky. They were well clear of any landfall and there was no danger of hitting submerged reefs or rocks.

They maintained a steady speed throughout the night and on into the following morning, now under a brilliant blue sky and a sun that seemed to blaze in its heaven. Prince Ibrahim had gone to his cabin for two very short breaks, but he spent most of his time on the deck of his ship, his brain seething with plans and counter-plans as he sought to picture the approaching confrontation in his mind.

It was mid-afternoon, and considerably earlier than they had expected, when they sighted the galley of the Order. Either the knights were supremely confident of their strength to overcome any conceivable enemies they might come across, or they had indeed lost a very large number of their oars. Prince Ibrahim gave orders for a short pull at maximum rowing speed until he could begin to distinguish individual figures on the enemy ship. It was flying the banner of the Order with a great white cross on a black background. Prince Ibrahim smiled dourly and ordered the Green Banner of Islam to be unfurled in the prow of his ship. After what had happened to the old Ottoman galley it was tantamount to an unofficial declaration of hostilities. Almost immediately the galley of the Order began to turn to face them. Whatever the number of oars they night have lost, their galley still manoeuvred well. Prince Ibrahim called Yakoub and Yusef to his side.

'We should have quite an advantage over them in speed. We shall row towards them, accelerating to battle speed, then sheer off to the right. Train your guns on their oars. I want to slow them down as much as possible.'

For a moment it seemed as though the two galleys would smash straight into each other but, at the last moment, both ships sheered off to the right. Prince Ibrahim heard the galley's guns boom as they veered. The Hospitallers had used exactly the same tactics, aiming their guns at the Ottoman galley's oars, just as they themselves had aimed at the Hospitallers'. Yakoub came racing towards him.

'We came well out of that, Lord. I think we have crippled twice of many of their oars as they have of ours. Shall we repeat the manoeuvre?'

'Yes,' Prince Ibrahim shouted back. 'Exactly as before, but this time use Greek fire as well. Aim it at the rowers. It will cause havoc and may cool their masters' tempers for a while.'

'They are your own people, Lord,' said Leonora softly. 'Have you no pity for them?'

He shook his head. 'There will be time for pity later, not now. Go now and help them get the Greek fire ready.'

Once again the two galleys raced towards each other. It was very evident now, however, that the Ottoman galley was much the faster through the water. Samuel had crouched down by the Prince's side, his face quivering with fear and retching violently. Prince Ibrahim forced himself to stand stock still and found to his own surprise that his hands were as cold as ice.

This time both vessels sheered off sooner than before, but the combination of the gunfire and the tubes of Greek fire threw the Hospitallers' ship into momentary confusion. It was clear now that a very large number of their oars had been smashed and it was several minutes before order was restored and their ship recovered a reasonable degree of balance.

'What now, Lord?' asked Yakoub, who was smiling now, baring his teeth in anticipation. 'I see they are putting out their nets, although how they propose to grapple with us I cannot see.'

'Nor I,' said Prince Ibrahim, 'unless they imagine that we plan to try and board them. That is a satisfaction I do not propose to give them. At least, not yet.'

Despite the damage they had sustained to their oars, the Hospitallers lived up to their reputation and brought their galley back under control. From where he stood, Prince Ibrahim could see galley-slaves being unchained, moved to other places and then be chained again by the ankles to their new benches. Broken oars were thrown into the sea and a few new ones, presumably kept in reserve, were placed quickly in position. But the fact remained that the enemy galley had lost at least a third of its oars and that its speed and ease of manoeuvre had been very substantially impaired.

Prince Ibrahim pondered carefully over his next move. The light, though still quite good, would soon begin to fade. It would not be easy to stay within sight of the enemy galley during the night. Nor could he afford to stay too close by her for the Hospitallers were still too formidable a proposition if ever it should come to boarding. The fact that they had put out their boarding nets suggested that that might well be their hope and objective. He could, of course, quite easily break off the engagement, claiming a moral victory, and leave the enemy galley to limp back to Rhodes. But that would be both disappointing and in some way dishonourable.

'We shall repeat the same manoeuvre one more time,' he said finally to Yakoub. 'Our best, our only hope of victory lies in immobilising them first. We shall accelerate up to battle speed and sheer down their starboard side. Have the tubes of Greek fire ready again to hurl at their rowers.'

The Hospitallers made no attempt this time to row to meet them, their galley moving forward only very slowly. As the Ottoman war galley sheered past them, seven or eight large and heavy nets and a number of grappling irons were thrown at them, but their speed was great enough to brush off all their attempts. The sound of oars breaking and snapping could be clearly heard and, above it all, the screams and yells of the galley-slaves as the canisters of Greek fire fell among them, bursting into flames with devastating effect.

As Prince Ibrahim gave the order to reduce speed and swing back round towards the enemy galley, he could see several small fires on board. Men were rushing around with large buckets of water and there was a manifest state of confusion as some of the knights could be seen taking off their armour to help in the work of dousing the flames and controlling the galley-slaves now driven into a frenzy of fear and panic by the flames which they were helpless to avoid or escape.

'Prepare for another attack, Yakoub,' said Prince Ibrahim jubilantly. 'It is too good an opportunity to miss. Allow our slaves a fifteen minutes' rest first. We must go past them again at maximum speed and must take absolutely no risk of them being able to grapple with us. Smash as many of their remaining oars as you can, and use Greek fire, but aim it this time, if you can, at the men on deck.'

There were more yells and screams on the Hospitallers' galley as they saw the Ottoman ship approaching at high speed. Again attempts were made to catch them with nets and grappling-irons, but it was done with less determination than before, and they had no difficulty in sheering past, smashing more of the enemy's oars and hurling onto their deck more than ten canisters of Greek fire that exploded like small bombs and set off another series of fires.

When the Ottoman galley, having swept past the enemy ship, turned back towards it, the scene before them was one of much greater confusion. They could see a large number of fires now; few oars appeared to remain intact on either side, and the vessel had a very slight list to one side. Although none of the fires seemed unmanageable, there was clearly a great deal of damage. Prince Ibrahim felt well pleased with the results he had obtained so far.

'We can wait now till morning, Yakoub,' said Prince Ibrahim curtly. 'They are in no position to escape or to try and attack us. But mount a careful guard all night and keep on as many lights as you need to keep the Hospitallers under observation.'

'And tomorrow, Lord, shall we finish them off? Slaughter them like pigs?'

'We shall see, Yakoub. Remember that we must take absolutely no chances. We are still no match for them if it comes to boarding, not as long as all their knights are in their armour.'

The light was fading fast now. Prince Ibrahim gave orders to keep the ship at a distance of some two hundred paces from the Hospitallers' galley, where several fires were still burning. The galley was floating aimlessly, seemingly incapable of maintaining any clearly set course. The sound of men shouting orders carried very clearly across the intervening distance. There heard many screams too, presumably from the men who had been burned by the large quantities of Greek fire that had been hurled at them. Prince Ibrahim tried to put himself in the place of the commander of the Hospitallers' galley. Short of a most unlikely rescue by another, passing, galley of the Order, he really had no chance whatsoever of victory, or even of survival, unless he could, somehow, board the Ottoman galley and make use of the overwhelming and crushing strength of his company of knights in full armour; but that, without any oars to propel and direct his ship, seemed an impossible task. As far as he himself was concerned, his best chance of victory appeared to lie in simply repeating the same tactics that had proved so successful, provided of course that his remaining supplies of Greek fire were adequate for the task. It was rather unheroic, but it had undoubtedly proved its effectiveness.

Prince Ibrahim slept little that night, preferring to stay on deck, with only a few occasional brief moments of snatched sleep. Throughout the night the sounds from the enemy ship continued to carry over the water. It could be seen that they had succeeded in dousing the last of the flames, but the smell of burnt timber was unmistakable. When dawn broke, it could be seen that the Hospitallers' galley was listing rather more, if still very slightly, to one side, and that its steering was quite evidently out of control. Nevertheless, it still remained a foe to be reckoned with. Prince Ibrahim contemplated the scene in silence for a while, his crew gathered expectantly in small groups below. Yakoub and Yusef stood eagerly by his side.

'We shall make one more attack with Greek fire,' Prince Ibrahim said finally. 'Then we shall see.'

As the big drum began to boom and the overseers exhorted the galley-slaves till their sinews cracked, the Ottoman galley picked up speed and raced towards the enemy hulk. There were reserves of Greek fire for several more attacks, Yusef had assured him, and the canisters were thrown almost in profusion as they passed alongside the Hospitallers' galley. Almost immediately the flames shot up in a dozen different places. On the listing ship the work of attempting to douse the flames had become much more difficult, and men lost their footing as they made their way on an increasing sloping deck to one or other of the fires. The screams of the galley-slaves rose higher than ever as they saw a terrible and hideously painful death staring them in the eyes. Most of the knights had thrown off their chain armour now to assist in fighting the fires, leaving only a very small number – six, seven, or eight at the most, as far as Prince Ibrahim could tell – in full armour. He believed the moment had come to move in for the kill.

'The time has come, Yakoub,' he shouted. 'This time we shall approach them from the larboard side where the vessel is higher in the water. Be ready with canisters of Greek fire as we come up to them. Then throw up the nets and the grappling-irons and board them wherever you can, between the flames. They will have the slope against them, only a handful of knights in full armour, and their minds at least half full of fears about the safety of their ship. May Allah be with us.'

The Ottoman galley's crew shouted jubilantly. It was only very rarely that an Ottoman galley had emerged victoriously from a combat with a vessel of the Order. Luck had, admittedly, been a little on their side, but that was quickly forgotten in the eager anticipation of a remarkable victory.

There were signs now of desperation on the deck of the Hospitallers' galley as they came up to it. They could see two of the knights hastily redonning their armour, but the fires that were burning in a number of places were inevitably distracting their attention. By now the galley was listing at an angle of some ten to twelve degrees, impeding movement and causing men to occasionally lose their balance as the vessel, floating without direction, was caught by a sudden puff or gust of wind. Prince Ibrahim was wearing only a peaked helmet and a light breastplate, just like the rest of his fighting-men.

As the ships came alongside each other, the Turks threw their nets over the enemy ship, in places throwing them over those that the Hospitallers had themselves put out futilely on the previous evening and had either neglected or not thought worthwhile to pull back in. They shouted wildly as they climbed up and over the netting. Only two knights came forward immediately to meet them, disregarding the canisters of Greek fire. These had caused several new fires and soon Turks and Hospitallers were jumping in and out of the flames in a satanic dance of death that seemed worthy of hell itself. Prince Ibrahim and Yakoub fought close together, their scimitars flashing as if in concert in the light of the sun and the flames of the fires. The knights fought with the courage and the steely determination that was the hallmark of their Order, but the odds had swung overwhelmingly against them. Divested of their armour for the most part, hampered by the angle at which they had to fight, and having to ensure that they kept at all times well clear of the grasping arms of their own half-demented terrified galley-slaves, they were forced back against the lower side of their own ship. There remained at this stage only two knights in full armour.

As Prince Ibrahim stepped back for a moment from the fray he saw to his astonishment that Leonora was standing close behind him, a scimitar in her hand and her eyes glowing with excitement. She was unrecognisable from the girl he had known before.

'Tell Yusef to bring two more canisters of Greek fire,' he snapped. 'We shall roast those two alive.'

Leonora gasped and gaped at him.

'Go. Immediately,' he thundered.

She turned and ran, and came back quickly with Khaled, the second of the men with whom Prince Ibrahim had fenced on his own ship, carrying the canisters of Greek fire. Prince Ibrahim pointed to the two knights still in chain mail. 'Throw one at each knight,' he ordered. The Bulgarian needed no second bidding and, taking careful aim, hurled the two canisters in turn, one at each knight. They burst into flames immediately. One knight threw his sword down and clawed desperately at his armour, only to be immediately cut down by one of the Turks facing him. The second knight, his surcoat ablaze, shouted out his Order's battle-cry and plunged overboard. He sank at once.

The remaining knights fought on but, without armour and outnumbered many times over, their cause was hopeless. Even so, not a single knight surrendered and they fought to the end when the last man fell before the combined attack of three Turks.

Prince Ibrahim looked round the enemy ship with a glow of pride. Pointing to the banner of the Order that still floated from the masthead, he ordered Leonora to hack it down. Now only the Green banner of Islam floated at the mastheads of the two galleys.

The fires were still burning in several places in the captured galley. It was too badly damaged to be taken over as a prize of war. Besides, there was still no formal state of war between the Ottoman Empire and the Order, and the sight of a captured galley of the Order being brought into Istanbul as a prize could well provoke an unwanted major diplomatic incident. It was better to let the vessel sink without any trace. Later, in time, word would, of course, spread. But it would, in all probability, be several months before word came back from Granada and, by then, many things might well have changed. It could then, in any case, be represented as a fit punishment for the unprovoked attack on, and the sinking of, the old Ottoman galley. Prince Ibrahim came to a firm decision. He would let the captured galley burn until it sank. Calling

Yakoub to this side, he gave orders to withdraw to their own vessel as soon as they had finished releasing any surviving galley-slaves and checking that all the knights were in fact dead.

It was, he reflected, a sad scene of carnage, fire, death and destruction, as he returned to his own ship and into his cabin, shouting to Leonora to bring him water to wash and to drink. He took off his light breastplate and threw himself onto his couch with a feeling of exhilaration. He had been tested in battle and felt, with justice he thought, that he come through the ordeal triumphantly. It seemed an extremely fitting way to say a final farewell to Istanbul and to a victorious Islam in the east. Perhaps he might even dare to hope that it would carry with it a glimmer of hope for Islam at bay in the west.

He heard Leonora come into the cabin, struggling slightly under the weight of a large bucket of water. He stripped and saw her stare briefly at his nakedness before turning and quickly leaving the cabin. For a moment he had completely forgotten her sex. He shrugged his shoulders with a wan smile. Placed as she was, he would not be the only man she would be seeing in the nude. But it had been thoughtless of him nevertheless.

He had only just finished washing and dressing when Yakoub knocked and entered.

'My congratulations, Lord, upon a victory that will resound throughout Islam. I am truly honoured to have served under so valiant a captain.'

'Leave out the flattery, Yakoub,' said Prince Ibrahim with a smile. 'Of course I am glad we won, but we did have fortune rather on our side. Without the damage the Hospitallers sustained, rather carelessly I imagine, in their first encounter, the result would have been very different. I would not have been so eager to seek to engage them then. Now, what news have you for me?'

'We have freed twenty galley-slaves, but at least ten of them are so badly hurt that they are unlikely to live for very long. There is also one knight, a Frank. He is only slightly wounded, and still somewhat stunned.'

'And their galley?'

'The fires are burning still. We can safely leave it to burn till it sinks.'

'Good. I will see this Frankish knight, and the galley-slaves we have rescued. See that they are given plenty to eat and drink, as much at least as they can manage, and plenty of warm clothing. What about our own losses?'

'Two of my men were killed, and seven wounded, none of them severely. We also lost four galley-slaves.'

'Well, our captured knight will take care of one of those four empty places. I am sorry about your men, Yakoub. They fought well.'

'They fought very well indeed, Lord, and died in a famous victory. It is the sort of death a soldier aspires to. But here comes our captive knight.'

Prince Ibrahim sat in silence as the captured knight was led into his cabin. He was tall, young and carried himself with a confident, even arrogant, air.

'I am the Chevalier Pierre de Foulques, knight of the Order of St John,' he said loudly in French, 'cousin to the Prior of the Langue or division of France. You may rest assured that the Order will be prepared to pay whatever reasonable ransom you may ask.'

Prince Ibrahim stared at him blankly. 'Tell him,' he said, turning to Leonora, hat if he wishes to speak to me, or to anyone on this ship, he will need to do so in Turkish.'

Leonora smiled. She appeared to be enjoying the Frankish knight's discomfiture as she translated Prince Ibrahim's words into her own broken French.

The knight frowned, but repeated his earlier words in a hesitant somewhat fragmented Turkish.

Prince Ibrahim smiled. 'That is better, Sir Knight. Unfortunately for you, I am not much concerned about a ransom. There is plenty of time for that. We are bound on a long voyage, which has already been badly delayed by the unprovoked attack by a galley of your Order upon an Ottoman galley and the massacre of most of its crew. You will have to be one of our company, I fear, for some little while. I have no doubt that Yakoub will be able to find you accommodation on one of the benches of our galley-slaves.'

'I?' the knight exclaimed. 'I, Pierre de Foulques, a galley-slave? This is an outrage. I have offered you a ransom.'

'Take him away, Yakoub,' said Prince Ibrahim, waving his hand. 'I wish to see no more of this talkative knight.'

Prince Ibrahim suddenly felt tired. He had been awake almost continuously for close on forty hours and felt a desperate need to sleep. He was alone now, save only for Leonora.

'Thank you, my page,' he said, 'for the water. You were very brave during the battle. I shall not forget it.'

'Lord,' she began, only to stop short suddenly.

'Yes?' he said. 'What is it?'

'Only this,' she resumed. 'You have trusted me, my Lord, absolutely. I shall not fail you. You see, I have nothing left to lose but my gratitude . . . that, and my dreams.'

'I believe you, Leonora,' he said warmly. 'But you owe me no gratitude. I have made you a promise, and I will keep it. Soon you will be able to go back to your own people.'

She shook her head, but said nothing more and stretched out her blanket close to the door.

'It is too late, my Lord,' she murmured a little later, 'but may heaven preserve you always.'

The next four days passed without any incidents. The regular practice sessions were continued, with a buoyant and elated crew, revelling over what they continued to see as their great victory over the Hospitallers. Such indeed was their confidence that Prince Ibrahim was led to believe that they would have been prepared to confront an entire squadron of ships of the Order. For Yakoub and his men he seemed to have assumed the mantle and aura of a minor deity. It was as well, he reflected, that he had Samuel there, with his doleful countenance and cold analytical approach to all matters, to remind him that he was just a simple mortal to whom fate had on this occasion vouchsafed a very considerable slice of luck. Leonora, he was relieved to see, was playing her part well. There was a spring in her step which had been totally lacking previously, and he even noted the occasional smile. This was particularly evident after a number of conversations between her and Samuel. He did not inquire, but he assumed that Samuel had been able to persuade her that she might be healed of her sickness. Throughout this time there was a clear blue sky, with only the occasional small wisp of cloud, and a hot sun that seemed to point stabbing rays at the Ottoman galley as it glided on its way through the water. The galley-slaves were rowing well, and Prince Ibrahim was content to demand no more than a reasonable cruising speed. They had performed extremely well in the battle with the Hospitallers and deserved some recompense.

It was during the following night, the eleventh since their departure from Istanbul, that the weather changed with great abruptness. Prince Ibrahim was woken by a sudden shuddering of the ship as a violent squall of wind and rain buffeted it from end to end. He leapt up from his couch, almost colliding with Leonora in the darkness.

'Get dressed, quickly,' he instructed her. 'I am going on deck. Come and join me as soon as you are ready.'

He opened the cabin door only to be drenched immediately by a huge spray of salt water. The sea appeared to be heaving in turmoil, throwing up phantasmagorical mountains of water that exploded into huge jets that cascaded downwards in trajectories of white and silver.

It was with great difficulty that he fought his way forward to the edge of the rearcastle of the ship, grasping at whatever supports he could find. The only light came from the three ship's lanterns, and the white and silver heads of the cascading waves. The galley was being rocked from side to side, its wooden frame groaning under untold stresses. He peered down at the galley-slaves below. Some of them were crying out loud in sheer terror, begging to be loosened from their chains. For a moment Prince Ibrahim's thoughts went to the proud knight who had so recently joined their ranks. A bitter smile crossed his face. The man would perhaps learn to be a little less arrogant in future as a result. He turned as he heard Leonora struggling forward to join him. He moved to help her but she waved him away with a wry smile.

The wind was steadily increasing in velocity and driving the ship in a southerly direction. There was nothing that could be done, except to render thanks for the fact that they were far from any shoreline and in no danger of hitting any rocks. However violent the storm, it was unlikely to last for long. Summer storms rarely did. Yakoub and Yusef had come forward to join him, clutching, like him, for support to one side of the rearcastle.

'We can ride out this storm, Lord,' said Yusef. 'The oars have been lashed to the side of the ship. We should not lose many of them. But I fear some of the galley-slaves may suffer. We cannot afford to lose too many of them if this very large galley is to maintain a reasonable speed.'

'We can do nothing until the storm has blown itself out,' said Yakoub. 'It is like a flooded dungeon down there.'

By midday the force of the wind had indeed abated, but it was still blowing too hard for rowing and the ship was being carried still further off course towards the south. Yusef calculated that they were some two hundred leagues off the coast of Africa and heading in the direction of the Bay of Sirte, to the east of Tripoli. Two hours later the wind had dropped sufficiently for Yakoub to be able to go and inspect the galley-slaves. He came back with a sombre look on his face.

'They have suffered quite badly, Lord. Three at least are dead and between ten and fifteen are too badly hurt to be of any more use. I have given orders for them to be thrown overboard, poor devils. At least they will be out of their misery.'

Prince Ibrahim nodded. 'How will that effect us? Can we cope with such a loss?'

'It is bound to slow us down, that and the fact also, of course, that we have been blown badly off course. The battle with the Hospitallers and the storm have between them, I would judge, set us back at least six or seven days. It is possible too that some of our food supplies may have been spoilt by all the sea water that came over our sides. I have set some of the men to bailing, but it is hard work for them. If our supplies have indeed been contaminated badly, then I fear we shall have to put in somewhere – Tripoli, Tunis, or wherever – so that we may replenish our stores, buy some more slaves and make good our losses.'

'Very well, Yakoub. Let me know as soon as you have come to a conclusion. Ask Yusef to try and calculate our distance from both Tripoli and Tunis. We are, in any case, still being carried in the direction of the former, whether we wish it or not.'

The clouds were becoming lighter in colour and beginning to break up, leaving space, here and there, for a touch of pale blue. It was a hopeful sign. Prince Ibrahim breathed in deeply. The loss of time was a pity, but he still felt invigorated and unconquered. Even the return of Yakoub with a downcast countenance did not dismay him. Yusef had come with him.

'It is as I feared, Lord. Most of the fresh water vats have been stove in or are contaminated. We shall have to call in soon for fresh supplies.'

'What do you think, Yusef, how far are we from Tripoli?'

'Normally we should get there in less than two days, Lord,' said Yusef. 'We should be able to start rowing soon, for the wind is dropping fast. But the galley-slaves are exhausted. It could take us longer. They have been badly affected by all those deaths. It is understandable.'

'Understandable perhaps,' said Yakoub, 'but it is not to be tolerated. It is we, not they, who will decide on the speed of this ship.'

'Allow them a few more hours' rest, nevertheless,' Prince Ibrahim ordered quietly, 'until the storm has completely abated, and give them some more extra rations, even if you have to watch the water. We must not forget that they served us well in the battle with the Hospitallers. How, Yakoub, is our captive knight? Has he survived so far?'

'He has, Lord, surprisingly well,' said Yakoub with a dour smile. 'He is a strong man. He has asked to see you again.'

Prince Ibrahim shook his head. 'He is a galley-slave now, Yakoub. He has no rights. When we reach Granada, he can write to his Order and see what ransom they are prepared to pay for him. Till then, he is to be treated like the rest of them. I do not like arrogance.'

Yakoub smiled his approval. Samuel, however, who had come up to them, gave a deep and audible sigh. Prince Ibrahim looked amused.

'Samuel, I think, does not approve. It is against his better financial instincts to subject such valuable merchandise to excessive risk. Is that not so, Samuel?'

Samuel spread out his hands. 'I am sure he would pay more to be freed of his fetters now, Lord. Why should we show generosity to the Order? They have plenty of funds.'

Prince Ibrahim laughed. 'If ever I fall heir to a kingdom, I will make you my financial treasurer and mentor, Samuel. But our knight must bide his time. I will see him when we reach Granada, not before. Come, let us have a game of chess to wile away the time till the wind has fallen. Leonardo will make us some coffee.'

This time Prince Ibrahim won easily. Samuel's game was lacklustre and his reactions slow. The combination of a missed financial opportunity and the rigours of the storm had, it seemed, been more than he could stomach. Prince Ibrahim waved him away. 'Go and rest, Samuel. You are no challenge today. By the time you wake up again, we shall be in calm waters. In the meanwhile, I shall teach Leonora to play. Come page, and attend your master.'

He was surprised at himself at how much he enjoyed her company. For a young girl, a royal princess, used no doubt to adulation and attentive servants since birth, who had been through such harrowing experiences, and who still now was under the shadow of a living death, she carried herself with pride, and even, he had to admit, with dignity. Whether it was her youth, her blood, or perhaps a new ray of hope, he was unable to tell. She was willing now to respond to his questions about Aragon and Castile, about the years of her childhood and her earlier aspirations.

'My cousin Ferdinand is ambitious,' she said on this occasion. 'He and Isabella are of one mind. They wish to unite the whole country and make Spain the new Rome. Ferdinand had plans for me too. I was to marry the son of the King of Navarre, to bind their house to ours. I met him once, my husband to be . . . and now not to be. He was a studious, courteous man, and not, I think, one made for blood and war.'

'Perhaps it will still happen, your marriage to him.'

Leonora shook her head. 'Not now. Ferdinand is ruthless. He will not risk offering damaged goods to Navarre. Such an insult would never be forgiven. All we Spaniards are alike in that respect, my Lord: proud, and proud to be proud. It is not for nothing that Their Catholic Majesties see Spain as the new Rome, and the saviour of Jerusalem in a new crusade that will go far beyond the confines of Granada.'

'So you too, child that you really still are, see no hope for Granada?'

'I am no longer a child, my Lord,' she remonstrated quietly. 'My innocence has been destroyed, beyond any redemption. I am sad for you at the fate that awaits Granada. But for Aragon and for Spain I am proud. I think you would also be so if you were in my place, for you are, I believe, a proud man at heart.'

'You are a princess of Aragon, Leonora, and true to your name. Perhaps we shall meet one day at the Spanish court when I go there as Ambassador from Granada. But that shall be as you wish. I will not know you there if you wish us to be strangers. But come, I was going to teach you chess. It is a fitting game for a princess.'

He dreamed that night of the court of Spain. A court of splendour, where gold and pearls shone alongside rich silken brocades, where damascened swords hung on the walls, and the hidalgos of Spain had a fierce and fearless mien. But above them, above the glittering richness of the scene and the gilded columns that towered above the throng, there hung a single iron crucifix with the limp body of their Christ. Queen Isabella and King Ferdinand were on their knees, genuflecting in deference to the figure on the iron cross. Leonora stood by their side, wearing the habit of a prioress, her eyes blazing with a sentiment that he was unable to define. Even in his sleep he felt the mailed power of Spain pressing down heavily upon him.

Yusef had been right in his forecast, and they reached Tripoli on the morning of the third day, fourteen days after they had first set out from Istanbul. It did not look like a big town, but there were a number of feluccas in and outside the harbour, and a number of men in long white burnouses were standing on the quayside as the Ottoman galley came alongside. Prince Ibrahim sent Yakoub ashore with gifts for the local Bey and a request to be permitted to revictual his ship with water, dried meats and fruit, and to purchase a number of male slaves to replace the galley-slaves lost at battle and in the subsequent storm. The Bey, it transpired, was an old man, content to stay in his harem, and little disposed to take note of the external world. Even the news of the Ottoman galley's exploit, which could no longer be kept a secret until their arrival in Granada, was insufficient to make him stir.

Prince Ibrahim left the buying of the slaves and the replacement of the galley's supplies entirely to Yakoub. It would, he was told, take the better part of two days. He had little wish to sleep on shore, but relished the prospect of a long hard gallop along the coastline. Inviting Samuel and Leonora to come with him, he instructed Yakoub to send one of his men to negotiate for the lease of three horses for the rest of the day.

The horses having been acquired, they set off at a trot, quickly leaving the rather sad town behind them. The sea sparkled in the sunlight on their right, while towards the left there were occasional sand dunes with, here and there, a caravan of poor traders. The wet sand by the edge of the sea provided an easy terrain for their horses and they often broke into short gallops. He noticed that Leonora was an excellent rider. For his part, poor Samuel had never been over-fond of horses and tended to trail behind.

'I understand that there are some old Roman ruins, a one-time port, some leagues along the coast,' he said to Leonora. 'Shall we go and visit?'

She nodded with apparent eagerness. 'Oh yes. How wonderful also to be able to escape from that galley for a while. It is not easy, my Lord, to act the page day in, day out.'

It did not take them more than three hours to reach the old Roman port. Samuel, who had painstakingly caught up with them, was the first to notice it. Although originally undoubtedly of considerable extent, it had been terribly ravaged by time and scavengers. Only the old harbour mole was still in good condition. But little remained of the granaries and docks that had once marked this site of Roman power. They dismounted and began to wander among the ruins. There was little to disturb, save only the occasional seagull as it went on its way.

'It is a sobering thought, Lord,' said Samuel, 'that it must be close to a thousand years since the Romans left. What a monument to their imperium. And to think that this port was built long before Christ or Mahomet had been heard of!'

'But not your Yahweh, eh, Samuel?' laughed Prince Ibrahim. 'Well, you perhaps have a point there, although whether it is one of any real significance is another matter altogether. What do you think, page?'

To his surprise, Leonora took his question very seriously.

'It is not fitting, my Lord, to make light of so grave a matter. There is only one true God. There can be no other. Jesus, Whom the Jews crucified, is the Son of God. They, he, your servant, are beyond redemption for their crime. You, My Lord, are our enemy. They . . . well, they are beneath contempt.'

For a moment there was absolute stillness between them. Samuel appeared to gulp. Prince Ibrahim, while angry, felt above all a sense of disappointment at her bigotry. He had not expected her to have such a blinkered approach.

'I think, master page, that I must remind you of your position,' he said evenly. 'I will not tolerate such prejudices. You will no doubt do as you please if ever you do return to Aragon, but here you will heed my commands. For me, Christians and Jews are one and the same. I see no difference between you and your sectarian quarrels and differences are of no consequence to me. Understand this, Leonora, and forget it at your peril.'

For a moment she made as if to reply, but then she shrugged her shoulders. Samuel said nothing, but there was an ugly look on his face.

They resumed their walk among the ruins in an awkward and embittered silence. It was close on half an hour before any of them spoke again. .It was Samuel who broke the silence with a sharp cry as he held up a small round object.

'A Roman coin, my Lord, a gold coin. And look, there are more.'

They turned back towards him, Prince Ibrahim quickly, Leonora at a pace that was somewhat hesitant. Samuel had scooped up the coins. There were six in all, gold coins of a good size. Samuel held them out to Leonora.

'Will you accept these, Princess, as a token of respect from one poor, unworthy Israelite?'

For a moment it looked as though she was about to dash the coins to the ground with indignation. But, suddenly, her attitude changed.

'I thank you, Samuel,' she said quietly. 'I am grateful.'

It was the tone as much if not more than the words themselves that began to heal the breach. Words now flowed between them more easily, washing away some of the lingering bitterness. Relief was in the air, as well as a kind of joy that was hard to define. It lasted for the rest of the afternoon and till their return to Tripoli as darkness was about to fall.

The incident, sordid perhaps though it had been, helped to set the tone for the rest of their short stay in Tripoli. Yakoub proved true to his word and by the late afternoon of the second day the reprovisioning of the galley was complete. Prince Ibrahim decided to leave immediately. He sent a curtly worded letter to the Bey and left without waiting for a possible, if improbable, reply.

Yakoub had purchased fourteen new slaves. They had been manacled to their benches, and presented a pitiful spectacle. Even their fellow galley-slaves seemed to sneer with contempt as they looked at their new companions in their distress.

'Not a prize lot, eh, Yakoub?' Prince Ibrahim commented drily.

Yakoub shrugged his shoulders. 'What can you expect, Lord, in a hole like this? But they will row, I can promise you that.'

It was, nevertheless, at a sedate pace that the galley set forth from Tripoli. Now that the news of their victorious encounter with a galley of the Order was in any case known, there was no longer any point in deliberately avoiding the great corsair ports of Tunis, Algiers or Oran, where an Ottoman galley was assured of a warm reception, all the more after an exploit that many would deem remarkable. At the same time, Prince Ibrahim wanted no unnecessary delay.

During the ensuing days they followed the African coastline, hugging it closely. There were occasional feluccas to be seen, but these generally sought to keep their distance from the big Ottoman war-galley. There was a certain elation and joyfulness of spirit on board, stemming very clearly from their victory over the Hospitallers. Even the galley-slaves had some cause to rejoice, for their treatment was very much milder than in more usual circumstances. Moreover, although Yakoub and his men deplored Prince Ibrahim's leniency of treatment towards his slaves, his personal prestige in their eyes had soared to such heights that his every order was obeyed to the letter. The galley-slaves themselves were only too aware of it.

They stopped for only two days at Tunis and again at Algiers, to take on fresh supplies of water and food. Their reception at the two principal corsair ports was in marked contrast to that they had received from the Bey in Tripoli. Here, there were tumultuous welcomes from famous corsair captains as well as from the local population as a whole. The slaves they had freed from the Hospitallers' galley elected for the most part to stay in Tunis. Ten of them had been well-known to the local corsairs and their praise of Prince Ibrahim was unstinted. They bore him no grudge for his use of Greek fire, having realised only too well how much it had contributed to his victory. It was indeed a terrible weapon of war and destruction and seldom allowed for the capture of enemy ships as prizes.

Prince Ibrahim felt obliged to go ashore in both Tunis and Algiers; he took Leonora with him on both occasions, even if his page's ignorance of anything more than a few words of Arabic or Turkish was bound to cause some surprise. Leonora was by his side when the corsairs of Algiers paid him the enormous compliment of offering him the captaincy of a fleet that was being prepared to ravage the coast of Italy between Genoa and Rome, with the hope and prospect of immense booty and wealth. He declined the offer politely, insisting that it was his duty and priority to return to Granada to assist in the defence of this last Moorish kingdom in Spain. His arguments were accepted with good grace, but Prince Ibrahim noticed with sadness that there were no spontaneous offers to come to the aid of Granada. It was to be hoped, he thought, that there would be a more positive response further west from the Kings of Fez and Marrakesh.

Prince Ibrahim did not in any way relax the daily military exercises as they progressed westwards and began to near their destination. He had decided to make for Malaga, the main port of the Kingdom of Granada. The Moslem Kingdom had few warships of its own and relied instead upon engaging corsair ships for periods of up to one year at a time. It was a costly operation but Granada was wealthy and had, in any event, no tradition of seamanship. There had been reports of some engagements with Castilian ships but Prince Ibrahim was taking no chances. It was his intention to sail boldly into Malaga harbour and hand over to King Boabdil a ship in fine fighting order for the year that Sultan Bayazet had placed it at Granada's disposal.

While personally buoyed up at the prospect of an imminent return to Granada, Prince Ibrahim could not but notice that his excitement did not appear to be shared by Samuel and even less so by Leonora. Samuel, he learned, had made use of his short spells on land in Tunis and Algiers to inquire about recent developments in Spain with regard to his own people. Such information as he had been able to gather, though scanty, had been depressing. The latent but unmistakable anti-Semitism that had been largely dormant in the first years of the Spanish monarchs' joint reign was now showing every sign of coming to the fore. Jews, like Moslems, were being required to wear special six-pointed stars on their clothes. The Inquisition was being strengthened and the new Grand Inquisitor, the friar Tomas de Torquemada, a former confessor of Queen Isabella, had taken up his position. There were rumours too of persecution, threats of expulsion and even of *auto-de-fe*, aimed particularly at supposedly insincere *Conversos* or Jews who had converted to Christianity under threats of death or deportation during the reign of Queen Isabella's grandfather, thirty or forty years before. Many of these reports were unconfirmed, but still the underlying message was grim and had filled Samuel with dismay.

Leonora, for her part, gave no reason for her relapse into gloomy introspection. But then, Prince Ibrahim reflected, there was probably not far to look for an explanation. Rejection by her family stared her in the face. After what she had told him, how could she expect it to be otherwise? King Ferdinand of Aragon clearly had high aspirations. There would be little room in his pantheon for a whore, even if she was his own niece with a title of princess in her own right. Samuel had assured him that he knew of several doctors among his own race who might be able to treat her. While nothing could repair the physical and mental damage that she had suffered, superficially she could, in all probability he thought, be healed. Prince Ibrahim made no attempt to broach the subject with her, but instructed Samuel to make urgent inquiries and appropriate arrangements for her as soon as they reached Granada.

It was on a gloriously sunny afternoon, thirty-one days after their departure from Istanbul, that they entered the harbour of Malaga. It presented one of the loveliest prospects that Prince Ibrahim had ever seen. Its fortifications were immensely impressive with three great fortresses, connected to each other, but capable of separate individual defence if the need arose. When well-provisioned and well-manned, it was considered impregnable. The harbour was busy with ships from Egypt, Morocco, Genoa and Portugal, and even one Castilian vessel. Carrying saffron, wax, hides, sugar, nuts, silks, gold and spices, the ships helped to make Malaga one of the richest ports in the Mediterranean and a key element in the wealth of Granada. In the distance beyond the city were the foothills of the Sierra Morena.

Turning to Leonora standing close behind him, he said softly: 'Is it not beautiful? For the moment this land still belongs to us. I pray to Allah that He will keep it so. But Their Catholic Majesties have their own designs. When we land, you are free to go. If you wish it, Samuel will escort you to a doctor, one of his race, who may be able to help you. The choice is yours, Princess.'

She did not hesitate with her reply. 'I will go with him,' she said quietly. 'Once I know his diagnosis, I will know what to do. Shall I see you again in Malaga?'

'That is also as you wish. I must hasten from here to Granada. If the King wishes me to go at once to the Spanish court, then that is where I shall go. I do not believe that it would be fitting for you to travel with a Moslem embassy.'

She nodded her head in agreement.

'No, that is not possible. But I shall see you again, somewhere, Prince Ibrahim. You may be assured of that.' She gave him a faint smile and walked towards the cabin they had shared for more than five weeks. It had been an extraordinary experience for him; perhaps for her also. Enforced intimacy had gone hand in hand, so to speak, with aloof politeness, ownership and, finally, manumission. She was, in many ways, quite an exceptional woman, and he realised with a certain wry suddenness that he would miss her greatly. He wished her well.

With a deep sigh he turned to other matters. There was the farewell to the crew and, above all, to Yakoub; orders to give on what to do until King Boabdil should have decided on how to use the galley so munificently given to him by the Sultan; and, not to be wholly forgotten, the fate of the knight of the Order who was still sitting manacled to one of the benches among his fellow galley-slaves. He smiled. That was a matter and, hopefully, a pocketful of gold, for Yakoub.

Although there was, inevitably, an element of sadness in leaving the ship that had given him taste of glory, it was nevertheless with a light heart that, with all his farewells made, he finally went ashore. Malaga, most of its white buildings glistening in the late afternoon sun, seemed to beckon him on. Within two or three days he would be back in Granada.

*Chapter Three*

# THE EMBASSY

His feeling of elation was, however, to be short-lived. It was in Malaga that he was first told of the internal dissensions and divisions in Granada. The governor of Granada, Ahmed al-Taghri, a close friend of Mohammed ibn Sa'd, popularly known as al-Zaghal, the brother of the former King, Abu al-Hassan, and uncle both to King Boabdil and Prince Ibrahim, spoke in contemptuous terms of the King and his mother, Queen Fatima. Admittedly, al-Hassan had been very foolish in doting so openly upon a young Castilian slave girl, Isobel de Solis, to the extent of making her his spouse and putting aside his first legitimate spouse, Queen Fatima, daughter of the previous King and immensely popular for that reason among the Moslem nobility of Granada. Upon Isobel, al-Hassan had lavished sumptuous gifts of jewelled bracelets, rings and necklaces, and pawed her like a lovesick cat in front of all his court. But Fatima had had her revenge and had him murdered as he slept. But Fatima's only child, Boabdil, was a weakling, lily-livered and a coward. Quite probably a traitor, too, to his country and his people. He had been foolish and careless enough to have fallen into an ambush and had been forcibly kept by King Ferdinand for three months as his housebound guest. He had been treated royally in his gilded cage and, at the end of the three months, had been freed by Ferdinand to return to Granada. But no one knew what secret agreements or undertaking had been reached between them, or how resolute Boabdil would be in the war for survival that was now generally seen to be on the near horizon. Boabdil's uncle, al-Zaghal, the fearless, was for a resolution as firm as that of the Spanish Kings. He favoured an immediate alliance with Fez or Marrakesh, or both, and the reinforcement of all the border garrisons, if necessary with volunteer troops from the neighbouring North African kingdoms. Granada, though small, with its population of not much more than three hundred thousand souls, was rich. It could afford to pay for mercenaries and alliances.

It was with a heavy heart, therefore, that Prince Ibrahim rode out of Malaga two days later. The governor, a man no less fierce and determined than al-Zaghal, had delighted in Prince Ibrahim's victory over the Hospitallers and furnished him with an impressive escort of fifty horsemen. With him also rode Samuel, who had, however, been absent for most of the two previous days. He had not heard again from Leonora, who had left the galley in the company of Samuel without a further word to him. With his attention focused primarily on the grim tidings about Granada, he had for a time almost forgotten her. Although outwardly indifferent, he could not wholly conceal from himself a slight feeling of pain that she had not found the time, or perhaps the inclination, for a more formal leave-taking. She had taken his gift to her of her freedom rather too naturally, however much he had meant what he said.

They rode in silence for the first two hours, Prince Ibrahim, intent upon his own thoughts and also drinking in, half unconsciously, the beauty of the land. This truly was el-Andalous, a paradise made for men on earth, an intimation of the glory of the next life for those who remained true to their faith. It was a land here of husbandry, of rich soil and produce, of vines, olives, orange and lemon groves, of thick green grass with streams that watered them all with munificence. There was a special scent in which delightful aromas were blended with magical potions. It was no wonder that the Christians called it another Eden, except that, for them, it would first have to be cleared of its infidel Moslem inhabitants.

They rode through small villages that bore no trace of raiding or fear. Virtually all the fighting, the commander of his escort had told him, was along the line of the border between Granada and Castile. Few raiding parties ventured more than a few leagues across either border, although there had been occasional major Castilian forays, led either by the redoubtable Beltran de la Cueva or the ferocious Marquis de Cadiz. But the border area was generally mountainous and very difficult terrain for horses. The aptly named Sierra Morena constituted a major obstacle. If it were indeed to come to a full-scale war, the Spanish armies would not find it easy to cut their way through the few mountain passes which were narrow, steep and strewn with boulders. The young lieutenant and the men of his escort seemed relaxed. They were well aware of the fact that the Spaniards could put many times their numbers in the field, and yet they were seemingly able to view it all with a surprising but cheering nonchalance.

A little later Prince Ibrahim signalled to Samuel to come and ride by his side. Perhaps Samuel knew in that perceptive way of his that his master was concerned about Leonora, for he himself came to the subject immediately.

'I accompanied the Princess Leonora to the house of a Genoese banker who acts in Malaga on behalf of Aragon, Lord. I understand that he agreed at once to furnish her with clothes and an escort to take her back wherever she wished. She thanked me and said she would visit the physicians whose names I had given her. She spoke of going first to Toledo, and only later, perhaps, to Aragon. She said she had no doubt that she would see us both again.'

'What do you know of these physicians, Samuel? Can they cure women like Leonora?'

'I do not know much about their skills, Lord, but I have heard it said that such diseases can be cured, provided help can be found speedily. I would be hopeful that in her case it will be time enough.'

They lodged that night in an inn a few leagues short of the town of Alhama. The inn was crowded with traders, pedlars and farmers taking their produce to the market in Alhama or on to Granada itself. Many of them spoke in loud voices, shouting their anger at the recent tax increases imposed by the King, or commiserating with one another at the ever-growing threat of war and the uncertainty of their future. These men's anxieties were in sharp contrast to the nonchalance of his escort. But then, he reflected, the people in the inn were generally older and stood more to lose in terms of livelihood and possessions. Prince Ibrahim mingled with them, asking questions. The news that he had just returned from Istanbul excited the interest of many of them. Even now, thirty-seven years after the event, the capture of Byzantium by the Turks remained a giant ray of hope in their hearts. What Islam had achieved in the east, it could surely match in the west. Many of the men there were carrying scimitars, swords or long sharp knives. All declared their willingness and determination to fight, provided only that they could find a leader. Al-Zaghal's name was often on their lips, but he was growing old and no longer as daring as he had once been. Granada needed a young military leader, able to inspire his men, and then they would show these Spaniards if they dared to invade Granada openly. Prince Ibrahim took careful note. If these men were in any way representative of the Granadan population as a whole, then there clearly was a will and a resolution to fight, needing only to be harnessed and mobilised. He went to his couch that night in a hopeful frame of mind and was able to ignore the snoring of his roommates as he thought ahead to what awaited him in Granada.

He felt a moment of sheer elation when, late the following afternoon, he caught his first sight of the Alhambra palace. It did not seem like five years since he had last set foot in it to receive instructions, such as they had been, from King Boabdil for his embassy to Istanbul. The sheer beauty of the palace took his breath away, as it had always done in his youth. If el-Andalous was the garden of Allah on this earth, then the Alhambra was the most exquisite of its flowers. In the delicacy of its architecture, in the beauty of its colours, and in the pure enchantment of its gardens, its creators had achieved an intimation of heavenly perfection. In beholding it one could have hope and faith in man's highest ideals.

Prince Ibrahim requested the lieutenant in command of his escort to notify the First Chamberlain, or Grand Vizier, of his arrival in Granada and to submit a request for an audience of King Boabdil. In the meantime he would go and call upon his sister, Ayala.

He found her, as he had expected, in the large rectangular house, not far from the Alhambra palace itself, where they had lived during most of his adolescence. Word of his imminent return had apparently reached Granada well before his arrival in the city. Ayala, who was sitting outside the entrance to their house waiting for him, threw her arms around him in sheer delight. For several moments she clung to him, her eyes wet with tears, before he could properly look at her. She was a beautiful woman, although there was an unmistakable touch of sadness about her eyes.

'Ayala,' he said quietly. 'I have missed your presence so much these last five years. Are you well?'

She nodded. 'Yes, I am well, now that you have returned, Ibrahim.'

They went through into the large courtyard with a wide circular fountain and a stone bench running around it. Scattered all over the courtyard were large bowls full of red and yellow flowers. Prince Ibrahim led his sister to the bench by the fountain and looked at her again. She was on the tall side, with a slim and elegant figure, brown hair and brown eyes. She was dressed in white, but with a gold necklace and two light gold bracelets round her right wrist.

'I have brought you back a gift from Istanbul,' he said. 'I hope you will like it.'

He clapped his hands for Samuel, who had waited outside the courtyard and who was carrying a box made of cedarwood. He bowed low to Ayala who gave him a brief smile of welcome. Prince Ibrahim took the box and presented it to his sister. For a moment she looked at him with the eager anticipation that he remembered from their youth.

'Open it then,' he said with a smile.

The cedarwood box was in itself an object of beauty and Ayala's eyes were wet with tears as she looked at it.

'It is the first present I have received since you left, Ibrahim,' she said as she opened it, and then gave a gasp of surprise and delight as she lifted out an exquisitely carved and shaped necklace of green jade. 'It is beautiful,' she breathed. 'Ibrahim, it is quite, quite beautiful. It must be worth a prince's ransom.'

She threw her arms round his neck again, embracing him with fervour while at the same time seeking to place the heavy jade necklace round her own neck. Against her dark skin the jade stones seemed to glow.

'The Ottomans are justly famous for their jewellery,' he said, 'and their jade necklaces, daggers and tiaras are simply quite fabulously beautiful.'

He led her back to the bench by the fountain. Samuel had disappeared discreetly and for a while Prince Ibrahim was content to watch his sister as she spoke of her life during their years of separation. For her, they had not been happy years.

'It is not that I was in any way maltreated, but King Boabdil has always made it clear that he had little time or liking for me. He has been a poor King, Ibrahim. He has not improved during the years of your absence. He hunts, drinks, covets gold, and spends most of the rest of his time with his women. He is jealous of the fame of his uncle and suspects that there are many in the land who would gladly see al-Zaghal on the throne. He has his own dealings with the Spaniards and no one knows what secret commitments he may have entered into during the months he spent as Ferdinand's compulsory guest. He does nothing to strengthen the defences of Granada, but is content to leave that mostly to others. Only occasionally he seems to flare up into short-lived bouts of fury, threaten to march on Cordoba or Valencia, but then falls back on cursing his lack of cavalry.

'And you he has neglected, completely?'

She nodded. 'Yes. There have been emissaries from Fez and Marrakesh to explore possible alliances and marriages. But al-Zaghal and I were never invited to participate in any of their discussions, nor even to meet them. I might as well not have existed.'

'And yet he has called me back from Istanbul. Why?'

'That I cannot tell you. Perhaps he has a use for you, or thinks he has, if you were to be prepared to be his tool. Perhaps an unwitting tool! Or perhaps he wishes to placate al-Zaghal who has long pressed for Granada to have an envoy at the Court of the Spanish Kings. I do not know his reasons, Ibrahim, but I do know that his feelings towards us are no better than they were five years ago when he as good as banished you to Istanbul. Rather, even, the reverse.'

'He is wasting your youth, Ayala,' said Prince Ibrahim angrily. 'I shall not let this continue. If Boabdil wishes me to go for him to the Spanish Court, then he must give proper recognition to your position here. He must find a suitable match for you, fit for a princess of his own House.'

'Ibrahim, Boabdil is not a king. He is a man of straw who blows this way and that. He is influenced by his mother, the old queen, who plotted against her own husband, and by the stars, by the sycophants who sit fawning all around him on their footstools. Sometimes, even, he is influenced by al-Zaghal, shamed into a moment of action. But those, alas, are moments that do not last for long. If you have forgotten this in your years in Istanbul, you will see it again for yourself soon enough. We have a scarecrow for a King; only our enemies are not crows, but eagles who are soaring high.'

'I can only pray, Ayala, that you are too severe in your judgment, although the words I heard from al-Taghri in Malaga were but little different from yours. We shall see how long he makes me wait before he summons me. But enough of Boabdil for today. We have so much to catch up on, you and I.'

They spoke until far into the night, reminiscing, wondering about the future, or talking about the glory of Istanbul. Ayala's eyes glowed with wonder as Prince Ibrahim described the great city, with its imperial aura and stupendous past, become now the symbol of a resurgent Islam. She shared his exhilaration at the prospect of Sultan Bayazet camping before the gates of Vienna.

They were given plenty of time to talk, reminisce and conjecture, for King Boabdil was clearly in no hurry to see him. When Prince Ibrahim inquired, he was informed that the King had gone on a three-day hunting expedition and that this would be immediately followed by a royal visit to the fortress of Bada in the east of Granada, where he would be meeting his uncle, al-Zaghal. Prince Ibrahim was invited to bide his time and to take rest after his arduous and reportedly adventurous journey back from Istanbul. As for the Ottoman galley, King Boabdil had written to thank the Sultan for his great courtesy and generosity and would shortly be appointing one of his own officers to its command. In the meanwhile, the galley remained inactive in the harbour of Malaga.

Prince Ibrahim spent his time talking to Ayala, playing chess with Samuel, and going each day to the military school at the Alhambra to fence. There, he was greeted with effusion, for his exploit in defeating the galley of the

Hospitallers had become famous throughout Granada. Many of his former schoolmates were keen to have sword-bouts with him. Although none of them spoke openly, and he himself was very careful to speak no words of criticism or disregard about King Boabdil, it very soon became evident to him that there was a widespread feeling of discontent and a low morale. Boabdil was held in low esteem, bordering on contempt.

Occasionally, he would stroll through the winding streets near the Alhambra palace to look at and admire the glittering and appealing wares of the Albaicin. Here there were brocades, taffetas, woollens, linens, leather goods of every shape and size, ceramics, jewellery, weapons of every description, and thick gold nuggets from as far away as the Sudan. The entire district was a tremendous treasure house in its own right, a haven of rich merchants and traders, dressed and apparelled in costumes as sumptuous as any he had ever seen in Istanbul. Women mingled here freely with men, and there were Moslems, Jews, Berbers, black Africans and Genoese in profusion, as well as quite a number of Castilians and Aragonese. Once Ayala accompanied him, but she appeared not to share the customary feminine passion for clothes, jewels and delicate fripperies. She preferred, she told him, to play the rebec or flute, or to read poetry with her poet friend, and sometime Grand Vizier, according to a past vagary or two of the King, one Ibn Zamnak, the greatest of living poets, in her view, in el-Andalous. Spurred on by his sister's enthusiasm, Prince Ibrahim went on three different occasions to listen to him as he recited the *kharjas*, the ballad-type songs that had reached the apogee of their development in the great flowering of the arts of el-Andalous some two hundred years before.

Ibn Zamnak was an elderly man with an unsavoury reputation. It was generally believed that he had connived to have one of his own predecessors as Grand Vizier poisoned, and that he owed his own several but short-lived spells as Grand Vizier up to the present time to a combination of blackmail and recourse to the evil arts. But he had a handsome appearance and the *kharjas* he recited, wistful and melancholy in their languorous beauty, touched Prince Ibrahim to the heart. Ibn Zamnak was currently out of the King's favour and often came to Ayala's house, where he was made very welcome. It was on one of these occasions that Prince Ibrahim met him for the fourth time and sat side by side with Ayala as Ibn Zamnak chanted in a low but lilting voice one of the loveliest of the *kharjas*:

'What shall I do, mother,
My friend is at the door.

Comes Easter yet without him
Tearing my heart for him.

As if you were a stranger's son.
You no longer sleep on my breast.

What shall I do or what will become of me?
My friend,
Do not leave my side.
Tell me what I shall do,
How I shall live,
Waiting for this friend;
For him I shall die.

So much loving, so much loving,
Friend, so much loving.
Beautiful eyes fall sick
And suffer such pain.'

Later that evening Ibn Zamnak plied him with questions about Istanbul and about its writers, poets and mysteries. He spoke with an air of regret, almost of depression. Spanish Islam, he said sombrely, was isolated, cut off, abandoned. Separate from and alien to the Christian kingdoms to the north, but foreign also to the peoples of north Africa and the eastern Mediterranean who were their brothers by race, culture and religion. Granada was like a brilliant silver shining shooting star that had lost its orbit and seemed destined to fall into a cold and hostile sea that would extinguish it forever. Despite Ibn Zamnak's unfavourable reputation, Prince Ibrahim was drawn to the man, with his poet's gift for words and a passionate love for the literature of Islamic Spain. He had the clear impression that his sentiments were reciprocated for, when Ibn Zamnak came to take his leave that evening he gave Prince Ibrahim the book from which he had been reading.

'Please take this book,' he said,' in memory of the glory of our cultural heritage, in which we can all share and find joy. You may rest assured, Prince Ibrahim, that when next the King deigns to take me back into his royal favour you will have a friend in me.'

It was not, finally, until the tenth day after his arrival in Granada that he was at last summoned to meet the King. The summons, when it came, was peremptory. Prince Ibrahim was to present himself at the palace within the hour. The royal herald, who had first gone to his house, had been directed by Ayala to the military school where Prince Ibrahim was fencing, as was his wont. He followed the King's herald immediately, taking time only to excuse himself to his fencing partners and to throw a cloak over his shoulders. Even so, the King kept him waiting – when they arrived at the palace, the King, he was informed, was taking a bath. This he apparently liked to do at his leisure, since another two hours passed by before Prince Ibrahim was finally permitted to enter the royal presence.

King Boabdil was seated on his throne, his head thrown well back, with two large hunting dogs at his feet. Two of his chamberlains stood close behind him and there were, Prince Ibrahim noticed, not less than ten royal guards in immediate evidence. At a sign from one of the chamberlains he stepped forward and bent down on one knee a few paces in front of the King.

'Welcome back, my dear nephew, from your sojourn at the Ottoman Court. I hope you found it instructive. I have written to thank the Sultan for his kind treatment of you, a minor princeling, I fear, at his Court and for his kind generosity in the matter of the galley. I understand you made use of the opportunity to demonstrate your military prowess. No, do not tell me about it. There are other more pressing matters.'

King Boabdil stopped for a moment as if to clear his throat, then motioned to one of the chamberlains to give him some water. He drank slowly, looking at Prince Ibrahim from beneath half-closed eyelids as he did so. Prince Ibrahim kept his face expressionless, seeking not to show his growing contempt for this jellyfish of a king. 'While you have been at the Ottoman Court,' the King continued, 'we have been struggling to maintain our country's independence against huge odds. That needs skill, Ibrahim, and tenacity, not just simple skills with sword or lance. I am not so short of good soldiers. But I have negotiated in person with the Spanish Kings. I have seen at first hand their cunning and know their objectives. But now I need to know more. Ferdinand and Isabella are not necessarily always of one mind, I think. The problems of Aragon are not always those of Castile. And what fate do they have in mind for us? What could we get by way of favourable terms or conditions in exchange ...' the King stopped abruptly, as if he had gone further than he had intended, but then resumed, '. . . in exchange for, say, a treaty of alliance, for loans to finance Castilian expansion in Africa, or elsewhere? You are to be my eyes and ears, my dear nephew, at the Spanish Court. See what you can learn and seek to direct their covetous eyes away from Granada. You will need of course a diplomatic weapon and for that you shall have gold. Gold in such quantities as will make the Spaniards gloat, for gold, I have learnt, is what they covet above all else.'

Prince Ibrahim shook his head. 'If I may contradict Your Majesty,' he said quietly, 'they covet this land, and honour, more than they do gold.'

'What do you know of the Spaniards, Ibrahim,' shouted the King angrily. 'You, abroad for the last five years, with no personal experience of either Ferdinand or Isabella, You would try to instruct me, your King? I had hoped that the Ottoman Court would have made you more respectful of your superiors.'

'I am yours to command, my lord King,' said Prince Ibrahim quietly, 'but you will permit me one question. Why then have you chosen me, so manifestly unfitted, for this important mission?'

King Boabdil's eyes seemed to become suddenly opaque. 'Because, my dear nephew, I need a Prince of the Blood Royal. The Spanish Kings are proud and arrogant. Any man who is not of our Royal House they would simply spurn. There is only my uncle and you who come into the reckoning. I cannot afford to send al-Zaghal. It could almost be seen or interpreted as a declaration of war; besides, he is my best commander. I cannot afford to lose him, or to let him go. His continued presence in Granada is quite indispensable. While you, my dear nephew, if I may say so without offence, are quite dispensable.'

'When do you wish me to leave, my lord King?'

'Why, now, at once. You will be provided with a retinue, befitting your estate as an ambassador to their Spanish Majesties. They can all be ready tomorrow. I will give you a letter of accreditation.'

'And my instructions?'

'To turn the eyes of their Catholic Majesties elsewhere. Use what skills you have, and all the gold I shall send with you. But keep them from Granada.'

Prince Ibrahim bowed. 'I shall seek to do so, my Lord, but I have a boon to ask.'

King Boabdil scowled. 'It is customary to ask for favours after a service has been rendered,' he muttered, his eyelids dropping lower.

'The Princess Ayala is also of your royal house. It would encourage me in my mission if I knew that her position was being recognised here in full.'

A dark crimson glow spread over the King's face. Prince Ibrahim saw him bite his lips with vexation, but he succeeded in controlling his anger.

'Very well,' he said, 'it shall be as you ask. But see to it that you do not fail me at the Spanish Court. And one point more, nephew. I would advise you to have no contact with your uncle al-Zaghal. His is a policy of war. It is not mine. See to it that you remember that. I will not need to see you again before you leave.'

The King rose and without another word walked out of the throne room, followed by his two chamberlains and all his guards, leaving Prince Ibrahim alone. He felt half-drained, as though he had been in close contact with a squid. And this man was the leader of Granada in its hour of peril!

He went back to Ayala in a sombre frame of mind. It was not that he necessarily disagreed with Boabdil's policy of peace, but his personal conception of that peace was that it should serve as a basis for bolstering Granadan independence, as precious time gained so as to forge an alliance with Fez or Marrakesh, or, if all else failed, to work towards a form of vassalship to Spain that would at least safeguard rights of religion and of property for all Granadans. The policy of Boabdil, it seemed to him, was one of pure appeasement, designed to maintain his personal position on the throne of Granada with no thought for the rest of its people. It left him with a feeling of distaste that affected his whole being. The delight he had anticipated from his return to Granada had all too quickly acquired a bitter taste and, were it not for the presence of Ayala, he would have been glad to have left immediately.

That had, admittedly, been the royal command, expressed in dismissive and peremptory tones, but days passed without any further word from the palace concerning his retinue, the gifts he was to take to their Catholic Majesties, or his letter of accreditation. It was doubtful whether Boabdil even knew where the Spanish Kings were staying at that moment. Perhaps he would be left to discover even that for himself.

It was, in fact, from Samuel that he first heard that the Spanish Kings had decided to extend their stay at Cordoba for six months longer. That in itself was an ominous sign that their minds were still bent on an early solution to their Granadan problem. Samuel, too, was in a sombre and downcast mood. *Auto-da-fe* were on the increase. A new royal edict compelled all Jews in Spain to wear yellow tunics, known as *sanbenitos*, inscribed with their names and misdeeds against the Christian religion, as well as high conical caps or *corozas*. Anti-Jewish sentiment was running high and there were rumours that all Jews were to be presented with a straightforward choice between conversion or expulsion. Even conversion did not bring with it a guarantee of safety from persecution, for all *conversos* were to be subjected to a careful and virtually continuous supervision by the Holy Inquisition. Samuel shuddered repeatedly as he told his tale of woe and disaster.

'It can only get worse, Lord,' he murmured. 'They are bent on a policy of religious purity. All of Spain must be purified in the sight of their Christian God, for only then can Spain receive His blessing and take the lead in the final crusade for the recovery of Jerusalem.'

'But your people are their financiers and bankers, Samuel,' said Prince Ibrahim. 'How can they be replaced? You have your network of contacts throughout Europe and even in many Moslem countries.'

'That is true, Lord, but now the Genoese and the Venetians have become the chief moneylenders and financiers in many European states. They are powerful and very sophisticated. The Spanish Kings believe them to be more effective. Besides, their combined political, religious and financial objectives override all other considerations. It has a message for Granada, too, Lord, and one that is, I fear, quite unmistakeable.'

'Granada is rich, in gold, if in little else,' Prince Ibrahim temporised.

'I know it is not for me, Lord, to proffer contrary views,' said Samuel meekly, 'but only prompt action now can save Granada. I do not know what should be done, but if nothing is done at all, then Granada is doomed and that doom will come very soon. Word has it that the Spanish Kings are assembling at Seville a large army with mule trains and carts for the transportation of provisions and materials. That can have only one possible objective.'

'King Boabdil has given no instructions save to keep their minds off Granada.'

Samuel shrugged his shoulders. 'Then he is no better than an ostrich, believing that if he buries his head in the sand the lion will not notice him. Believe me or not, Lord, as you will, but Their Majesties of Spain have their eyes fixed very clearly on this particular ostrich and they would not lose sight of him even if he buried himself totally in the sand.'

It was not till three days later that one of King Boabdil's chamberlains at last brought news that all was ready for Prince Ibrahim to set out on his mission. He was to seek out Their Majesties of Spain as envoy of Granada, with representative and limited negotiating powers. He was to have an escort of twenty attendants and was to take their Spanish Majesties gifts of gold, silver and carpets. It was believed that the Spanish Kings were still at Toledo, but Prince Ibrahim was to take such steps as he could to establish confirmation of this. Samuel laughed bitterly as he listened.

'Still at Toledo! Why Lord, it is more than two weeks that they have already been at Cordoba.'

'We cannot appear to be disregarding the King's commands,' said Prince

Ibrahim quietly. 'We shall ride from here due north towards Jaen. From there we can either continue northwards towards Toledo or strike westwards towards Cordoba. We shall leave tomorrow at daybreak.'

He took a sad leave-taking of Ayala. He had told her of the King's promise to give her a fuller role at his Court, but neither he nor Ayala had any great faith in his words. At least this time, he was able to comfort her, he would be closer to her and, in case of desperate need, he would be able to return and be with her quickly.

His retinue, when he inspected it the following morning, was reasonably impressive. Out of the twenty men in the escort assigned to him, twelve were men-at-arms. The remaining eight comprised a secretary, two cooks, two body-servants, and three black slaves. There was, of course, also Samuel. The horses that had been provided for them were fine animals, and the jackets, blouses, gowns and cloaks of the escort made for a smart appearance. The carpets, gold and silver he was to present to the Spanish Kings were carried on the backs of pack-mules. He could only hope that these gifts would be of finer quality than the presents King Boabdil had sent with him to Sultan Bayazet five years previously. There were, in addition, three diamond rings of exceptional size; these had been entrusted by the King, personally, to the secretary.

Ayala rode with them for the first hour until the road began to narrow and snake its way through the high trees of the lower mountain range.

It was silent among the trees. Although it was peacetime, Prince Ibrahim decided to take no chances, but detailed two of his men-at-arms to ride some fifty paces ahead. They advanced at a gentle walking pace. The journey to Jaen could be expected to take three to four days, for some of the terrain to be traversed was very rough. Nearer the border with Castile, the risk of skirmishes or ambushes would be much greater so that very careful precautions would have to be taken.

They camped beneath the trees that night, round small log fires to keep out the first autumnal chills. Prince Ibrahim went round the men of his escort, chatting easily to them. Most of them were young men, seemingly well-pleased to have been assigned to this mission and keen, too, to see the Castilians at closer quarters. Nearly all of them had been engaged in some previous skirmishes with them. However, Prince Ibrahim was less favourably impressed by his secretary, an older man called Sharif, light of build and elegant in his dress and manners. There was a lack of directness about him that the Prince found unpleasant. The fact that he had doubtlessly been assigned the role of secretary of the mission by King Boabdil in order to keep a close watch on Prince Ibrahim only served to increase the Prince's suspicions.

The following day brought with it a different terrain. The pack-mules with their heavy loads had frequently to be helped, and their rate of progress slowed down appreciably. They were out of the woodlands now, but there were steep ascents and descents with crevasses that sometimes widened alarmingly. The sun, however, was still hot and the sweat clung to their clothes. Later in the day they came to an area with small streams with fast-flowing water that seemed at times to burble on their way. Prince Ibrahim ordered a halt and they took it in turns of six or seven to strip and lie in the cool water. They had passed only a few small hamlets where the local inhabitants had been friendly, but watchful. There had been, they said, occasional raids by Castilian soldiers, but none in the very recent past. But there were, as had often been the case before, rumours of a massing of Castilian soldiers beyond the border.

It was, in fact, not until the fourth day of their journey that they began to draw close to the border with Castile, and they were still a few leagues short of it when they stopped to make camp for the night. This time Prince Ibrahim doubled the number of sentinels and ordered all the fires to he stamped out. Occasionally through the night they heard the distant sound of galloping horses, but no one came near their encampment.

After they had resumed their journey the following morning, they came suddenly to a small village, called Zafra, where several fires were burning. There were loud cries of women wailing and shrieking. Ordering his men-at-arms to follow him, Prince Ibrahim spurred his horse on into the centre of the village. There a small number of Spanish soldiers were rounding up a group of villagers with the clear intention of carrying them off. The bodies of two dead villagers lay on the ground and a third had been forced to lie with his head across a fallen tree trunk. A Spanish soldier had his sword raised high and was about to behead him.

The sound of the approaching horses made the Spaniards look up and shout out in alarm. But it was too late. Only eight in number and unable to take to their horses in time, Prince Ibrahim and his men swept down upon them, cutting five of them to the ground and seizing the other three. The villagers swarmed round them, some grabbing their legs and feet and kissing them as they wept with relief and gratitude. Prince Ibrahim heard that the Spanish raiders has fallen upon the village at dawn. The two dead men had been on watch but had clearly been taken by surprise. The man who had been about to be beheaded was the Alcalde of the village. He had dared to rebuke the raiders and had already been severely beaten about the body. He was, however, still able to walk, albeit with some difficulty.

'What do you intend to do with them, Lord,' he asked, pointing to the three Spanish soldiers who had been captured.

Prince Ibrahim looked at the man's haggard face. The desire of revenge was visibly burning in his eyes and Prince Ibrahim followed his gaze as he looked at the group of villagers who had been rounded up for deportation and subsequent slavery, but who were now laughing, praising Allah and singing.

'I think, Alcalde, that I will give them to you. It will be for you to hold them to ransom, or to punish them as you and your fellow villagers think best. I am only pleased that we came in time to be able to help you.'

'Thank you, Lord, for your generosity,' said the Alcalde with fervour. 'I shall consult with my villagers, as our custom requires, but I have no doubt about their verdict.'

The three prisoners had at first looked on with a certain disdain. While villagers and other ordinary folk were frequently tortured, raped or sold into slavery, captured soldiers were accustomed to being exchanged or ransomed. Even when captured by villagers whom they had cruelly wronged, the lure of money or the sheer basic need of money in order to survive after an enemy raid was usually enough to ensure their protection and their lives. But the tone of the Alcalde's voice and the look of profound hatred on his face as he looked at them was enough to warn them of the peril they were in.

'We are soldiers in the armies of Spain,' they said almost in unison. 'Touch us if you dare. Our murder would be avenged ten times over and more.'

'Methinks, sirrahs, that you are ill-placed to speak of murder,' said Prince Ibrahim acidly. 'Silence. It shall be as these villagers decide.'

The Alcalde had been right. It did not take the villagers more than a few minutes to decide in favour of vengeance. The three should hang, and so also should the bodies of the five dead marauders. Prince Ibrahim nodded his consent and drew back his men. As they withdrew one of the Spanish soldiers broke free and threw himself at his feet.

'Mercy, great Lord. I am the son of Beltran de la Cueva. My father will pay any ransom you ask.'

Prince Ibrahim started back in surprise. Beltran de la Cueva was a campaigner known for his exceptional ferocity and as a scourge of Granada; he had led raid after raid, sometimes deep into Granadan territory. He had stormed several castles, often putting their defenders to the sword. A brilliant soldier who had struck terror into his enemies' hearts, he was also a figure of loathing and hatred.

'You must speak to the Alcalde,' said Prince Ibrahim curtly. 'It is out of my hands.'

'I will give you one hundred thousand maravedis,' said the Spaniard breathlessly to the Alcalde. 'Even more, if you will but let me send word to my father.'

Many of the villagers gasped while some of the men in Prince Ibrahim's escort gaped in amazement. It was a princely sum. Even the Alcalde hesitated.

'How can you be certain that your father will pay so huge a sum,' he asked curtly, 'and where would it be delivered, and how?'

'Wherever you wish,' said the young Spaniard, a wave of relief spreading over his face. 'You can send one of my men with a message.'

The Alcalde shook his head. 'No. These men are to die. You will write a letter to your father which will be delivered to him by a safe hand. You will say in it that the ransom is to be delivered to us here by a company of not more than eight men. We shall be watching very carefully. At any sign of double-dealing, you will be the first victim. Is that clearly understood?'

The Spaniard paled. For a moment he appeared to be about to reject the Alcalde's terms, then he lowered his eyes. 'I agree,' he murmured.

His two companions, who had at first looked on with rising hope, now looked at him with contempt, They said nothing, but their expressions were contemptuous beyond description. Without a further word they turned their backs on him.

'We are ready,' they said simply.

Prince Ibrahim looked at them with a certain admiration. Freebooters, killers, robbers, all of these things could, rightly, be said of them, but they were nevertheless brave men who knew how to die. They were, he knew, the real representatives of Spain, soldiers by whom personal honour, as fashioned by their own code, was prized above all else.

The executions did not take long. They strung up the bodies of the five dead men first. There was little or no breeze and their bodies gyrated only slowly on the long ropes dangling down from the trees. Then they came to fetch the two living soldiers. Even the villagers, it seemed, were impressed by their bearing in the face of death. They tied their hands behind their backs and hauled them up to a height of some fifteen feet before they let them go. The sound of their necks snapping could be clearly heard. The young de la Cueva let himself fall to the ground and covered his eyes with his hands. Prince Ibrahim sighed. The young man had been dishonoured beyond any possible redemption. Perhaps his father would even refuse to pay the ransom and leave him to die; but there could be no doubt that he would seek to wreak a terrible revenge. The young de la Cueva, his only son, had perhaps saved his life, but he had forfeited his right to honour.

Prince Ibrahim was about to signal to the men of his retinue to move on when they heard the sound of a large body of horse rapidly approaching. They were evidently galloping fast. The villagers began to tremble with fright, fearful that their liberation from the threat of captivity might prove to have been short-lived, while Prince Ibrahim ordered his men to close in behind him with their weapons at the ready. It was a tense moment until cries of 'Al-Zaghal, al-Zaghal' rang out loud and clear. Prince Ibrahim craned his neck to catch the first sight of his great-uncle, brother of the former King, Hassan, and known as the foremost warrior of Granada. He had only the vaguest recollections of him, dating back to his childhood, since al-Zaghal had spent but little time at the court of Granada. Much of his time he had spent across the sea in Morocco at Fez. In King Hassan's prime he had been the commander of the Granadan army as it fought to keep back the Castilians in short campaigns between equally short-lived truces. Three years before, he had returned from Fez and semi-exile to become once again the commander of the Granadan forces and Granada's most feared military chief. He now rode straight up to where Prince Ibrahim was standing.

'So,' he said in a deep booming voice, 'you are my great-nephew Ibrahim, back at last from Istanbul. I should not have recognised you. And whom have we here?' he added, pointing to the young Spaniard still on his knees on the ground.

'Greetings then, my uncle,' said Prince Ibrahim coolly. 'This is the son of Beltran de la Cueva. We have captured him. He is to be ransomed by the villagers.'

Al-Zaghal boomed with a laugh that seemed to travel up from his belly. 'The young de la Cueva! Well, congratulations, nephew, although it is rather a pity you did not hang him along with the rest of his band. Perhaps I should pay his ransom for him, then I could roast him a little and send his well-gnawed ribs back to his father. But I fear I shall have to forego that pleasure. My other nephew the King would not be best pleased. But come, let us be seated and eat. My men have brought plenty of provisions. You shall tell me all your news. It is not every day that Granada finds a new young hero to add to its ranks.'

The evening turned into a feast. To Prince Ibrahim's surprise, al-Zaghal and his men drank wine and drank it in considerable quantities and without the slightest compunction. At his uncle's playful insistence he too sipped a glass but found the taste too sour, and little to his liking. Besides, for him the words of the Koran were to be taken literally.

It was not long before his uncle turned, inevitably, to the subject of Granada and its fate.

'Boabdil is an ass, an incompetent bungler, who is throwing Granada to the winds. All he can think about is his own fat carcass, his gold and his women – that is when his mother, Fatima, will let him. She is worth ten of him, but her only concern is for her son and pandering to his wishes. For centuries now we have been on the retreat. First we lost out provinces beyond the Pyrenees, then Catalonia, then the region immediately to the south of it which the Spaniards call Old Castile, then Toledo, Zamorra and, not so long ago, Cordoba and Seville. It is a tragic tale of unmitigated disaster and woe. And Why? Because we let it happen. We could have stopped it all, Ibrahim, if only we had stayed united and counterattacked. We could have driven them back. Now they are too strong and we too weak and few in numbers. But if we are resolute we can nevertheless still keep what we have. To do it we have to show the Spaniards that the cost of the seizure of Granada will be so high that it will cripple them for a generation, or longer. They have other worries besides Granada. They have their rivalry with Portugal in Africa and the Atlantic, with Navarre which, like us, is small but capable of resistance, and with France which wants to seize Aragonese lands to the north of the Pyrenees. But to survive we must make ourselves feared. There, Ibrahim, lies our salvation, not in cowardly posturing. Not in acting like the young de la Cueva who has dishonoured not only himself but his father also.'

'You are aware, uncle, that the King has sent me on a mission to the Court of the Spanish Kings?' said Prince Ibrahim questioningly.

'Of course. That, indeed, is why I am here. I came to look for you on your way to Jaen.'

'To stop me, or to advise me?'

'To speak to you, Ibrahim. To see for myself of what kind of mettle you are made, and I thank Allah that he has made you a man and not a poltroon like our wretched King. Of course you must carry out your mission and go to the Court of our enemies. If you can prevail upon them to leave Granada in peace, then I shall be one of the first to applaud you. But if they could be convinced that in us they have a real tartar, that would be even better.' He fell silent for a moment, then sighed. 'The odds against us, sadly, Ibrahim, are greater than I care to think about, or acknowledge. But I for one would rather die a free Granadan than live under an alien yoke. If it ever comes to that, each one of us will have to find his own salvation. Mine, I know, is to fight to the end. Boabdil will manoeuvre untiringly to save his own bacon. You, you Ibrahim, will similarly have a choice to make. But come, we have spoken long enough. I am glad to know that a real man will represent us at the Spanish Court. Tomorrow our paths will separate, you to go on your mission, while I return to Boda on the eastern frontier. But we shall assuredly meet again, Ibrahim, and hopefully know better times for Granada.'

Prince Ibrahim was sad to see his uncle leave on the following day. He seemed a man of exceptional strength and determination. For him, the issues were manifestly clear-cut and his course a totally obvious one. In contrast, the devious underhand manoeuvres of King Boabdil seemed to make one a party to dishonour. He sighed. It was going to be a difficult line to keep when he got to the Spanish Court. Their farewells were sincere, but unemotional and short. The villagers were the only ones to cry and show any grief at their departure, but they were at least partially reassured by al-Zaghal's promise to be mindful of their need of protection.

Some three hours later Prince Ibrahim and his escort reached the frontier with Castile.

A small fort marked the spot but, although undamaged, there were no soldiers to guard either it or the frontier. Prince Ibrahim shrugged his shoulders. It really made very little difference; if the reports they had heard were true, it would not be long before they would be encountering forces of the Spanish army, and so it soon proved to be, since it was only shortly after passing the fort and frontier that they saw a patrol of six horsemen in the distance. Prince Ibrahim immediately motioned to one of his men to hand him the white banner which he had been given as a signal to make to the Spaniards when he met them, and rode forward alone at the head of his retinue with his men riding behind him in a double file with the pack-mules between them. The road here was wider and in good condition and they were able to ride forward quite easily in their relatively wide broad formation. It was not, however, until their white banner had been clearly distinguished that the enemy patrol rode forward to meet them. Their leader, an older man, with a touch of grey at the temples, greeted them courteously.

'You are welcome to Castile. I see you carry a flag of truce?'

'I am Prince Ibrahim Ibn Sa'd, sent by the King of Granada as envoy to the Court of their Spanish Majesties. I have my credentials with me.'

'Then you are doubly welcome. I am the Marquis Juan de Santillana, brother to His Eminence the Cardinal Mendoza, Archbishop of Seville. I am the commander of the Castilian forces in the province of Jaen. I should be honoured if you would accompany me there.'

Prince Ibrahim could see a number of soldiers as they approached the town, but they were not in such numbers as to suggest preparations for an imminent march on Granada.

Santillana took them to a large palatial building constructed in the Moorish style in the centre of the town.

'This palace belongs to my brother the Cardinal. It is at your disposal as long as you are in Jaen. I will send word of your arrival immediately to Their Majesties in Cordoba.'

'To Cordoba?' Prince Ibrahim repeated, glancing at Samuel.

'Yes, they have been there for the past three weeks.'

Santillana accompanied Prince Ibrahim on a tour of the palace. Although in need of some restoration it was generally in a good state of repair. It was, Santillana said, little used although there were plans to give it to one of the great Spanish Orders of chivalry as a base for a southern commandery. He was careful to avoid any reference to the fact that the palace had clearly been built during the time that Jaen had been a Moslem city. Santillana, who seemed to be of an expansive disposition, said that one of his own sons was a knight in the Order of Calatrava. Prince Ibrahim knew that the knights of Calatrava were reputed to be the most formidable of the three great Spanish military Orders of chivalry: Calatrava, Santiago, Alcantara, their names rolled like thunder over the battlefields and, like their distant cousins the Hospitallers, they had an unmatched reputation for valour and fearlessness. These military Orders had played a leading role in the Christian Reconquista and the dour and unstoppable drive south that had reduced the once great Moslem Iberian empire to the small enclave of Granada.

Santillana insisted that Prince Ibrahim and his retinue should accept his full hospitality. He undertook to provide supplies of meat, vegetables and fruit for all, and invited Prince Ibrahim, personally, to dine with him in the house that he occupied nearby. Prince Ibrahim accepted the invitation, curiously and uncomfortably aware of the fact that, with the exception of Leonora, this would be the first time in his life that he would eat with a Christian.

Santillana was again in an ebullient and even exuberant mood. He received Prince Ibrahim with great ceremony. A huge silver bowl with water, slightly perfumed with roses, was brought to him as he entered. After he had washed his hands he was led to a richly furnished and decorated room, brightly lit with perhaps some twenty Moorish lamps. He refused an offer of sherry or spiced wine, but accepted a glass of water.

'You will, I am sure, be made most welcome by Their Majesties,' said Santillana courteously as they took their places at a long and massive rectangular oaken table. Silver platters and goblets had been placed on the table together with long thin knives with silver handles. Servants now brought in two large silver candelabra which they placed at either end of the table. 'These are glorious days for my country,' Santillana continued. 'Our Spanish Kings are the glory of Europe. They seemed destined to usher in a golden age when all the world will be redeemed. Nothing can stop us.'

'I have indeed heard that your Kings are held in high esteem,' replied Prince Ibrahim politely. 'I count myself fortunate in being permitted to attend their Court.'

'I am a Castilian, Prince, and I serve Her Majesty, Queen Isabella. But together with His Majesty King Ferdinand of Aragon, she is forging a new Spain. United, our two countries have become the champions of Europe. France, Portugal, England, they all stand in awe of us and seek peace and our friendship. The Holy Father in Rome has sent his blessing to our Kings. They will fulfil the prophecy that out of the west will come the hero-king who will recover Jerusalem so that all men may be free to go there and glorify God the King.'

'I have not heard of this prophecy,' said Prince Ibrahim, 'but great though your Kings may be, how can you hope to recover Jerusalem? You may have won great victories here and in the west, but in the east the Ottoman Empire will not so easily be overcome. And even here in the west, there is discord between Castile and Portugal, between Aragon and France.'

'No longer, Prince. Do not allow yourself to be deluded by fanciful dreams. The Royal Houses of Castile and Portugal will soon be united through marriage when the Princess Isabel, our Queen's much loved eldest daughter, marries the Crown Prince of Portugal. At the same time negotiations are taking place between King Ferdinand of Aragon and the French King that will lead to recognition of Aragon's suzerainty over the province of Rosellon, north of the Pyrenees. No, Prince Ibrahim, in this world only Granada stands between us and the mastery of the whole Iberian peninsula and our onward thrust into Africa. Can you wonder that we have great faith in that prophecy?'

'You are indeed fortunate in your Kings,' said Prince Ibrahim with a slight smile, 'but your ambitions would appear to be very great.'

'Not too great, Prince. We Spaniards are a proud people. We would scale the heavens themselves if our Kings bade us do so.'

For a moment Leonora's words came back to his mind. She too had spoken of her countrymen's pride. It seemed to be there, embedded in the marrow of their bones. Was it pride or arrogance, or perhaps some special Iberian combination of the two?

The meal was sumptuous. Squid, in small rolls and fried, were followed by oysters, langoustines and lobsters, and they, in turn, by mullet, carp, bream and tunny. Then came a profusion of meat dishes: beef, lamb, veal, fowl of various kinds and gaily coloured piles of tomatoes, beans, peas, cabbages and peppers. Santillana drank considerable quantities of wine, Prince Ibrahim noticed, but was scrupulous in avoiding pressing it on his guest. It seemed to have little effect on him, although he grew less talkative and more pensive as the evening wore on. He was a good trencherman too and ate with gusto. Prince Ibrahim, for his part, ate sparingly. The food was certainly of the highest quality, but he felt little hunger and found little pleasure in eating with his country's enemies.

'My brother the Cardinal will be particularly pleased to meet you,' said Santillana as the evening drew on.

Prince Ibrahim looked at him questioningly.

'My brother's ambition is to leave Spain as a wholly Christian country before he dies. He is sixty years of age.' Santillana chuckled. 'He fears he may not have many more years. He will want to ask you how many Moslems would be willing to convert and become members of a greater Spain.'

'I fear,' said Prince Ibrahim coolly, 'that if he were to ask me such a question, my reply would not give him great joy.'

'But why not? You must surely realise that Granada will soon be crushed. Why else should you have been sent on this peace mission of yours? Your King, who is a wise man, understands the situation well enough. I was present when King Ferdinand spoke with him. King Boabdil is clearly a man of good sense.'

'I think, my lord Santillana, that these are questions that give rise to very delicate issues. If you mean that King Boabdil is anxious to find an accommodation with Their Majesties of Spain, then I could agree with you. But neither he, nor anyone else, can tell the people of Granada to abandon their faith in favour of Christianity. That is a matter for each individual to decide for himself. But I fear that I am wearying you. Thank you for your gracious hospitality. I will retire to rest. Tomorrow we may perhaps speak again.'

As he rose from the table, Santillana rose with him. Courteous to the end, he accompanied Prince Ibrahim to the palace where he and his retinue had been housed before bidding him a good night's rest.

They waited three days at Jaen before the messenger Santillana had sent to Cordoba returned with permission far Prince Ibrahim to proceed and confirmation that Their Majesties of Spain would graciously consent to receive the envoy of King Boabdil.

Prince Ibrahim spent those three days talking to the men of his retinue and, occasionally, after obtaining the authorisation of Santillana, going for short rides or walking round Jaen. Although Santillana unfailingly provided a small escort of Castilian soldiers, he himself made no further effort to meet Prince Ibrahim. It was though a curtain had been drawn between them. Sharif, the secretary, twice asked him whether he wished to record any part of the conversation he had had with Santillana, but on both occasions Prince Ibrahim declined his offer.

'There is nothing to tell, Sharif, except that he is a very proud Castilian nobleman, devoted to Their Spanish Majesties, brother to Cardinal Mendoza, and father to a knight of the Order of Calatrava. As you can imagine, his is not a very optimistic vision of our future.'

Even Sharif had smiled at that formidable list of negatives. No doubt he had drawn some conclusions of his own which he would in due course be reporting back to King Boabdil; but for the present he could have only very little to go on.

Prince Ibrahim played chess again, on two occasions, with Samuel, and won both times. Samuel's depression seemed to have settled on him like a monk's cowl that hid his real face and left him looking blank and characterless. He declined the invitations to go on any of Prince Ibrahim's walks about Jaen, seeking instead permission to stay inside the palace.

They set off on the fourth day, within a few hours in fact of having received the favourable reply from the Court of the Spanish Kings. Santillana and a large body of soldiers went with them, enclosing them completely. It was, said Santillana, a measure taken to ensure their safety, although they in fact saw very few Spanish soldiers during the next two days. They crossed over the Guadalquivir river early on the second day in a small fleet of boats that plied backwards and forwards until all the Granadans and their Castilian escort had been ferried across. The water level in the river was comparatively low, and the boats were scarcely necessary, but Santillana's orders were strictly obeyed.

The countryside between Jaen and Cordoba was rich and lush. This, too, had once been a part of el-Andalous, but had been reconquered by the Christians some forty years before by Queen Isabella's grandfather, King Alfonso X. It now formed a part of the province of New Castile. Prince Ibrahim's hand fastened on his sword hilt as they passed the front of the occasional church that was clearly a converted mosque. It was like seeing the obliteration of a nation. How many of the people living there, he wondered, in the places where he was now passing by, were still Moslem at heart? Who could tell? Only a war could provide the answer and even then, how many would actually dare to proclaim their true faith until such time as it became clear that Granada had at least a chance of victory? The Holy Inquisition had done its work well. There were moments when the odds stacked against Granada seemed insurmountable and Prince Ibrahim came close to sharing Samuel's black mood of despair. But he fought back against it with determination.

In these rich lands he saw plenty of activity. There, also, they saw more soldiers. Sometimes, long columns of them marched slowly along the country paths and tracks, like ugly snakes wriggling and crawling with poison in their fangs. There were tears in his eyes when they first caught sight of Cordoba with its Roman bridge and, soon afterwards, the erstwhile great mosque, the largest there had been in Spain, now with its heart ripped out and soaring pillars in its place, and become a Christian cathedral. He dashed his hand across his face. Tears could not be permitted in front of the pride of Spain. He had to don a mantle of apparent facile indifference, of an arrogance as great as their own, or perhaps even greater. Yes, he determined, that would be his attitude from then on. He would not simply just match their arrogance, he would trample upon it with a greater arrogance of his own. King Boabdil's mission would have to live with that as best it might. Again Leonora's words came back to him. She had said that he too was a proud man; well, perhaps he would be able to prove her right.

It was not really a transformation. Perhaps Leonora really had been right and had simply recognised that part of him better than he had known it himself. He began by informing Santillana that he and his retinue would wait outside Cordoba until the preparations for their reception had been completed. He would call upon their Spanish Majesties at their earliest convenience, but requested time to prepare himself in a manner befitting this great honour. If Santillana was surprised at the greater aloofness in Prince Ibrahim's voice and bearing, he showed no sign of it. He merely smiled and went to carry the message to his sovereigns.

This time Prince Ibrahim was not kept waiting long. Word came back within three hours that the Granadan embassy was welcome and to be formally admitted into the city, that the palace of the Marquis of Cadiz was to be placed at their disposal, and that Their Spanish Majesties would be graciously pleased to receive the Granadan envoy at nine o'clock on the following morning. Two knights from the royal household had been assigned to lead them on their way through the streets of Cordoba. The streets were crowded now and many faces turned to look at the visitors from Granada that had come into their midst. Prince Ibrahim set his face hard. Although the pain of the grief of what had been lost was welling up inside him, he was determined to be unyielding. While he saw buildings and occasionally even faces that attracted him, he kept his eyes fixed resolutely forwards. He was suddenly playing for high stakes. He had to be strong. Arrogance, he reminded himself repeatedly, had to be met with even greater arrogance.

But he had not yet mastered control of himself and his emotions to the extent that he would have wished. He slept fitfully that night in the Marquis's palace. His mind was full of conjectural images of the Spanish Kings. Of course he expected them to be proud, but then they were Kings among kings. They were spoken of with awe. Their ambitions were limitless: the islands in the Atlantic, Africa, new lands still to be discovered, and, above all, Jerusalem. They were of the stature and the ilk of Sultan Bayazet.

He rose early the next morning. The palace of the Marquis de Cadiz was a sumptuous new building, constructed since the re-conquest of the city by King Alfonso. The hospitality of the Spaniards was, he had to admit, on a grandiose scale. Prince Ibrahim was impressed despite himself. His body servants brought him water from the large ornamental garden that stretched out on one side of the palace. Although this was not a Moorish building in style, the love of water had manifestly survived the *Reconquista*. Prince Ibrahim gave careful thought to his dress for the occasion of his first meeting with the Spanish Kings. It was important for him to appear at once ceremonious and independent. He had heard that the Spanish Court loved dark colours, deep reds and purples. He would go in sharp contrast, deliberately in white, slashed with green, with a dagger made of green jade that he had purchased in Istanbul on the same occasion as the necklace he had brought back as a gift for his sister, Ayala.

It was Santillana who came to escort him to his audience. It was, he was informed, to be a short presentation of his credentials. Their Majesties could not spare more than a few minutes, but had desired to demonstrate their good will towards King Boabdil by granting an immediate audience to his envoy. Prince Ibrahim bowed but said nothing in reply. Even a short interrogation was likely to be a daunting experience.

His nerves were raw and on edge when he was ushered into the small chamber where King Ferdinand and Queen Isabella received him. For a moment he returned their gaze steadily with equanimity, then he bowed low before kneeling down on one knee, close before them.

'You are welcome to our court, Prince Ibrahim,' said King Ferdinand smoothly. 'You bring us tidings from your King?'

'I bring a message of peace and goodwill, Your Majesties, and a letter from my lord King, nominating me as his envoy to Your Majesties and requesting that I may be received as such. The letter speaks of King Boabdil's love and true devotion to Your Majesties.'

'There will be much for us to discuss, Prince Ibrahim,' said Queen Isabella, speaking for the first time in a voice that was at once melodious and strong. 'Granada is ever in our thoughts and we pray daily to God that He may give that issue a favourable outcome.'

'Word had reached us, Prince,' said King Ferdinand, 'that you are a man of action, that you captured a galley of the Order of the Knights of St John, and that you were involved in a skirmish with some Castilian soldiers.'

Prince Ibrahim bowed. 'These reports are true, Your Majesty, but they may have omitted the fact that in both cases my men and I reacted to an act of aggression.'

'It appears that in the second incident you captured the son of our noble lord, Beltran de la Cueva, and handed him over to the common men of the village.'

'To the common men of the village where he had slaughtered two villagers and was about to behead a third, and carry off the rest of the population to slavery, my lord King. He deserved to be punished and may count himself fortunate that he will be ransomed.'

'What ransom do you seek?' asked Queen Isabella.

'I want no ransom, Your Majesty. The ransom must be paid to the people of the village he raided.'

'You are a young man, envoy of Granada, and you speak with remarkable firmness,' said King Ferdinand quietly. 'It seems you are also a man of a violent disposition. I wonder whether King Boabdil has chosen his envoy wisely.'

'It is not for me, Your Majesty, to question my lord King's appointment. I can only endeavour to carry out his commands.'

'You may retire, envoy of Granada,' said Queen Isabella. 'You may stay at our Court, for the present at least. We shall consider how long your stay here can serve a useful purpose. You may attend major Court functions and receptions. On all other occasions you are to come to our presence only if commanded to do so. You may move about Cordoba as you will, but only after informing the Marquis de Santillana of your intentions. He will be personally responsible for your safety and that of your retinue. We would greatly regret any unfortunate incident. We shall expect you to attend our Court ball tomorrow evening.'

With that Queen Isabella gave him her hand to kiss. Prince Ibrahim bowed low and retreated from the chamber. He had scarcely noticed what the Spanish Kings had been wearing. Externally he had, he believed, succeeded in keeping his composure. Internally, he was trembling with emotion. These were truly great Kings. It no longer surprised him that Santillana and Leonora had spoken about them in such terms of respect. He could have wished that they sat, as Moslem Kings, on the throne of Granada.

Sharif questioned him closely on his first meeting with the Spanish sovereigns. At times it bordered so much on an interrogation that Prince Ibrahim felt compelled to rebuke him. He had not inquired as to how Sharif was to send back his reports to King Boabdil, nor would he condescend to ask. It was enough to be sure that some form of communication existed, perhaps even with the active connivance of Ferdinand and Isabella. He told Sharif the truth, almost literally word for word, as he remembered their conversation. The secretary showed no emotion other than his very persistent curiosity. He was particularly keen to know whether the Spanish Kings had made any reference of special moment to King Boabdil, but did not seem in any way concerned to learn that this had not been the case. Prince Ibrahim was even inclined to believe that the secretary had been quite relieved.

Samuel was no less eager in his questioning, although his only real genuine interest was to know whether anything had been said, perhaps indirectly, about the status of the Jews. While he readily accepted Prince Ibrahim's comment that it would have been a surprising topic for the Spanish Kings to have mentioned or broached to a Moslem, he was nevertheless clearly disappointed.

'Perhaps they will object to the presence of a Jew in your retinue.'

'I doubt that,' said Prince Ibrahim. 'They will hardly seek to dictate who should be included and excluded in a delegation from what is still another sovereign state. Besides, they probably do not even know that you are a Jew.'

'That would surprise me, Lord. If no one else had told them, I think your secretary Sharif will make sure that the fact is brought to their attention. Remember, Lord, I am not an official member of your retinue, only your personal servant. Sharif has no direct hold over me. I think that hardly suits him, although he may overlook it as long as he believes me to be of no significance.'

'You seem to have little fondness for Sharif.'

'I have a strong dislike of spies, Lord, and Sharif has been sent to spy on you. I am sure he is very clever. King Boabdil will have learnt to choose his spies well, of that you may be certain.'

'So what would you have me do, Samuel? I could, of course, send him back to Granada with a personal message for the King, except that for the present there is no special message to send.'

'I would suggest, Lord, that you should make much of him. Allow him often about your person. Consult him, or at least appear to do so. He will never be your friend, but at least it may make him less of an enemy.'

Prince Ibrahim nodded. It seemed good advice. He put it into effect straightaway and Sharif returned with the smile of a contented cat. 'Ah, Sharif,' said Prince Ibrahim with a smile that hurt his lips, 'I have thought of one item that I did not mention to you. Their Majesties have commanded me to attend a ball tomorrow night. It would be very helpful to know who may be there. Also any advice you might be able to give me about their particular interests would be very much to the point. I would appreciate your full cooperation, Sharif. You are in King Boabdil's confidence, I know. We must all work for the best interests of Granada, must we not?'

'I think I can get all the names you want, Lord,' said Sharif confidently. 'The whole royal family will be there. I mean the royal children, the Infantas, the Princess Isabel, her sisters, the Princesses Juana, Catalina and Maria, and, of course, Prince Juan, the heir to both thrones; the Cardinal Mendoza, Archbishop of Toledo and elder brother of the Marquis de Santillana; the Marquis de Cadiz, the Grand Master of the Order of Calatrava and the Grand Masters of the Orders of Santiago and Alcantara; the Guzmans; the High Constable Benevento; Nicola Franco, the Papal Legate; the Franciscan friar, Jimenez de Cisneros, confessor and close confidante of Queen Isabella; and also . . .' he hesitated for a moment, his eyes veiled, although whether from concentration or contained amusement it was impossible to tell, before resuming, '. . . and also, in all probability, the lord Beltran de la Cueva. And then also, of course,' he added, almost as an afterthought, 'the new Grand Inquisitor, Tomas de Torquemada.'

'I see that you are indeed well informed, Sharif,' said Prince Ibrahim with a faint smile. 'My congratulations! Have you any advice as to how I might approach any one of them?'

Sharif appeared to hesitate. For a brief moment Prince Ibrahim had the impression that the secretary was on the point of revealing perhaps the first of his cards, but, if so, he was quickly disappointed.

'I think, Lord, that on this first occasion little more is called for than the conventional niceties. There will be time enough thereafter to test the waters.'

'Thank you, Sharif. I think it would be as well if you were to attend me tomorrow evening. Please inform the Court Chamberlain. You will, no doubt, be permitted to wait in the outer chamber.'

Sharif's face remained expressionless. 'It shall be as you wish, Lord.'

Prince Ibrahim sat well back in one of the tall high-backed chairs that were to be found in most of the rooms of the palace, all of them decorated with the arms of the Marquis de Cadiz. He felt a certain strangeness about sitting in a chair belonging to one of the bitterest enemies of Granada. A strangeness and yet, at the same time, there was a certain excitement to be derived from it. Prince Ibrahim tried to relax. He really was in the thick of it now. Ambitions, dreams, intrigues, treachery, all of these seemed to be present in a vast cauldron that seethed and bubbled with a venomous ferocity. But there was also time to think and to decide what he would do. He had to master and control his feelings, curb his impulses, and play a waiting game. Pawns in chess could become castles, or even queens. Hemmed in though he was, he was not yet bereft of hope. Granada was a pearl fit only for kings. He would endeavour to keep it so.

He summoned his body servants. Were they spies also? he wondered idly. In the pay of Sharif and, through him, of Boabdil? But what if they were? He could bear that thought, although it was ironic that out of all those whom he had met since his last days in Istanbul, the only ones in whom he felt he could place any trust were Yakoub, the Anatolian, and Leonora, a Christian princess become a whore by force of evil circumstance. There was also, of course, old Samuel, the Jew, who was probably reliable enough, up to a point, and as long as the interests of his fellow Israelites were not at stake. He thrust the thoughts away, out of his mind. He was alone at the Spanish Court, and would have to face the challenge unaided. His mind went back suddenly to the words of the *kharja* recited by Ayala's poet friend, Ibn Zamnak, 'So much loving, friend, so much loving, beautiful eyes fall sick, and suffer much pain.' Strange that while reciting that poetry to himself it should be Leonora's face that came back to him, troubled and unclear as if reflected in a pool of water into which a piece of granite had been thrown, cracking the surface and leaving only distorted images.

*Chapter Four*

# AT THE COURT OF THE SPANISH KINGS

Santillana came early the following evening to escort him to the palace of the Dukes of Medina-Sidonia where Their Catholic Majesties were staying and where the ball was taking place. Prince Ibrahim had dressed for the occasion in a black hose and a dark green doublet slashed with silver, and wore a heavy gold chain that had come from King Boabdil's treasury.

Santillana greeted him with a noticeable less effusive manner than before. 'His Eminence Cardinal Mendoza, Archbishop of Toledo, my brother, has expressed his wish to meet Your Excellency,' he said. 'His Eminence will wish to know the precise purpose of your mission. He is a close and trusted adviser to Their Majesties.'

Prince Ibrahim thanked him, glancing as he did so at Sharif who was standing a couple of paces behind him. As usual, his face was completely devoid of any kind of expression. In a sense, the man made him feel as though there was a poisonous viper permanently on his trail.

The lanterns provided bright lights as they approached the palace. Although very large, it had been built in a sober style that impressed by its elegant simplicity rather than any grandiose or exultant display of gold and carving. Already a sizeable throng of guests were amassed in the outer rooms, awaiting the arrival of King Ferdinand and Queen Isabella. Prince Ibrahim was struck by the exuberant richness of the guests' clothes, but Santillana gave him little time to think or to observe, and led him straight to a small vestibule to one side of the palace where Cardinal Mendoza and one other ecclesiastic were waiting expectantly for him.

Cardinal Mendoza greeted him with at least some slight superficial impression of warmth in his voice. 'I am glad to be able to welcome you to Granada, Prince Ibrahim. You have, I know, already paid your respects to Their Majesties.

This is Father Jimenez de Cisneros, Father Confessor to Her Majesty, the Queen.' He looked for a moment at Sharif who had followed Prince Ibrahim into the small vestibule, but then appeared to ignore his existence.

'You will be aware, Prince, that I am one of Their Majesties' principal advisers. It is in that capacity, and not, therefore, in that of a prince of the Catholic Church, that I was keen to have this meeting with you. I, as you can see, am an old man. Wisdom, it is said, comes with experience, and experience with age. I note, Prince, that you are a very young man. I will presume, therefore, to offer you a word of advice which I assure you is well-meant. It would be imprudent, and highly damaging to your mission, to act in any way in the interests of the Jews. They are still numerous in our Spanish kingdoms but, unless they convert quickly, their days are numbered.'

'All Jews must vanish before the last day,' said the friar in short staccato tones. 'You must know, Prince of Granada, that this is a land of prophecies. Take good note of that. The first of these prophecies I have just told you. The second is that the *Encubierto*, the Hidden One, sent by our God to destroy all unbelievers, to conquer Granada and Africa, and to raise God's standard in Jerusalem, is about to return. There are those who believe our gracious and most holy monarchs are a joint embodiment of the *Encubierto*.'

'I am not aware of these prophecies,' said Prince Ibrahim calmly. 'Like all prophecies, they should no doubt be very carefully examined and assessed before being given too much credence.'

'You are a Moslem, Prince,' said Cardinal Mendoza, 'and not a Jew. Your faith, even though it is different from ours, is one that we can salute. Our differences can, if necessary – and if we find no other way forward – be resolved honourably on the battlefield.'

'The Jewish race are like the charnel house of Satan,' hissed the friar.

Prince Ibrahim looked at him with distaste. 'For a holy man of God, you are strangely full of hatred,' he said. 'To us, the Jews are no different from other men.'

'They were the crucifiers,' said the friar, 'the crucifiers of Jesus Christ, the Son of God.'

'I do not seek to alter your views, Prince,' said Cardinal Mendoza smoothly, 'but only to counsel you in the best interests of your mission. Refrain, therefore, I beg of you, from any expression of sympathy for the Jews. It would be wise not to let it be known widely that you have a Jew in your retinue, since this could well be misconstrued. That, I fear, would not be helpful in the accomplishment of your mission. Their Majesties have determined that their realm shall be purified. You should know that an official edict will shortly be promulgated stating that all Jews must either convert to Christianity and provide convincing evidence of the sincerity of their conversion, or leave the country. Relapsed *Conversos*, and we know that there are a number of them who have secretly continued to practice their own evil rites, will be severely punished. Already, there have been several spontaneous *auto-de-fe*. There will be another, rather more official, here in Cordoba in three days' time. I would advise you, Prince, to attend.'

'I?' exclaimed Prince Ibrahim. 'But what has this to do with me, or my mission here in Cordoba?'

'If Spain is to be purified, it would be unfortunate if those who refuse our offer of conversion were simply to resettle, a short distance away, in Granada. From there, they could plot and scheme, perhaps even harbour evil thoughts of revenge. By attending an *auto-de-fe* here in Cordoba, your presence would be seen as a clear signal to the entire Jewish community that they should not look to Granada as one of their preferred places of escape.'

'Many have already come to us,' temporised Prince Ibrahim.

'That we know, and regret,' said Cardinal Mendoza smoothly. 'But that is a problem for another, future, day. For the present, it is with the Spanish kingdoms, as they are currently constituted, that we must deal.'

'I understand what you are saying, Your Eminence,' said Prince Ibrahim coldly. 'You would, no doubt, expect me to ask what room your policy of purification leaves for any Moslem who still lives in Spain.'

'It has become a matter of great joy to us, Prince, that many former Moslems have become good and worthy Christians. Those who did not wish to convert have, for the most part, left our realms. Any that remain, indeed all of them, are free to stay; but they are like lost souls, condemned to spiritual and social isolation. Eventually they will convert or leave.'

'And any that should lapse?'

'I have to tell you, Prince, that as far as I am aware, they have not lapsed. We have no problems with converted Moslems. After all, for any for whom conversion is inconceivable, Granada is not far distant, nor even the kingdoms of Morocco, where they can find their own kin, ready no doubt to receive them.'

Prince Ibrahim clenched his fists. He felt his anger rising in his throat. Whether meant to be deliberately insulting or not, the words of the Spanish prelate were like slaps across his face. But, openly at least, he could not risk offending Cardinal Mendoza at this stage of his mission.

'But come,' the Cardinal continued, 'it is time to go. I have already detained you far too long. I hope the pleasures of the ball will give you a few hours' pleasant relaxation from your onerous responsibilities here in Cordoba.'

Despite his age, Cardinal Mendoza moved with a kind of easy elegance that was almost feline in its pose and grace. He took Prince Ibrahim by the arm to lead him towards the great hall of the palace where the ball was taking place, leaving the friar and Sharif to follow behind. Prince Ibrahim wondered what kind of account of their meeting Sharif would be sending back to Boabdil. He felt a sudden tinge of anxiety about Samuel. Although no direct threat had been made, the fact that Samuel was not an official member of his retinue was now a definite cause for concern. Fortunately, Samuel was the sort of man who would heed such a warning.

The great hall of the palace of the Dukes of Medina-Sidonia was ablaze with lights. There were candelabras, separate self-standing high candles, rushes and flares, making a small ocean of light within which the great of the land – nobles and their ladies, clerics and courtiers – seemed to swim like tropical fishes in richly coloured vestments. At the far end of the hall a tall dais had been erected for King Ferdinand and Queen Isabella. With them were their son, Prince Juan and three of his sisters, the Princesses Isabel, Catalina and Maria. With them also was Prince Alfonso, son of the King of Portugal, the betrothed of the Princess Isabel, a marriage designed and planned to bring about a closer union between the Spanish kingdoms and Portugal. Cardinal Mendoza led Prince Ibrahim towards the royal dais.

This time Prince Ibrahim could not but notice their dress. Even in the great heat of the hall generated from the innumerable lights and the massed heaving press of sweating bodies, Queen Isabella was wearing a scarlet cloak over a velvet underskirt, a brocade overskirt, and a broad-brimmed and richly embroidered hat under which her hair was gathered in a silken net. She looked much more like a queen about to ride out among her people than a monarch presiding over a ball. Sitting by her side, King Ferdinand was dressed in black velvet but with a brilliant sash of emerald green across his chest and with a heavy gold chain round his neck. The Infantas were in heavy brocade dresses, their young bodies motionless as they watched the swirling throng all around them. Prince Ibrahim looked longest at Prince Juan. About sixteen years of age and the pride of both his parents, he was delicate in appearance although elegantly dressed and elegant, too, in manner. There had been rumours, or so Prince Ibrahim had been informed, that the young Prince's health was giving rise to some concern.

For the next half hour or so the Cardinal stayed close by him, making introductions interspersed with brief, often very witty comments about this or that member of the assembly. There was an extremely definite solemnity about the entire proceedings that Prince Ibrahim found wearisome, even though he was greeted courteously enough. Only a few persons seemed surprised at, or even interested in, the presence at court of an envoy from Granada. The conversation, as far as he could hear and judge, was mainly about the forthcoming royal wedding and its effect upon relations with the neighbouring kingdom of Portugal. The Canaries, Madeira and Africa were often on people's lips. There was talk of a famous Portuguese mariner, one Vasco da Gama who, or so rumour had it, had sailed to the furthest southerly extremity of the African continent and, after rounding it, sailed into a completely new ocean, opening up the prospect of a new route to the Indies and beyond to distant Cathay. Prince Ibrahim listened with his mind in a whirl. Solemn and formal the Spanish court might be, but there was also a hum of excitement, of adventure, of unconfined ambition, that was in utter contrast to the stratified and introspective absorption of Granada.

Sharif had been correct in his forecast. Among those to whom he was introduced by the Cardinal as the evening progressed were the Guzmans, the Papal Legate Nicolo Franco, the High Constable Benevento, Alonso de Cardevas, the Grand Master of the Order of Santiago, and Tomas de Torquemada, the new recently appointed Grand Inquisitor. It was this man who impressed Prince Ibrahim the most. They spoke only briefly, but the impression left by the new Grand Inquisitor was indelible. The man had the look of an ascetic, but with the mien and bearing of a prince among princes, and with a presence that dominated over all those around him.

Prince Ibrahim had just been rejoined by Santillana who appeared to have been detailed to take over the role of his escort from the Cardinal, when one of the King's pages came to summon him to King Ferdinand's presence. Prince Ibrahim hastened to obey. Although Queen Isabella and three of the Infantas were still seated well above the throng of surrounding courtiers on the high dais, King Ferdinand and the Princess Isabel had stepped down and were mingling, seemingly quite freely, with the crowd.

'Ah, Prince,' said the King, 'there is one matter about which we wish to hear from you. Come.'

The King led the way out of the ballroom to a small audience chamber where he and the Queen had received him the day before. But, on this occasion, the King was accompanied only by the Princess Isabel and there were no guards to be seen. There were no seats so that they all had perforce to remain standing.

'We understand that you brought back with you on your galley from Istanbul to Granada my cousin, the Princess Leonora de Antequera,' said the King.

'That is indeed correct, Your Majesty.'

'Why?'

'To rescue her from the situation she was in.'

'In Istanbul?'

'Yes.'

'What was her situation?'

'I think, Your Majesty, that it would be more appropriate to address that question to your cousin.'

'My cousin is unwilling to see me. She has asked for our royal authorisation to enter a convent. She has given no reasons for wishing to do so. All we know is that the ship in which she was travelling to Rome was captured by pirates and that she was taken first to Tunis and then to Istanbul. Now, you understand why we are asking you these questions?'

Prince Ibrahim thought back to what Leonora had told him, of how she would be seen as soiled and unworthy by her cousin the King, and of how she would be rejected by him. But it was not for him to interfere; nor, however, would it be honourable for him to reveal the full sordid details of her life in Istanbul.

'I met the Princess Leonora in a situation of great distress almost immediately before I left Istanbul to return to Granada,' he answered slowly. 'In fact, I was on the point of leaving. I had gone ashore one last time to have a final look at the city where I had spent the previous five years, and I found her lying in the street. Seeing her condition and learning who she was, I offered her a passage on my ship. She accepted.'

'And on your ship?'

'She travelled as my page, disguised as a boy. She was in no danger, except for the danger we all faced in a sea-battle with an enemy galley.'

'Ah yes,' said the King, 'a galley of the Order of the Hospitallers. Your exploits are becoming rather numerous, Prince, and well-known.'

'What was my cousin doing in Istanbul?' asked Princess Isabel, who had been listening intently to the conversation.

Prince Ibrahim looked straight at her. She had her mother's build and a wide open face with intelligent eyes. She carried herself with considerable arrogance.

'I believe she had been sold as a slave,' replied Prince Ibrahim. 'When the corsairs in Tunis learned that she was not to be ransomed, they took her to the slave markets of Istanbul where they were looking for a better price.'

'My cousin, a common slave,' breathed Princess Isabel, her eyes widening in horror and disbelief. 'Father, did you know this?'

The King made a vague motion with one hand. 'I knew Leonora had been sent to Istanbul. I sent a trader secretly to Tunis to negotiate a ransom. I could not leave our cousin to rot in their jails, or worse. But he arrived too late, and we have no contact with Istanbul. But we still do not know,' he continued, turning back towards Prince Ibrahim, 'what happened to her there.'

'That, I fear, I cannot tell Your Majesty,' said Prince Ibrahim quietly. 'Only the Princess Leonora herself can tell you that.'

'Cannot, Prince, or will not?'

'I cannot, Your Majesty. It is not my secret to reveal. But she will, I am convinced, be prepared to tell you herself, if only you will give her time.'

'Very well, Prince. I can see that you are not prepared to tell us. We should warn you, however, that if we learn that you were in any way responsible for her distress, your status as envoy of Granada will not save you.'

'You do yourself no honour by that remark,' replied Prince Ibrahim coldly. 'If Your Majesty will excuse me, I will return to the ballroom.'

'Wait, please wait, Prince, one moment,' Princess Isabel broke in before he had time to turn, and, placing one hand on his arm, went on, 'I, for one, am convinced that you will have treated my cousin honourably. I believe that my father, the King, believes it too. But he is angry, aggrieved, appalled by what has happened to her, as I am also. We now know that she was a slave. It is the rest that we do not know, and yet fear to know. She herself, you see, has so far told us nothing.'

Prince Ibrahim looked at her hand that was still on his arm. 'I understand, Princess,' he said after a moment, 'but it is she who must tell you all herself, in her own time.' He bowed low to the King, and left them in the antechamber to go back into the main ballroom where the throng was even greater than before. Santillana was near the door, and had seemingly been waiting for him to emerge, but he made no immediate effort to come closer to him. Prince Ibrahim looked around for the Cardinal but was unable to see him in the jostling crowd. Mostly they were – both the men and the women – clustered in small, dense groups. Only here and there, around one of the great lords, were there much bigger clusters of twenty or even thirty courtiers, all trying to catch their master's eye and press their suits.

Prince Ibrahim strolled slowly about the great hall, occasionally having to push past a near solid wall of human beings in order to be able to advance. There was a pungent, powerful smell of human bodies, their sweat and body odours mingling disagreeably. A few of the women carried pomanders which they applied incessantly to their nostrils, but for the vast majority there was no such relief. But Prince Ibrahim had to admit to himself, nevertheless, that the display of royal power and domination was impressive. Occasionally, servants in the livery of Castile attempted to penetrate into the hall with large trays of wine, beer and water. Prince Ibrahim took a glass and sipped the cool water gratefully. The conversation all around him was continuous and sparkling, and he even heard his own name mentioned, although with a certain indifference, as though he, and his arrival in Cordoba, were of little importance. There was, he concluded, little point in staying any longer. From the point of view of his embassy to the Spanish Court it could scarcely be described as having been an auspicious occasion. No doubt Sharif would hasten to communicate the news of the poor beginnings of his mission to King Boabdil.

He had not gone far towards the main entrance when both the Cardinal and Santillana came suddenly to his side. Both of them, he noticed, had singularly taut expressions on their faces. They were, however, not looking at him but at a tall broadly-built middle-aged man, dressed in fine silks, who was thrusting his way towards them. His features were hawklike and aristocratic and courtiers were giving way to him with an air of deference. There was a barely contained look of fury on his face, and he was gripping a velvet glove in his right hand. He was within two paces of Prince Ibrahim when Cardinal Mendoza stepped adroitly between them.

'My lord de la Cueva, this is Prince Ibrahim, Ambassador to the King of Granada to the Court of Spain. He has already been received by Their Majesties and has presented his credentials to them. Prince, you doubtless know of the lord de la Cueva, by repute at least. He is one of Spain's finest soldiers.'

It was with a visible effort that de la Cueva brought his voice under control. 'I understand,' he said in a harsh cutting tone, 'that you were concerned in an affray on the border as you came to our country, as a result of which two Spanish soldiers were hanged and another, my son, is being held to ransom. I do not believe Their Majesties will tolerate for long at their Court a man who so abuses his ambassadorial privileges.'

'Your son,' replied Prince Ibrahim in an equally cutting tone, 'was leading a band of marauders, looting and burning a Granadan village in a time of peace. Two villagers had been murdered. A third was about to be beheaded, and a group of men and women were about to be led off into slavery. This was on Granadan territory. Your son was fortunate to escape with his life, but he offered to pay for it, handsomely. He clearly had no wish to die.'

'My son is a brave man, as he would prove to you himself if he were free, and you not skulking behind your ambassadorial clothes.'

'Your son showed little sign of valour. He pleaded on his knees for his life. He was contemptible.'

'Liar! You will pay for those words! You vile infidel, an ambassador you may be now, but one day, soon, I will have you whipped like a mongrel through the streets of Granada.'

'I am aware, de la Cueva, of your reputation for bloodshed, ferocity and savagery, but at least you are said to be brave. It must be galling for you to know that you have a son who is a coward, a disgrace to himself and to your house. But Allah directs his punishments as He sees fit.'

De la Cueva's face had gone white. With an indescribable howl he pushed Cardinal Mendoza aside so that he almost fell and slashed Prince Ibrahim across the face with his glove, gashing his cheek so that it bled.

'It seems, de la Cueva, that you are after all no better than your son. You must know that I cannot fight you now. But this I swear to you, and to all those present here: the day I am free from my duties, and obligations, as envoy of Granada, I will meet with you, or your son, or the two of you together, wherever you wish.'

'It shall be to the death,' shouted de la Cueva between gritted teeth.

Prince Ibrahim disdained to answer but turned his back on him to speak to the Cardinal. All around them a large circle of courtiers seemed disappointed that no further immediate action could be expected.

'It would appear, Your Eminence, that there are unexpected perils at the Court of Spain. You will, of course, inform Their Majesties of this incident, as I shall King Boabdil. He will, I am sure, be very disappointed and vexed at this insult to this country's representative.'

'I shall most certainly draw this matter to Their Majesties' attention,' said Cardinal Mendoza, who still seemed a little shaken at the way he had been rudely shouldered to one side. 'But I would beg of you to recognise that my lord de la Cueva was under particularly strong emotional stress. He had only just been informed of his son's capture, and of the demand for ransom. Your own words, Prince, did little to soothe his troubled spirit. It would be well if the matter could rest there.'

'I will not insist on an apology, my lord Cardinal, but I hope that if we do meet again, de la Cueva will know how to curb his tongue. I cannot answer for the consequences if he does not. But it is high time I left. I will bid you good night, Your Eminence.'

Prince Ibrahim bowed and walked into the outer courtyard where he saw Sharif waiting for him. He sighed inwardly. The prospect of another discreet covert interrogation by his secretary left him with a feeling of nausea. But he was joined also by Santillana and four pikemen.

'My lord Cardinal's orders are that I should escort you back to your residence,' said Santillana with a slight smile. 'He hopes there will be no further . . . incidents this evening.'

They walked back in silence to the palace of the Marquis de Cadiz. As they reached its entrance Santillana bowed. 'Good night, Prince. If I might be permitted to say so, it would be as well to be always on your guard against Bertran de la Cueva. He is not a man to forgive what he regards as a deadly insult to his honour or that of his family. He is no friend of mine and I will keep a watchful eye on his activities. But the danger for you, Prince, is real.'

Prince Ibrahim murmured a few words of appreciation. He felt tired and irritable, both with others and with himself, and there were still long sessions with Sharif and Samuel to come. Both, in their separate ways and for entirely different reasons, were unavoidable. 'Call Samuel,' he said brusquely to Sharif, 'I would speak to you both.'

It was very silent in the palace. Two of the soldiers of his Granadan escort were visibly on duty and he was told that his personal body servants were preparing his rooms and that the cooks were in the kitchens. He walked through into one of the palace's several spacious side rooms, off the main central courtyard, and sank down into a large and comfortable Moorish style chair. He had not long to wait before Sharif and Samuel joined him. He motioned to them to come and sit close by him.

'I have news for you, Samuel, especially. The rumours you have heard about the expulsion of your people are correct. Their Spanish Majesties have decreed a policy of purification. All Jews must become converts or leave. Lapsed converts will be punished and will almost certainly go to the stake. I am commanded – no, not commanded, but strongly advised – to attend an *auto-da-fe* here in Cordoba in three days' time. Your own presence in my retinue is, I sense, tolerated, but on condition that you conceal the fact that you are a Jew. You, Sharif, will no doubt find an opportunity to report on these developments to our King in Granada. You heard the words of Santillana as he escorted us back from the royal palace. Bertran de la Cueva, the notorious father of the young de la Cueva whom we captured at the village of Zafra near the border, is set on revenge and will do all he can to harm us. We must set a permanent guard and close all exits and entrances to the palace here.'

'But we are so few,' said Sharif. 'How are we to resist him?'

'I do not believe that he would dare to attack us openly as long as it suits Their Majesties to have me here as envoy of Granada,' said Prince Ibrahim. 'But that situation could change at very short notice. We can only hope that their lust for the gold of Granada will be enough to ensure our safety.'

'Will you go there, Lord, to the *auto-da-fé*?' asked Samuel, looking as pale and fearful as Sharif.

'I do not think that I have any choice,' said Prince Ibrahim quietly. 'Do not forget, Samuel, that I am here as the envoy of Granada. King Boabdil claims that he wants peace above all else. My refusal to attend, when specifically invited, could be seen, or presented, as an intentional affront to Their Spanish Majesties. No, I fear that I must go.'

'And I?'

'You Samuel, had best stay inside the palace walls. You are not an official member of my retinue. The Spaniards know it. It would be foolhardy to venture out of the palace in daylight unless you are with me.'

'I cannot hide, skulking here, while my brethren are led to the stake,' whispered Samuel. 'Let me go with you. I beg it of you, Lord.'

'Very well, Samuel, you shall accompany me, but I must have your most solemn oath that you will neither speak nor move without my express permission.'

'I promise it, Lord,' murmured Samuel.

'And you, Sharif,' asked Prince Ibrahim, 'do you also wish to come? It will not be a pleasant experience.'

Sharif shrugged his shoulders. 'These men have chosen to die. It is their choice, and their privilege. My nerves will not fail me.'

'Very well. You will both accompany me. You may go now, Sharif. Prepare the report for King Boabdil and ask for an official courier to take it to Granada. We have no secrets from Their Spanish Majesties, at least not for the present. Santillana will, I am sure, be only too pleased to help.'

After Sharif had gone, Prince Ibrahim and Samuel went out into one of the palace's many courtyards and sat for a while in silence. Apart from the hooded light from two small lanterns there was near total darkness. Occasionally a tiny moth would flutter across the pale beam of light coming from the lanterns, its minuscule wings appearing diaphanous and silvery. Only here and there, among large banks of swirling clouds, there gleamed stars that were like pinpricks of light in the pervading gloom. In the distance voices could still be heard. Sometimes they were raucous and loud, ugly vulgar mouthings, bespattered with curses and sometimes ending in a sudden scream. Other sounds were gentler, sometimes lilting and musical, soothing and caressing to the ear.

Prince Ibrahim closed his eyes. He had heard enough about *auto-da-fe* to dread the impending prospect. To have to watch men, bound and helpless, die in agony would not be an easy burden to bear. Cruelty, even savage cruelty, had always been an ordinary part of his life, never distant, and he was prepared to recognise both its inevitability and its necessity. He was himself prepared to be cruel and to have to confront cruelty if or when it was turned and directed against himself. But to see men, and perhaps women also, burnt alive, to smell their flesh as it roasted, men and women whose ability to harm or to hurt had been utterly destroyed or extinguished, was not for him. He sighed almost audibly. If it was difficult for him; he could well imagine how much more difficult it had to be for Samuel. He regretted now having brought him to Cordoba. It had been a foolish decision on his part and it would have been prudent to have left him behind with his sister, Ayala. There was little he could say to him now, to help or to comfort. He leaned over and patted Samuel's shoulder gently with his hand.

'I am so sorry, Samuel,' he said quietly. 'I did not think it would come to this.'

He felt Samuel's body stiffen under his hand.

'I am afraid, Lord,' he began, 'afraid and racked by a desire for revenge. I know myself to be a pitiful creature. I am your slave, Lord, but also a man riddled with fear. I cry for my people who are to die so cruelly and, at the same time, I tremble for myself. I want to run, to escape, to hide back in Granada, and yet I want also to go to the *auto-da-fe*. May heaven have pity on me.'

They continued to sit. Gradually the sounds from outside the palace grew fainter and fainter, until at last they ceased altogether. It was not going to be easy to get through the next three days. Prince Ibrahim's thoughts roamed and wandered back to what King Ferdinand had said about his cousin Leonora. He was not really surprised at her apparent decision to become a Christian nun, but it seemed to him a tragic waste of a young life that had once held such rich promise. What would become of her, he wondered? He did not believe that she would accept simply to fade away as a lady abbess of some remote provincial nunnery. He could not help but wonder whether her decision had been forced upon her by her doctors' inability to cure her. Samuel had expressed confidence in her recovery, but he could only surmise. Even if mercifully cured, the King could well have insisted upon her becoming a bride of Christ. Whatever the reasons behind her decision, he could not resist the hope that he would see her again. The image of her standing by him on his galley, her closeness in the final battle with the Hospitallers, were memories that simply kept on recurring.

The three days, waiting for the *auto-da-fe*, passed with a wearisome slowness. There was a growing, deepening atmosphere of depression that was not easy to combat. While Prince Ibrahim went out occasionally, accompanied each time by an escort of Castilian pikemen, the absence of freedom of movement was such that each time he returned quickly to the palace; but within its walls there was little cheer or relief.

Samuel was silent and seemed to be sinking into an bottomless coma, answering only when physically prodded or shaken. Sharif flitted in and out of his room like a shadow, often disappearing for several hours at a time. He had, he reported, spoken with Santillana and received his authorisation to send his report by courier to Granada. He had not shown him his report, and Prince Ibrahim did not ask about its contents, simply informing Sharif that on the next occasion he would use the opportunity to send a letter to Ayala. In the meanwhile he sought to fill his time with regular fencing bouts with members of his retinue and grappling with one of the several Castilian manuscripts in the small library of the Marquis de Cadiz. The Marquis' tastes were apparently very wide-ranging, since his manuscripts ranged in subject matter from religious themes to military strategy, astrological computations and medicine. Although there was much in the terminology that he was unable to decipher or fully understand, the manuscripts themselves, with their thick reams of paper and beautifully illustrated texts, exerted a great fascination over him.

The day before the appointed time for the *auto-da-fe*, Santillana brought him a personal message from Their Spanish Majesties that Prince Ibrahim was invited to join those accompanying the procession of the penitents from the *Casa de los Conversos*, where they were being held, to the field on the outskirts of Cordoba where it was expected that the final act of the *auto-da-fe* would be watched by thousands of Granadans.

'Their Majesties have accorded you a great honour,' said Santillana. 'I shall come and escort you to the *Casa de los Conversos*. You should be ready to leave here at noon. The town will be crowded.'

'I shall be accompanied by two members of my retinue.'

'Very well. I shall inform Their Majesties. I shall provide an adequate escort for the occasion.'

Santillana kept to his word. Noon on the following day had just struck when he rode up to the palace entrance with an escort of twelve pikemen. Wordlessly, Prince Ibrahim, also on horseback, and accompanied by Samuel and Sharif on foot, moved to join them. Santillana and Prince Ibrahim rode at the head of the column, followed by four pikemen, with Samuel and Sharif sandwiched between them, the eight remaining pikemen making up the rear. They went off at a slow pace through streets that were rapidly filling with huge crowds of people, shouting and gesticulating but already half-inebriated by the excitement of the gruesome spectacle that they had come to watch. They paid little attention to Santillana's party.

To reach the *Casa de los Conversos* it was necessary to traverse the centre of the city. The crowds here, many of them having made their way over the old Roman bridge over the Guadalquivir river, were even denser, so that their progress was extremely slow. Santillana, however, seemed unconcerned. Prince Ibrahim wiped his brow. It was already hot and the packed masses all around them added to the stifling feeling brought on by the glaring heat of the sun. Soon, Prince Ibrahim's attention was drawn to what seemed like a huge unbroken structure, but as they drew nearer it he could see that there were at least two large archways with heavy swing doors. Armed soldiers were on duty and were letting the occasional person through. Santillana simply stretched out his hand to show the guards a heavily embossed ring that gained them immediate admittance. Once through the archway the crowds were much less dense, and yet the atmosphere seemed, if anything, to be even more emotionally charged. He could see the *Casa de los Conversos* now; it was a very big building on five floors with narrow windows and a mournful, even threatening appearance. Santillana motioned to them to stop when they were still some hundred paces or so from the building.

'We must wait here,' he said, 'until we can take our place in the procession. We shall be near the heart of it. Their Majesties clearly wish you to see all of it at very close quarters indeed. It is as well, Prince, that you are a hardened man of war.'

Prince Ibrahim did not reply, but he looked behind him to where Samuel and Sharif were standing among the pikemen. Sharif looked unconcerned, his eyes roving restlessly over the crowds, while Samuel looked pale, almost white, with his hands clasped behind his back. He was dressed in baggy, sombre clothes and wore a headdress that hid much of his face. For a moment his eyes met those of Prince Ibrahim; he tried to smile, but the smile turned into a grimace before he hastily lowered his eyelids and turned away.

They stood there, slowly baking in the sun, for close on half an hour, before a series of shouts of command, together with the clashing of arms and shields, provided the signal for the grim-looking doors of the *Casa de los Conversos* to be thrown open. The first to emerge were a group of Dominican monks, walking three abreast, in long black serge habits, their cowls drawn tightly over their heads, their hands folded away into wide loose-hanging sleeves, and the white flash of their feet clearly visible through their sandals. Prince Ibrahim counted eighteen of them as they moved away on what he had been told would be a Calvary of at least a league. They had begun to chant a hymn, the *'Venite Creator'* in deep loud voices that carried easily to where he was sitting on horseback. Santillana's horse, immediately next to him, neighed loudly as if in reply.

As the monks moved away, there were sudden cries not far from where they stood, followed by cheers and jubilation, announcing the arrival of Their Majesties. King Ferdinand and Queen Isabella were riding in a totally open carriage, sitting bolt upright and occasionally raising one arm as if in response to the near delirious cries of their subjects. Behind them came more carriages, some open, some closed, in a seemingly endless accompanying convoy. With them came a squadron of cavalry, magnificently accoutred, riding black caparisoned chargers. Riding at their head, Prince Ibrahim recognised Bertran de la Cueva.

The long line of carriages drew up just short of the *Casa de los Conversos*. No one descended from the carriages, but doors were thrown open so that those seated inside could watch in comfort. As if the arrival of Their Spanish Majesties had been an agreed signal that those inside the *Casa de los Conversos* had been waiting for, a second group of Dominican friars, again walking three abreast, now emerged. They, too, were chanting the same hymn but, unlike the first group, now one monk in each line of three carried a crucifix high above his head. Later it would be passed in turn to each of the other two monks in the row so as to share equally the burden of carrying the heavy cross. Immediately behind them came a group of nuns, clad in white habits, carrying a long tapering candle in their right hand. Only after they had passed did the first of the penitents appear: for a moment he seemed like some exotic, and yet at the same time, spectral figure as the sun shone on the long yellow smock that covered his entire body, topped by a tall pointed conical yellow hat. He, also, was carrying a candle, but a candle that was long and thick which he was required to hold up aloft. Behind him came another, and then another and yet another, until Prince Ibrahim had difficulty in keeping count of their number. There were women among them, although it was often difficult to detect the sex of the penitents as they filed slowly forward. They walked in a long single file, with two to three paces between each one of them. Behind them all came Tomas de Torquemada, the Grand Inquisitor, holding a missal with both hands and reading out loud from it in a deep rich voice that boomed across the intervening space. More monks and friars brought up the rear as the melancholy procession wound its way out of the *Casa de los Conversos* and moved slowly on towards the northern outskirts of the city of Cordoba.

After the last of the monks bringing up the rear of the procession had left the *Case de los Conversos*, the long line of carriages came suddenly to life. De la Cueva and his horseguards swung in behind the royal carriage carrying King Ferdinand and Queen Isabella, and led the way at a leisurely trot past the long line of monks and penitents to go straight to the field where three huge stands had been erected round a flattened central area; there, forty poles had been hammered deep into the ground and were already piled all around with brushwood awaited the arrival of the penitents. Behind the royal carriage there came all the others, the dust rising in dark-brown and grey clouds as their wheels rolled over the dry earth beneath. Only when the last of them had gone did Santillana give the order to move. While he and Prince Ibrahim rode on, the pikemen, with Samuel and Sharif still closely encased between them, marched smartly behind them at a fast walking pace. The dust from the carriages was still thick in the air and clung to their nostrils, making several of the pikemen cough and splutter.

Moving quickly as they were, it was not long before they caught up with the monks and friars at the rear of the column of penitents. They, too, were chanting hymns; 'Canticles of Glory to the Lord,' shouted Santillana as they passed them by. Prince Ibrahim looked at them with curiosity. Could these men of God really believe what they were saying? Could they really believe that burning the *Conversos* alive was the way that led to their God? No, that was simply not possible. The only explanation that made any sense was that this was the naked use of terror to fulfil political goals and ambitions, and prime among them was the conquest of Granada. It was clear enough why he had been summoned to witness this example of the subjugation and purification of non-Christian Spain.

When they came abreast with the Grand Inquisitor, Santillana doffed his plumed hat and bowed in his saddle. Torquemada momentarily raised one hand as if in blessing, although never stopping for a single moment to read from the missal he was holding in the palms of both hands. When giving the blessing he pressed the lower part of his right arm against the missal so as to prevent it from slipping. His face had a look of absolute determination, almost of dedicated triumph. Prince Ibrahim did not salute him, but turned his head away, away and a little way ahead to where the last in the line of yellow-robed penitents was shuffling painfully forward.

He could see some of them gasping for breath, short, sharp gasps that made their faces grimace and their eyes water. He could imagine them racked with fear as they groped their way forward, their heavy candles swaying with their uncertain movements. He could see that some of them were stumbling, their high conical yellow caps knocked askew and making them objects that were at once comical and distressing. Some of the monks who had set off in the first group, at the head of the procession, had fallen back to help keep the line of penitents in proper order. At first they used soft words and spoke in gentle tones, but their patience was soon exhausted and they did not hesitate to buffet and shout angrily at any poor wretch unable to continue. Prince Ibrahim felt his revulsion turning to bile in his throat. He forced himself to close his eyes until they should have passed beyond the line of penitents and tried to drive out of his mind the thought that when he was to see them again only a little while later that same day it would be in even more heart-rending circumstances. He did not look round at Samuel but felt a great wave of pity for his servant.

They had to mark time for a while as they came alongside the group of nuns in their long white habits. To Prince Ibrahim these sisters of mercy seemed utterly incongruous in this pageant of death. Their white, virginal, pure natures were, presumably, intended to underscore the contrast between purity and the rotten corruption and decadence of the tottering penitents who were following after them. To Prince Ibrahim it all appeared like a grim mockery, a satanic display of political power politics, in which the chosen brides of Christ and the condemned Jews were nothing more than pawns, whose lives or professed convictions mattered as little as a slaughtered chicken's feathers in the farmyard breeze. And yet, it was to a community of this kind that Leonora was proposing to commit the rest of her life. It could surely not be allowed to happen.

They were kept waiting for close on half an hour within sight of the field where the *auto-de-fe* was to be staged, as the King and Queen, with their courtiers and attendants, took up their assigned places in three great stands that had been especially erected for the occasion. They remained slightly to one side of the white-clad nuns since the whole procession had been similarly brought to a halt. At least, thought Prince Ibrahim, it would give the line of penitents a moment of respite, even if each extra moment of life could only be filled with the terror of what still lay ahead. He wondered whether any mercy would be shown at the last moment, as a sign perhaps of magnanimity on the part of the Spanish sovereigns. It seemed improbable. This whole elaborate and macabre procession, with its chanting and its symbols, with the vivid victimisation of the penitents, was deadly in its dramatisation and its intent, and was unlikely to leave any room for a sudden surge of pity. He was suddenly made aware of Samuel standing close by him. He was trembling slightly and there were tears in his eyes. Prince Ibrahim leaned down from his saddle to put his hand on his shoulder.

'Lord,' he whispered, 'I cannot answer for myself.'

'I know, Samuel, that this must be like so many daggers in your heart, but you must bear it with stoicism. There is nothing that you can do here and now; later, we can consider whether we can help some of the others. But today you must watch, with me, this tragedy unfold in silence. Must I remind you that you gave me your promise?'

Samuel looked up at his face for a moment as if to speak. Then he sobbed violently and turned away. For a moment Prince Ibrahim was on the point of summoning him back, but then he decided to let the matter be.

Two short blasts on a horn gave the signal that Their Spanish Majesties had taken their seats and that the procession could resume its melancholy march. Santillana motioned to Prince Ibrahim to follow him and led the way to the central stand where King Ferdinand and Queen Isabella sat under a gold-coloured canopy in the middle of the first row.

'You are to take a place near Her Majesty,' said Santillana curtly. 'Your men will be sitting immediately behind you. The space between the Queen and the two Infantas and yourself is reserved for the Grand Inquisitor. Please follow me.'

Without waiting for an answer, he leapt to the ground and led the way round to one side of the central stand where a solid wooden stairway led up to the level where the King and Queen were seated. Santillana escorted him to his seat, only four places removed from Queen Isabella, who had the Infantas Isabel and Maria seated next to her. The next seat in the row, next to Prince Ibrahim and on his left side, was clearly the one reserved for Tomas de Torquemada.

Prince Ibrahim bowed to the Queen and to the two Infantas and took his place. Santillana was on his right, and he recognised several other leading courtiers sitting further along the front row of seats. This demonstration of the Spanish Kings' determination clearly had him, and through him Granada, as one of its main targets, even if it was not the only one or probably not even the main one. Looking round, he saw Samuel and Sharif had been placed immediately behind him, with a guard on either side. He wondered at mere servants being given such apparently honourable places but assumed that this was no more than a matter of convenience for Santillana; in all probability their small segment of the royal stand would be the subject of a special exercise in exorcism to remove any stains resulting from the presence of infidels.

Behind the monks and the nuns, in seemingly endless numbers, there came at last the long file of penitents. Their arrival was the signal for a barrage of shouts and invective. 'Pigs,' 'Filthy Jews,' 'Abominations of nature,' and other epithets that Prince Ibrahim could not comprehend were hurled at them like so many verbal missiles. Prince Ibrahim looked and listened with contempt. It did no honour to Spain to have recourse to organised riff-raff and bullies on occasions such as this. He had not expected the Spanish Kings, or their advisers, to sink so low. It came as a fleeting moment of relief to see from the manifest anger on Queen Isabella's face that she too shared his feeling of nausea and contempt. She wanted her triumph, of course, but not at the price of mass popular and common hysteria that could only besmirch and bedraggle the proud banner of Castile.

It was while Prince Ibrahim sat watching the penitents stumbling forward that the Grand Inquisitor came to take his seat. For a short while he spoke to Queen Isabella and the two Infantas, explaining to them the rest of the afternoon's proceedings in a gentle sanctimonious patter that was at once explicit and honeyed, with words like forgiveness, tolerance and mercy dripping like sugared plums into a basinful of carefully distilled poison. Only when he had finished did he turn and pay attention to Prince Ibrahim.

'Ah, Prince of Granada, you have done well to come and join in our triumph,' he began smoothly. 'That is indeed wise on your part, for it will help you to understand, and not misjudge, what may seem to some to be a policy of harsh and needless cruelty. They make a sorry spectacle do they not?' he went on, pointing to the penitents as they were being herded together like animals in a pen within a few feet of the royal stand. 'They have condemned themselves,' he resumed, 'irredeemably. We offered them the Christian kiss of peace and clasped them to our bosoms. But they were double-faced, kissing us in return and swearing to eat the bread of Christ, while continuing in secret to pursue their old accursed faith and plot against the destiny of Spain. Now they have gone too far and must face the penalty for their treason and dishonesty. They were given the chance to repent, to deny the crimes of their forefathers, but they spurned all our offers. There can be no hesitation now if we are to march to God's glory to re-conquer Jerusalem from its pagan occupiers. Spain is the chosen vessel of God; as such its purity must be unalloyed. Granada belongs to Spain. Its return to our fold cannot be stopped, any more than the great wheel of time can be stopped. Be mindful of all this when you send your reports to your King and be mindful above all of the inescapable destiny that requires all the Spains to speak with one voice, whether it be a military voice, a political voice, or, Prince of Granada, a religious voice.' He gave a sudden smile that momentarily gave his features a look of calm benevolence, in such total contrast to the words that he had just spoken that Prince Ibrahim could only marvel and stare. 'The time has come for the purification of our blood. Today is but a step in that direction, but it is a huge step. With it we have set out on a road from which there shall be no turning back.'

Prince Ibrahim followed Torquemada's gaze as he turned towards Their Spanish Majesties. King Ferdinand had risen to his feet and, as he did so, an absolute hush fell on the vast assembly. The King raised both arms to heaven. '*Deus vult,*' he thundered. '*Deus vult.* We must obey His commandments. We must strive to fulfil His purpose. God in His great goodness has sanctified our country. He has set us proud goals. With His help these goals are within our grasp. But we must also be worthy of His great love for us and the signal honour that He is prepared to bestow upon us. For that we must be wholly pure. Pure in heart, in mind and in soul. Impurity can only defile us and make Him turn His face from us in sadness and disappointment. We cannot and we shall not fail Him.' King Ferdinand turned towards Torquemada. 'My lord Grand Inquisitor, you may proceed.'

Tomas de Torquemada, in rising, seemed to assume gigantic proportions. His eyes glinted and he exuded such a dark menace that even the Spaniards sitting near him appeared to cower. He struck Prince Ibrahim, sitting so close by him, almost like some elemental force in human shape that was suddenly to be savagely unleashed. It would know no pity, for pity was a concept foreign to its savage nature. Prince Ibrahim almost trembled in his turn as he waited for Torquemada to speak.

The Grand Inquisitor began quietly enough. 'It is, Your Majesties, with God's grace that we are gathered here today. When the Almighty called you to your thrones, and you were jointly crowned King of Aragon and Queen of Castile, a great mission was vouchsafed you. A great destiny awaits our country. It is God's manifest will that Your Majesties, who have in your august persons united our previously fragmented kingdoms, should recover the whole of Spain and go on from there to lead all Christendom to the recovery of the Holy Places in Jerusalem. Your banners have been bravely unfurled. May they wave one day soon by the side of the church of the Holy Sepulchre in Jerusalem.'

A cacophonous torrent of cheering, applause and clapping seemed to burst from the massed bands of spectators. King Ferdinand and Queen Isabella smiled and waved, while the group of penitents stood in a half circle below the royal stand, trembling but still erect, their faces white and drawn, but with a bearing that won grudging admiration.

Torquemada, who had remained standing, waited for the noise from the tumultuous crowd to subside. Then he raised is arms as if in supplication. 'But these great honours are not lightly given. God has given us His great love and called us to deeds of service that will echo down the arches of time and win for those who are His true servants eternal life in His holy presence. In return, He requires us to purify our hearts, to cleanse our minds and bodies of all impurities, to become vessels – if not of perfection, for that only He can ever be – then at least of heartfelt endeavour to do His will and live by His law. On this there can be no hesitation, no holding back, no room for accommodation. Today we are witnessing the process of purification in progress. It will not always be easy. There will be times of pain and anguish, when pity will struggle with duty, but we cannot afford to weaken, and thereby fail both us and Him.' Torquemada paused for a moment while a great silence seemed to hang like a massive rock of granite in suspension over the vast multitude of people gathered there. 'Our God is above all a God of mercy. He has bidden us to be patient and forgiving. Once already we have held out our hands in friendship and in peace to this group of sinners and renegades who stand condemned before us. But they jeered at our meekness. They spat in secret upon our Christian faith. By so doing they defiled the blood of Spain, imperilled our purity, and put in jeopardy the great destiny that is ours. They deserve death and the torments of hell. They are the abomination of desolation of which the prophet Daniel spoke. And yet, and yet, despite the vile impurity of their deeds, our God offers them one more chance of salvation.

Let any man here who will do so, abjure now, in front of us all, from all taint of idolatry and vow to be a true son or daughter of Jesus Christ our Lord, and a true servant of Their Spanish Majesties, let him step forward, I say, and his life may yet be spared.'

This time the silence was short-lived, quickly broken by shouts of anger as a group of monks yelled their anger at this apparent offer of pardon and escape from the just and righteous flames of the funeral pyres. But almost immediately Bertran de la Cueva and his men came round at a gallop from where they had been waiting in attendance behind the royal stand, and order was speedily restored. De la Cueva looked straight at Prince Ibrahim as he galloped past, a sardonic smile on his face. Who is the poltroon now? it seemed to say, and Prince Ibrahim felt the barb strike deep into his flesh.

When de la Cueva and his men had gone, it could be seen that five of the penitents had stepped forward. There were three men and two women. They were still holding their candles high in front of them, but their faces seemed to glow with hope. At a sign from the Grand Inquisitor they fell upon their knees, planting their candles by their side.

'May God's grace be praised,' thundered Torquemada, 'that at least these five persons have seen His light and repented. Swear,' he shouted at the five who knelt cowering below him, 'swear that you renounce forever the evil idolatry of your past lives, beg forgiveness for your past hypocrisy, and vow to remain true till death to our Lord Jesus Christ and His Holy Church.'

The five each raised one arm towards Torquemada. 'We swear all this,' they said out loud, their voices fortified by hope.

'Your lives are spared,' said Torquemada, 'but you cannot hope to escape all punishment for the grievous sin of having once already denied Our Lord. For that you three men will go to the galleys. You women will be assigned to the household of Her Majesty Queen Isabella, to use as she may think fit. May you be forever grateful for this unmerited but gracious mercy.'

One of the men leapt up and screamed. 'That is not mercy. It is a living death. Torquemada, I spit on your mercy. May you one day rot in your Christian hell.'

Torquemada did not move. Instead two of de la Cueva's men rode back towards the still shouting man and beat him with the flat of their swords till he lay a bleeding mess upon the ground. At a signal from de la Cueva a number of foot soldiers encircled the group of penitents and dragged them towards the lines of stakes that rose like stunted pillars out of the ground in front of the stands. Each stake had its own pile of faggots piled up high around it. The four penitents who had abjured were kept separate from their battered companion, roped together and made to kneel on the ground in front of the royal stand. Then they were made to watch as the near crippled man who had cursed Torquemada was lifted screaming by two of the soldiers and dragged by his feet to the nearest stakepost. His cries were those of a man in agonising pain.

There were again loud jeering shouts from the crowd as the other thirty-five penitents were led in their turn to their stakes. 'Let the devils roast!' they shouted, while others joked that they wanted the pigs' trotters while they were still hot, and others again that the sows should be cooked first, and to a turn. The crowd was finding its good humour now, its baser instincts excited by the prospect of imminent agonising death scenes. Their victims, looking, praying for an escape route that no longer existed, flailed helplessly. As the flames began to lick up around them, they turned their heads this way and that, the flames scorching their flesh as the piles of brushwood burned and crackled, the orange flames glowing against their yellow smocks. Soon all thirty-six fires were burning fiercely so that the acrid smell of burnt flesh grasped at their nostrils and made many of the avid spectators splutter uncomfortably. For a while the screams became louder and louder with an intensity that made even some of the monks turn away their heads, until eventually they became unrecognisable as noises made by human beings. But the majority of the crowd did not lose their good humour or their jollity. Bets were being taken as to which fire would last the longest. Some even ran forward to throw on a few extra faggots, reviling their victims as they did so.

Prince Ibrahim vomited. He clasped his eyes in front of his eyes, but was unable to blot out the horrific vision. He did not believe that he would ever be able to obliterate from his mind that contorted dance of death. Torquemada tapped him on the shoulder. 'For a man of war, tested and proven in battle, you have a weak stomach, it seems. A good commander should know that there are times when only extreme severity can ensure discipline, for without discipline there can be no final victory.'

Prince Ibrahim did not reply. He felt physically unable to speak. He looked down to see his own vomit on his clothes and on the ground at his feet. He felt himself to be a man debased, not so much humiliated as psychologically annihilated, smashed into a hundred pieces that could never be entirely restored to their former state. It was only with a superhuman effort that he was able for a moment to open his eyes. He was aware of Torquemada by his side, smiling whimsically as he looked at him. But he could only focus on the unbelievable horror of the spectacle in front of him.

Only a few of the fires were still burning, and even there the flames were flickering much less brightly than before. Some of the stakes were still standing, the calcinated corpses of the dead penitents still slumped against them. Mostly, however, the stakeposts had themselves collapsed or been consumed by the flames so that the charred remains of the bodies lay, unrecognisable, on the ground amid the ashes and the blackened stumps of wood. The crowd was manifestly jubilant. Glory had come to Spain. The great work of purification of the nation had been set in motion and nothing could now stop its successful accomplishment. Glory be to God. Hallelujah. Glory to the cause of re-conquest, and on to Jerusalem.

Prince Ibrahim struggled against his nausea. He felt sick to death. He felt himself to be utterly contemptible. And yet, he was the envoy of Granada. He had somehow to react, to asset his independence, or that of his country, and its complete rejection of the bestiality he had just witnessed. Whatever the cost he would speak the truth to Their Majesties of Spain. Painfully he made his way towards them, brushing past Torquemada as he did so. He could sense rather than see the Infantas staring at him in disgust. For them too, clearly, it all become just a spectacle, a simple scene in the unfolding drama of the *Reconquista* that was to lead to total Spanish hegemony throughout the Iberian peninsula.

He made to stride past them when he heard the sudden scream. Even as he turned back, his mind seemed to have realised what had happened: Torquemada was lying on the ground while Samuel struck at him repeatedly with a small dagger.

For a moment Prince Ibrahim, like all the others in the immediate vicinity, stood as if in shock. But even as he stood there stock-still, he registered in his mind that Samuel was raising his dagger yet again to strike another blow at his victim. With a snarl of anger he forced himself to leap forward. Hurling himself upon Samuel he threw him to the ground and slammed his head against one of the massive wooden supporting posts of the royal stand. Samuel grunted, his legs drummed briefly against the floor, and then he lay completely still. There was a murderous fury in Prince Ibrahim's head: that Samuel should have committed such an act was unforgivable. Men were pressing in closely now all around them. He saw King Ferdinand and sank to his knees, but the King ignored him and went directly to Torquemada's side. The Grand Inquisitor half risen to his feet and was smiling weakly.

'I am not so easily removed, Majesty,' he said quietly. 'God still has work for me to do. But it is fortunate that I was wearing a coat of mail beneath my cassock, or this wretched dog would indeed have claimed a great victim.'

'Heaven be praised, Torquemada,' said the King warmly, 'but you must take care to rest and be sure that you are fully recovered. In the meanwhile, we have our guests from Granada to deal with.'

'Your Majesty, if I may request one favour, I beg you to believe that Prince Ibrahim is not to blame. He sat by my side throughout the *auto-da-fe*. He can still be a useful channel, a useful vessel for the purification of Granada that must now inevitably come about, as surely as night follows day. Punish rather the Jew, the man Samuel, who has shown us all once again the loathsome baseness of his tribe.'

King Ferdinand nodded. 'It shall be as you have requested. You may consider yourself fortunate, Prince of Granada, to have such a friend to plead on your behalf. As for your man Samuel, he must die. We shall make an example of him.'

The King motioned to one of the guards to summon de la Cueva before turning back to Torquemada and helping him to rise slowly to his full height. There were tears of relief in the King's eyes. 'How shall he die, Torquemada?' he asked. 'It is for you to judge.'

Two of the guards had lifted Samuel to his feet. The blood was streaming from one side of his face where Prince Ibrahim had flung him against the solid wooden post. His eyes were half veiled and he was trembling violently.

'I am ready to die,' he shouted suddenly. 'I wanted to die, but to take this monster with me to hell. You, Lord,' he screamed, pointing a finger accusingly at Prince Ibrahim, 'you prevented me. You are the man who stopped me. May you be accursed for that!'

One of the guards hit him with his fist on the mouth, and then hit him again until the whole of his face was covered in blood.

'I think, Majesty, that this wretch should suffer the same fate as his fellow tribesmen. There are four spare piles of brushwood. That is three more than we need.'

'No,' screamed Samuel, 'not that.'

His eyes flitted from person to person. 'You, Lord,' he said, turning to Prince Ibrahim, 'do not let me die in that way.'

'There is nothing I can do, Samuel,' said Prince Ibrahim shortly. 'You have not only condemned yourself, but you have put our whole mission in jeopardy. His Spanish Majesty is right. I agree with the sentence passed upon you.'

Samuel continued to scream as the guards took him away. De la Cueva had come with four of his men on horseback and supervised the preparation of a single and exceptionally large pile of brushwood. This time there was to be no central post, but Samuel was simply thrown into the middle of the pile while de la Cueva and his men remained standing close by. Torquemada raised his right arm and flaming rushes were thrown onto the pile of brushwood. There was a faint roar as the flames leapt up, bright and golden in the afternoon light. Samuel was screaming more loudly than ever, his voice no longer sounding wholly human, and the sounds he was making unintelligible. Twice, blunderingly, he attempted to break loose from the burning brushwood, his clothes and hair on fire, but de la Cueva and his men prodded him back with long spears as if were a bull being branded. Then, abruptly, the screaming stopped.

The King, Torquemada and Santillana had gone over to where Queen Isabella and the two Infantas were still sitting quietly, seemingly calm and demure. For a moment it occurred to Prince Ibrahim to wonder how they could all have borne to watch such a scene with apparent equanimity. They did indeed seem totally unconcerned, save only for the safety of Torquemada.

Left to himself Prince Ibrahim climbed down from the royal stand and walked slowly towards the smoking brushwood pile where Samuel had been burned to death. Among the still occasionally flickering flames, his charred body was very visible. De la Cueva had dismounted and came towards him.

'So this is how you defend your servants! Do you still claim to be more courageous than my son? On you, too, men will spit with contempt and I shall give them the example.' He spat on the ground. 'Soon your embassy will be finished. I shall be waiting for you.'

Prince Ibrahim said nothing. There was too much truth in what de la Cueva had said. Samuel had been a good and loyal servant. No, he had been more than that. He had been a friend, and he had not lifted a finger to save him. There was, admittedly, very little, if anything, after what Samuel had done, that he could have said or attempted on his behalf. But he had not even tried, and had even felt relief that his awful death had left his embassy, temporarily at least, in some semblance of order. But he knew also that Samuel's death, or rather the manner of it, had broken something in himself. For his wounds ever to heal, there would need to be a magical, if not a providential, balm.

*Chapter Five*

# THE GATHERING STORM CLOUDS

That night Prince Ibrahim slept uneasily. The vision of the victims of the *auto-da-fe* was as if etched into his mind, but it was Samuel's face that stayed with him the most, his face and the last words that Samuel had spoken to him: words spoken with bitterness – hatred, almost – words spoken with such intensity that it still made him recoil in disbelief. He had returned to the palace placed at his disposal like a man unconscious of his surroundings although he could distinctly recall the escort of pikemen assigned to him by Santillana and, of course, Sharif. He had gone immediately to his private rooms, unwilling to speak to anyone. The chessmen still set out on one of the tables were a poignant reminder of the servant who had died in so brutal a manner, whom he had been unable to help and had, in a sense, even disowned. De la Cueva's taunts still hurt, even though Prince Ibrahim had been able to largely convince himself that there was nothing he could really have done to save Samuel's life. He recalled Sharif on the way back to their palace quarters complimenting him on his action. It had, he had said, saved the embassy, and saved King Boabdil from any possible charge of conspiracy. Prince Ibrahim was less certain. It had never been clear in his mind why Their Spanish Majesties had agreed to receive him, or indeed any official Granadan envoy. The fact, however, remained that they had done so, and the Grand Inquisitor's words, after Samuel's assassination attempt, suggested that he too was in favour of continuing formal diplomatic contacts with Granada. Perhaps it was all simply a cunning subterfuge designed to lull King Boabdil into a false sense of at least temporary security.

Prince Ibrahim's thoughts went back to Samuel. The man had been a servant, an inferior, little better than slave, but he had come as close to being a friend as anyone he had ever known, save only for his sister, Ayala. For a second the image of Leonora floated in front of his eyes. Yes, Leonora too; despite the extraordinary circumstances of their meeting and of their enforced companionship, he somehow knew she was very close to him. He could sense an unspoken, not wholly avowed, longing in himself to see her again. But these were idle, ridiculously sentimental thoughts. It was essential that he should force himself back into facing the forbidding reality of his present situation.

He rose early the next morning and, after picking at some bread and fruit, summoned Sharif to come to him. He came almost at once, like a man who had been expecting a call and sensed his own heightened importance.

'One possibly important detail is still unclear to me, Sharif,' he said. 'How did Samuel come to have a dagger? Did he have it hidden on his person?'

'Lord, just before he leapt at the Grand Inquisitor, Samuel knelt down and appeared to be loosening one of his shoes. It was a small dagger, he may very well have had it concealed inside one of his shoes, or strapped to his leg. I was paying little attention to him at the time. As soon as he rose up again he made his attack on the Grand Inquisitor.'

'And you had no reason to be suspicious?'

'That he was carrying a dagger? No, Lord. He had been behaving very strangely, but that was nothing new. He knew very well what kind of an ordeal lay ahead of him.'

'He gave little thought to us, or to our mission here, but I cannot but grieve for the manner of his death. It was fiendish.'

'To the Spanish Kings the Grand Inquisitor represents the hand of their God,' said Sharif coolly. 'It is not surprising that they were without mercy for anyone who sought to harm him. But I do not believe, Lord, that this attempt at assassination will seriously harm your mission here. It is my belief that both His Eminence the Cardinal and the Grand Inquisitor see in your presence here an opportunity to prepare the way for the peaceful conversion of Granada. Of course Spain wants Granada, and they have the power to seize it when they wish. But it is not enough for them to annex it; they would prefer to annex its people also, provided they abjure their religion and become good Christian souls. They do not look upon us in the same way as they do the Jews. We are seen by the Court and the Church here in Cordoba as less resilient, more ready to abandon our faith. They have reason for their thinking in this way; many former Moslems in New Castile have indeed become Christians. A number are even enrolled as Christian soldiers. Spain is not so rich in manpower that it would willingly forego the acquisition of two to three hundred thousand new Christian citizens. It is the same, I imagine with the Christian Church.

Think what a victory that would represent for them! That would indeed be a powerful manifestation of their God's grace and a major milestone on the road to Jerusalem.'

Prince Ibrahim looked at him thoughtfully. It was the first time that Sharif had spoken his thoughts so openly. Disagreeable though the picture was that he had painted, it contained more than a small ring of truth.

'And my role in this, as seen by the Grand Inquisitor and his friends?' he said inquiringly.

'You, Lord, are a Prince of Granada. They believe your standing to be high with King Boabdil. They hope that you may help to persuade him that Granada should accept Spain's terms. They would no doubt be prepared to be very generous to all those who contribute to a gloriously successful finale to the *Reconquista*.'

Again Prince Ibrahim looked at him in silence. More than just the cat's ear was poking out of the bag now. Sharif's face might be as expressionless as ever, but there could be no doubting the covert meaning of his words. It was a clear invitation to play the Spaniards' game. If true, it went far to explain King Boabdil's actions, his apparent hesitation and continual equivocation. This almost certainly had been the theme of the discussions between the Spanish Kings and Boabdil during the time the latter had spent in Spain as a supposedly honoured guest. Perhaps they had already come close to a final agreement that circumvented the determination of men like al-Zaghal and all those others who were ready to fight to the death for the independence of Granada and their Moslem religion.

Sharif was in King Boabdil's camp. Prince Ibrahim had been certain of that from the very beginning. But not until now had he really suspected the full extent of Boabdil's likely accommodation with the Spanish Kings. Granada was indeed rotten to the core when its own King had sunk so low. Sharif struck him as a common turncoat, a vulgar spittle-licker; all that was clear enough, but extremely clever at the same time. But perhaps after all he was doing King Boabdil an injustice. It was hard to believe in such treachery and duplicity. He needed time to think and to try and obtain confirmation of suspicions that were now coming near to being a certainty in his mind. He dismissed Sharif with a wave of the hand. It was only at the Spanish Court that he could learn more, and access to it had not been forbidden him. It seemed inadvisable to ask for a meeting with the Cardinal or with the Grand Inquisitor, but he would send word through Santillana, expressing again his regret at what had happened, that unfortunate, regrettable incident, and the hope that the Grand Inquisitor was now fully recovered. Such a goodwill message on his part was very likely to result in an invitation to call upon some, if not all, of them – all the more so if Sharif's analysis of the Grand Inquisitor's motives and line of approach was correct, as Prince Ibrahim was himself nearly convinced was indeed the case.

And so it proved. Within three hours of his message of commiseration having been dispatched, Prince Ibrahim received a reply couched in warm tones and inviting him to a reception at the palace of the Dukes of Medina-Sidonia that same evening to celebrate the Grand Inquisitor's miraculous escape from an assassination attempt by a member of the vile tribe of Jews. Prince Ibrahim had received the invitation he was looking for, but it was with a taste of gall and ashes in his mouth that he set off for the palace.

The reception was once again in the great hall of the palace, only on this occasion it was on a very much smaller scale, with only a hundred persons or so being present and not a single woman among them. As Prince Ibrahim entered, King Ferdinand and Prince Juan were talking animatedly to a small group that included the Cardinal, the Grand Inquisitor, and Jimenez de Cisneros, the Confessor to Queen Isabella, whom he remembered for his particularly vicious anti-Semitic diatribes during their first encounter in this same palace. Upon seeing Prince Ibrahim enter, Cardinal Mendoza came straight towards him.

'You are very welcome, Prince, after yesterday's terrible event. By God's grace the Grand Inquisitor has been restored to us in full health and quite unharmed. It was with great pleasure that we noted your concern on his behalf. Be assured that we bear you personally no grudge. You were in no way at fault. Quite the contrary indeed, with your commendably prompt action to immobilise that vile would-be assassin. But come, His Majesty wishes to thank you in person.'

Prince Ibrahim bowed low as he approached King Ferdinand.

'Prince,' said the King, 'you have our royal gratitude for the action you took to assist the Grand Inquisitor. He is very dear to our hearts. We must thank you also for the gifts of gold you brought us from King Boabdil. We have now had an opportunity to inspect them. It was a gracious gesture on his part which the Queen and I greatly appreciate. We would ask you to transmit our royal thanks to your sovereign in your next dispatch. We also have an item of news we wish you to convey to King Boabdil which will, we are convinced, give him great cause for satisfaction. We shall shortly be announcing the official betrothal of our daughter, the Princess Isabel, to Crown Prince Afonso of

Portugal. It is another great step forward towards the unity and single-minded purpose of our whole Iberian peninsula. We should of course be glad to invite King Boabdil to the wedding which will take place in six months' time. You also, Prince Ibrahim, would be a welcome guest on that occasion.'

'I thank Your Majesty,' said Prince Ibrahim. The news was not surprising, but it marked the end of any hope of a resumption of hostilities between Castile and Portugal. Much worse than that, however, it brought much nearer the risk of Portugal siding with Spain in its campaign to re-conquer Granada and placing its formidable navy at Spain's disposal in order to blockade Granada ports. It left only the currently remote possibility of a conflict between Aragon and France over the possession of Rosellon as a vague ray of hope for Granada. That, or a treaty with Fez or Marrakesh in the hope that the Moorish kingdoms would prefer to fight the Spanish Kings on the Spanish mainland rather than risk a Spanish invasion in due course of Morocco.

The King had resumed his conversation with the Grand Inquisitor and Friar Jimenez de Cisneros, leaving Cardinal Mendoza to occupy himself with Prince Ibrahim. The Cardinal passed one arm round his shoulders.

'We must speak more often, Prince, you and I, for there is much that could be of mutual benefit, for you, and for us. Unnecessary bloodshed is abhorrent to us, as indeed was yesterday's *auto-da-fe*. That, too, would have been unnecessary if the men and women who died had kept their word and not reneged on their professed faith. But there will be time enough for us to talk. I know very well how distressed you must be at this moment. Talk to me instead about Granada, about its people, about its customs, about its hopes for the future.'

Prince Ibrahim breathed deeply. He felt like a man confined to a room with barred windows that were moving slowly but inexorably inwards upon him. Both the Cardinal and the Grand Inquisitor were masters of their art. He believed that he had heard enough now to know their real objectives. But, for the present at least, their approach was not unlike an intricate ritual dance, with individual steps that could go forwards, backwards or sideways, but with a definite purpose and sense of direction nevertheless. For his part, he felt he had no option but to play their game for the moment with some appearance of enjoyment.

'Granada, Your Eminence, is a city and a land of great beauty. You must know that our people have a great love of water. You spoke yesterday of purification. For us and, I believe, for all peoples who have the desert in their ancestry and in their blood, water is the crystallised essence of life. It is a thing of rarity in the desert but where we find it, trapped as it were in crystal emerald green, it is both the elixir of life and a jewel of incalculable value. So it is that you find it in our architecture, in our gardens, in our houses, in the very notions of our everyday lives. In Granada we have brought water to the desert so that it has become a garden of delights. This art has reached perfection in the gardens of the Generalife by the Alhambra Palace. It is a place of magic where nature and men have combined in a matchless perfection. I have heard some Christians describe it as the garden of Eden. But that it could never have been, for the gardens of the Generalife are too perfect, and too pure, to have ever been the home of a conniving serpent. Granada, my lord Cardinal, is as close to heaven as any man can hope to be in this life.'

Cardinal Mendoza, who had at first begun to listen with an expression of benign interest, was now looking at him in open surprise.

'Why, Prince, you are a real poet at heart. Or perhaps you should have been a minstrel, for your words are like music when you speak of Granada. You must indeed love it dearly.'

'Yes, Your Eminence, I do love it dearly. Do most men not love the country of their birth? All the more so when it has been so wondrously endowed with beauty as Granada. For us, it is one of the gardens of Allah, and perhaps even the finest of them all.'

'I did not for one moment expect to learn so much from my simple question, Prince. Tell me, do all Granadans feel like you?'

It was Prince Ibrahim's turn to smile. It was a wan smile, but it gave him a moment's satisfaction to see the sudden look of concern on the Cardinal's face.

'My Lord Cardinal, you know very well that for the past five years I have been absent from Granada. Much has no doubt happened during that period of which I am not yet fully aware. You will have other sources of information. You must not place too much credence on my words. But I would say that a very substantial majority of Granadans feel as I do. Certainly they did. But who can say to what extent circumstances of all kinds may not have led some to modify their views?'

'And those that felt, or feel, like you – are their minds open to change?'

'My Lord Cardinal, you have in Castile and Aragon your great orders of chivalry. The knights of Santiago, the knights of Alcantara, the knights of Calatrava. They are the flower of your young Spanish manhood. Their courage is indomitable, their bravery universally acknowledged, their faith firmer than any rock. You are truly fortunate in their splendour. But I would beg you to believe that we Moslems also have men in our midst who can, and do, feel just as strongly. It is not for me, a man only recently returned to his country, to tell you how many feel like this, but I can most solemnly assure you that we do not feel ourselves to be a vanquished people.'

Cardinal Mendoza looked him straight in the eye. 'There is, if you will allow me to say so, Prince, much that I like about you. You are a man full of surprises, and I cannot as yet see clearly how you fit in, or could fit in, to our greater design. It puzzles me why King Boabdil chose you as his envoy, for I do not recognise your King as being among those whom you have just described. It is, of course, not for me to decide on our country's policies, even if I am close to Their Majesties, and, together with the Grand Inquisitor, their closest counsellor on all matters pertaining to religion. But this, Prince, I can tell you, for it is no secret. The time is very near when great decisions for Spain will have to be taken. You will have heard us speak of the call of destiny. That is no idle or bombastic talk. It is God's will that we must heed. In that great destiny there are consequences, unavoidable and inevitable, for Granada. I would say only this to you at this time: weigh them carefully before you make your own final judgement. It benefits a man little to die in vain and in so doing to bring the land he loves to ruin and destruction. There must be other ways. Good night, Prince, for I must leave you now. We shall speak of us all this again, and soon.'

Prince Ibrahim watched him go over to rejoin the Grand Inquisitor and Friar Jimenez de Cisneros. The King was no longer to be seen, and had presumably left the assembly to return to Queen Isabella. Once again he felt drained and exhausted. It seemed like an unending vista of loneliness that stretched out in front of him, without, it seemed, a single ray of hope. But he would not yield. Bowing to the Grand Inquisitor as he passed him on his way out of the great hall, he contrived a jaunty smile. Whatever King Boabdil's secret machinations might be, he swore to himself that he would never dishonour his role as envoy of Granada.

Outside, his escort of six pikemen was waiting. The men of his escort were often the same, but their faces wore a sullen expression as though the fact that they had been assigned to protect an infidel Moslem cast a slur upon their manhood.

The next four days passed uneventfully enough. Prince Ibrahim resumed his fencing bouts and had occasional long sessions talking with Sharif. The *auto-da-fe* and the death of Samuel had left a heavy mark upon him. He also resumed his walks about the town. Santillana accompanied him on several of these occasions so that his escort could follow at a fair distance and so enable Prince Ibrahim to feel less constrained. Santillana made no attempt to press him and left him free to wander about the city as he wished; but he talked with apparent openness about the movements of the King and Queen and was the first to give him warning that the day for the formal betrothal of Princess Isabel to Prince Afonso of Portugal had been brought forward and would now coincide with a solemn declaration of dedication of Spain to a new crusade.

'A crusade?' repeated Prince Ibrahim. 'Against whom?'

'We do not think of it in those terms, Prince. It is not necessarily against anyone in particular. It is, instead, a dedication of our peoples to the purification of Spain, to the realisation of an exclusively Christian faith in this country and, ultimately of course, to the recovery of Jerusalem.'

'And Granada?'

'That, Prince, you should discuss with my brother, the Cardinal, and with Their Majesties. But there is one other piece of news that may be of interest to you. The Princess Leonora, who has begun her novitiate, has come to Cordoba to be present at her cousin's betrothal to Prince Afonso. I understand that she has spoken most favourably of you and of your treatment of her, both in helping her to escape from Istanbul and on board your galley. King Ferdinand will be grateful to you for that.'

For Prince Ibrahim it was like a sudden surge of joy. Amid the seemingly unending catalogue of misfortune, misery and setbacks, the image of Leonora and the thought of seeing her again soon was like a rainbow in the storm.

Taking his leave of Santillana he returned to his quarters to tell Sharif about the imminent betrothal and the launching of a new crusade.

'You must send a message at once to Granada, Sharif. King Boabdil should know of this at once. Our embassy here would seem to serve little purpose now.'

'If you will permit me, lord, I do not think anything irretrievable has been lost. A crusade against Granada, the crowning glory of the *Reconquista*, has always been the Spaniards' aim. Their power and their strength are overwhelming and there is nothing to stop them.

'Lord, allow me to speak openly. I am King Boabdil's trusted servant. You must know that he has long had contacts with the Spanish sovereigns. If it were left to him there would be no war, but Granada would find its place in the new Spain peacefully, without bloodshed and, I dare to hope, with few men driven into exile. But there are those who think differently – his own uncle, al-Zaghal above all, who would rather see Granada engulfed in flames than passing peacefully back to Spain. You, lord, are not only a Prince of the Royal House but a hero to the people of Granada. Your choice will weigh heavily on the scales. Forgive me if I have spoken out of place, but you are King Boabdil's envoy.'

'I was sent here by the King, but I am also the envoy of Granada.'

'For me, lord, there is no distinction between the two. I am sure that King Boabdil would be deeply grieved if he were to learn that you are of a different mind.'

Prince Ibrahim cut short his reply. King Boabdil, and no doubt Sharif, had clearly made their calculations. They had no wish to fight. That much was very obvious. Perhaps they would find it easy to live under Spanish rule, in comfort no doubt as a reward for their comprehension and co-operation. But there was also al-Zaqhal and those like him, all men of sterner stuff. This was of course the choice confronting him: to fight or to swim with the tide. Sharif all this while had been observing him closely.

'I have noted your words very carefully, Sharif,' Prince Ibrahim said at last. 'I think you are right when you say that a time for decision is drawing near. It will not, I think, be long before the Cardinal and the Grand Inquisitor set out their terms.'

'When they do, Lord, it will be a time for circumspection. Granada cannot afford heroic impetuosity. It is sometimes better to live with one eye than to walk blindly to one's death.'

'I have never doubted your perspicacity, Sharif,' said Prince Ibrahim drily. 'I shall not fail to mention it to the King. Strange, is it not, that it should be the Spaniards who are our enemies who have honour as their lodestar. I envy them that, Sharif, for it is honour that determines whether a man is worthy of the name. Cruel, hideously and sometimes unbelievably cruel they may be, but honour is their second god.'

'A dead man's honour, Lord, is of little consequence.'

'But a live man's dishonour, Sharif – how would you rate that?'

Prince Ibrahim waved his hand as an indication that their discussion was over. He walked slowly over to his own apartment. For a while he stood playing idly with the chessmen that still stood in orderly ranks upon the chequerboard. There could be no escape from war. He would complete his mission for King Boabdil, but after that there would be only one possible course, to join al-Zaqhal and fight. For a little while he played a game with and against himself, in which he was both attacker and defender, but played like that chess was too far removed from war. Setting his own ambuscades was a good exercise for his brains, but avoiding them was of course too easy. It was Sultan Bayazet who had stimulated his interest in maps. But where the Sultan had pored over the maps of Hungary to prepare his offensive against Vienna, he would have perforce to seek the best lines of defence. The region known as *Las Malistas* on the western side of Granada was notorious for its narrow gorges and marshlike terrain. It was in many ways the most likely, if by no means the only, route which an invading Spanish army would take. It was a relief to him to try and imagine how that sort of terrain could best be used to devise a strategy to foil a would-be invader.

Thoughts about map study were still uppermost in his mind when Santillana called on him the following morning, bearing an invitation to the formal betrothal of Princess Isabel to Prince Afonso of Portugal with, simultaneously, as an event that would surely win favour for the young couple in the eyes of God, the proclamation of a new crusade. The combined ceremony was to take place in the palace of the Dukes of Medina-Sidonia on the following day. Prince Ibrahim took the news with apparent calmness, simply requesting Santillana to inform Their Spanish Majesties that he accepted their invitation and would be present at both ceremonies.

Summoning Sharif, he instructed him to send another message to King Boabdil. For him also the time for prevarication was running out, for once the crusade had been launched, even if only in name, he would have little choice but to reveal his hand.

It was Santillana once again who came the following morning to escort him to the solemn high mass in the cathedral. Prince Ibrahim was told that the call to a crusade was to be made from the cathedral steps as soon as the mass was over and the newly betrothed couple had emerged into the open. In the streets enthusiastic crowds were singing and chanting, waving banners and calling lustily for King Ferdinand and Queen Isabella. Many were wearing large rosettes of red and yellow flowers. The streets were full of bunting and girls flaunting ribbons and garlands in a wild frenzy of colours and excitement. Instruments of all kinds were to be seen and heard, with pipes, ocarinas, cowbells and flutes in particular evidence. There could be no doubt about the people's enthusiastic support for both the betrothal and the crusade. On both these scores Spain was evidently totally united.

Inside the great hall of the palace of the Dukes of Medina-Sidonia fifes and kettledrums reverberated as the multitude of guests were escorted to their places. Once again, Prince Ibrahim had been assigned a place of honour, seated in the third row immediately behind King Ferdinand, Queen Isabella, the King and Queen of Portugal, the Princess Isabel and Prince Afonso, Prince Juan and many of the noblest families of Castile, Aragon and Portugal. He had Santillana on his left and Friar Jimenez de Cisneros on his right.

Once all those invited had taken their seats, there was a loud and prolonged blast from twelve trumpeters, six of them dressed in the livery of Castile and six in that of Aragon. Then King Ferdinand and the King of Portugal rose, both magnificently dressed, attired in robes of ermine and wearing golden crowns that glittered brilliantly with the reflected light of day and an innumerable number of rush flares placed all around the walls of the great hall.

'This is indeed a great and glorious day for all our countries,' King Ferdinand began. 'Throughout history certain peoples have been selected by Divine Providence to take up the burdens of leadership for the greater benefit of all men. Today it is the turn of our countries. Consider how we were divided and weak until only a few years ago. Then we were at war with our brethren in Portugal; even our own Spanish kingdoms of Castile and Aragon have known unity for less than twenty years. If we are now to carry forward the torch of destiny with fortitude and with pride then we must, at the same time, forge unity among all three of our countries. For this reason it is with an immense joy in our hearts that Queen Isabella and I welcome the betrothal of our dear daughter Isabel to Crown Prince Afonso of Portugal. In little more than one hour's time we shall celebrate their future union in the cathedral of this city, in the sight of God and beseeching His blessing upon them. But now, on behalf of all the kingdoms of Spain and Portugal assembled here before you all, we announce to you with pride and joy the betrothal of these two young princes. May all happiness be theirs and may heaven's blessing rest upon them all the days of their lives.'

King Ferdinand stepped forward and was followed by Queen Isabella, Princess Isabel and Prince Afonso. Taking his daughter's right hand King Ferdinand placed it in the right hand of Prince Afonso, embracing each in turn as he did so. There was a tumultuous applause with men and women clapping and cheering as the Prince and Princess were embraced in turn by Queen Isabella and then by the King and Queen of Portugal. All six then formed a line so that the multitude of guests could file slowly past to offer them their congratulations and best wishes for the future. Prince Ibrahim took his appointed place in the row of well-wishers and, when his turn came, offered them Granada's hopes for a future that would be marked by mutual amity and respect. His words were received with smiles, but only Princess Isabel spoke in reply to thank him and adding only that there was a surprise awaiting him later that day.

They walked on foot from the palace to the cathedral through the massed and cheering crowds on the streets, who showered them with flower petals as they passed. The royal party led the way, followed by all those who had attended the betrothal in the palace in a long sinuous line of three to five abreast. It was with a gnawing feeling in his chest that Prince Ibrahim approached the erstwhile mosque, now converted into a Christian cathedral. He had debated within himself the morality of entering a former mosque that had been defiled by the Christian conquerors of a former Moslem territory, in order to be present at a ceremony that could not but be detrimental and injurious to the country he represented. But for the present, he was still King Boabdil's envoy to the kingdoms of Spain and there could be no possible doubt as to what King Boabdil would wish him to do.

As he entered the cathedral he felt as though this was yet a further dishonour that had been set upon his shoulders. It was only the central part of the mosque that had been dismantled and then rebuilt as a Christian cathedral, leaving the rest of the building virtually unaltered from its former state. The bitterness in his soul hardened as he saw the Christians massed inside and leaning against the pillars designed by their Moslem builders to make men strive to reach up and out to the power and glory of Allah.

Inside the cathedral it was as bright as in the blisteringly hot afternoon sun. Thousands of candles glittered, their flames flickering and sparkling against gold plates, ornaments, chalices and crucifixes that seemed ubiquitous in what had become for Prince Ibrahim an accursed monstrosity of a building. The royal party had taken their places before the high altar with its massive reredos with paintings of the Annunciation, the birth of Jesus, and the Virgin Mary's bodily ascension to heaven. Several processions of priests came from opposing directions towards the high altar, each one preceded by six young boys in red cassocks and white cottas swinging heavy incense burners that left great clouds of incense swirling in their wake. They, in turn, were followed by larger processions, led respectively by Cardinal Mendoza, the Grand Inquisitor, Jimenez de Cisneros and one other high ranking prelate whom he did not recognise, all of them magnificent in their episcopal glory, moving very slowly as the cathedral's organ began to play, rolling its sonorous music over the huge congregation.

Prince Ibrahim watched in silence as Cardinal Mendoza, Tomas de

Torquemada and Jimenez de Cisneros mounted the altar steps to begin the celebration of high mass. The solemnity of the occasion was indeed awesome, with the thunderous volume of the organ alternating with the singing of the choir and the prayers and responses of priests and congregation.

Prince Ibrahim felt the incense pinching at his nostrils. Some of the people round him were spluttering behind their hands or holding small linen cloths. He watched them all kneeling, rising, genuflecting and sitting according to the ritual of the mass while he remained seated in their midst. He had come this far, but to play the marionette on this gruesome stage was more than he could bear.

He had long ago been told about the mysteries of the Christian faith and knew a little about the so-called Ordinary or order of the mass. Looking around him there could be no doubt about the sincerity of the faith of these Christians. Almost all of them rushed to take communion, cupping their hands in front of them or kneeling and putting out their tongues so that the officiating priests could place the host upon them.

It was towards the end of the mass that he sensed a sudden excitement and tenseness all around him, rippling through the entire congregation like the forerunner of a vast outsize wave about to crash upon the shore. By the high altar the Cardinal, Tomas de Torquemada and Jimenez de Cisneros had been joined by a man whom he recognised as the Papal Nuncio to the courts of Aragon and Castile, Nicolo Franco. Prince Ibrahim, too, was tense now, his eyes glued to this man.

Nicolo Franco took a small step forward. He was not a tall man, but strongly and even more powerfully built, with broad shoulders and commanding features. In his right hand he was holding a folded piece of parchment which he proceeded to unroll as a near total silence fell upon the congregation, with only a short and quickly stifled cough.

'*Frates*,' he began, 'beloved brethren in our Lord Jesus Christ. On this great and auspicious day for your kingdoms, in the presence of your eminent and illustrious sovereigns, I am indeed happy to be the bearer of good tidings. The Holy Father in Rome has charged me to bring you the Bull that lays upon you all the glorious dedication of your souls to a new crusade. I do not need to tell you of the threat to Christendom from the East, of the menace of the Turks after their capture of Byzantium and their imminent move upon Vienna. The time has come to strike back, and our counter offensive starts here in the West. God, my brethren, has vouchsafed you all His Holy Blessing and given you the mission to drive out the infidel from this land and to put your hands to His Holy Purpose and the recovery of Jerusalem. This is the crusade that I preach. This is the Holy Father's Bull, and with it the indulgences for all those who will partake in this most holy crusade.' The Papal Nuncio stopped for a moment while all around him men wept with joy and some knelt in a state close to ecstasy, their eyes glowing with emotion. Then he resumed, 'But I also have one other message. You, Your Majesties,' he continued, addressing himself directly to King Ferdinand and Queen Isabella, 'have dedicated your reigns to our Christian cause. It is thanks to you that a great hope has been kindled here in the West that will offset the peril in the East, and that will one day soon restore Jerusalem to our faith. The Holy Father has therefore decreed that from this day on you should adopt the style and be known as *Los Reyos Catolicos*, dearest to his heart and the most stalwart bulwark of our Holy Mother Church.' The Papal Nuncio went over to where King Ferdinand and Queen Isabella had sunk down upon their knees. Raising them by the hand, he embraced each one of them in turn as the choir intoned the *Te Deum*, in which the whole congregation joined in a frenzy of excitement that made many faint with the power of their uncontrollable emotions.

Prince Ibrahim had remained seated throughout the Papal Nuncio's peroration. The words and their meaning had sunk in deep. It was hard to see what scope they left for any negotiation. This was a declaration of war to come. Even as he sat there, priests had begun to bring in large baskets full of crosses made of stiff red linen that were intended to be worn on the jackets or surcoats of all intending Crusaders. Men were flocking forward in their dozens, tears still streaming down their faces, reaching out for the red crosses and clutching them to their chests. Even some of the women were following their example. It was time for him to leave this festival of jubilation that spelt the onset of doom for Granada. Squaring his shoulders, he turned to go. It was like fighting against a human current as the congregation thrust enthusiastically forward, with their faces glowing, every man and woman's, all eager, it was clear, to grasp one of the red crosses.

It was by dint of pushing and shoving with brute force that he finally battled through into the periphery of the cathedral where the rows of graceful pillars, of medium height, recalled the one-time mosque. There were relatively few people there, most having no doubt joined in the joyous stampede towards the high altar. Those who were still sitting there on narrow high-backed chairs were all women, mostly nuns. Prince Ibrahim paid them little heed until he became subconsciously aware of someone staring at him, fixedly and unwaveringly. He felt the tremor that ran through his body as he returned her gaze. He watched her move slowly towards him, alone, motioning to those around her not to follow. As she came near to him, she lifted the veil from her face. Even before she had done so, he knew. The woman in nun's clothing was Leonora.

She came right up to him, her face immobile, her arms held tightly against her body.

'Leonora,' he said quietly, savouring the music of the syllables of her name. 'Leonora. At last we meet again.'

She nodded. 'It could not be otherwise, Prince. You have been too often in my thoughts. – even more so since the *auto-da-fe*. I cannot find the words to express the sadness I felt at Samuel's death. He was a good friend to me. You should know too that I took his advice. I shall be completely healed. It was he who gave me the courage to hope and to go to a doctor of his race. I wish that it had been in my power to save him.'

'I cannot forget how he died. There is a small spring in me that is broken. But you heard what was said here just a few minutes ago. A crusade has been preached, and launched. There will be many more *auto-da-fe* and many more will die horrible deaths. And you, Leonora, what will happen to you? I was told that you intend to take the veil and become a nun. That grieved me.'

For a moment her eyes seemed to lose their immobility and he saw the glimmer of a smile.

'That was my intention,' she answered quietly, 'but it is so no longer. My cousin Ferdinand is prepared to allow me back at Court. He has been much less ferocious than I had expected. Perhaps he has a feeling of guilt that he left me to my fate and that it was a Moslem prince who rescued me. I had indeed thought to become a novice, to begin my novitiate and become a Cistercian nun, but it is no longer my wish.'

'I am so glad. So you will live at Court?'

'My cousin Isabel has asked me to become one of her ladies-in-waiting. I have agreed and will join her in a few weeks' time. Perhaps later, after her wedding, I may accompany her to Lisbon.'

'May I call upon you, Princess, at Court?'

'You should not call me by that title, Prince Ibrahim. For the moment I am still known as Sister Teresa. But when I see you I shall always see myself again as Leonardo the pageboy. Do you still recall those days, Prince, on your galley?'

'Our positions and our roles were very different then, Princess. No, I shall never forget those days.'

'It is time for me to go,' she said suddenly.

'To go and collect a red cross?' Prince Ibrahim asked bitterly.

She shook her head gently. 'No. I shall not wear a red cross. I shall say that it does not fit the habit I am wearing. But my debt of gratitude to you, Prince Ibrahim, is the real reason for my refusal. Whatever the future may hold, rest assured that you have one friend in this country. I have no powers of my own but my prayers, for what little they may be worth, will be for you.'

Slowly he raised her right hand and put it to his lips. He saw the tears well up in her eyes and looked away quickly.

'I shall call upon you as soon as I may,' he said, 'if that is permitted by Court etiquette.'

'It will be perfectly proper for you to pay your respects to the Princess Isabel,' she said quietly. 'You can see me there. Adieu, Prince, for the present. May God have you in His keeping.'

He watched her as she went towards the great throng, the other nuns in her group following after her. There was a sudden lightness in his heart. He did not dare to try and begin to analyse its cause. Deep within him emotions were stirring and visions beginning to form that were too phantasmagorical to be ever possible. But the lightness of heart was unmistakable.

He walked out of the cathedral doors with a new purposefulness. Outside, a vast crowd was cheering and gesticulating loudly. The preaching of the crusade clearly appeared to have overwhelming and enthusiastic popular support. There would be many among them hoping to be able to profit soon from the spoils of Granada. The air felt heavy and oppressive. Looking up at the sky he saw that thick black clouds were rolling up from the west, moving very quickly and partially blotting out the sun. Already far in the distance he could detect the rumble of thunder. He could feel the occasional speck of rain on his skin.

There was no sign of his customary escort. Either they had been swept away by the contagious exhilaration of the massed spectators, or they had not expected him to leave before the end of the ceremonial proceedings. Prince Ibrahim shrugged his shoulders. He was not afraid to make his way back alone to his own quarters, but he had not gone more than a few paces when he heard heavy footsteps and a loud cry of derision behind him. When he turned round, it was to see Bertran de la Cueva and his son, the latter with a look of venomous triumph on his face.

'So, Prince, this is where we find you skulking. My son saw you slinking out of the cathedral. No doubt Their Majesties will be interested to learn that the envoy of Granada deemed it unnecessary to stay till the end of our ceremony of national dedication. But you will, no doubt, as envoy of Granada, wish to rejoice with me in my son's safety and the knowledge that those who held him captive have been very severely, and most fittingly, chastised.'

The younger de la Cueva laughed. 'You would have some difficulty in finding Zafra again, Prince, I fear, if you were to return by the same route to Granada. You see, this time, there was no upstart interference. Oh yes, my father paid the ransom they asked. We met their terms, as the saying goes; we sank for a day to their stinking level, treating with them as though they were our equals and not just squalid village oafs and villains. But in their rejoicing at our humiliation they omitted to mount any guards. We returned that same day, Prince, and reclaimed the ransom my father had so generously paid. Most of your peasant friends, are, I fear, no longer of this world. But we did spare a handful to bring back as slaves to sell to our good Portuguese friends. So you see, Prince, your foolish extravagant impetuosity has cost your peasant friends dear. Perhaps you will reflect upon another occasion before crossing a de la Cueva.'

Prince Ibrahim looked at the younger de la Cueva with revulsion. Poor villagers. He should have hanged the coward on the spot. He could imagine only too well how he would have relished his revenge upon those poor villagers in Zafra, too simple-minded to suspect such swift and terrible retaliation. But de la Cueva's taunt was only too true. His action had initially saved a small number of villagers from slavery. But had thereafter led to their total destruction.

'It seems, father,' continued the younger de la Cueva, 'that our popinjay has lost his appetite for words; our special fare of the last few days has been too strong for his stomach.'

'Perhaps,' said Bertran de la Cueva, 'he is rueing his proud words. What was it again, Prince, that you boasted? Was it not that you would meet both of us together, father and son, in a duel to the death? Well, it seems that fate has given you that chance. Or would you perhaps prefer to forget your popinjay's boast? Oh, I know what you will say: that you are still the envoy of Granada and have an ambassador's immunity. But after today's events I do not believe that Their Majesties would feel in any way impugned if your ambassadorial status were to be temporarily waived. The wheel, Prince, has turned full circle. You have for sure the option of evading it, for a while, but at the price of being branded a loudmouthed vainglorious stage-strutting poltroon.'

Despite his feelings of revulsion, Prince Ibrahim felt himself able to remain totally calm, as though some icy coolness had somehow come to encase him. Father and son stood together before him, close together. The look on Bertran de la Cueva's face was arrogant, vengeful, determined to wreak humiliation on the man whom he held responsible for the dishonour of his son. The younger de la Cueva looked equally arrogant, but behind his posturing the fear in his heart was not completely hidden. Prince Ibrahim gave a harsh laugh.

'I marvel at your courage, hidalgos of Spain, daring, together, to challenge me. But let me assure you, if you are right and Their Majesties will give their consent, I am prepared to meet you tonight, tomorrow or at any time you wish. My only regret, de la Cueva, is that while I know you to be a beast in human form who is at least courageous, your son is more contemptible than the lowliest peasant in this whole land of Spain. I pity you as his father.'

'You shall hear from us within the hour,' Bertran de la Cueva hissed at him, spitting out the words. 'We shall see then how you crow.'

'Against an old man in his dotage and a yellow-livered cur, what risk do I run in combat?' said Prince Ibrahim contemptuously. 'Believe me, de la Cueva, I shall not seek to evade your challenge. I welcome it as much as your son, coward that he is, is regretting it. Why, man,' he added disdainfully, 'you are already shaking with fear. I will kill you like the cur you are.'

Thrusting them both, father and son, to one side, Prince Ibrahim walked into the crowd. They made way for him, generally with respect. The de la Cuevas were, it seemed, little loved or esteemed, even though Bertran de la Cueva had the reputation of being exceptionally brave, if also reckless and uncaring of the lives of his own followers.

It was the first time since his arrival in Cordoba that Prince Ibrahim had walked unaccompanied through the streets of the city. The raindrops which had been slowly increasing in size and in intensity now turned suddenly into great sheets of water as the thunderstorm that had been rolling in from the west burst with a sudden savage series of explosions over the city. Men scurried for shelter, the rain streaming down their bodies, soaking their clothes and already forming gushing rivulets in the narrow streets. Prince Ibrahim paid no attention. The elemental forces of the thunderstorm, the forked flashes of lightning and the crescendo of human yells and screams seemed like an appropriate apocalyptic accompaniment to the gruesome horrors of the past few days. He, too, was utterly drenched when he reached his own quarters, but the storms of nature had set a light to his own inner feelings. He felt himself to be burning inside with a more intense hatred than he had ever experienced before. He felt no fear whatsoever about the outcome of any duel.

Sharif was waiting anxiously for him in his private quarters but quailed at the look on his face. Prince Ibrahim waved him away. 'Later, Sharif, I will talk to you later. I shall consider what message we should send to Granada. But I fear we are moving very quickly towards war.'

Sharif made no attempt to argue, but left the room immediately. Prince Ibrahim stared out through the open casement at the continuing storm. If anything, it had increased in intensity, the deep resounding thunderclaps ricocheting among the walls of the city's taller buildings, booming like guns in an uneven broadside. The clouds had tints of indigo and black that were slashed through with fine silver threads that forked and flashed as the lightning struck. The rain was like a curtain now, at once transparent and opaque according to the light. And yet the awesomeness of the spectacle was not frightening but rather comforting, as if this was somehow the deity's disavowal of the bestialities committed that day and the day before by the men whom it had created.

It was, in fact, not until noon on the following day that Santillana came to him, bringing a message from King Ferdinand and Queen Isabella. The request for an exceptional temporary suspension of normal diplomatic procedures was granted, but for one hour only on the following day when Their Spanish Majesties would not be present in Cordoba. The duel was seen as a personal affair of honour between Prince Ibrahim and the House of de la Cueva. It could be taken that the outcome of the duel would have no bearing on relations between the kingdoms of Aragon and Castile on the one hand, and Granada on the other hand.

'I have been instructed to select a suitable venue,' added Santillana. 'Their Majesties are concerned that this incident should pass off as quietly as possible. I will be your second if you wish it.'

'Thank you, Santillana. I accept. I believe that, by your laws of chivalry I, as the challenged party, have the choice of weapons.'

'That is correct, Prince.'

'Then I choose sword and dagger. The fight is to be without protective armour of any kind.'

Santillana raised his eyebrows. 'No armour at all, Prince? There could well be serious injury.'

'If I am to fight against the two de la Cuevas simultaneously then I must have maximum freedom of movement. It may also make them a little more circumspect.'

'Very well, if that is what you wish. I shall go and inform your opponents. I shall return as soon as the venue and the time have been agreed.'

Prince Ibrahim strolled slowly through the palace gardens. The heavy rain had left huge pools of water and the plants and flowers, with the raindrops still clinging to them, glistened in the early morning sun. He nodded absent-mindedly to his body servants sitting on low stools, munching large slices of watermelon. It was not long before Sharif came up to him; for once, there was an expression of concern, or even outright agitation, on his face.

'Lord, you cannot fight a duel. What would become of us if you were to kill Bertran de la Cueva, or his son? Spain would treat it as a declaration of war. All our careful work of the past few years would be undone. You must decline to fight.'

Prince Ibrahim looked at him quizzically. 'Your concern, Sharif, is most touching, and your confidence in my victory most reassuring. It is possible, nevertheless, that they will kill me. How would Granada stand then? Unharmed?'

'Lord, I beg of you, do not fight. Wait at least until we have consulted with King Boabdil. As his envoy, you are in duty bound to do so. You have not the right to jeopardise the safety of Granada for the sake of personal squabbles that are of little matter.'

'Their Majesties of Spain have agreed that there shall be a temporary suspension of my embassy. De la Cueva and his son have insulted not only me, but Granada also. I cannot believe that King Boabdil would tolerate the dishonour that our silent toleration of such an insult would inevitably bring. You must write to King Boabdil, Sharif, and tell His Majesty that there was no alternative. Tell him that if I die in this duel, my last thoughts were for the freedom of Granada.'

'Lord, at least let me . . .'

'Silence, Sharif. The matter is closed.'

He watched Sharif turn away. Anguish and bitterness showed visibly on his face. There were factors at play that he could only dimly perceive. Sharif's concern, and the words he had just spoken, made it only the more evident that some kind of understanding, and perhaps a great deal more than that, had been reached between Boabdil and the Spanish Kings. Sharif obviously knew a great deal, but it was equally obvious that he was totally committed to the interests of King Boabdil, and that they were also manifestly his own. More than ever, Prince Ibrahim felt himself to be groping in a fog of intrigue and double-dealing that augured ill for the survival of Granada. These were sombre thoughts with which to confront the de la Cuevas. He was surprised himself at his total absence of fear of the pending encounter. It was not that he was ready for death. Despite the gloom and depression surrounding the probable fate of Granada, he had no death wish, but rather the contrary – a longing that swelled up inside him to battle on until the end, however bitter that might be. Perhaps it was his feeling of contempt for the younger de la Cueva, whom he virtually discounted – a coward, he was convinced, always ran true to kind. Even the presence of his redoubtable father would not turn the son into a man of courage.

His mood did not change later that day when Santillana returned to let him know that the duel was to take place by the bank of the Guadalquivir at eight o'clock the following morning. He would call for him some thirty minutes earlier with a closed carriage. Cardinal Mendoza had ordered an escort of not less than fifty foot soldiers to ensure the absence of spectators or any form of popular demonstration.

Santillana was, once again, true to his word. Punctually at half past seven the following morning a carriage drew up outside the palace of the Marquis de Cadiz. Prince Ibrahim, who had risen at six, walked at once to meet him. For the first time since they had met near the frontier of Castile and Granada, Santillana grasped him by the hand. Prince Ibrahim held the Spaniard's hand firmly for a moment in his own. He had come to respect Santillana. They exchanged only a few words as the closed carriage rattled over the cobbled streets of Cordoba and then on by the river bank to the appointed field. Cardinal Mendoza and the escort of fifty foot soldiers were already there, as was a small handful of courtiers. The Cardinal was evidently prepared to tolerate their presence, but only at a considerable distance. He greeted Prince Ibrahim with a wan smile.

'I fear, Prince, that you are too stormy a petrel. I assume you have no interest in a reconciliation? It is not too late to step back. It is my duty to tell you so, in case that should be your wish.'

Prince Ibrahim shook his head. 'I thank Your Eminence, but the time has come to let matters take their course.'

The Cardinal nodded. 'I fear you are perfectly right. Ah, here come Bertran de la Cueva and his son.' They stood silently for a few moments waiting for the two men to join them, accompanied by their seconds. Prince Ibrahim stared straight past them.

'My lords,' said the Cardinal, 'I am here on the instructions of Their Majesties to see that this duel be conducted honourably. It is my duty to urge you to examine in your hearts whether you cannot forgive each other for any injuries and exchange a kiss of peace. Regrettably that does not seem to be the case. The rules of combat are straightforward. You are to take up positions five paces apart, facing each other. When I give the signal, you are free to move against each other as you wish. You may move anywhere within the confines of this field which, as you can see, is now ringed with soldiers. Any man attempting to break through them will be driven back. I hope that whosoever wins will show mercy to his opponent. My lords, it is time for you to take up your positions.'

Prince Ibrahim walked some ten paces forward without a backward glance, then turned and waited, almost nonchalantly, for his opponents to take up their positions. Cardinal Mendoza wasted no time but, taking Santillana's sword in his right hand, brought it swiftly down to the ground as the signal for the combat to commence. Santillana and the courtiers chosen by the de la Cuevas as their seconds stayed by the Cardinal's side, their eyes glued to the area where the three contestants were moving cautiously towards each other.

The older de la Cueva was the first to attack. Uttering a series of loud cries he launched a succession of heavy blows, wielding his sword rather in the manner of a sledgehammer, raising it high about his shoulders and bringing it down at Prince Ibrahim with tremendous force. It would have been a dangerous tactic to employ in a man-to-man combat but Prince Ibrahim was unable to take advantage of his opponent's moments of great vulnerability each time his sword came sweeping down to the ground lest the younger de la Cueva should dart in and strike him from the side. It was immediately very clear to him that their tactic was indeed for the father to bear the brunt of the direct engagement while his son hovered on one side or the other, waiting and watching for an opportunity to strike home, jabbing occasionally in the meanwhile to distract Prince Ibrahim's attention as much as possible.

It had been Prince Ibrahim's intention to try and deal first with the older de la Cueva, leaving the son to the end but, as the combat proceeded, he decided upon a different tactic. Bertran de la Cueva, although still very strong, was suffering from the fury of his initial assault. He was of an age when most men would have chosen to fight on the defensive. Here, however, he was carrying almost the whole burden of the attack. Had his son been a braver man the fight would already have been over with their joint victory. Prince Ibrahim began to fall back more rapidly towards the edge of the field, encouraging the older de la Cueva to redouble his efforts. It was not long before he was rewarded by seeing the beads of sweat glistening on his forehead and hearing his breathing grow heavier with a loud panting noise. His son, too, was advancing, dancing on the balls of his feet and still jabbing with his sword with an airiness that was almost comical. He had a smile on his face now, imagining perhaps that his terrible father had the measure of their opponent.

It was the moment for which Prince Ibrahim had been waiting. Stepping well back, he gave a sudden leap to one side so that he came within a pace and a half of the younger de la Cueva. Arching himself forward he drove his sword up and into his stomach. It had been the work of three seconds, or less. The younger de la Cueva fell to the ground with loud shriek. Prince Ibrahim pulled out his sword and leapt back before the older de la Cueva had fully comprehended what had happened. For a moment his eyes met those of Prince Ibrahim with a look that was at once full of hatred and of pleading. Prince Ibrahim leaned on his sword and motioned to his opponent that he could kneel down by his son's side. Bertran de la Cueva placed his hands tenderly round his son's head and raised it slightly. There was a bloody red froth on his lips and his eyes were half-glazed. Prince Ibrahim could see the blood welling out of his wound in his stomach. He knew then that at least one of the de la Cuevas would soon be dead.

Prince Ibrahim looked towards the spot where Cardinal Mendoza and their two seconds were standing. They did not move, making no sign of any kind, but waited. They were right, of course. The combat was not yet over. The older de la Cueva's reputation was that of a beast in human form. His son's death could only inflame his thirst for blood. He had been responsible for the death of countless Moslems. This was no time for pity.

'Rise, de la Cueva,' said Prince Ibrahim coldly, 'or I shall spit you as you lie.'

Bertran de la Cueva rose to his feet and in a single flashing movement hurled his dagger with his left hand straight at Prince Ibrahim's chest. Almost by instinct he swerved to one side but only to feel the dagger cut deep into his left shoulder like a red-hot pincer. The pain was so intense that he was forced to drop his own dagger which he had been holding in his left hand. He knew that it was a serious wound and that he would have to finish the combat virtually there and then if he was to survive. He uttered no sound but jumping forward launched in his turn a series of sweeping blows from right to left and back again that had de la Cueva reeling. In trying to fall back he stumbled over his son's outstretched arm. Without hesitation and before his enemy could recover his balance, Prince Ibrahim brought his sword down with all his remaining strength upon de la Cueva's neck, virtually severing it from his shoulders.

The older de la Cueva was dead before he hit the ground. Prince Ibrahim stood over their prone bodies. The younger de la Cueva was still breathing, although his eyes were almost completely closed. Remorselessly Prince Ibrahim raised his sword and drove it down into his heart. Then he made to move towards Cardinal Mendoza but his knees buckled under him and he sank to the ground. He had won a bloody victory, but at what cost?

Santillana was the first to reach him, but his words were like blurred sounds in his ears. He was losing consciousness, and yet he knew that his wound was not fatal. He could only hope that his enemies would observe and respect their own code of honour. Somehow, with Santillana there, he was hopeful that they would.

*Chapter Six*

# PRINCESS LEONORA

Prince Ibrahim felt himself being supported by Santillana as he struggled to stand up again, but awareness of his surroundings seemed to alternately focus and then fade away again as he attempted to marshal his thoughts. The duel was over, but there remained Torquemada to speak to. He felt himself swivelling his eyes trying to locate him but it made the blood rush to his temples, thudding and beating inside his head so that the pain brought tears to his eyes. He could hardly feel his left arm, although he knew it was there, hanging limply by his side. He groaned. How was he to pursue his mission now? How would his victory be portrayed, presented or perhaps treacherously misportrayed? He sensed that his vision was becoming more obscured as though dark lenses were being brought closer and closer to his face. Try as he would, his thoughts wandered, veering this way and that, a vague fear clutching at his heart that somehow a nerve had been touched and his vision irretrievably damaged. But no, that could not be. Only his arm had been gashed by Bertran de la Cueva's dagger.

Santillana was clearly finding his weight too heavy to bear. As he lowered him to the ground, Prince Ibrahim sank again to his knees. For a moment he remained there, kneeling still, but even that effort was too great. He had to lie down. Gingerly, he allowed himself to slide on to the ground, resting mainly on his right arm. He could hear Santillana talking to him. His voice was soft and almost tender, caressing, but he was unable to distinguish any of the sounds. He attempted to nod in acknowledgement but the movement seemed to increase the pain in his eyes. If only he could sleep, and rest. The giant form looming over him was, he fancied, that of the Grand Inquisitor, but he could not be certain. Despite the pain, his consciousness was ebbing away. He was indeed in the Spaniard's hands.

The Grand Inquisitor looked down at the prone figure. Santillana was down on one knee, one hand under Prince Ibrahim's head, raising it slightly so that they could both look at his face.

'He has a deep wound in his left shoulder,' he said to Torquemada, 'and is losing a lot of blood. He will need careful nursing.'

The Grand Inquisitor nodded. 'Have him carried to the *Casa Santa*. We shall tend him there.'

Prince Ibrahim, floating in and out of consciousness, felt himself being lifted. Every so often he could distinguish a few of the words being spoken by persons close to him, but his mind was unable to focus upon them or to establish any connecting link. It was easier to lapse into emptiness and to reject any attempt at thinking. Even in moments of full consciousness he kept his eyes firmly closed. There were moments when he could feel the sun on his face; it felt warm and comforting, encouraging a drift into a renunciation of effort. He felt as though he should try and combat it, but the struggle was too uneven. He was conscious of sighing deeply, but then his whole mind seemed suddenly overwhelmed with blackness.

In the days that followed he was occasionally conscious of time passing while, at the same time, losing all notion of it. He sensed, rather than felt, that he was lying on a low couch, alone in a room, although there were persons who came in periodically and forced liquids and light food into his mouth, tended his wound and washed his whole body. He felt too tired to resist, although he found the very thought of food repellent. Little by little he was, however, able to focus more on his surroundings. The room was middling in size but with a large wide window that appeared to look out over a garden, for he could clearly distinguish a number of tall trees that seemed to stand in rows like brown and green soldiers on parade. The walls of the room had been painted in a stark white, broken only by an immense black iron crucifix. The first time he consciously realised what it was Prince Ibrahim recoiled, but the longer he lay there the more it attracted his attention. The figure of Christ nailed to the cross was that of a man in agony and great torment. From several days before, the words *Casa Santa* came back into his mind and he came to understand that he was lying in the palace of the Holy Inquisition. His initial reaction was one of indifference since it was evident from all the attentions he was receiving that they wanted him to live. It was only slowly, as the days went by and his mind gradually returned to a fuller awareness, that he began to wonder why they had chosen this place in preference to the quarters that had been assigned to him and his embassy in Cordoba, or indeed to a hospital for soldiers hurt in battle. The room contained only one piece of furniture other than his couch: a big oaken cupboard stood in one corner, away from the window, and served as a general worktable for basin and ewer and several jars with ointments with which they regularly rubbed all round his injured shoulder. While his wound still hurt, the intensity of the pain had greatly subsided. His shoulder remained, however, heavily bandaged and still made him start abruptly with the pain whenever he attempted to move.

Prince Ibrahim had lost all reckoning of time. The first time he realised it, was when he first became aware of Torquemada's presence in his room. It was early one morning and it was a full minute or two before he fully recognised the figure standing upright by the side of his couch. For a moment their eyes met and held each other, before Torquemada spoke.

'I see that you are recovering, Prince. I am glad. There are many serious matters for us to discuss as soon as you are well enough to do so. For the moment you must still rest. But I will come again soon. Much has happened in all the time that you have been lying here.' He raised his hand in a gesture of farewell, turned and went out of the room.

Prince Ibrahim repeated the words Torquemada had spoken slowly to himself, over and over, trying to force their meaning into his brain. He forced himself to sit upright, gritting his teeth as he felt a spasm of pain in his shoulder. It passed quickly, however, and he continued to sit, bolt upright, focusing his eyes on the trees beyond the window of his room. For the first time he was aware of a tingling in his arms and legs, as though the desire for action was beginning to return. He began to try and keep a closer record of the passing of time, forcing himself to recall the images of his duel with the de la Cuevas. He remembered very clearly killing them both, the memory of it still etched quite vividly in his mind. It filled him with a kind of spasmodic exhilaration.

Despite the alleged urgency it was, nevertheless, another three days before Torquemada came again. Prince Ibrahim had just been brought his midday meal of hot soup, fried fish, bread, onions and grapes. Once or twice they had brought him wine and beer which he had left untouched. Since then they had simply brought him water that had a slightly brackish taste. Torquemada came in alone and for a moment the two looked at each other again in silence as Prince Ibrahim continued to eat his meal.

'So, Prince, I am glad to see that you have a good appetite. It is fitting that you are building up your strength again for I fear there are perilous times ahead for you. You will need to be well fortified.'

'How long have I been lying here?'

'Thirteen days. You have been unconscious or only barely semiconscious for much of the time. You did not appear to understand much of what was said to you.'

'I know that you came three days ago.'

'I have been five times in all, Prince. This is my fifth visit. There is much to tell you, and much to discuss.'

'I can recall similar words, Your Eminence, from your last visit.'

'Good. Then there is no time to be lost. I will begin now, if you can attend me?'

Prince Ibrahim nodded. His mind felt clearer although Torquemada's words had had an unsettling effect upon him.

'You should know that the day after the duel, Granadan soldiers, led by al-Zaghal, took the town of Jaen by surprise. The entire garrison was put to the sword, save for one man. Al-Zaghal proceeded to send King Boabdil, his own sovereign, an ultimatum: either he should join him in a holy war against Castile or he should abdicate and make way for his uncle who was prepared to fight to the last ditch for his country. King Boabdil capitulated, or so it would appear, so that now both he and al-Zaghal are currently inside Castile territory with large forces of horse and foot-soldiers. We know al-Zaghal of old, and of his hatred for Spain. But of King Boabdil we are less certain. So, with you incapacitated, Their Spanish Majesties have written to him, selecting Sharif as messenger. He left four days ago. So far we have received no further news.'

'And my embassy, that of Granada, here in Cordoba?'

'Is terminated, Prince. After al-Zaghal's act of aggression there can be no room for any Granadan embassy; unless, of course, he were to be disowned by King Boabdil, his nephew, and suitably punished.'

'And my own position as envoy?'

There was a brief moment of silence before Torquemada replied, but it did not seem to reflect any hesitation on his part as to what he had to say but rather the manner of it. 'Let me answer you, Prince, with a question of my own. You are clearly a man of ability. You have been long absent from Granada, but there are certain secrets that cannot be kept for long. When King Boabdil stayed at our court as an honoured guest he was quite outspoken in his willingness, indeed his desire, to bring an end to a situation that had become, as he himself put it, politically and culturally grotesque. He showed himself to be exceptionally broad-minded, without religious bigotry or fanaticism, or the type of zeal that refuses to recognise hard military facts. In short, if I can try and say in a few words what transpired after many hours of discussion, an agreement was reached between my sovereigns and your King. What was not settled, however, was its timing or its manner of application. I can see from your face, Prince, that you follow my meaning. I would imagine that I am not telling you anything that you did not know or, at least, had not guessed before?'

Prince Ibrahim ignored the question, but Torquemada nodded his head as if answering his question to his own satisfaction. 'What I have just told you is a fact. There are documents and papers in your King's own handwriting to prove it. What is less clear to us is the extent to which King Boabdil still proposes to honour his agreement with us. We are puzzled by his choice of your person as ambassador to Spain but we knew that Sharif was in his confidence and that gave us some cause for reassurance. We assumed that he had nominated you as someone whom his own people would readily accept. This became all the more true when you returned from Istanbul as a hero. Perhaps he thought you would rally to his cause, but we have no means of knowing, at least not so far, of whether that could ever be the case. But now we have this unexpected and quite unforeseen development with the news that he has joined – or would appear to have joined – with al-Zaghal in an invasion of Castile.

'You asked me, Prince, what had become of your mission. The answer, I fear, is that you are very ill-placed. Your King has violated the truce between our countries, and that at a time when his ambassador had been received with friendship at our court. A number of our subjects have been killed. Others have probably been sent back to Granada to be sold as slaves. By his action, all your privileges have been forfeited. Many here hold you responsible, at least in part, for the hurts we have suffered, and are calling for an exemplary punishment. The relatives of the de la Cuevas have petitioned Their Majesties for your head. It is not so simple a matter to refuse them what they claim as their right.'

'Is this why you have had me tended so carefully? You could have let me die, honourably.'

'A man can die in many ways,' said Torquemada sententiously, 'but the manner of his death can become a political gesture, full of meaning for the other side.'

'I hope you will believe me, Your Eminence, when I tell you that I am not afraid to die.'

'I know you to be brave, Prince, and to be a man of integrity. It is for these reasons that I will be open with you. Spain is determined to repossess Granada. We cannot be stopped. Its return to Spain lies in our destiny and is commanded by God. But we do not seek Granada's destruction or the exodus of all its people. Spain is prepared to be generous, to be accommodating and to greet Granadans as fellow-Spaniards and fellow-Christians. For those whose consciences may require a period of reflection or meditation we are prepared to wait. Your King is, or was, prepared to accept such a proposition. It was not an act of cowardice, Prince, on his part, but rather one of great courage, taken in the best interests of all his subjects. Reflect for a moment on the alternative: war, leading to inevitable defeat, despoliation, exile or slavery. It is our hope – my hope – that you also will see it in practical, emotional and unbigoted terms. Our God is great. He is One. Perhaps our two faiths are not so fundamentally antagonistic. I would like your help, Prince. Give us that and not only will you be safe from any vengeance, but the way will be open to you to become a grandee of Spain, a captain in the greatest army the world has ever known, with the entire world as your horizon.'

Prince Ibrahim pushed away the tray that still lay in front of him. It was a most extraordinary proposal. It was easy to see how King Boabdil had been tempted, and how he had yielded to that temptation. But it was the kind of persuasion that carried with it the stench of treachery in its train. But then, even now, how was he to judge Boabdil's behaviour? The possibility remained open, as indeed the Grand Inquisitor had himself recognised, that King Boabdil's apparent acceptance of Spanish inducements had been no more than skin-deep, and might just conceivably have been a simple ploy to win more time for Granada. But if that were really so, there was no evidence that he had put it to good use. For his own part, there could be no accommodation with Spain. The only question was whether to say so bluntly and openly now, or to prevaricate. Torquemada had been forthright in his approach. His impulse was to reply in kind, regardless of the penalty that plain speaking might bring with it; but that would not necessarily coincide with the best interests of Granada.

'I see that I have given you food for thought,' said Torquemada pleasantly, 'it would be unreasonable of me to expect an immediate reply. But please believe me when I tell you that the situation for Granada is perilous and requires on your part a speedy adjustment of mind and intellect, not so much for our sakes as for your own and those of your fellow Granadans. You, Prince, can play a leading part in such a process. Destiny, it seems to me, has chosen you for a role of either saviour or destroyer. I can only hope that you will be farsighted enough to make the right choice.'

Prince Ibrahim felt rather than saw Torquemada look at him inquiringly as though he was half expecting some kind of response. The temptation was indeed still there to reject the offer with contempt – the words were there, bubbling in his throat as much as in his mind – and it was only by gritting his teeth that he was able to refrain from spitting them out. Torquemada did not appear to be aware of his internal struggle; he was perhaps a man too deeply inebriated with the stimulus of his own mental and emotional fervour.

'You will need time, Prince, to consider your position, and that of Granada. I had not expected it to be otherwise. Indeed, it raises you in my estimation. Now that you are on the way to recovery from your wound you should have a change from the religious solemnity of the *Casa Santa*. Please believe me when I tell you that we brought you here for your own safety. The de la Cuevas have many friends for whom revenge would be sweet. I have thought carefully about where you could best go for your convalescence. I discussed the matter with the Princess Isabel. She tells me that Princess Leonora, or should I say Sister Teresa, still has three months' recuperation to complete before joining her as her first lady-in-waiting. She has not yet formally withdrawn from her novitiate although it is now her known and stated intention to do so. In the meanwhile she has been assigned as a companion to the Abbess of the *convent de la Sangre de Nuestro Señor* in Seville. You are to be transported there. The sisters will be responsible for your welfare and for your safety. I shall come and see you there very soon to hear your answer to my proposal. I take it there is nothing you would wish to say to me now before I take my leave.'

'I can only thank Your Eminence for your patience,' replied Prince Ibrahim in a thick voice.

Torquemada nodded. His face was unsmiling as he rose and slowly went out of the room. Perhaps he was less confident of Prince Ibrahim's response than he had appeared to be; or, perhaps, the matter was of such little importance in relation to his overall strategic thinking that he had already thrust Prince Ibrahim and their conversation out of his mind.

Prince Ibrahim relaxed and sank back deep into his couch. How strange were the ways of fate! First, Leonora had to all intents and purposes been his prisoner; and now, in effect, he was to be hers. But regardless of their respective roles, he could not but feel the blood coursing more rapidly through his veins at the prospect of being with her once again, however different their positions or surroundings.

It was Santillana who called on him the following morning to prepare him for the journey to the *convent de la Sangre de Nuestro Señor*. He seemed like a man in excellent humour and greeted Prince Ibrahim effusively.

'You are seen as one of the paladins of old,' he said jovially as he entered the room. 'The story of your duel with Bertran de la Cueva and his son is known by now throughout the Spains and no doubt well beyond. I am not surprised the Grand Inquisitor is keen to win you over to his side. I hope it for my sake too, for I have been given the command of one of the three armies that is to march against Granada.'

'Does that mean outright war, then?'

Santillana shook his head. 'No. At least, not yet. But Their Majesties have decreed that the capture and massacre at Jaen must be avenged. My orders are to advance towards Malaga. But you may rest easy. It will take time to assemble the necessary number of men, equipment and, above all, the horses and pack-mules to transport all our weapons and provisions. By then it may be that your King will have withdrawn and offered compensation, and we can all return to the status quo.'

'You have come to see me moved?'

Santillana nodded. 'Yes. I think you will like the convent. It is a comparatively recent building but set in very beautiful gardens by the banks of the Guadalquivir. From it you can see the harbour of Seville with all its ships. If it lacks the sheer perfection of the gardens of Granada, it is still not an altogether unworthy rival. You will find it restful and soothing for both body and mind.'

Prince Ibrahim looked up at him. 'I take it the Grand Inquisitor has informed you about the proposal he made me?'

'Yes, he has indeed. He clearly holds you in the greatest esteem. There are not many Moslems to whom he would willingly accord so much time or attention.'

'You are a man of honour, Santillana. Would your honour not be tarnished by such a proposal from an enemy?'

Santillana started as if in surprise. 'An enemy! You are mistaken, Prince. Torquemada does not look upon you as an enemy, but rather as a man to be convinced, to be won over in the best interests of his own people. He is not looking for traitors, Prince, but for men of vision who will participate willingly in the venture of Spain. Your Moslem faith is no bar to that, as long as Granada is a part of the main, irrevocably committed to the rest of the kingdom.'

Prince Ibrahim closed his eyes. He felt suddenly tired, not so much drained as loathe to make any further effort of concentration. Santillana placed one hand in his side. 'Rest, Prince, we shall carry you in a litter. The road from here to Seville is quite straight and smooth. If we leave now we shall be in Seville before nightfall tomorrow.'

The road ran for the most part close to the bank of the Guadalquivir and had, as Santillana had said, a good surface that allowed for an easy, comfortable journey. The countryside was rich in olive, orange and lemon groves, where the crickets chirped in the evening twilight and ships and barges appeared to glide magically in the waters of the river. They camped that night in the open beneath a sky that glittered with a million stars. There was a heavy scent of perfume from the pomegranate trees close by their encampment. Prince Ibrahim turned in the direction of Mecca to pray to Allah, to Allah the all-merciful, the all-compassionate. All would be as He had decreed, but he prayed nevertheless for help for Granada.

They reached the *convent de la Sangre de Nuestro Señor* late in the afternoon on the following day. The light was still good so that it was possible to look out on the trees and plants in the gardens that surrounded the convent buildings on all sides. The Abbess, a distant cousin of Santillana and his brother, Cardinal Mendoza, greeted him kindly. She looked very old with wrinkles in her face that puckered as she looked at him.

'You are welcome, Prince, to our convent. May you find rest and good guidance in the midst of our Christian fellowship. We are all of us children of the one true God, I truly believe.'

'I thank you, lady, for your gracious words,' he replied.

The Abbess gave a gentle smile. 'One of the sisters will show you to the room you are to occupy. Food will be brought to you there. You will forgive me if I go now to attend to my other duties, but I shall see you later tonight. Sister Teresa will join us then.'

'Sister Teresa is the name under which Princess Leonora is still known here,' murmured Santillana. 'As the Abbess has said, she will join us for dinner. Normally, the Abbess, like all the nuns in this convent, eats only once a day, at noon. Today, exceptionally, they will break their fasting rule. Come, let us go to your room.'

The room on this occasion was in total contrast to the one in which he had lain for thirteen days and nights in the *Casa Santa*. Here, stark simplicity had been replaced not just by comfort but by outright opulence. The room was large with wide windows that overlooked the luxurious convent gardens where orange, lemon and oleander trees grew in rich profusion. There were bougainvillea creepers, their purple flowers thrown like richly glowing scarves across sylvan glades. There were peacocks among the trees, their gorgeous tails spread out like near diaphanous fans of green and blue. Inside the room thick oriental carpets covered the floor, deadening all sound, their patterns reflecting the hangings on the walls that were similarly of eastern workmanship. A high bed made of oak stood in one corner, while the other furniture in the room consisted of a table, two reclining chairs and a prie-Dieu, all equally of oak and exquisitely carved. Above the bed, but scarcely visible behind its high canopy in brilliant tapestry, there was a crucifix that seemed carved in alabaster. A tall jug of water and a plate piled high with fruit stood on the table.

'You will probably wish to rest for a little while, Prince,' said Santillana. 'I hope the room is to your liking. The Abbess has asked that we should join her for dinner at eight tonight. If you require anything at all you have only to ring the bell on the table there. One of the nuns with nursing skills will be constantly on duty to attend you.'

Prince Ibrahim went over to the window, letting his back rest against one of the two heavy oaken chairs that stood one on each side of the table. The pain from his shoulder was much less now, but he felt very tired after the two-day journey from Cordoba. Or, perhaps, rather more than the fatigue of the journey, it was still the harrowing memory of his last conversation with Torquemada. How long, how long he wondered, would the Grand Inquisitor give him to consider his proposition? He had spoken of seeing him again soon. Four days? Five days? A week? It was very unlikely to be any longer. With the armies of Spain on the move, Torquemada would want all his pawns in place as soon as possible. While it was perhaps not open war as yet, as Santillana had said, it was only too clear that it could no longer be far away. It was an agonising situation in which, he swore to himself, he would be guided solely by the best interests of Granada, whatever the cost to himself.

It was now almost totally dark outside, with only the occasional pinprick of light in the convent gardens, when a knock on the door came as a signal that it was time to go down for dinner. He felt his heart beat faster at the prospect. He had no choice but to go as he was, for his boxes and travelling trunk had not yet been brought to his room. A basin and a ewer of water had been placed in one corner of the room. He washed his face and hands quickly before stepping out into the corridor where one of the grey-habited nuns was waiting for him. She motioned to him, without speaking, to follow her.

She led him past the main refectory where the nuns were gathered for their silent daily meal, put back this day from midday to evening, interrupted only by readings from the New Testament, to a small but once again luxuriously appointed dining-chamber that was slightly to one side with doors leading to a terrace that overlooked the convent gardens. The glass doors had been thrown open and there was an almost intoxicating scent of blossom wafting its way gently into the room. Santillana and the Abbess were already there. Both had glasses in their hands. Santillana came towards him immediately.

'Prince, I presume I cannot tempt you to a small glass of Jerez, the drink of this province? It has, let me assure you, a taste of velvet. No? What else can we offer you? There is the juice of pressed oranges, or lemons?'

'Thank you, my lord Santillana, but a glass of water will do very well.'

Although small, the dining-chamber had been equipped with a massive six-legged oaken table. Four equally massive chairs had been placed in position around it, while a further six identical chairs were arranged close against the walls of the room. The Abbess, dressed in a grey habit that would not have disgraced a pauper, and wearing only a long thin gold chain with a squat wooden crucifix dangling at the end and that she repeatedly pressed close to her breast, gestured to him to sit down.

'I am sure that you must be very hungry. Sister Teresa will join us shortly. There is no need to wait for her.'

She clapped her hands and almost at once four serving-girls dressed in long black gowns came in, each one carrying a small cup of soup from which the steam was still rising. Prince Ibrahim had scarcely raised his spoon, however, before the door was quietly opened again. It was Princess Leonora. She also was clad in a long grey habit almost identical to that of the Abbess, but without the wooden cross. She did not look at him as she entered. The Abbess motioned to her to take her place at the table, opposite to her and to Prince Ibrahim's right.

'May we all be properly thankful to our God for his bounteous mercies,' said the Abbess lifting her eyes upward, 'and be grateful to Him always. Praise be to God.' She made the sign of the cross, with Santillana and Princess Leonora following her example.

'It cannot happen very often, Prince,' said Santillana, 'that a Moslem prince is invited to eat at a Christian table, especially in a Christian convent. I would like to think that our meal tonight has a certain symbolic value for the future of our relations.'

'I am grateful for the hospitality that I have been shown,' said Prince Ibrahim with a slight smile.

'It is His Eminence the Grand Inquisitor's express wish that you should be received here as an honoured guest,' said the Abbess. 'He has our total confidence, and obedience, convinced as we are of his total Christian commitment. Sister Teresa has been charged with your special welfare. It is a task she has accepted without demur. You should know that she sees it as having a part to play in her redemption from sin. It is nonetheless praiseworthy for that.'

Princess Leonora continued to eat in silence. The soup was followed by both fish and meat dishes, served on platters of pewter with great accompanying piles of beans and sprouts. Prince Ibrahim ate sparingly. Santillana spoke in an almost singsong monologue, praising the food or embarking on tales of the hunt in the mountain ranges of Spain. The Abbess appeared to look on approvingly but spoke very little, although her eyes seemed to have Prince Ibrahim under constant surveillance. He, for his part, interjected the occasional comment, but was happy in the main to leave Santillana as master of the table. Princess Leonora was inscrutable, and yet hers were the only words or thoughts that could matter for him.

The meal ended as it had begun with a brief prayer of thanks to God. The Abbess was the first to rise. 'I bid you good night, Prince. You will be escorted back to your room. As from tomorrow morning you will be in Sister Teresa's charge, but I shall see you again very soon.' She rose and left, Sister Teresa following her without a word.

Santillana smiled. 'You are to be left in peace, it seems, Prince. I also will bid you good night. I have no doubt we shall meet again very soon.'

Prince Ibrahim followed the serving-girl who was carrying a tall candle to light the way back to his room. She placed the candle on the table and left. He noticed that his trunk and boxes had been placed against one of the walls while he had been at dinner. He was glad to be alone. He felt very tired and wanted to think, even though it was the image of Princess Leonora that kept on dominating his thoughts. There was the key question of King Boabdil's position and the true nature of his apparent reconciliation with al-Zaghal. It was hard to believe in a genuine conversion on Boabdil's part to the cause of war. But if that was indeed the future, then Granada's limited resources of manpower demanded that it should be a defensive war, leaving it to the Spaniards with their enormously superior numbers to run the risk of exposure. Out in the open, against the heavy Spanish cavalry and their massed infantry battalions, the Granadan army stood no chance. He dozed off with his mind in turmoil, but also full of foreboding.

Despite his apprehensions for the future, Prince Ibrahim slept well. Perhaps the more tranquil atmosphere of the convent and its sharp contrast with the ascetic rigour of the *Casa Santa* provided at least a partial explanation of the difference; he could not, however, totally dissimulate from himself the relief he felt at being at least temporarily out of the immediate vicinity of Torquemada. The Spanish cleric was truly a formidable figure. Mendoza and Torquemada would indeed have been formidable and dominating figures in any country. The friar Jimenez de Cisneros too – austere, fanatical and repellent though he found him – was undoubtedly a man of high calibre and seemingly totally devoted, like the other two, to the greater glory of Spain and its aggrandisement. They were fearsome antagonists.

One of the nuns entered in the early morning and brought him a small tray with water, bread, a bunch of dates and two oranges. She did not reply when he spoke to her but placed two fingers across her lips, although whether as an indication of a vow of silence or of unwillingness to converse with an infidel he had no means of knowing. When he had finished eating she took away the tray and then returned almost immediately to renew the bandages round his shoulder. She was gentle in her touch and the pomade which she rubbed into his arm was soothing to the skin. When she had finished she put a new bandage round his shoulder and arm, tying it more tightly than before so that it felt more painful when he struggled to his feet. The nun waited till he was standing upright before leaving the room, gesturing to him to stay where he was and closing the door behind her. Prince Ibrahim wondered how long it would be before Princess Leonora would appear.

In fact, he had not long to wait. She entered without knocking, still clad in her habit, her face framed by her nun's coiffe. He found himself wondering to what extent her hair might have grown since their journey on the galley. The recollection of it all made him smile.

'As you know, I have been appointed your keeper, my lord Prince. It is a strange reversal of fortunes, is it not? But come, for this morning you are to walk in the convent gardens. My lord Torquemada is most anxious that you should regain your full strength as quickly as possible.'

'My lord Torquemada,' repeated Prince Ibrahim slowly. 'It is good of him to be so solicitous about my health.'

'I think he has high hopes that you will be persuaded to help him in the enterprise of Granada, on which he has set his heart. But we must go. Can you rise easily without help, or shall I get you a stick?'

'Thank you. I can walk as long as the ground is relatively flat.'

'Then I shall help you down the steps into the garden, but, once there, you will have to be your own master.' He placed his right hand on her shoulder as they walked down the steps. He counted them; there were fifteen in all. Her nun's habit felt coarse and rough in his hand.

'You are still wearing a nun's habit,' he said quietly. 'May I ask why?'

'That, my lord Prince, is a complex matter. There is weakness in it, and repentance, a longing for consolation and a dream, or an escape from a dream. I am not wholly certain myself. But it is not for much longer. My official novitiate is only to last until the Princess Isabel and her fiancé, Prince Afonso, leave for Portugal. They are expected to leave in a few weeks' time. I shall go with them, but in secular dress. The past – my past – will have been erased.'

There had been no joy in her voice as she spoke. If the bitterness of the first few days after their departure from Istanbul had not returned, neither it seemed had any kind of reconciliation with herself come into her soul. They walked slowly on among the citrus, olive and oleander trees, their scents enveloping them in what seemed at times almost like incense. The grass under the trees had been left untended and was in places more than ankle-high. Here and there an occasional chicken clucked its disapproval as they disturbed its matinal peregrinations through the garden. They came suddenly upon a small fountain with stone goblins spouting forth water from their mouths. Several wooden chairs stood nearby and, as if moving in concert, they both sat down, some little distance apart.

'Some of the nuns come and sit here in the evening, after Vespers,' said Princess Leonora. 'It is a place of great beauty and peace. If I were ever to become a permanent member of the community I think I would come here very often.'

'But you will not stay. I am glad you have decided that way. You are too young, too beautiful, too much alive to reject the world.'

'You are not of our faith, my lord Prince, and cannot understand what moves us. I have indeed decided to abandon my novitiate – in part because my cousin, the King, would have it so, and in part also because I feel myself to be unworthy. I would have been a nun on false pretences, sheltering behind the convent walls out of fear of what the outside world thinks of me, hiding from their fingers pointing at me in scorn and in disgust. That would have been my reason, not the love of Our Lord Jesus Christ and the wish to follow Him and His teaching. I want my own wishes, in that respect at least, to take second place. So I shall obey Ferdinand's command, in the interests of Aragon and of Spain.'

'Is that then what governs you, Princess? Are love and duty to Spain your highest goals?'

For a moment she looked straight at him, her face white against the grey of her coiffe, only her eyes glowing, but, whatever she was about to say, she checked herself.

'You ask unanswerable questions, my lord Prince,' she said after a moment. 'I can only tell you that I am still wrestling with myself. But we should go on. It is not enough exercise for you simply to walk such short distances and then just sit and talk. Come, Prince, and let us walk on.'

They walked at a steady pace. The convent gardens were immense. There was a wide path that ran alongside the Guadalquivir. They could see boats passing on their way to and from the harbour, plying up and down the river in an almost endless procession. From some spots along the banks of the river they could see the Giralda tower, built when Seville was still a Moslem city and from where the muezzins had been wont to cry their call to prayer. Now it was a Christian guardhouse. Was a similar fate to befall his beloved city of Granada? Prince Ibrahim saw that his companion was looking at him and following the direction of his gaze. No doubt she sensed the feelings in his breast, but she did not speak. Both of them had their own thoughts, for they said little more to one another on the way back to his room. Only when they reached it did she speak again.

'Tomorrow there is to be a *corrida*, a running of bulls, in the main city square, close by the Alcazar. The Abbess is content that you should go and watch it. If you wish it, I will accompany you.'

'Without a guard?'

'There is no need for guards, my lord Prince. You cannot escape from Seville. Even if you had fully recovered from your wound, no Moslem, alone, would stand a chance of escape. No, we do not need guards, at least, not yet.'

Prince Ibrahim nodded. Escape from Seville did indeed not seem to be an option for one man on his own.

'So,' she insisted, 'do you wish to go to the *corrida*? It will stir your blood, and perhaps for a moment ease some of the pain in your heart.'

'Yes, Princess. I would welcome that.'

She smiled and left without a further word. He did not see her again that day. One of the nuns, whom he had not seen before, accompanied him on a further walk in the convent garden and brought him his dinner in the same dining-room where he had eaten the previous evening with Santillana, the Abbess and Princess Leonora; this time, however, he was left to dine in solitude. A lot of wine had been placed in uncorked bottles on the table but he ignored them. The art of temptation, he reflected, had to be in the Christians' blood.

The next morning he was woken early. Yet again, it was another nun, and yet again she did not speak. Although he was given to understand that there was no need for any excessive haste, it was clear that the invitation to the *corrida* had not been an idle one. The nun helped him to wash and dress; he had selected a dark blue doublet and only slightly lighter leggings, with a dagger in a heavy jewelled scabbard at his side. The doublet was loose and easy-fitting so that it slipped easily over his bandaged shoulder. It was perhaps too much finery when accompanying a woman dressed in a coarse-spun grey-coloured nun's habit, but he felt all the better for it. Perhaps one day fate would permit him to see Princess Leonora dressed as her station in life demanded.

Leonora entered his room briskly, calling to him that it was time to go. If she had noticed his dress, or his dagger, she showed no sign of it. Outside a small open carriage was waiting with a coachman standing by its side. They stepped in and almost at once set off for the *corrida*.

The entire city seemed to be of a similar mind. Men on horseback, carriages and carts, both small and large, were hastening in the direction of the central square. But the closer they got to it, the more difficult their progress became, as the crowds grew so thick that their further passage seemed well-nigh impossible. People were shouting, some in anger, some in anticipation and some no doubt for the relief that shouting gave them from the heaving, bruising masses of humanity all around them. Prince Ibrahim looked at his companion questioningly but she only shook her head with a faint smile on her lips. Abruptly, and without warning, the coachman swung to the right through a domed archway whose twin doors had been thrown open as though by means of a prearranged signal.

'These are the stables next to the cathedral,' Princess Leonora said. 'From here we can simply walk through the cathedral and out into the square. You will be particularly well-placed, as will I. For this morning at least I shall be a princess of Aragon, in mind and spirit if not in dress.'

He followed her as she walked quickly through the stable yard and the cathedral itself. This was the second Christian cathedral he had traversed. There was a heavy scent of incense and in some of the side-chapels priests were celebrating low masses before groups of the faithful. He was glad Princess Leonora was walking so quickly. When they emerged from the cathedral he saw that they were on a kind of elevated platform overlooking the square, with the elegant walls of the Alcazar towards their right. Wooden barriers had been set in place to mark off a sizeable open area in the middle of the square. A few soldiers stood on guard by two gates leading into the enclosure, while all around the perimeter men and women were already packed close together, jostling and yelling, their faces already damp with sweat from the combined effects of heat and excitement.

As they took their seats in the front row, drums started to beat to the accompaniment of tumultuous swaying and cheering. Almost immediately, a single, huge, black bull charged into the midst of the arena, evidently released from somewhere beneath the platform where they were seated. All around him Prince Ibrahim could see people quivering with excitement; glancing at Princess Leonora sitting beside him, he could see that she was no less intoxicated with anticipation.

For a little while it seemed as though nothing more was to happen. The bull, excited by the noise of the crowd, made an occasional rush to the edge of the stockade. Once a man vaulted over the barricade and jumped down into the arena. The bull charged straight at him and he leapt back onto the surrounding barrier to a loud hiss of disapproval. This was followed by a further quick roll of the drums. With that, one of the gates leading into the arena was thrown open and a single man, dressed in tight figure-clinging hose and a thick padded jacket sown with sequins that flashed and glittered in the sun, strode boldly forward. He was carrying a red cloak over his left arm while his right arm was raised up high, his hand gripping a long and finely tapered sword.

For the first few moments the bull appeared to pay no attention. The man continued to come forward, moving slowly, but now holding out his red cloak like a fan or web, shouting the while brief, staccato words that Prince Ibrahim was unable to understand. Then, suddenly, the animal charged. With a dramatic swirl and flourish the man twisted his body while the bull hurtled past him, the red cloak seeming to lie for one moment on his back. The spectators shouted their approval as coins were thrown onto the floor of the arena. The man waved one arm and then turned back to face the bull a second time. Again the animal charged and again the man seemed only to swerve his body by a fraction as he sidestepped it, his red cape seemingly goading the bull to a frenzy of irritation. Prince Ibrahim found himself admiring the man's footwork and his courage; as the bull's charges became each time more frenzied and the animal snorted and pawed the ground in mounting irritation and fury, the man was coming closer and closer to it, at times even turning his back towards the bull, still with his red cape outstretched and seeming to sense without looking the exact moment to swerve or step fractionally to one side. Princess Leonora was shaking with excitement, both her hands gripping the wooden railing that ran along the entire length of the raised platform immediately in front of them.

While continuing to admire the man's skill, Prince Ibrahim found it hard to understand the crowd's evident absorption in the spectacle, waiting for a moment of high ceremonial drama which could only end in death, just possibly that of the man or, so very much more likely, that of the bull. Even as he wondered, the drums beat once more and a total hush fell upon the expectant crowd. This time the man had thrown his cape over his shoulders and was advancing towards the bull, holding his sword in both hands well above his head with its tapered blade pointing at the animal's head. It was as if the bull could read the man's murderous intent for it snorted more violently than before, pawed the ground as if to summon up its greatest strength and charged. The man did not move from his position but, lunging forward at an angle halfway between the vertical and the horizontal, met the bull's onrush with a single brilliant driving stroke of his sword into the animal's brain. For a moment man and beast stood locked together in a macabre statue of death, then, slowly, the bull rolled over onto the ground, its legs still moving slightly, the blood streaming from its head. The man had wrenched out his sword, pulling himself upright as the bull collapsed at his side. Taking his cape from his shoulders he waved it in triumph and in salute to a crowd that was delirious in its applause. Prince Ibrahim noticed that without having been aware of it he too had moved forward in his chair. He sank back into it with mixed feelings while all around him men and women were standing, gesticulating and shouting their approval of what had most definitely been for them a masterful display of bullfighting. It was several minutes still before Princess Leonora turned to him.

'The man you have just seen is from our family estate near Toledo. He is one of the finest bullfighters in Spain, if not the finest. Men like him can earn a great deal of money as you can tell from the number of coins that have been thrown into the arena. He is entitled to keep all of them, although it has become an accepted practice to donate some to the Church to thank the Virgin or a particular Patron Saint for their protection. It can be very dangerous. Many bullfighters are killed or badly gored. It is not our custom to rescue them if they are gored by a bull.'

'I have never witnessed anything like it,' said Prince Ibrahim, 'although I have read accounts of men in northern European countries occasionally fighting bulls with their bare hands. They must be giants.'

Princess Leonora nodded. 'That is true. I have heard of it also. But here it is different. Here there are regular *corridas* with men who quite specifically learn to become bullfighters. Also I think that our bulls are larger and fiercer. I do not believe that even a northern giant could tackle one of our bulls with only his bare hands. There will be six runs in all today, but we shall stay only for the first four.'

Prince Ibrahim sat in steadily growing amazement as the day progressed. The individual bullfights seemed to him to be very much alike, with the same posturings, deftness of footwork, displays of bravery, and pawings and bellowing by the bulls, that all seemed to follow a pattern in which there was very little change. But this was evidently not the view of most of the spectators. Individual feints and movements, a step forward taken more quickly or more slowly, the elegance in wielding the cape and handling it so as to enrage the bull and set it on its mad onward rush, and perhaps above all the studied perfection of the final scene of death, all of these were discussed and assessed, commented upon in loud approving or disapproving voices and translated into great largesse or, sometimes, a great paucity of coins thrown into the arena.

It had been in many ways an arresting and a revealing day, but he was not sorry when, after the fourth bull had been duly dispatched, Princess Leonora said that it was time to return to the convent. She, for her part, was visibly still half-trembling with the thrill of adventure and the taste of death.

They spoke very little on the way back. Princess Leonora's face was flushed and she repeatedly raised her hands to her head almost as if her hair was straining against her coiffe. Idly, Prince Ibrahim found himself wondering once again how much her hair might have grown since her return to Spain.

'I hope you had entertainment, Prince,' she said suddenly as they neared the convent. 'Tomorrow we can ride out of town into the country, if you wish it?'

'Alone? Is that safe?'

'You need have no fears,' she said fiercely. 'I am a princess of Aragon. No one would dare lay his hands on anyone in my charge.' The look in her eyes as she spoke was the same as he had seen in their battle with the galley of the Hospitallers. She did indeed look like a princess of Aragon. 'Tonight you will dine alone. If there is anything you require, you have but to tell the serving-women. I shall meet you at the stables after breakfast.'

It was as he watched her go that he became really consciously aware for the first time how huge a place she had come to occupy in his mind and outlook. Twice now they had been thrown together by external forces. This time, like the last, was doomed to come to an end and, almost certainly, in a much shorter space of time. Was it her misfortune, the tragedy of her young life, or the horror of her contamination with syphilis, that had so attracted his attention? Or perhaps, rather, her outstanding courage and determination? Whatever the explanation, he felt a bond with her, an Aragonese, related to the ruling House of the country with which his own was effectively on the point of war, that he had never experienced before with any other human being. It was a bond that made no sense, that could not logically nor reasonably be translated into any kind of direct relationship even if she were to feel sentiments similar to his own. They were each of them prisoners of their own worlds and there was no visible bridge between them. Be that as it might, tomorrow he would see her again, and with that thought he had perforce to be content. In the meanwhile, he tried to concentrate his thoughts on Torquemada and the reply he would shortly have to give him. Neither of the two main alternatives – refusal to cooperate, or apparent disloyalty to Granada – were pleasant to contemplate, but it was hard to see how a choice could be avoided.

Princess Leonora was once again in her grey nun's habit when they met at the stables on the following morning, but this time she had with her one of the convent serving-girls carrying a hamper.

'We shall eat by the river bank,' she said with a laugh, 'that way we can take all the time we want for our ride. It is very beautiful by the river and we shall see all the ships as they come up and down from Seville.'

It was true. The bank of the Guadalquivir was a garden of its own, with oleander roses, bougainvillea, and tall white marguerites in huge clumps and with branches in profusion. The sun seemed to sparkle on the water and catch the sails of the ships. Although there were ships almost without number, Prince Ibrahim counted few galleys. Most of the vessels here were sailing-ships, with one or two masts and large areas of canvas, even if some of it was rolled up when the ships left the open sea and came into the estuary of the Guadalquivir. It was not difficult to see the signs of wealth brought by this huge volume of trade and activity. The coffers of the Spanish Kings would be very full and able to finance quite easily the war against Granada.

They rode in silence most of the time. He noticed with admiration that this time Princess Leonora was riding side-saddle. She had the seat and carriage of an Amazon as they alternately walked, trotted and cantered their horses. Princess Leonora had placed the basket of food behind her on her horse and this precluded her from galloping. Occasionally she would point to a building, or a landmark, or even a ship, drawing his attention to a particularly quaint house or strangely-shaped outcrops of rock.

When at last she stopped it was at a small headland that jutted a little way into the stream so that the water on their side of the river swirled noisily, sending currents rippling towards midstream. Princess Leonora seemed in a gay mood as she unpacked the hamper of food.

'We shall eat well, Prince, shall we not? See, there is bread, cakes, butter, dates, oranges, honey, cold meats, smoked fish, pomegranates, and water and wine to drink. The wine must be for me, I think, Prince, for your abstemious habits are well-known in Seville.' She took a large loaf in her hands and, breaking it into pieces, passed one piece to him.

'Thank you,' he said quietly. 'This must be a place of contentment.'

'I have always loved water. When I was small we lived for a while near the Ebro river in Aragon, in the north. We spent entire days there sometimes, swimming, diving and sunning ourselves on the banks – until I grew too old and my *duenna* thought it was no longer fitting for a young girl to be tumbling naked in the water with her future serfs and servants.' She laughed. 'As if it mattered, given what happened to me later.'

'Princess . . .' he began, but she cut him short.

'I have put it all behind me, Prince. I have become reconciled with myself and can look again at the future with a purpose. But I do not wish to talk about myself. It is you of whom we must speak. I am in your debt.'

'You owe me no debt, Princes Leonora. Any man would have done as I did.'

'No,' she said firmly, 'only but a few men and, indeed, I can think of only one. But now it is you who are in danger. I will help you if I can, and if you will let me.'

'Why should I be in any danger?'

'I am not blind, Prince. Do you think I cannot guess why the Grand Inquisitor has sent you here? – That I cannot guess his purpose with you, or how you must be torn? I think I know the character of the captain on whose galley I sailed, on the floor of whose cabin I slept without fear, and whose bravery I admired. I will tell you more. I know that your king is a traitor, a turncoat and a coward. I know the estate near Cartegena that he has been promised, for life. He may indeed be in Jaen at the moment with his troops, but neither King Ferdinand nor Queen Isabella really doubt his desire to abide by the deal he struck with them. Where does that leave you, Prince? Shall I tell you, if you have not already told yourself? You are the last resort of Granada, the only commander who can, perhaps, stave off defeat, for a while, although even you cannot prevent its ultimate fall.'

'Why are you saying this to me?'

'Because, Prince, I can do no other. I cannot help myself.'

'What do you mean, Leonora?' he asked quietly.

She shook her head. 'I cannot – I must not – say any more. I should implore God's forgiveness every day so that I may one day be rehabilitated. But this I will tell you, so that there shall be no secret between us. I took Samuel's advice and saw two learned Jewish doctors. They were able to treat me and to cure me. I am no longer contaminated, though God knows that the memory of the past will be with me for as long as I live. So I live on, cured in body, but not fit for any man, and the subject of revulsion for all those who know my secret.

'Can you deny it, Prince? Can you deny that you still do not see me as the whore whose life you saved in Istanbul?'

Prince Ibrahim rose and lifted her to her feet. Slowly he pulled the coiffe down to her shoulders, revealing her hair. It had grown considerably since they had shorn her on the galley. 'I swear to you, Leonora, by all that I hold most sacred, that I see you as a woman of honour, of courage and of beauty, whom I respect in every way.'

Princess Leonora put her hand to her hair with the gesture that he had seen her make so often in the past two days.

'What would my lady Abbess or the Grand Inquisitor say if they saw me like this,' she gasped with a half-smile. 'I am failing in my duty to them. You see, Prince, you have still to hear the worst about me. I have been cast in the role of temptress, to tempt you into the Spanish web. A contaminated princess of Aragon, even if superficially cured, is no longer a fit mate for a Christian prince. But as a prize to be flung to a Moslem vassal who has proved his worth, why, that would be another, and quite acceptable, matter. It has even, in our Christian eyes, a certain poetic justice.'

Prince Ibrahim looked at her with horror in his eyes. 'No,' he breathed, 'that I never suspected.'

'But it is the truth. Now you know how low I nearly sank, for you see, Prince, the thought did not displease me. I even dared to hope it might become true.'

'You would have married me, a Moslem?'

'Oh, they have you as a Christian. That would be part of the price that you would pay. Aid King Boabdil in his surrender, and abandon your Moslem faith. And in return for these trifling sacrifices you would become a grandee of Spain and receive a contaminated Spanish as your consort.'

'How do you know all this, Leonora? I cannot believe it!'

'I am the cheese in the mousetrap,' she said wildly, 'but a human cheese that knows how and why it has been placed in the trap. You must hold me in such contempt.' Gently she disengaged herself from him and knelt down by the side of the basket. For a moment she picked up one of the oranges, then threw it on the ground and began to pull her coiffe back over her hair. For a little while neither of them spoke. Tears were welling up in Princess Leonora's eyes, while Prince Ibrahim's mind was a whirl with thoughts in which elation and despair contended for the mastery. But he knew he owed it to her, despite himself, to be no less sincere than she had been.

'Leonora, listen to me,' he began quietly. 'Before today I was already convinced that our destinies were locked, inextricably. The stars in their motions may be inscrutable, but I do not believe that we have been thrown together only to part again. But you should know me as I am, as a Moslem, as a Prince of the royal House of Granada, and as one who would fight, if he can, to the very end for the independence of his country. If I hid these feelings from Torquemada it is because my death or incarceration would be of no help to Granada. But I know very well that I shall have to give him an answer soon, and I fear that I shall have no choice but to refuse his proposition. I imagine he will then throw me to the de la Cuevas for their vengeance, but I have at least the means to protect myself from them.'

'Then escape. Flee from here.'

'Alone? Still able to only partially use my left arm, and with hundreds of soldiers in pursuit? It would not be long before I was ignominiously captured.'

'Alone? Who speaks of alone? I will come with you. Together, Ibrahim, we have a chance.' Her eyes were glowing now as she rose to her feet, her hands reaching out for his.

'Leonora,' he whispered, 'can this happiness be ours?'

'Yes,' she shouted exultantly, 'yes, a hundred times yes. Whatever the future may bring we shall be together and snatch at least the happiness that lies in our grasp.' Passionately she threw her arms round him, her lips seeking his, her eyes aglow. 'I think I have loved you since you raised from the ground in that vile street in Istanbul,' she murmured, 'but I never dared to let you guess the truth. I was afraid that I disgusted you and that you would spurn me as unclean. I am still afraid, Ibrahim, but now I also have some hope. All I ask and long for is to be yours for as long as you will have me.'

Prince Ibrahim shook his head in disbelief. 'You must not speak like this, Leonora,' he said hoarsely. 'For me too that night in Istanbul was a watershed, although I think that I only came to realise it after our battle with the

Hospitallers. You have been so often in my thoughts, and in my dreams. But then it all seemed like a totally impossible dream.'

'We must plan carefully, Ibrahim,' she said gaily, 'to make our dreams come true. There is not much time. The Grand Inquisitor will not wait much longer. We must forestall him and be gone from Seville before he returns.'

'It is a perilous choice, Leonora. It means death, and perhaps worse than death, if they catch you. You must think carefully before taking so great a risk.'

'Risk?' she repeated. 'There is no risk. I know what sort of life awaits me in Spain. Their Majesties have allowed me back at Court, but only provided I leave immediately to accompany my cousin Isabel when she leaves for Portugal. I may have been released from the prospect of immurement in a convent, but I shall be seen for ever, for the rest of my life, as a piece of damaged royal merchandise. No, Ibrahim, there is nothing in such a life to cherish. And to set against this, I have you as my purpose in the life that you have given back to me.'

'I have little future to offer you, Leonora. Even if we reach Granada safely, you will find yourself in a Moslem land soon to be invaded by your compatriots. I do not know how long we may be able to hold out, but there can be only one possible ending.'

'I do not care, Ibrahim. Wherever you go, I shall be content to follow. You are my life now.'

He drew her to him, folding his arms round her till she gasped for breath. He could feel her body, lithe and supple, against him, the soft roundness of her breasts and the pressure of her thighs. He felt the onrush of the male, the blood beating at his temples and a dizziness in front of his eyes. It was only the sound of voices, loud and raucous, from a boat near the river bank that broke the spell and brought back the harsh reality of their situation.

'We must wait, my well-beloved,' he said softly.

She smiled. 'That is what I always wish to be, Ibrahim, your well-beloved. I think I know what we should do. We shall ride back to the convent. Tonight you shall dine alone. I shall tell the Abbess that tomorrow I propose to take the light carriage and go out towards the Sierra Morena mountains to the village of Loreja, where my family has an estate that I remember visiting as a child. There is a castle there that is one of the most forbidding that I have ever seen. It seems rather appropriate to our circumstances. It is about a four hour drive and will please the Abbess who is a firm believer in the mortification of both spirit and flesh. I shall ask for a coachman, Sanchez, whom I know well.

He will drive us. I shall bring a large hamper of food, money, and tell Sanchez to take two of the best horses in the convent stables. As soon as we are some way out of Seville, we shall turn east and make for wherever you desire. Once we are well clear we can take the horses and gallop away . . . to our future together.'

'And your coachman?'

'Sanchez? I shall think of some ploy.'

'The Abbess must be very sure of your loyalty.'

'The Abbess believes, like Torquemada, that I seek revenge.'

'On me?'

'On you, and on all Moslems.'

'They will come after us, Leonora.'

'Let them come. With luck we shall have enough of a lead to escape. If not, then my dearest, we shall die together, for I do not intend to fall into their hands alive.' She kissed him again, passionately, on the lips. 'That, too, is an earnest of what is to come. But for now we must hurry and hasten back to Seville.'

She gathered up the food left over from their midday meal and, saddling their horses, they set off on their way back to the *convent de la Sangre de Nuestro Señor*. Once again they spoke very little, but their glances were continually for each other and Prince Ibrahim felt the joy streaming through his whole body.

It was not an easy matter to dissimulate it as they rode into the convent gardens. He left Leonora without a word. He passed by the Abbess close by the refectory and bowed silently, praying that he had kept his face expressionless.

Alone in his room, Prince Ibrahim grappled with his own thoughts. Suddenly, escape had become a real possibility, and escape, not just alone, but with Leonora as his willing companion and accomplice. It was an exhilarating notion. For the present he determinedly closed his mind to all the hidden perils of the longer term where there could be little hope of happiness. But in the shorter term there was a radiant glimpse of paradise. He started to look through his trunks and boxes. Soon all their contents would belong to the past, never to be seen or wanted again: hoses and shirts, circlets of silver, gloves, hauberks and jewels, daggers, slippers from Istanbul, two curved swords of Turkish manufacture, and body linen. He ran his hands over it all. It mattered little what he was to wear that evening, though he would look his best for appearances' sake. As for the following day, it would be a choice of the stoutest, strongest clothes he had, and at least one poniard. He took up in turn each one of his four daggers. They were all fine weapons but two green jade daggers given him by Sultan Bayazet, equal in perfection of workmanship to the necklace he had given to Ayala, were irreplaceable. He would have to take them both. He proceeded to put everything back in place. It would be foolish indeed to do anything now that might attract special attention. There would be time enough to make his final selection in the morning. He sank down slowly onto his couch to try and compose his thoughts. If all went well, by that same time the following day they would be well clear of Seville.

There was the question of which road to take. There could be little doubt but that once their escape was discovered, the Spaniards would come after them. In that regard it was fortunate that Torquemada had appeared to be more than half-convinced of his willingness to accept his terms and also, of course, saw Leonora as being completely on his side. The Spaniards would be a little less on their guard as a result, and they might well be able to count on a four to six hours' start. There were, he knew, large concentrations of Spanish troops between Cordoba and Jaen, and also towards the south round Cadiz and Palos. The obvious way to go, therefore, was due east, which was also the most direct route to Granada. It was also the most inhospitable and meant traversing the area knows as *Las Malistas*, to the west of the Granadan town of Zahara and some way north of Malaga, the region Santillana had been appointed to command. The drawback was that it was, nevertheless, in so many ways the most obvious route for him and Leonora to take that much of the Spanish pursuit would be concentrated there. But the longer Prince Ibrahim pondered the matter the more he concluded that they had no real choice. Whatever the risks, it was the only route that made any sense.

The expectation of another solitary dinner that night was short-lived, even if the grey-habited nun who came to summon him to his meal was, as usual, expressionless and unspeaking. As on his first night at the Convent, only four days previously, the Abbess and Santillana were already seated at the table. There was, however, this time, no fourth place set. For a moment Prince Ibrahim's heart beat faster. Could it possibly be that they had become suspicious of his or her intentions? But the smile of easy contentment on Santillana's face was somehow reassuring. He greeted Prince Ibrahim warmly.

'I hope, Prince, that you have rested well and that Sister Teresa has proved herself to be an inspiring companion. She told me that you had been impressed by all the activity on the Guadalquivir. Spain is already a great naval power. We intend her to become an even greater one in the future.'

'I was indeed very impressed,' said Prince Ibrahim truthfully.

'Good,' beamed Santillana. 'I am glad to hear you say that. You will, of course, have realised, Prince, that if it were ever to come to war with Granada, we should have total supremacy at sea. Granada would be blockaded immediately.'

'If it comes to war,' repeated Prince Ibrahim. 'Do you now then consider that to be inevitable?'

Santillana's smile grew broader. 'We have heard nothing from King Boabdil, although he and Al-Zaqhal have abandoned Jaen and retreated back across the border into Granada. But Their Majesties are growing impatient, and Nicolo Franco, the Papal Legate, has reminded us quite forcibly of our dedication to a new crusade. I think that you can draw your own conclusions.'

'Yes,' said Prince Ibrahim laconically.

'Also, and this is the main reason for my presence here tonight, Prince, my army corps has been ordered to assemble at Cadiz and I have little time to lose. But the Grand Inquisitor bade me tell you that he will be here tomorrow night. He expects then to receive your answer to his proposition.' He hesitated for a moment. 'Unless, of course, you have already come to a conclusion and wish to tell me this evening. I could send a messenger to His Eminence.'

Prince Ibrahim shook his head. 'You must forgive me, my lord Santillana, but I cannot tell you yet. It is not an easy choice. I had hoped for more time.'

'The Grand Inquisitor is not famed for his patience, saintly man though he undoubtedly is. But then he carries on his shoulders great cares of state and church, and we must be mindful of that.'

'I am sure Prince Ibrahim will come to the right decision,' intervened the Abbess. 'Sister Teresa has given me encouraging reports of our guest's recognition of the very positive role he is in a position to play, and of course of the potential rewards. I, for one, cannot believe that he could fail to appreciate the hospitality of our convent.'

'Sister Teresa has been very patient, and forbearing,' said Prince Ibrahim quietly. 'She makes me very aware of the power of Spain.'

'Then she has done well,' said Santillana. 'The Abbess tells me that tomorrow you are going with Sister Teresa to Loreja. The road to Loreja branches off to the west a league or two south of Seville. I will accompany you, therefore, that far, tomorrow morning. Till then the Abbess and I will bid you good night.'

Prince Ibrahim rose and bowed as they left the small dining-room, and then sank back into his chair. Santillana's initial presence on the following morning would be a nuisance. He wondered whether Leonora was already aware of it. Still, irritating though it was, it called for no change to their plans. As he followed one of the silent grey-habited nuns back to his room joy and exhilaration sent the blood coursing through his veins.

*Chapter Seven*

# A GLIMMER OF HOPE

There was, quite exceptionally, a slight haze when Prince Ibrahim woke the following morning. As usual, one of the grey-habited nuns brought him a tray with bread, butter, dates, two oranges and a carafe of water. He ate slowly, relishing the thought that if all went well these were among his last moments in captivity. Escape might be full of danger, but at least it offered a ray of hope for the future.

As he walked down the stairs to the main courtyard and on into the stable-yard, there appeared to be a real buzz of activity, very different from the more customary serenity of convent life. Unusually, the Abbess was there, with three of her senior sisters, talking with some animation to Santillana. With him was an escort of twelve armed soldiers, standing by the side of their horses.

Santillana waved to him cheerily. 'Sister Teresa will be here in a moment. She is delighted to have our company for at least a small part of the way. I am sorry I do not have the time to accompany you to Loreja.'

'I hope you will find your trip to Loreja instructive, Prince,' said the Abbess with a cold smile. 'Do not forget that tonight we are expecting His Eminence the Grand Inquisitor. But then, of course, how could you forget? Sister Teresa would not allow you to forget.'

'Here comes Sister Teresa,' said Santillana with a smile. 'I am sure, Reverend Mother, that she is working diligently to further the wishes of His Eminence.'

'She is a good daughter of Our Holy Mother Church,' said the Abbess equably. 'I am sure that she knows very well where the requirements lie for the salvation of her soul.'

Prince Ibrahim said nothing but stood with his head bowed submissively as if in deference. A little way behind Princess Leonora stood a small open carriage, its two horses neighing in anticipation. They were remarkably fine horses. Prince Ibrahim could only hope that neither the Abbess nor Santillana would consider them to be too fine for the outing that was planned. Neither of them, however, seemed to consider it worthy of mention.

'Duty, alas, calls, Reverend Mother,' said Santillana briskly. 'Perhaps fate will allow me to come back soon to this haven of beauty and tranquillity. Let us hope that there will be only a minimum of bloodshed. We shall be looking to you, Prince, to make that come true. Farewell, my Lady Abbess.' Gallantly he raised her hand to his lips before ordering his men to move forward. 'My escort will ride ahead of the Prince and Sister Teresa. I will ride alongside your carriage,' he continued. 'I trust that will be a pleasant arrangement for everyone.'

Prince Ibrahim bowed formally to the Abbess and took a seat in the carriage. Sister Teresa knelt down in front of the Abbess and kissed the cross she held out to her before joining him in the open carriage and ordering the coachman to move off in his turn.

They set off at a gentle walking pace out of the convent gardens and out into the streets of Seville. There was a bitter irony, it seemed to Prince Ibrahim, in the company of Santillana and his escort at the start of what was intended to be his flight from Spanish captivity.

Santillana was in sparkling good humour. Most of his remarks were addressed to Sister Teresa, whom he treated with a gallantry that was more in keeping with a princess of the Blood Royal than a temporary novice in a religious order. He certainly acted as though her assignation as lady-in-waiting to Princess Isabel, soon to be the bride to the heir to the throne of Portugal, had signalled her complete rehabilitation at the Court of the Spanish Kings.

'Look,' said Santillana, pointing to three barges that had just come into view, 'those three boats are laden with cannonballs. If ever it comes to a siege, they are big enough to pulverise the thickest walls in Granada. Heed that well, Prince, for the cannons that are being produced now at our ordnance plants near Toledo are, I am reliably informed, at least as fine as any you may have seen in Istanbul.'

Prince Ibrahim followed his directions. Santillana was only too right. The barges were laden with cannonballs of a greater dimension than he had ever seen before. He doubted whether there was a single fort in Granada with walls strong enough to resist such a bombardment beyond three or four days. Although he smiled nonchalantly, in his heart he seemed to feel the odds grow even more heavily stacked against Granada.

Once outside the city walls, Santillana gave the signal to his escort to move on at a trot. Princess Leonora ordered her postillion to follow suit and conversation with Santillana became somewhat more difficult. Prince Ibrahim leaned against the back of his seat and closed his eyes. He could only pray that Santillana would not change his mind and that when the road forked off to Loreja he and his men would indeed continue on their separate path. Princess Leonora, for her part, evinced no concern but maintained quite an animated exchange with Santillana, into which the latter continued to slip the occasional shaft of gallantry. More than once he spoke of her forthcoming journey to Portugal as chief lady-in-waiting to Princess Isabel, and hinted that he would hasten to be by her side as soon as his mission to the borders of Granada had been completed. She remonstrated with him gently, but in a tone that held no real rebuke. Santillana's regret when they came a little later to the fork in the road sounded genuine.

'Alas that I cannot accompany you further. But my orders are quite imperative. So I will bid you both farewell, but not, I hope, for long. You, my Lord Prince, I trust I may see again very soon, not as I had once feared on the field of battle but as a trusted friend and ally in finding a peaceful solution to the question of Granada. I have great hopes for it, and for you. For you, Princess, if you will permit me that form of address, wild horses will not keep me from the Court of Lisbon as soon as my duties allow it.'

Prince Ibrahim jumped to the ground to shake Santillana's hand. The Spaniard too had dismounted and the two men looked each other in the face. Prince Ibrahim smiled. Santillana had won his respect. His behaviour throughout had been courteous, correct, and even generous. He regretted the element of deceit that he felt he was practising in allowing the Spaniard to think that he might become a willing collaborator in the Spanish cause. He had said, and would say nothing to support such an assumption, but refraining from an outright rejection came close, in his own personal reckoning, to deliberate deception.

'Thank you, Santillana,' he said, 'for your courtesy. I cannot say what the future holds, but I shall always think of you as a true Spanish hidalgo.'

'Is that all you can say to me, my Lord Prince? I had hoped for a warmer signal from you before we parted.'

'You will have to forgive me, Santillana. Formally, I still see myself as the envoy of Granada. King Boabdil has not recalled me. I could still have an official role or duty to perform. Only time will tell.'

'Then we must part in uncertainty,' said Santillana in a noticeably less cordial tone of voice. 'I can only hope that you and your King will choose the path of caution and salvation. When destiny beckons, as it is beckoning now to Spain, there can be no room or time for hesitation.' Turning towards Princess Leonora, who had remained seated in the carriage, he bowed before vaulting back onto his horse and giving the signal for his company to more on. He did not look back.

'I fear he may be suspicious,' said Princess Leonora, getting down from the carriage to stretch her legs. 'You did little, Ibrahim, to persuade him to the contrary.'

'I know. I realise I am not a good liar, Leonora.'

Impulsively she took him by the arm. 'You would not be the man I honour if you were,' she said softly. 'But come, we must make a start on our ride to Loreja. There are some woods a league or two further on. There we can abandon our carriage and Sanchez and make our dash, my dearest, for freedom. Come.'

Quickly they climbed back into the carriage, Princess Leonora shouting the while to Sanchez to drive off. He clucked his tongue and the horses broke into an easy trot. With a smile she clasped his hand in hers. He could feel her trembling but her face was glowing. 'Soon,' she whispered, 'soon we shall be on our road to freedom.'

It was not long before they came to the small wood to which Princess Leonora had referred. She jumped down with alacrity.

'Sanchez will unharness the horses,' she said excitedly. 'Take the hamper with the provisions and the horse blankets. Sanchez will carry on from here on foot to Loreja to tell them we shall be there later in the day. We will abandon the carriage there beyond the first line of trees.'

Sanchez, a bright-eyed, intelligent looking man of perhaps some forty years of age, nodded in agreement and, having unharnessed the horses, immediately set off at a brisk walking pace. They watched him for a minute or so before mounting their horses and heading back at a modest walking pace towards the road that led from Seville down to the coast. Leonora was confident that close to the junction of the roads they would find boatmen willing and able to ferry them and their horses over to the far side of the Guadalquivir.

Her optimism proved to be well-founded. Fortune, for the present at least, seemed to be with them. The Seville road was empty when they reached it, and a boat able to ferry them and their two horses was tied up by the river bank. It was Princess Leonora who haggled and prevailed upon the ferryman to agree to take them over to the opposite bank for four maravadis. It was when they actually set foot on the far bank that the smell of freedom seemed suddenly to take on a purer and much more potent scent. They waited only for a moment to quieten their horses before breaking into a gallop, their voices shouting in unison with the exhilaration of the moment.

They rode without stopping, alternately galloping and walking their horses for the next three hours. They had no fear of immediate pursuit but wanted to put the maximum distance between themselves and the Guadalquivir before nightfall. The nearest town to them in Granadan territory was Zahara, situated just beyond the actual frontier and, Prince Ibrahim estimated, approximately the same distance away as Cordoba; only here there was no major road and much of the terrain was rugged and criss-crossed with gulleys that occasionally plunged quite suddenly to very considerable depths. There were a number of bridlepaths that were readily accessible, but which often required them to make big detours. This was the beginning of the region known as *Las Malistas*, much of which was notorious for its ravines, wetlands and marshes that covered a large area in western Granada and thus presented a particularly taxing obstacle for any would-be invader coming from the west. This, as Prince Ibrahim mentioned to Leonora with a wry smile, was a route that might quite conceivably be taken by Santillana and his corps if, or when, war was officially declared.

They rode on for over three hours without a break before stopping to eat and rest their horses. Although the place where they stopped was on relatively high ground and there was no one in sight, Prince Ibrahim remained on his guard. It disturbed him that their only weapons were the green jade daggers he wore on his belt. The sun felt hot on their backs and almost induced a feeling of security. Leonora smiled and, as she smiled, suddenly pulled her nun's habit from her head. It was as though a magic wand had been waved, magically transforming her back into the shape and dress of the page Leonardo, clad in jerkin and hose, but with hair that now reached considerably lower down.

'Is this perhaps an improvement?' she asked with an impish smile.

He nodded vigorously. 'You were not made to become a nun, Leonora. You are too much alive; a creature of life, born to love and to be loved. We should live our lives to the full, whatever the emotional cost.'

'Regardless of the risks? We are set on a dangerous path, Ibrahim, you and I. By abetting your escape, by fleeing with you, I am making myself an exile from my own land forever. Ferdinand was prepared, to my very great surprise I must admit, to overlook my personal disgrace. But this new offence he will never forgive. But you too, Ibrahim, as a man who walks by himself and now become a total outcast, are one for whom the future must inevitably mean uprooting and exile from the land of your birth. Perhaps this is one of the things that has brought us together.'

'All things, dearest Leonora, are as Allah wills them. If it is His will that our lives should be thrown and blended together, then all the armies of Spain and Granada will be powerless to prevent it. I did not myself believe that fate had cast us together in Istanbul only to part us from one another as if our meeting had been no more than one event among others. Now I know that I was right and that, for better or for worse, our lives are inextricably linked.'

Leonora looked at him with an expression of solemnity. 'I have always prayed since my early childhood that I would one day meet a paragon among men in whom honour, courage and personal commitment were blended into a single whole. I never dreamed that my hero would be a Moslem Prince for whom I would give up everything else in life.'

'Leonora,' he whispered, 'you are too generous. I am not worthy of such sacrifices.'

She placed her fingers over his mouth. 'It is for me to judge, Ibrahim. But we should ride on. I should be very surprised if Torquemada did not send a large troop of men after us. Perhaps we will find a village or hamlet where we can spend the night.'

Prince Ibrahim nodded. She was right and they had already tarried too long. They rode on in the same way as before, walking or trotting their horses, with occasional short canters or gallops when the terrain permitted. Some of the gulleys now were quite fearsome and there were times when a sudden treacherous stretch of marshland came almost to the very edge of the single track where they had perforce to ride in single file. Twilight was just beginning to fall when a sudden turn in the path brought them to a small cluster of houses. For a moment their hopes of a good night's lodging rose, but these were short-lived as the realisation sank in that the village had been raided and gutted. While much of the structure of the houses had survived, doors had been stove in, walls smashed and the contents ransacked. One house had clearly been used as a kind of makeshift charnel-house; inside it were piles of dead bodies, rotting in the heat with a stench that was nauseating and unbearable. The horror of it made them blench. Prince Ibrahim went inside two other houses. There prayer mats had been defiled on the floor. Although they were still in what was officially Castilian territory, the inhabitants of the village had clearly been Moslems. From the state of decomposition of the bodies he reckoned the slaughter of the villagers could not have been carried out more than three or four days before. This presumably meant that there was a fair chance that there were still some Castilian soldiers somewhere in the vicinity.

He lifted Leonora back onto her horse and led the way to a narrow but reasonably flat path that appeared to descend quite quickly. Soon they heard the sound of gurgling water and almost immediately came to a small rock pool where two streams came together so that their combined waters tumbled over a double and roughly circular line of boulders. The light was fading very fast but there was still light enough to see, if rather dimly, how beautiful and idyllic was the spot, with carpets of wild flowers in an absolute riot of colours surrounding the rock pool.

After Prince Ibrahim had tethered the horses, he bent down low, one ear to the ground, straining to hear the least sound in the distance, but he could distinguish nothing beyond the gurgling of the water and the occasional neighing of the horses. He considered it unlikely that the men who had perpetrated the massacre in the village would have stayed in the near neighbourhood. Besides, the probability was that some of the villagers, and particularly the younger women and the girls, would have been carried off to be sold as slaves. Even so, there would be little sleep for them that night.

They took down the blankets and spread them on the ground close by the rock pool. There was more than enough food left for their evening meal, even if there was a risk that they would have to start rationing their remaining supplies on the following day. Leonora came and sat down by his side. Her face was white and taut.

'Which side committed these murders?' she murmured.

'The villagers were Moslems. They had clearly not converted to Christianity. They paid their penalty for that.'

'Then the killers must have been our men. Castilians?'

'Yes.'

'It is horrible.'

For a little while neither of them spoke. With the rising of the moon there had come a small ray of yellow golden light that played spectral fantasies on the surrounding rocks and grass. It was as if their faces were being bathed in an angelic light with golden haloes for their heads. The water in the rock pool, too, was like a golden mirror. For a while Leonora looked at it all in silence, then, abruptly, she rose. 'Only the water will cleanse me, Ibrahim,' she said. 'I feel almost as I did in Istanbul. Tainted. But this water, in this place, in your presence, will cleanse me for all time. I feel it.'

Quickly, but methodically, she took off her clothes. Prince Ibrahim watched her, spellbound. When he had seen her naked for the first time as she lay spreadeagled on the couch on board the galley, even then, when his mind had been full of the horror of her enforced service in the brothels of Istanbul, he had found her beautiful. Lithe, slim, her breasts like little ripe gourds filled with kukkurush, her past shame swept away by a growing bond of comradeship and mutual trust, he felt an overwhelming realisation of his love for this extraordinary Christian princess. She did not look at him, but ran to the rock pool and plunged into it with a splash that seemed to send golden sparks into the air. Instinctively, without consciously thinking, he followed her example, taking off all his clothes, until he too was completely naked and plunged into the pool. The water, although quite deep, did not come up to his full height. It was not so warm as he had expected, due no doubt to the constant inflow of water that came cascading into the rock pool only soon to flow out again into a wider stream below. In the golden moonlight, the water in the pool was almost mirror-like, while at the same time soft and velvety to the touch. Leonora swam towards him, lazily for the first few strokes, then with a furious flurry that brought her to him. Prince Ibrahim crushed her against him, his lips pressed on hers as their two bodies coalesced into single human flesh. He lost all count of time, fear and reason as he possessed her, forgetting the horrors of the village and the perils that surrounded them. His only conscious thought was that this moment was a true intimation of paradise that he wanted to make eternal.

When at last they made their way out of the pool it was to walk back hand in hand to the place where they had eaten. Prince Ibrahim untethered the horses which had been grazing contentedly to let them roam around them. They sat down close together and he draped one of the blankets over their shoulders. 'We should try and sleep, my beloved. We have another hard day's travel ahead of us tomorrow,' he murmured, his hands clasping hers and his lips seeking the yielding softness of her breasts. She nodded and waited for him to smooth down the blanket. He marvelled at her total confidence in him, in her trusting him so absolutely. He possessed her again, almost reverently. 'My beloved,' he whispered, 'my love for you will last for ever.' He sat by her side as she slid into sleep. He had never before felt so happy. Never had he dreamed of such love, where adoration, sexual passion, admiration and respect were so commingled. Unbelievably, after what had gone before, it had turned into a perfect night to dream of love under the golden light of the moon, the bubbling of the water, and the immediate proximity of this beautiful and lovely woman to love and possess as he desired.

Prince Ibrahim succeeded without difficulty in keeping awake. He had, to help him do so, he reflected, the stimulus of love as well as that of danger and a regained freedom.

It was hard to resist the renewed call of their bodies when Leonora awoke, but reason prevailed and they set off resolutely on their way further east towards the Granadan border. The going tended now to become even harder and more inhospitable than on the previous day. There were times when the path they were following disappeared completely and they had only the angle of the sun to guide them on their way. For hours on end they saw no sign of human life or habitation, only an occasional bird of prey, sometimes an eagle soaring high above them in the direction of the Sierra Morena. There were places without number where bandits or outlaws could have fallen on them unawares. They could do little more than hope that in this benighted land they were the only travellers. Often their eyes met and they clasped hands, but both realised the foolhardiness of yielding again to their desire for each other's body when the risks were so high.

It was late in the afternoon that they came to a small keep, but with massive walls that had been built near the top of a rounded hill slightly to one side of what had suddenly become a much wider and seemingly well-used path. Their approach had clearly been observed and presently a group of six horsemen emerged from the keep and rode straight towards them. Their commander was a tall black-bearded man wearing a Moorish costume. He and his men rode straight up and surrounded them.

'Who are you, and why do you come here?' he asked in Arabic in an aggressive, barking tone of voice.

'I am Prince Ibrahim Ibn Sa'd, returning to Granada from the Court of the Spanish Kings. I am accompanied by a page given to me by the Castilians.'

'Prince Ibrahim,' repeated the man. 'We have heard much about you. You are indeed welcome.'

His name had acted like a talisman. The six men's faces were beaming as they escorted them back to the keep. It had been built, they were told, by the Spaniards soon after their conquest of Cordoba and was known as the *Torre Negra*. It had been stormed by Granadan soldiers some five years before and a small garrison of twenty men stationed there. The official Granadan border was some twenty-five leagues further to the east and the town of Zahara a league or two further still. In reality, however, there was no such thing as a clearly defined border and there had been no attempts so far by the Spaniards to establish settlements on the eastern side of the Guadalquivir. The road to

Zahara, said the commander of the keep, was in good condition.

'We would be honoured, Prince, if you and your Castilian page consented to spend the night with us. My name is Qasim Abbas and I am the commander of this fort. My room is at your disposal. You must in any case be tired. Your horses also.'

'Thank you, Qasim,' said Prince Ibrahim with a smile. 'We are grateful for your offer and accept it with pleasure. I should be interested to see how life is led on an exposed frontier outpost like this. You must all be brave men.'

Qasim's room turned out to be small but tastefully furnished with Moroccan rugs on the floor and silk hangings on the walls. There was also a low Moroccan divan and two wooden stools. Two wide apertures in the wall brought plenty of natural light into the room. Wooden frames – used, they presumed, to block the apertures in winter and cold weather – were placed immediately below them. Although the light was beginning to fade, they could still distinguish the pools and wetlands of *Las Malistas* stretching away towards Zahara. As they were looking, four men brought in a large tub of water slung on a metal pole over their shoulders and placed it in the centre of the room. The water was hot and there were faint wisps of steam rising from it.

They took it in turn to bathe. The tub was sufficiently deep for one person to sit in it, the water rising almost to shoulder height. Again, Prince Ibrahim marvelled at the perfection of Leonora's body as he watched her undress and step into the bath before subsiding slowly, flower-like, into the warm lapping water of the tub. She held out her hands to him.

'Fortune has been with us so far, my beloved,' she said smilingly. 'Let us make good use of it tonight, and every night that may be granted to us.'

He kissed her as she sat in the water. 'You are beautiful, my Princess, beyond imagining. I am the most fortunate of men. But how blind I was for so long on my own galley!' He smiled at her. 'You were in my power then. I should perhaps have made better use of my opportunity.'

She rose, the water running down her body, and looked at him lovingly. 'No, Ibrahim, no. That would have been dishonourable, as well as dangerous for you. I can never forget that I am a Princess of Aragon. It is at the very core of my being. As such, I must strive and look for the highest. Only a man of honour, whom I could admire and honour, could have won my heart. You are my paragon. It could not have been, and must not be, any other way.'

It was, he reflected as he sat later that evening among the men of the garrison of the *Torre Negra*, a mutual requirement. Beautiful though she was, with limbs and breasts that made him reel with desire, it was the steel in her character that made his longing for her more than simple sexual lust. He had left her to rest in their room for there were no women in the *Torre Negra* and any accidental disclosure of her sex could have had uncontrollable consequences. The men of the garrison gave every appearance of being hard-bitten soldiers, veterans of many years of often savage border fighting. There were frequent encounters, he heard, with Castilian patrols, with no mercy being shown on either side. They showed little emotion when he told them about the massacre of the Moslem villagers. They had known the village and sometimes stayed there overnight. But the border region was like that. The killings were unending and usually carried out with savage brutality.

He was woken the following morning by loud shouts. Going to the top of the tower he found Qasim Abbas and several of his men looking out over the parapet. A troop of about forty Castilian cavalry had halted just out of bowshot from the keep.

'They have come after you, Prince,' said Qasim Abbas. 'Well, they can have little doubt but that you are here. But there is not a great deal they can do at the moment. They are not strong enough to attack us, nor even to besiege us.'

'Perhaps they will offer you prize money – a thousand gold maravadis – who knows? It would make you a rich man, Qasim Abbas. The Spaniards have great faith in the power of gold.'

'We shall soon learn. They are sending a herald to parley.'

They watched in silence as a single rider, holding a lance with a white flag fluttering from it, brought his horse slowly to the edge of the tower. He seemed a young man still, confident and full of poise.

'I bring a personal message from His Eminence the Grand Inquisitor, Tomas de Torquemada, to Prince Ibrahim Ibn Sa'd,' he shouted. 'We have reason to believe that he is in this tower.'

Prince Ibrahim stepped onto the parapet; at once Qasim Abbas and one of his men leapt up beside him, as though fearful for his safety.

'His Eminence bade me tell you that he regards you as a traitor to your King and country, as a man of no principles, who lapped up the generosity of Spain and absconded behind the skirts of a whore. For that you deserve to die.'

Even as the herald finished speaking, Prince Ibrahim heard the whistling of crossbolts. Instinctively he leapt back down from the parapet, but for one of Qasim Abbas's soldiers it was too late and he fell to the ground with a crossbolt embedded in his skull. Qasim Abbas gave a low curse as he too fell back with a crossbolt in his right arm. 'Return fire,' he roared. 'Kill that herald.'

Several shots were aimed at the herald who had put spurs to his horse as soon as he had finished speaking, but they all missed. Qasim Abbas was able to rise unaided. 'By Allah, these are dogs and sons of dogs. May they rot in their eternal hellfire,' he exclaimed. He clasped one arm with the other. 'I think it is only a flesh wound.' He went on with gritted teeth, 'But you see, Prince, what manner of foes we have? I blame myself. I should have suspected something of the sort.'

Prince Ibrahim watched as two of Qasim Abbas's men seemed almost to wrench the crossbolt out of their captain's arm. He groaned once, loudly, and had to be held by his men, but he made no other cry as they poured oil on a deep gaping hole that had been gouged in his arm and proceeded to bandage it, lashing it firmly against his chest. 'We are hard men out here, Prince,' said Qasim Abbas in a low but steady voice. 'I only wish that there were more of us.'

Prince Ibrahim, who had been joined by Leonora, watched as they led Qasim Abbas to a room next to the one, his own, which had been assigned to them. Two scouts, sent out to check on the movements of the Spanish cavalry detachment, returned with the news that they appeared to be heading back to the west, apparently in a buoyant mood. It was possible, indeed probable, from their apparent jubilation, that they believed Prince Ibrahim to have been one of the victims of their crossbows.

Although loath to leave Qasim Abbas and the garrison of the *Torre Negra*, Prince Ibrahim decided to continue on at once to Zahara and then from there to Granada. There was nothing he could do here to help, and Qasim Abbas's men were quite manifestly able to look after their captain as well as themselves. The overwhelming likelihood was that there would be no Spanish soldiers to the east of the tower, and that the road to Zahara would therefore be comparatively safe, if often difficult and treacherous where it came uncomfortably close to pockets of quicksand. Qasim Abbas, who had been heavily drugged, was in a deep sleep when they went to visit him in his room. Prince Ibrahim left him one of his green jade daggers as a parting gift.

'Tell Qasim Abbas,' he said to one of his men, 'that I leave it in gratitude for the hospitality that we have found here and in recognition of your bravery.' The tower's garrison cheered and waved as he and his page rode out and took the road to Zahara.

They rode hard for the rest of the day. The heat was intense and there were a number of occasions when they were compelled to dismount and lead their horses with great caution by the side of the quicksands that looked like inviting pools of pale yellow water that occasionally gurgled, almost as if in merriment at the deviousness of the disguise that nature had vouchsafed them. Prince Ibrahim looked round often in his concern for Leonora but she, although terribly pale, followed him without hesitation. But there were also moments of relaxation when the terrain became suddenly hard and firm, with now and then a clump of trees where birds chirped in the branches and the world took on a much kinder hue. Prince Ibrahim took careful note of the terrain as they passed through it. It was clear that an invading force would not find it a simple matter to traverse *Las Malistas* if it was resolutely defended. It was, in many ways, an ideal defensive terrain.

It was late in the afternoon by the time the nature of the land changed again with the wetlands, marshes and quicksands of *Las Malistas* giving way to a gently rolling countryside, studded with olive and citrus groves. They passed in quick succession through several small villages where there seemed to be no thought or fear of war, and where children played undisturbed in the streets. Clearly no Spanish soldiers had yet penetrated this far into Granada. The villagers greeted them with polite and friendly words, replying readily to their questions and responding to their greetings. Zahara, they learned, was still another four to five hours' ride. They accepted gratefully the offer of the headman of the village to spend the night under his roof. They ate sparingly and slept on rugs spread on the floor, fully dressed, with only their hands clasped in the darkness as they lay close together in whispered dreams of love.

They reached Zahara the following day at noon. Zahara was the sixth largest town in the kingdom of Granada, but one of the poorest. Here too, however, Prince Ibrahim found that his fame had preceded him and he was welcomed as the young hope of Granada in the conflict that most of its citizens were now expecting imminently with Spain. Of the willingness and readiness of the men, and women, of Zahara to fight there appeared to be no doubt. Many had suffered in earlier times from Castilian invasions or marauders, and there were few who did not have to mourn for relatives killed or carried off into slavery. Prince Ibrahim spoke to many of them, urging them not to be dismayed by rumours about the size or ferocity of the Spanish armies, but to remain steadfastly determined to fight them to the death.

It was while he was in Zahara that he learned to his surprise and pleasure that Ibn Zamnak, whom he had met at the house of his sister, Ayala, and whose poems he had so greatly admired, had been appointed by King Boabdil as his new Grand Vizier. It made his determination to press on to Granada with the utmost speed all the greater.

Men generally reckoned on a further two days of hard riding between Zahara and Granada. After the first ten to twelve leagues, the richness and beauty of Andalusia came suddenly to its glorious best. Here, in truth, was the garden of Eden, the dreamland of the Hesperides, where heaven and earth seemed to have become as one. Prince Ibrahim's heart rose as they traversed it. He looked with pride at Leonora and exulted in the unparalleled beauty of his native land. He wanted to sing in celebration of its perfection, lingering with delight over each individual pearl in its crown of loveliness. He saw Leonora smile in appreciation of his exultation, and smiled in his turn at her understanding of him.

That night they stopped at a hostelry for travellers, where they mingled with large numbers of itinerant traders, vendors, soothsayers and quackdoctors, peddling a miscellany of wares and nostrums that intrigued a host of passers-by. Once again, they slept on rugs, fifteen or more of them to a room, without undressing. They smiled at each other, a little ruefully, the same thought in both their minds. Their escape had been conducted under a sign of abstinence. Once during the night she drew his hand to her and, having carefully loosened her doublet, placed it on her bared breast. Involuntarily Prince Ibrahim grasped her so firmly that she almost yelped with the pain. He had to thrust his other hand, balled into a fist, into his mouth to stifle his curses at his own brutality. Afterwards she whispered her forgiveness as they lay motionless side by side with more than a dozen men snoring all around them.

The following morning they rose early for the last lap of their journey to Granada. Prince Ibrahim was able to bathe unashamedly in a shallow stream that ran close by the hostelry, while Leonora coped as best she could as several other men came out of the hostelry and stripped in some cases to the skin within a few paces of where she was standing. One or two looked at her in some surprise, but since modesty among younger men was not an uncommon feature, her apparent reticence occasioned no special comment. Even so, Prince Ibrahim deemed it prudent not to eat at the inn but rather to purchase some bread rolls and fruit and ride straight out of the town and on to the road to Granada. They ate as they rode.

It was some six hours later that they rode into Granada. The city seemed clad in beauty. Long streaks of brilliant bougainvillea were strung as if haphazardly in the streets. The sun was near its zenith with a dry heat that warmed them to the very core of their bodies. Leonora looked around her with fascination. Granada was alive with men, women and children, walking, running and shouting. There was no sign of fear or trepidation, but rather a kind of reckless rhapsody of human activity, determined to enjoy the wonders and treasures of Andalusia.

'I think we can best go first to the house of my sister, Ayala,' said Prince Ibrahim with a smile. 'We shall have to consider how to prepare the Court of Granada for the arrival of a Princess of the Royal House of Aragon.'

Leonora nodded her agreement. 'I hope your sister is like you. But I am surprised at the women here. I had assumed that they would all be wearing the veil, but I see that only a very few in fact are doing so.'

'Granada is more a city of the west than of the east,' replied Prince Ibrahim. 'The original Arab invaders of Spain were relatively few in number. Our ancestors were able to conquer this country because of their superior cavalry, better discipline and, above all, a totally fearless dedication that carried all before them. But they were in a minority, and many of them intermarried with the local indigenous population. They converted to Islam, but the outward symbols of Islam were never as evident here as in Morocco or in the rest of North Africa.'

'Does your sister speak Castilian?'

'Yes, not with complete fluency, but very well nevertheless. It has long been the practise of our nobles to learn Castilian. Many of the foreigners here speak it more easily and readily than they do Arabic.'

'I think I will find it easier to adapt than I had expected.'

'Granada is like a pearl of glittering beauty, matchless, I believe, in its radiance,' Prince Ibrahim said quietly. 'But in its very radiance lies its undoing. Granadans have grown indolent and the city is coveted by its enemies. I fear its radiance may soon be dimmed.'

'I hope not, Ibrahim, for my sake and even more for yours. Surely such a glorious treasure can be safeguarded, whatever the future may hold.'

Prince Ibrahim did not answer but took her right hand in his and raised it to his lips. They were approaching the house of his childhood where he had left Ayala only eight weeks before to set off on his mission to Cordoba. This time there were armed guards round the house. One of them stepped forward as they rode up to the main entrance. There was no sign of recognition on his face.

Prince Ibrahim leapt down from his horse and motioned to Leonora to do likewise.

'I am Prince Ibrahim Ibn Sa'd,' he said imperiously. 'Is the Princess Ayala at home?'

The man's eyes seemed to come alive. 'My lord Prince,' he said, bowing from the waist, 'then it is true that you have returned to Granada. Allah be praised. The lady Ayala, your sister, has gone to the nearby mosque, as she does daily, to pray for your safe return.'

'I am glad to see guards on duty here. On whose orders are you here?'

'On the orders of the Grand Vizier, my lord Prince.'

'Ibn Zamnak?'

'As soon as he was appointed, only two weeks ago, he assigned a platoon of men to guard this house. He comes here himself at least once a day.'

Prince Ibrahim nodded as if in approval, then strode on into the inner courtyard with Leonora close behind him. Three more guards were sitting by the fountain. They rose as Prince Ibrahim approached.

'Go, one of you,' he said, 'and tell the lady Ayala that her brother has returned and would speak with her. Tell her that I will wait in the inner courtyard.'

A large number of small shrubs and plants, many of them in gaily coloured tubs, had been placed round the sides of the smaller inner courtyard. In one corner there stood a small table with two chairs with green velvet cushions. There was a chessboard on the table with chessmen drawn up in an unfinished game. Prince Ibrahim examined it with interest. The player playing black was in a perilous position. He turned on hearing a sudden peal of laughter behind him.

'You cannot have known of my strength at chess or you would not look so surprised. Yes, I have been well taught and Ibn Zamnak finds it hard to keep me at bay.' With that, Ayala threw her arms round her brother's shoulders. 'Praise be to Allah that you have returned safely. We heard from Sharif that you were to be executed. I was so terribly afraid for you.'

Prince Ibrahim looked tenderly at his sister. 'I am safe and well, as you can see. As for Sharif, I am most curious to hear what tales he has been spreading. He is a creature of our treacherous King Boabdil, a poisonous serpent and a dangerous one. But first, Ayala, I would have you meet the Princess Leonora of Aragon, my saviour and my betrothed.'

Ayala turned in amazement towards Leonora who had been standing quietly a couple of paces behind Prince Ibrahim and his sister, like the page she was, or, ostensibly, had been. For a moment the two women looked at each other without speaking before Ayala held out her arms.

'Welcome,' she said in a somewhat accented Castilian. 'The woman who saved my brother's life and whom he has chosen as his betrothed is very dear to my heart. You are indeed welcome in this house.'

Leonora smiled, though there were tears in her eyes. 'You are very gracious, Ayala – may I call you so? As Ibrahim's sister I must love you, but my heart already tells me that we shall be much more than just sisters in name.'

'Come and let us all sit down. Oh, but I must not spoil our chess game. Ibn Zamnak is only a move or two away from total ignominy. I would not willingly deprive myself of the gloating pleasure of yet another victory over him at chess.' Ayala clapped her hands for servants to come and ordered them to bring out another table and three more chairs. 'Let us sit here and you shall be able to tell me all about your return from Cordoba. Ibn Zamnak will be here soon and he too will be anxious to hear it all. He and Sharif are at daggers drawn.'

'Sharif?' said Prince Ibrahim questioningly.

'Sharif has become Boabdil's confidante and court favourite. He has the King's ear, his favour and, some rumour, much more besides. But he is common, a man of mean social origin, and even Boabdil, weakling though he is, surely must have the sense to realise that he cannot give that man any official position at Court. But he has him about his person at all times, with access to him and his private apartments at all times that the Grand Vizier does not have. Ibn Zamnak, as Grand Vizier and High Court Chamberlain, has, I firmly believe, the best interests of Granada at heart. Sharif, like his master, thinks only of himself. It is as well for you, Ibrahim, that you have Ibn Zamnak and al-Zaghal on your side, for Sharif, on his return from Cordoba, would have had you branded as a traitor to your King and country, and as a man thinking only of your personal honour and glory. For what it is worth, Boabdil probably believed him and probably still does. But, for the moment at least, al-Zaghal and the Grand Vizier have the support of the majority of Granadans.'

'For the present?'

Ayala shrugged her shoulders. 'Who knows for how long? Boabdil's pusillanimity is well-known. Although he has never said so openly, there are many who know only too well that his sole concern is to save his own skin, but with the requisite degree of comfort. But al-Zaghal has his following too, of those who are determined to fight it out. Ibn Zamnak is of a similar mind. At the moment they have the ascendancy. Just.'

Prince Ibrahim nodded sombrely. 'I learned a good deal about Boabdil's attitude in Cordoba. Sharif's role, also, soon became clear enough. The rest of us will have to take our decisions soon, for it will not be long now before the

Spanish Kings declare their hand and march openly on Granada. A holy crusade is being preached and the Christian cross blessed that will lead their armies against us.'

'You do not sound very optimistic, Prince Ibrahim, but I am very glad nevertheless to see you back in Granada.' The words had been spoken in a low but beautifully modulated voice. Prince Ibrahim did not need to turn round to recognise Ibn Zamnak, the poet, the lover of his sister, and now the latest Grand Vizier of Granada.

'May I first of all, Grand Vizier, offer you my heartfelt congratulations. Granada is fortunate to have you as Grand Vizier in this hour of trial.'

Ibn Zamnak smiled in his turn. 'The situation is not without its humorous side, with the poet turned statesman, or even soldier, in his country's hour of need, as you rightly put it! We are, I fear, surrounded by those who are more concerned to change their garlands each night before they go to bed with their latest conquest than by the fate of Granada. It is high time you were back, Prince Ibrahim, for there are not very many men of your calibre here. But who is this by your side?'

'I have the honour to present to you, Grand Vizier, the Princess Leonora of Aragon, who is shortly to become my wife.'

'You, a Prince of Granada, to wed a Princess of Aragon,' repeated Ibn Zamnak in amazement. 'I do not understand. It cannot be with Spain's consent. What does it mean?'

'I will tell you the whole story of our meeting. But you need not have any diplomatic concerns. Their Spanish Majesties will not seek to claim her back or to make her presence here a *casus belli*. But that the armies of Spain will soon be marching against us is, I fear, inevitable and unavoidable. Their forces are gathering, their commanders appointed, and their plans made to blockade all our ports.'

Ibn Zamnak sighed. 'You only confirm what I feared and what we knew in our hearts was coming. You had best come with me tomorrow, Prince Ibrahim, to the royal council. His Majesty King Boabdil has called a special session for tomorrow afternoon. Al-Zaqhal will be there, as shall I, and as will also your former secretary at the Court in Cordoba – Sharif the infamous! I shall inform the King of your return and of my decision to invite you to the Council meeting. But forgive me, Princess,' he continued, turning towards Princess Leonora with a courtly bow, 'this is a poor way to express our welcome to you. The bride-to-be of Prince Ibrahim must be welcome in our midst. I can see that he has known to choose not only great beauty but also great fortitude, for only a lady of great courage would have come to Granada at a time like this. You have brought us not just yourself but a ray of hope.'

Princess Leonora glanced for a moment at Prince Ibrahim before replying. 'I am grateful, Grand Vizier, for your kind words, as I am to Princess Ayala for her sisterly greeting. I am of the Royal House of Aragon and a stranger in your midst. But it is my fondest hope that I can be of some help and comfort to you all.'

'I, too, have news for you, Ibrahim,' said Ayala. 'Since Ibn Zamnak was made Grand Vizier, King Boabdil has permitted me to return to his Court. He has also given his royal consent to our wedding. We hope that it can be arranged soon, the dangers confronting Granada notwithstanding.'

Ibn Zamnak concurred. 'Very soon, I hope. I suppose it is my duty to inform the King of your return with a Princess of Aragon even if, as you say, there will be no call by Spain for her return. I will consider the matter. For it to be true, she must indeed have offended the Spanish Kings very deeply. I will let you know, Prince Ibrahim, at what time you must be at the Alhambra palace tomorrow.'

'One more question before you go, Ibn Zamnak. What has become of the Ottoman galley and her crew?'

'Need you ask? The galley has never once moved since you left Malaga. The crew are still there. A rough bunch, as I have heard.'

'Rough, perhaps, but tough fighting men, of that I can assure you. They may yet serve us well.'

Ibn Zamnak made no reply but, after bowing ceremoniously to Ayala and Princess Leonora, turned and walked quickly away, leaving Prince Ibrahim alone with the two women.

Ayala took Princess Leonora affectionately by the arm. 'I shall be glad to have you as my sister.' Then, turning to Ibrahim, added, 'She will stay with me, Ibrahim, will she not, till you are married? She will teach me to speak Castilian correctly, and I shall instruct her in the ways of Granada.' She hesitated for a moment. 'The ways of Islam are very different from those of your Christian faith.'

'I know only this, Princess Ayala. My life was destroyed. Ibrahim has given it meaning again. He has become my sun, my world. Without him I would not exist. So, you see, marrying a Moslem, or embracing Islam, has no terrors for me.'

'Then I am happy for you, as well as for my brother. But I am being unforgivably remiss. You must both be exhausted. Come, let us eat, and then

182

I will show you where you can rest for as long as you wish.' Ayala clapped her hands and immediately servants came into the inner courtyard carrying jugs of water and iced cordials, sweet cakes and dried fruits.

Prince Ibrahim sipped slowly from a glass of water and listened to the two women talking together. It was perhaps the first time in many weeks, or even months, that he had felt so completely relaxed – ever since, in fact, the day that he had set sail from Istanbul to return to Granada. It had been, when seen now calmly in retrospect, an extraordinary contrast between the halcyon existence he had been able to lead at the Ottoman Court and the fraught uncertainty of his mission to Cordoba. It was, he knew full well, only a brief lull before the hurricane that was swiftly gathering. Boabdil and Sharif could be expected to accuse him of having failed miserably in his mission. In a sense, he had indeed been a failure, for he had not been able to budge the Spaniards even one small iota from their predetermined intentions. But he knew, as Boabdil and Sharif did, that it had in any case been a hopeless task from the very start. And he knew – and they both knew that he knew – of Boabdil's secret dealings with Ferdinand and Isabella. While he had no hard evidence of treachery on their part, his awareness of their double dealing gave him at least a small psychological advantage which he had every intention of using if he were to be pressed or unjustly accused. The unknown factor for him was the extent to which Boabdil's manifest desire to save his own carcass – and, in so doing, surrender as quickly as possible to any Spanish onslaught – was shared by ordinary Granadans. But for that he could presumably look to Ibn Zamnak for reliable guidance.

He looked up from his musings to see Ayala and Leonora still in close conversation. They were speaking quietly, so that much of what they were saying to each other escaped him, but that it was of a serious nature and that it dealt directly with him, was quite unmistakable. It pleased him to see that they had clearly warmed to one another.

Despite their fatigue, they continued to talk long into the night. Ayala was inquisitive about life at the Spanish Court and about their escape. Her eyes had always been the mirror of her soul, and now they betrayed her feelings of anger, compassion, and the shared moments of passion or distress, as Leonora and he – but mostly Leonora – described their experiences of the past few weeks. It doubtlessly affected Ayala's dispositions for the night for, although she placed him and Leonora in separate rooms, they were separated by only a narrow corridor. The house, Ayala told them, was well guarded, but its only current occupants were the three of them and her eight servants, all of whom slept on an upper floor. They had only to ring if they required anything during the night.

Prince Ibrahim found that clean linen had been laid out for him on the bed in his room. It was a large room that overlooked the bigger outer courtyard where three soldiers remained on guard duty. Beyond their occasional movements there was little activity and virtually no sounds from the streets beyond. A large ewer and basin stood in the corner of the room and the fatigue seemed to roll off him with the day's grime as he washed. The thought of Leonora waiting for him across the corridor made the blood tingle and course through his veins. For a few hours at least he would be able to put out of his mind Granada and all its perils.

He went noiselessly across the corridor. Leonora's door was ajar. He knocked on it gently before entering. He recognised the room as one that had once been used by his mother to store some of the tapestries she specially loved. Two of them, both of hunting scenes, were still hanging on the walls. The room was smaller than his own and the bed with its heavy brocaded curtains was near to a window that overlooked the inner courtyard, where they had sat for so long that same evening. The bed curtains were still open on one side and he could dimly make out Leonora's form beneath the bedclothes. She put out her arms to him.

She was naked beneath the bedclothes. Gently he stroked her hair, her shoulders and her breasts until the blood beat in his temples. He murmured her name, again and again, kissing her lips and her eyes, pressing her close to him, feeling her body taut against him, the warmth of her sex and his own manhood, his body filled with such convulsions of passionate desire that it reached out simultaneously in ecstasy and pain. And yet he could not stop, as though an insatiable and relentless lust had gripped him while she clutched him to her in a moaning frenzy in keeping with his own.

When at last it was over, he lay motionless beside her, his body drained, it seemed to him, of all power, leaving him oblivious to the world. When he woke the first signs of dawn were appearing. Leonora was lying close against him, breathing lightly but still in a deep sleep. He kissed her gently before rising and returning to his own room.

A messenger from Ibn Zamnak called before he had finished dressing later that morning. The King had decided to bring forward his council meeting and Prince Ibrahim was required to be at the Alhambra Palace by noon. King Boabdil had expressed irritation at the fact that he had once again gone first to see his sister before presenting himself at the palace. The King was likely to be in an exceedingly ill-humour. To be set against this, however, was the fact that al-Zaqhal would certainly be present. Prince Ibrahim gave a small sigh of relief.

He left without seeing Leonora or Ayala. He was glad in a way, for he would probably have had to try and soothe their fears. He recognised, too, that in many respects this could be a real moment of truth for him, that would reveal his worth – or lack of it – and determine his whole future course of action. The time for prevarication was passed. Today he could well have to choose between compromise and confrontation. He knew that if that were so he would not hesitate.

He rode alone to the Alhambra Palace, waving aside the offer of two of Zamnak's guards to accompany him. The Alhambra, as he approached it, was as magically, enchantingly beautiful as ever, with its gardens that seemed to climb to the skies and scent the air with sweet perfumes that made men dream of paradise

King Boabdil's palace was well guarded. Repeatedly he was asked to give his name and the purpose of his visit. Immediately outside the Alhambra he was told to dismount and to hand over any weapons. Then he was escorted into the courtyard of the lions and told to wait. The scene around him was one of sheer delight – of a beauty, it seemed to him, that was unmatchable on earth, for here men had fashioned a miracle of mosaic, marble and delicacy of carving and tracery that made the senses reel with admiration.

Somewhat to his surprise, he was not kept waiting long. It was Ibn Zamnak himself who came to fetch him and lead him to a small chamber in the rear of the palace where King Boabdil, al-Zaqhal, al-Taghri, the governor of Malaga, and Sharif were already seated round a large oval-shaped table. Prince Ibrahim bent down on one knee before the King

'So,' said King Boabdil in a loud voice, 'so, you have returned from the embassy on which we sent you to the Court of Spain. You returned, we understand, yesterday and yet we have received no report from you. Are we to deduce from this lack of diligence that your mission was unsuccessful?'

'I understand that Your Majesty has already been informed of many developments at the Spanish Court by your secretary, Sharif, who left somewhat prematurely.'

'Secretary Sharif has indeed given us much useful information. He showed great discretion in leaving Cordoba at the moment of your disgrace, yours and that of your man, Samuel.'

'Disgrace?' repeated Prince Ibrahim slowly. 'Who spoke of disgrace? Is that how this caitiff, this tapeworm of a man described the insult to Your Majesty's ambassador by the Spanish knight, Bertran de la Cueva?'

There was a sudden guffaw. 'Well spoken, Ibrahim,' said al-Zaqhal. 'Do not concern yourself with Sharif's rantings. He is nothing but a lickspittle and muttonhead with the stench of onions and the guts of a violated she-ass. What our dear sovereign Boabdil sees in him is one of the lesser mysteries of the age. Come now, Boabdil, let us turn to serious business. Ibrahim was our ambassador, as you rightly said. Ask him for his report and forget Sharif.'

King Boabdil nodded. 'You may speak,' he said curtly.

'The mission to Cordoba was impossible from the start,' began Prince Ibrahim firmly. 'Their Spanish Majesties are determined on the conquest of Granada, as it is their belief that the hour to do has struck for Spain. With their daughter Isabel's betrothal to the Portuguese Crown prince, they have no fears for their western frontier. King Ferdinand is convinced that he can keep the French at bay in the north. But, above all, there is a conviction that this is a holy crusade, blessed by the Pope and the whole of Christendom, that at least partially offsets the losses in the east to the Turks. No Christian prince will dare to take advantage of Spain's preoccupation with Granada since they would immediately be branded as friends and abettors of infidels and run the risk of papal excommunication. About my reception, as your envoy, by Their Spanish Majesties, I have no complaint. But it was made very plain to see that the plans for the so-called re-conquest of Granada are well advanced. We have the choice of peace, provided we convert dutifully to their religion and accept the extinction of Granadan independence, or war against great and fearful odds with the certainty of death, slavery or exile if we lose.'

King Boabdil's face was cold and his fingers drummed against the sides of his chair with obvious irritation. 'There was no need to send you to Cordoba, Prince Ibrahim,' he said icily, 'if it was only to return with so galling a report. But I was given to understand by Secretary Sharif that your mission, difficult though it undoubtedly was, forfeited any hope of success through your man Samuel's attempt upon the life of the Grand Inquisitor and your own subsequent selfish duel with Bertran de la Cueva and his son. These events, it seems to us, were inexcusable breaches of your position of diplomatic privilege.'

'Samuel's attempt upon the life of the Grand Inquisitor was indeed unforgivable, Your Majesty, even if the tension and the provocation to which he was submitted were, I believe, more than any man worthy of the name could be expected to bear. He paid a dreadful penalty for it. As for myself, I was challenged in such a way as would have reflected dishonourably upon

Granada and, Your Majesty, upon yourself, had I not responded. I honestly believed, and still believe, that as the accredited envoy of Granada, there was no other course of action open to me. But I would also add this: neither Samuel's attempt upon the life of Torquemada nor the outcome of the duel that was forced upon me, affected in any way the Spanish decision to move against Granada. That decision, Your Majesty, had already been taken. It is unavoidable and it is about to be translated into action.'

'And Their Spanish Majesties said nothing else? About our own position?'

There was a veiled look in King Boabdil's eyes as he put his question. Sharif, sitting close behind the King, was ashen-faced. Prince Ibrahim hesitated for a moment before replying. How could he repeat here what he had heard about Boabdil's pusillanimity, his probable treachery and faithlessness? In his own heart he believed it all to be only too terribly and horribly true. But to say so now, openly, in the presence of al-Zaqhal, could have the direst consequences.

'They expressed uncertainty about Your Majesty's willingness to fight,' he temporised.

'And how, Prince, did you reply to that?'

'I replied, Your Majesty, that in my poor opinion Granada would resist to the bitter end.'

King Boabdil smiled. To Prince Ibrahim it seemed like a smile of relief, of a relaxation of inner tension. When Sharif made a slight movement as if seeking the royal permission to speak, King Boabdil ignored him.

'We shall reflect, Prince Ibrahim, on what you have said to us by way of explanation of your conduct of your embassy, but we will wait for your full written report before giving our final verdict. Sharif has already provided us with a very full and valuable account that will facilitate checking and verifying all the details. But for the rest of our council meeting today let us consider the action we should now take.'

Al-Zaqhal, who had shown increasing signs of irritation as he sat listening, laughed harshly. 'At last, nephew. I am glad you have come to the end of your of your long, totally unnecessary and humiliating inquisition into the activities of your envoy and cousin. You must have proved yourself an apt pupil during your sojourn as a guest of Ferdinand and Isabella. But my information is similar to that brought by Ibrahim. Spanish troops are massing round all our borders, in the east, north and west. I do not believe that they will wait much longer before invading in force. We must be ready for them.'

'How, and with what?' asked King Boabdil coldly.

'We have some twenty-five thousand men. We can fight a defensive war, close to our own bases. Our enemies will have much longer lines of communication, often over difficult terrain. But we should also make another approach to our co-religionists in Fez and Marrakesh. If Granada falls, they must surely realise that they will be the next in line. It is important above all that we keep Malaga, for it is through there that men and supplies from North Africa can most easily reach us. We should not need to immobilise too large a force there, for it is virtually impregnable.'

'What do you say to all this?' asked King Boabdil, turning to the Grand Vizier, who had sat motionless and silent through all the discussion that had taken place so far.

'The first question, Your Majesty, is whether to fight or to seek a peaceful settlement, securing the best terms we can for all of us here in Granada. It is my view, and I do not think that Prince Ibrahim would disagree, that Their Spanish Majesties would be prepared to be quite generous in terms of property and religious observance if they could acquire Granada without fighting. They would be pleased to avoid the risk of a bloody campaign, expensive in money and in the lives of their soldiers. Granada is not the end of the line for them. It is perhaps an option that is open to us.'

'Never,' shouted al-Zaqhal, 'never, by Allah.'

'It is indeed an option, uncle,' Prince Ibrahim said quietly, 'but it needs to be examined in full. I have no doubt that, initially, terms such as those described by the Grand Vizier would be obtainable. But I have spoken with Tomas de Torquemada, and have been a witness to his profound influence with King Ferdinand and Queen Isabella. The Grand Inquisitor is like a man of iron, an incorruptible, a stoic who knows no deviating from his goal. He has no personal interest in our lands or in our problems, for these are, to him, like summer chaff. No, it is our souls and our salvation, as he sees it, that he lusts after, and the price of our survival in Granada will be the negation of Islam and conversion to Christianity. He is generous in his own peculiar way, for to those who are willing to convert he is prepared to offer a full and equal part in the great quest that he sees beckoning for Spain.'

'What quest?' snapped Sharif venomously before King Boabdil could stop him.

Prince Ibrahim looked at him with distaste. 'We must not underestimate our enemies, either in their strength or in the convictions that fire their purposes. I would have thought that you would have noted that there are many in Spain who believe that their God and their destiny are calling them to great things. There is talk of sending fleets out into the Atlantic ocean to find a new sea route to India and Cathay, of launching a new crusade for the recovery of Jerusalem, of suzerainty in Europe in a new awakening of the old Roman Imperium. They may well prove to be all just flights of national passions, but they are undoubtedly underpinned by a real and growing sense of power.'

'And yet,' said the Grand Vizier mildly, 'you, Prince, would recommend resistance against such a great power, and choose to fight the Spaniards.'

'Yes,' replied Prince Ibrahim immediately. 'For me there can be no choice. I could not live under Spanish domination. If we fight, there is at least a chance that we shall survive, with luck perhaps, if Allah wills it, and if we fight well.'

There was a brief silence. King Boabdil shuffled uneasily in his chair. Twice he turned as if to speak to Sharif, but both times he refrained as if unwilling to seek Sharif's advice in front of men who so visibly and openly held him in contempt. Prince Ibrahim could see the King almost visibly struggling to find words, or a formula, that would release him from the meeting. He seemed finally, however, to come to a decision.

'We shall put it to a vote, to all of us, Sharif included. Then we shall see. Sharif has been my confidante for the past three years now and I can vouch for his ability. You will all of you treat him and his views with the respect that his position as my confidante requires. Sharif, how do you vote?'

'For peace, Your Majesty.'

'And you, my brother?'

'For war.'

'One each so far,' said the King gently. 'And you, Prince? Although I do not really need to ask.'

'War,' said Prince Ibrahim curtly.

'And you, Grand Vizier?'

It seemed to Prince Ibrahim that both the King and Sharif were confident that Ibn Zamnak would side with them. Looking at him, there was an evident struggle in his mind. Perhaps it was the part in him that loved peace and beauty, and abhorred all thought of war and destruction. But it was the duty of the poet also to cherish high ideals and to castigate dishonour. Above all, however, this was the man who desired Ayala's hand. She would have no place in her heart for a poltroon. Ibn Zamnak had no choice.

'War,' he said firmly.

There was a flash of dismay on King Boabdil's face, while Sharif almost started from his seat. But the King recovered his poise almost at once and turned with a polite smile on his face towards al-Zaqhal.

'You have a majority, Uncle, for your view, so that I am absolved from voting. You shall be our ambassador to the Courts of Fez and Marrakesh and ask for their urgent support for our cause. I shall personally take command of the forces defending the city and port of Malaga with eight thousand men. You, Grand Vizier, shall take the northern front, until al-Zaqhal returns, and you, Ibrahim, the west and the region of *Las Malistas*. When you return, Uncle, you shall have overall command of all the fronts, excepting only Malaga. The decision has been taken. You will all send reports to us here, or in Malaga.'

King Boabdil rose to signify that the council meeting was over and strode quickly out of the room. Sharif followed him without a word.

'You seem to have created a surprise, Ibn Zamnak,' said Prince Ibrahim, 'an unpleasant surprise for His Majesty judging by the expression on his royal countenance.'

The Grand Vizier shrugged. 'The King is too much inclined to judge all men by his own standards. My tenure of this high office will probably prove to be of brief duration, but our time is running out in any case. In these circumstances I prefer to act according to my conscience.'

'Well spoken, Ibn Zamnak,' said al-Zaqhal. 'We must strike while we may. Our men should be deployed at once, and arrangements made for their equipment and supplies. After the King has taken his eight thousand men we shall be left with only some seventeen thousand men among our three fronts. It is my opinion that the main initial Spanish thrusts will come from the north and west. We should make our preparations accordingly. I shall draw up my detailed proposals and send them to you within two days. I hope we shall be able to agree them quickly so that I can set off for Fez before the end of this week.'

Prince Ibrahim rode back to his sister's house with an uneasy mind. Although pleased at the formal decision to resist the Spanish invasion and to fight, he remained deeply concerned at King Boabdil's marked reluctance and his decision to place himself with a third of the entire Granadan army in Malaga. While the strategic importance of Malaga could be neither denied nor exaggerated, Prince Ibrahim could not believe that the city with its massive fortifications was in any immediate danger of a Spanish attack. The Spaniards, with the help of their Portuguese and Navarran allies, would no doubt seek to blockade the city from the sea, but a full frontal assault on its formidable defences was improbable and close to inconceivable. The King's decision would weaken the general morale of his soldiers and it raised niggling doubts once again in his own mind about Boabdil's reliability. It left Prince Ibrahim in a very troubled state of mind. About his own proposed command in the region of *Las Malistas* he felt no qualms. It was a position of gratifyingly high honour, even though he did not himself believe that the Spaniards would make their main thrust – or even a really major one – through such exceptionally difficult terrain. His thoughts went back fleetingly to the *Torre Negra* and the attempt on his life. It would be ironic if the Grand Inquisitor were to select that particular route and if their next encounter were to be in the neighbourhood of that forbidding border outpost.

Leonora and Ayala were waiting for him when he returned. They were poring over an Arab manuscript with Leonora giving her future sister-in-law her first lesson in Arabic script. The two women rose as he approached and Leonora threw her arms round his shoulders.

'After the last five days I am no longer used to being without you, Ibrahim. I want to be by your side always, as we were on the galley, and in *Las Malistas*, whatever the dangers.'

He kissed her tenderly before turning to Ayala.

'What news, brother?' she asked. 'What conclusions did the King's council reach?'

'To resist invasion. It was Ibn Zamnak's vote that won the day for the cause of resistance. It seems as if you have chosen a good man, sister.'

Ayala gave a wry smile of satisfaction. 'I am glad he voted so,' she said, 'although war is a dreadful prospect. But capitulation would have been worse. I console myself with that thought.'

'What does it mean,' asked Leonora, 'for you, Ibrahim?'

'I am to command our soldiers in the west.'

'When do you leave?'

'Soon. My uncle, al-Zaqhal, is drawing up our plans and dispositions. It will be a time for parting, my beloved, but for a short time only.' He hesitated for a moment. 'Sorrow at parting is part of the tragic joy of our human existence.'

'No,' she said vehemently, 'no, Ibrahim, where you go, there I shall go also. Already once I have been your page, on board the galley that brought us back from Istanbul, and then again on our escape from Seville. I have known danger, and much worse, and shall not be afraid. You will have no cause to blush for me. I shall come with you in a man's clothes and stay by your side.'

'Leonora,' he exclaimed, 'it is impossible. This time it will be totally without pity and without any niceties. If you were to be captured . . .'

Leonora went pale and, for a few moments, her face lost some of its resolution, but she recovered quickly. 'They will never capture me alive, Ibrahim.

My disguise will be very thorough, have no fear. I shall not be easily recognised.'

'Did the King not wish to see Leonora?' asked Ayala. 'The Spanish Kings may indeed have renounced her, but she remains a Princess of Aragon nevertheless. It would be like him to seek to use her as a bargaining counter.'

'He never once referred to her,' said Prince Ibrahim. 'I can only assume that Ibn Zamnak has not yet reported her presence here to him. But you are right, Ayala; Boabdil would be capable of such meanness. It seems, my well-beloved,' he said, turning back to Leonora, 'that your case is accepted and that you shall come with me. In fact, we shall leave immediately for Malaga. I understand, Ayala, that the crew of the galley that brought us back from Istanbul is still there. They have been left in total idleness, unused, ignored. They are fine fighting men, and I would willingly recruit them to come with me to *Las Malistas* if they can be so persuaded. If we ride hard we can be back in two, at the most in three, days' time. By then al-Zaqhal's dispositions should be ready. You, Ayala, must tell Ibn Zamnak of our plans and he can inform al-Zaqhal.'

'But will you not need clothes and money, and what if word were to come from the King?'

'You can tell him the truth: that I have gone to recruit good fighting men to fight for Granada. As for money, I have sufficient with me, and we can travel in the clothes we are wearing. Come, Leonora.'

He took her hands in his, kissed Ayala fondly and led the way quickly down to the stables. Fifteen minutes later they were on their way to Malaga.

*Chapter Eight*

# THE INVADERS

They reached Malaga in the afternoon of the following day, having galloped with relays of horses for almost ten hours without a break. Leonora's exhaustion was unmistakable, but she had refused all his suggestions for stopping or resting. Their one overnight stay, at a bright and cheerful hostelry, had been of the briefest duration. It was another warm and beautiful day as they came into Malaga, the city and its three towering fortresses giving it an air of absolute impregnability. They clattered on, without stopping, to the harbour where he had disembarked from the Ottoman galley on his return from Istanbul and where the ship was reportedly still moored.

His information proved correct. There was, however, little left of the ship's former proud appearance. The sails hung limply from a single mast, flapping only from time to time in small and very occasional puffs of wind. Crates and boxes were scattered all over the deck and Prince Ibrahim counted at least three swords just lying there unsheathed. There was no one to be seen on the deck of the ship. Dismounting from his horse and passing the reins to Leonora, Prince Ibrahim went on board, the vessel's planks creaking under his feet. The sound of his footsteps seemed to echo through the whole length and breadth of the ship.

Prince Ibrahim walked slowly along the central plankway from where he had spoken to the galley-slaves. They had all gone, sold no doubt, although whether by the ship's crew or by those in power in Malaga there was no immediate way of knowing. Not that it mattered a great deal. He climbed up to the rearcastle where he had stood so often during the adventurous journey back from Istanbul. Here again there was no one to be seen. The galley had become a ghost ship, inhabited only by memories. He went back down to the poop and picked up one of the swords lying there. There was a thin film of dust on it so that it had clearly been left lying there for some considerable time. He was still holding it in his hand when a sudden warning cry from Leonora made him hasten to the side of the ship. She was pointing to a tall white building some three to four hundred paces away from where a group of about twenty men had emerged. All, or nearly all of them, were carrying weapons. Prince Ibrahim vaulted over the side of the ship and ran to Leonora's side. The men were running now, coming quickly towards them, but remaining in a group and making no effort to encircle or surround them. They heard loud cries and then two of the men in the front began to shout.

'They are some of the crew,' he said, turning to Leonora with a smile. He could recognise them now, one by one, as they drew near. There was Yakoub, the captain of the fighting men, and the two with whom he had fought on his first day on board the galley.

'Lord,' said Yakoub in a loud voice, 'at last you have come back. We had almost given up all hope.'

'I am very glad to see you all again, so very glad,' said Prince Ibrahim warmly. 'But I see only some twenty of you. Where are all the others? And what has become of the galley-slaves?'

Yakoub shrugged. 'We do not know. Some of the crew have gone across to Africa. A number are no doubt still here, somewhere in Malaga. A few days after you left us the governor of Malaga came down to the ship and demanded that all the galley-slaves should be delivered to him. They were led away in chains. The Hospitaller seized two Granadan soldiers and threw them overboard before diving after them into the water. The archers shot at him in the water and claim to have killed him, but his body was never recovered. Perhaps he sank to the bottom. We were told to await further instructions and provided with quarters in that tall white building yonder. There is plenty of food and we are left to our own devices. But we are rotting away, Lord, and nobody here seems to give a damn.'

Prince Ibrahim looked round the faces of the men standing there. Almost without exception they were smiling now, anticipation on their faces.

'You will all of you remember my page Leonardo,' he said, smiling in his turn as he saw them all nod pleasantly at his companion. How odd it was, he had time to reflect, somewhat idly, that Leonora seemed fated to spend most of her time with him in male attire. But perhaps it was as well.

'Men,' he resumed, 'I have been appointed by King Boabdil to command the Granadan forces in the west. It is of course a land command. We are, in any case, enormously outnumbered at sea by the Spaniards and their allies so that for the present at least there can be no prospect of fighting them at sea. You are all brave men. I have seen you in the heat and fire of battle. We have fought together against the mightiest and bravest soldiers of our age, and overcome them. I invite you now to come with me as my personal guard in the campaign that is most assuredly coming against Spain. I could ask for no better companions. What do you say? Will you come?'

There was a loud tumultuous chorus of 'Yes' from the gathered sailors. 'I speak for all of us, Lord,' said Yakoub. 'We are your men, everyone of us.'

'Thank you,' said Prince Ibrahim. 'I cannot stay with you now. I have to return at once to Granada. I came only to see you and to ask you to join me. Gather your belongings, take provisions for three days and make for Granada. I will procure horses for you and send you money and more food. When you reach Granada, go to the office of the Grand Vizier. Come as quickly as you can.'

'And the galley?' asked Yakoub.

'The galley we must leave here. There is no alternative.' Prince Ibrahim hesitated for a moment. 'If,' he resumed gently, 'if you are thinking of your eventual return to Istanbul, only Allah knows when, or how, that may be done. Our thoughts, I fear, must be for today only.'

'We have no reason to delay,' said Yakoub. 'We can leave at daybreak tomorrow.'

Prince Ibrahim drew a purse from under his belt. 'I have only these sixty pieces of gold. Take them as an earnest of what is to come. Farewell men. I shall look to see you again in a few days' time somewhere near our western border with Spain.'

He waved, Leonora followed suit, and they were off on the gruelling ride back to Granada. He kept close by her side, for several times he saw her reel and sway in the saddle. This time they stopped for eight hours in the same hostelry where she slept without stirring. He lay close by her side, occasionally caressing her head and shoulders. Tiredness weighed on him also, with aching eyes and buttocks that were raw in places with riding, and yet he was unable to sleep for more than an hour at a time.

This time, when they entered Granada, they went straight to the Grand Vizier. Ibn Zamnak welcomed them warmly. King Boabdil, he told them, had gone off for a few days' hunting. He had spoken to the King several times about Princess Leonora, but His Majesty had expressed little interest beyond saying that he would wish to see her, probably, after his return to the Alhambra Palace. Al-Zaqhal had departed for Fez and had left instructions about the disposition of all Granadan forces. To Prince Ibrahim and his command on the western front he had assigned a total force of three thousand men. The main force under the Grand Vizier himself was to go north, close to the town of Jaen. There were increasing reports of a large massing of Spanish troops just across the border there.

'When do I get my men, and where are they now?' asked Prince Ibrahim.

Ibn Zamnak smiled. 'Al-Zaqhal has left me in overall charge, subject, of course, to the supreme overlordship of His Majesty.' He smiled again and shrugged. 'But His Majesty has other concerns. I will do what I can for you. You can have and take five hundred men at once. There are provisions for them also. As for the rest, I shall assemble them as quickly as I am able to do so. When do you plan to leave for the border?'

'Tomorrow.'

Ibn Zamnak looked at him in surprise. 'So quickly? That will not please the King.'

'I am not concerned, Ibn Zamnak, to please the King. My concern, and my duty, is to be prepared to meet the Spaniards.'

'And also a little to keep Leonora from King Boabdil's grasp?' murmured Ibn Zamnak.

Prince Ibrahim stared straight back at him. 'Yes. Perhaps that also.'

'You cannot keep her sex or her identity a secret forever. Already there are a large number of people who know.'

'Probably. But I cannot risk leaving her here alone in Granada. Nor would she be willing to stay. There is one favour I would ask of you, Ibn Zamnak. I have recruited at least twenty men, and possibly a good many more, from my old galley crew. They are presently making their way to Granada. I have promised them horses, equipment and provisions. May I ask you to provide them with what they need, and send them horses under escort? My sister and I will repay you.'

'There is no need for any payment, Ibrahim. Granada's coffers are not yet so depleted that they cannot pay for twenty more defenders.'

'Thank you, Ibn Zamnak. The men should come and join me at Zahara as soon as possible. My intention is to make them my personal bodyguard. But for now, dear friend, farewell. I shall go first to take my leave of Ayala, but then we shall go at once to the western borders.'

Ayala urged them to delay their departure until the following morning. 'You must think of Leonora,' she said in a half-scolding voice. 'She is not made of iron, whatever you may believe of her. Besides, I would spend one night more with my sister-to-be. You can surely spare us that much, Ibrahim!'

He yielded readily enough. There were indeed quite sound reasons for waiting a little longer, until the Grand Vizier had, in fact, assembled his five hundred men and until the twenty or more men of his former galley-crew had arrived from Malaga. But it was as though he knew – or felt through some sixth sense – that the Spaniards were on the move, and he was anxious to be in place and have the maximum time to reconnoitre the terrain through which their troops would have to pass. For that, he needed to be on the spot – for that, and of course, for Leonora's safety. She had become too dear a treasure to entrust to the hands of men like Boabdil and Sharif.

It was a night of tenderness, of quietude and an underlying tinge of sadness. Ayala, Leonora and Ibrahim sat and talked in the inner courtyard. His departure this time was synonymous with the advent of war and a future fraught with uncertainty. The questions of how to act or what to do in the case of eventual defeat were in all their minds, but not one of them spoke of it. Were they, all three, he wondered, like Granada itself, behaving just like ostriches and burying their heads in the sand, or was it a form of reckless fearlessness in the face of the threat of extinction of the world they knew and cherished?

When they set off the following morning in the direction of Zahara, they were accompanied by six sumpter-mules laden with gunpowder and two muleteers sent as a parting gift by the Grand Vizier. With them had come a short letter with the news that Ibn Zamnak had learned that King Boabdil had dispatched Sharif on a secret mission to the Court of the Spanish Kings. He, Ibn Zamnak, had not been officially informed and could only presume that the King was negotiating on his own behalf. Prince Ibrahim read out the contents of the letter to Leonora.

'A house divided is a house condemned to fall,' she said softly. 'What will you do now, Ibrahim?'

'Fight,' he said savagely. 'Then we shall see.'

The beauty of Granada was as paradisiacal as ever, with groves of olive trees, of pomegranates, oranges and lemons that seemed to breathe the serenity and promise of eternal peace. It was almost impossible here to think in terms of war. It was no wonder that the Spaniards did not want the destruction of this Granadan Eden but much preferred to incorporate it as the most priceless of all the jewels in their crown.

Prince Ibrahim was minded to make Zahara, initially at least, the principal base of his command. The town was small, compact and moderately well fortified. When garrisoned, it would be capable of standing up to any attacking force not equipped with artillery. It had excellent storage capacity for food, horses, weapons and all other supplies. For himself he selected a large house in the centre of the town that was the personal property of King Boabdil. He summoned the leading citizens of the town to inform them of his appointment as commander of the western approaches to Granada. He then ordered them to make sufficient labour available to reinforce the city walls and to clear out the houses and buildings he would specify as quarters for the troops who would shortly be coming and needing to be billeted, as well as for storage purposes, and to ensure that there would, additionally, be sufficient food placed in store to enable the inhabitants of Zahara to withstand a siege of several weeks' duration.

A few of the leading citizens of the town protested loudly and vehemently and selected one of their number, a particularly vigorous and arrogant man, not much older than Prince Ibrahim himself, to act as their spokesman. He was, Prince Ibrahim learned, a Genoese renegade, still known under his former Christian name of Frescobaldi.

The following day Frescobaldi led a delegation of citizens of Zahara, walking in unannounced to the room where Prince Ibrahim was poring over some rough makeshift maps of *Las Malistas.*

Frescobaldi came straight to the point. 'I fear, Prince, that the burden you are proposing to place on this town is not acceptable to its inhabitants. We shall be sending a written protest to His Majesty. In the meanwhile we have decided not to make any of our horses, buildings or barns over to you or your men. We see no need to do so. This house, which belongs to His Majesty, should be large enough for your purposes.'

'I see,' said Prince Ibrahim. 'And the soldiers who are being sent here to fight in the defence of Granada, on your behalf, what of them?'

'What indeed?' murmured Frescobaldi. 'I suggest that they bivouac in the fields outside our town, or on the frontier. That is, after all, where I would imagine that you plan to engage any invaders who may, perchance, come this way.'

Prince Ibrahim smiled politely. 'I note what you say, good people. Perhaps I should point out that as the appointed commander of the western approaches; His Majesty King Boabdil will expect me to take all necessary measures to ensure the proper defence of his realm, to the best of my ability, and yours.'

'That, my Lord, is a matter for you. We have no wish to interfere. Equally, however, we have no wish to be interfered with.' With a slightly insolent sneer Frescobaldi turned on his heel and, followed by his party of fellow citizens, walked out into the street.

Leonora looked at Ibrahim solicitously. 'I have been only a few days in your beloved country, Ibrahim,' she said quietly, 'but I fear Granada is like a golden apple on the outside with a worm at its core. First your King, now these people here in Zahara. Perhaps they do not represent the majority. These people prefer peace, with assurances of ease, comfort and money. It is not with the likes of them that you will be able to resist the armies of Spain. Theirs, I can assure you, is a very different sort of mettle.'

'Granada must fight,' he said between gritted teeth. 'Granada *will* fight.'

'*Some* Granadans will fight,' she gently corrected him. 'Some. The question is how many. Already here, where you had planned your base, you are not wanted. "Go and camp in the fields" is their message; "Do not bother us." Surely you realise this?'

'I do not care for their message,' he answered grimly. 'I shall have my base here over their bodies, dead or alive. They will not enjoy today's little triumph over me for long.'

'What can you do?'

'Nothing today. But tomorrow, or the day after tomorrow, or the day after that, when my galley crew arrive, then they will sing a different tune here.'

'But Ibrahim, that will change nothing. You will only turn these people against you all the more. They have already made clear their preference for an easy accommodating settlement with Spain. If you compel them to obey you, they will betray you at the first opportunity.'

He looked at her and nodded. 'I think you are quite right, Leonora. But I do not intend there to be such an opportunity.'

Prince Ibrahim oversaw the muleteers as they stocked the gunpowder in one of the rooms in his house. There were twenty-four boxes in total, each one weighing some fifty pounds. It represented a formidable arsenal. To the muleteers themselves he offered employment for the duration of his command on the western front. Rather to his surprise they accepted with alacrity. Their positive response, however small and insignificant a matter in itself, contributed towards a raising of his spirits.

They rose even further when, two days later, twenty-four men from the Ottoman galley crew rode into Zahara. They had been well-mounted by Ibn Zamnak and well equipped. With them came a train of thirty more sumpter mules carrying weapons, salt, smoked fish, dried meats, bags of onions and animal skins.

'I bring you greetings, my Lord Prince, from the Grand Vizier,' said Yakoub with a smile. 'He expects to be in a position to send you at least five hundred men within a week to ten days, and the rest of your command within a month. He requested that the train of sumpter mules and their muleteers should be sent back to Granada. He has need of them there.'

'It shall be done. Welcome, Yakoub, and welcome all of you, my good friends, to Zahara. The first task will be to find quarters for you all. Yakoub, leave eight of your men here on guard with Leonardo. The rest of us have a call to make.'

Frescobaldi's house, not more than three hundred paces distant, was square-shaped with thick walls and a high parapet along the sides of its flat roof. Four armed men stood by the main entrance. Prince Ibrahim went straight towards them.

'Open the door,' he ordered curtly. 'I am now the governor of this town.'

The four men stepped in front of the heavy wooden door and drew their swords. Without a further word Prince Ibrahim drew his own sword from its scabbard and ran one of them through the body. With a loud shout his galley crew members followed suit. Then they pushed the bodies of Frescobaldi's four retainers aside and smashed open the door with axes. Frescobaldi, his wife and three children were on their knees and he raised his hands in supplication.

'Forgive me, my lord Prince,' he moaned. 'I beg for your forgiveness. I shall be your man forever.'

For a few moments Prince Ibrahim looked at him in silence. 'No,' he said at last. 'No forgiveness. This town needs an example and you will be it. But you may die the easier, Frescobaldi, if I promise you that your wife and children will not be touched.' He thrust his sword into Frescobaldi's chest and waited until he lay quite still.

The summary death of Frescobaldi and the manner of it cowed those who had been his associates into total, immediate, submission. It left Prince Ibrahim free to concentrate on the requisitioning of quarters for the billeting of his men, both the twenty-four from the galley and the five to six hundred expected to arrive soon, and for the selection of suitable storage facilities. The assistance he had requested for the strengthening of the town's defences was now provided, often, it seemed, without a grudge and sometimes even with considerable apparent spontaneity.

This marked the beginning of a period of intense activity for Prince Ibrahim. The close on six hundred men, when they arrived exactly one week later, were a motley crowd. Some, perhaps a third or just over, were indeed professional and seasoned soldiers who had fought against the Spaniards and the French. The majority, however, were young Granadans, keen to fight but with no experience of war. Finally, there was a group of about fifty ex-convicts released from the stone quarries on their promise to fight to the death for Granada. Prince Ibrahim went round every man in person, speaking to them all individually and seeking to gauge their temperament and reliability. He had decided to form them into companies of one hundred, each one with its own captain. He appointed Yakoub, whom he felt he could trust implicitly, as overall commander, responsible and answerable only to himself. He had enough horses to mount only one of the six companies. The rest would have, perforce, to serve as infantry but, given the nature of the terrain of *Las Malistas*, there was in any case only limited scope for the use of cavalry. It did underscore even more, however, the need to engage the enemy in the rutted terrain of *Las Malistas*. Once through it, in the open flat and rich plains, the sheer weight of the Spanish cavalry, artillery and infantry would be overwhelming.

Prince Ibrahim insisted on training every day. He himself was tireless and the men around him were seemingly inspired and driven on by his example. After the first week he went regularly with one company after another into the nearer stretches of *Las Malistas*, often going as far as the *Torre Negra*. Qasim Abbas, the commander of the tower, was recovering well from the wound he had sustained from Prince Ibrahim's would-be assassin. He was jubilant at the arrival of the Granadan troops and looked forward with keen anticipation to forays across the wilder stretches of *Las Malistas* and, perhaps even beyond, deep into Castile.

Prince Ibrahim took Leonora with him every time. He was keen that his men should come to look upon the presence of his young page at all times as something automatic. Despite the strain manifestly put upon her by the need at all times to conceal her true identity, Leonora showed no sign of cracking under the pressure. It was really only in the room that they shared that she was able to relax her guard and, even there, there was a need for vigilance. Often at night as they lay together, her naked limbs intertwined with this, he ran his hands over her breasts, marvelling at their exquisite softness, but praying at the same time that the stout jerkin and shirt she wore would not reveal their twin swelling shapes. Leonora, however, seemed relatively unconcerned, having apparently become as fatalistic as any Moslem.

At first the pattern changed little as one week followed another and the heat grew steadily more intense as they moved towards high summer. A hundred or so more men had come to join Prince Ibrahim's command, but with them had come the news from Ibn Zamnak that King Boabdil was reluctant to send him any further reinforcements, preferring to keep the bulk of his army for the protection of Malaga and the defence of the northern border where he expected the Spaniards to invade in great force. There was no word about Sharif's mission or about al-Zaqhal. Prince Ibrahim cursed, but there was, as he said bitterly to both Yakoub and Leonora, little he could do short of riding back to Granada to remonstrate, and he had no illusions about the sort of reception he would get there.

As a result of frequent reconnoitring, he had by now become familiar with large stretches of *Las Malistas*. He had several times been back to the village whose Moslem inhabitants had been massacred and where he and Leonora had first come together in the rock pool only a few hundred paces from the scene of carnage. Despite the ghoulish memories of the village itself it was there, or just beyond it, that he had noticed an opportunity of waylaying an advancing invading force. The path leading round and up to the village from the western side – that any invader would necessarily have to take – was narrow with high and rocky slopes on either side. The path climbed quite steeply before widening to give access to the small plateau on which much of the village had originally been built. At the bottom of the steep incline that led up towards the village, two tall pillars of rock pointed up skywards. If these two could be blasted with gunpowder so as to collapse and so form a partial barrier, and if his own men could hold the plateau up above, then any Spaniards caught between them would be trapped, like rats.

Prince Ibrahim discussed the plan with Yakoub and his senior captains. They all agreed that it was a worthwhile plan, provided the Granadans kept perfectly silent as the invaders moved forward, and provided, also, that the invaders did not constitute so large a force that they stretched back well beyond the two pillars. That was manifestly true, but it was agreed nevertheless that there was sufficient merit in the plan to warrant bringing a large number of barrels of gunpowder from Zahara and storing them in one of the houses in the village. It was agreed at the same time that, since they would in future be coming quite frequently to the area where the stench of putrefying bodies was still very strong, they would bury all the dead in one large communal grave. It proved to be a particularly gruesome task that made more than one man faint from nausea.

The work of burying the dead and transporting the barrels of gunpowder from Zahara to the village had been completed only a few days when one of the scouts, whom Prince Ibrahim sent out regularly almost as far as the

Guadalquivir river, brought in the news that a very considerable Spanish advance force appeared to be moving in their direction.

The following morning a messenger from the Grand Vizier brought the tidings that a large Spanish army, led by King Ferdinand and Queen Isabella in person, had moved south from Jaen and had crossed the border into Granada. Clearly, the Spanish invasion of Granada had begun in earnest.

The next morning, Prince Ibrahim, taking Yakoub and Leonora with him, rode out to observe the approaching invading force. Dismounting and hiding behind a thick clump of trees, well above the Spanish columns, they were able to observe them quite easily. They counted some fifteen hundred soldiers, including some two hundred cavalry, as well as a number of pack-mules with their attendants. Across the distance they could faintly hear men shouting and some occasional laughter. There appeared to be little or no attempt to send scouts on ahead or to mount any kind of flanking watch. It could, hopefully perhaps, be presumed that the Spaniards expected no opposition of any kind before reaching the fort of the *Torre Negra*. They were, moreover, advancing at a very modest pace.

Prince Ibrahim and his two companions returned to their encampment and began to lay their plans with infinite care. As it was not yet possible to estimate with any degree of precision how long the winding Spanish column would take to reach their position, it was decided to prepare the trap to be effective as from the following afternoon. Four pits were dug, two on each side of the long incline that led up to the village. The barrels of gunpowder were lowered carefully into them and the ground covered with a tangle of broken branches, pieces of rock and leaves. A party of twelve men, all of them from the crew of the Ottoman galley, were hidden close by. All twelve were volunteers, for their discovery by the Spaniards would certainly mean a slow and painful death. Their Herculean task would be to drag out and place the barrels of gunpowder in position as soon as the leading Spanish troops had passed and to throw in the lighted rushes that would cause them to explode and hopefully send the pillars of rock crashing to the ground. Four companies were posted on either side of the long incline under strict orders to remain in hiding until they heard a pre-arranged signal of three short blasts on the horn in quick succession. A special contingent of one hundred men was held back in the village itself, and would spread out over the plateau and go to its very rim as soon as they heard the sound of explosions below. That, at least, was the outline of the plan.

It was a little after noon on the following day before Prince Ibrahim had completed his dispositions. The horses, all one hundred or so of them, had been taken back to a safe place several leagues beyond the village, lest their neighing would have been heard by the Spaniards and arouse their suspicions. Prince Ibrahim, Yakoub and Leonora lay flat on the ground at the top of the incline, straining their ears for the least sound in the distance. All movement, whatever the men's needs, had been forbidden.

The hours ticked away with infinite slowness so that time seemed to be almost standing still in the glaring sun. Only the occasional drone of a bumble bee disturbed the silence. From the six hundred and twenty men there came not a sound. It was uncanny, but Prince Ibrahim felt a surge of pride in his heart. The labours of the past two months had been immense and intense, but the discipline and sense of purpose of his small band could not be faulted.

It was another two hours, and the sun past its zenith, when they first began to hear the clank of armour, the neighing of horses and the deep booming tramp of soldiers marching at they filed along *Las Malistas* in their direction. After a while they could distinguish men's voices, with sudden shouts or cries, an occasional snatch of song, and orders barked in short stentorian tones. Prince Ibrahim did not dare to raise his head. From where he was lying, at ground level, he had a clear view of the start of the incline several hundred paces below him, but no further. He could feel the sweat gathering under his armpits and running down his body in little streams that itched and tickled. The silence of his men remained absolute.

The first to appear were four horsemen, riding now two abreast as the path widened. They looked up and about them but were clearly unperturbed. Behind them was a gap. Prince Ibrahim began to fret impatiently. If the gap became too great his trap could not be sprung. The four riders had covered some fifty paces before those leading the rest of the Spanish column made their appearance. Prince Ibrahim started in surprise as he recognised the two men at its head. Santillana was riding bareheaded, his face turned towards his companion, who was wearing his vizor half closed. But the huge, bulky shape of the man was enough to tell Prince Ibrahim that this was the Grand Inquisitor – Tomas de Torquemada, no less – who was now riding straight towards him. Prince Ibrahim caught his breath. Even with the element of surprise in his favour, this promised to be a bloody encounter. Men of the ilk of Torquemada did not surrender.

The Spanish column continued to file forward, and it became apparent that it was as Prince Ibrahim had feared, and that the length of the Spanish column was greater than the length of the incline up to the plateau where he and his company of one hundred men were waiting. But with the four leading Spanish horsemen now only some fifty paces away, he dared wait no longer. His original plan had perforce to be changed.

Leaping up he shouted, 'Granada, Granada,' and hurled the spear he had by his side at one of the approaching horsemen, as Yakoub blew his horn three times to give the signal to those hidden at the base of the incline to blast the rock pillars. Almost simultaneously the four hundred men, two hundred on each side of the incline, leapt to their feet to fire arrows and throw spears and stones at the Spaniards caught between them.

For the first few minutes there was confusion and even a hint of panic in the Spanish ranks, but the infantry of Spain had not gained its formidable reputation lightly or undeservedly. Within minutes, order had been restored. All their horsemen had dismounted and, like the infantry, were holding up their shields in long parallel lines as they sought to fight their way up to the edge of the plateau. Prince Ibrahim could see Santillana clearly, marshalling his men and leading them forward. The Grand Inquisitor had disappeared from his sight, although Prince Ibrahim had not seen him fall. The noise had reached a crescendo, with men screaming war cries intermingled with curses, imprecations and cries of 'Allah' and '*Santiago y Dios*'. Prince Ibrahim took good note. The presence of a company of knights of the Order of Santiago was rather more than he had expected or reckoned on.

Despite their bravery, the Spaniards were fighting at a great disadvantage. From each side of the long gully incline, arrows were continuing to fly. At such short distances even the strongest armour provided only limited and partial protection. The steepness of the incline and its relative narrowness severely hampered their freedom of movement. Suddenly, above the fracas, came the thunder of explosions. Looking down towards the bottom of the incline, Prince Ibrahim could see dense clouds of smoke with an acrid smell that attacked his nostrils. The two pillars, however, were still standing. Soon, some of the Spanish troops would be fighting their way forward along the heights on either side of the gully. It would necessarily now be a case of each man for himself, but for the moment at least it was still Granada that held the ascendant.

The light had suddenly begun to fade as heavy clouds rolled up from the north and there was now little hope that the Spaniards would be able to storm their way on to the plateau before dark.

A similar conclusion had evidently been reached by the Spanish commanders. Two loud blasts on a horn were followed by a slow and measured retreat back down the incline. Prince Ibrahim could see men still falling as they were hit by arrows or boulders on their way back down to the bottom. He could not but admire the disciplined order in which they retreated, although they made no attempt to help any of their badly-stricken comrades, leaving them to lie where they fell. Prince Ibrahim waited till the last of the enemy soldiers had retreated to the bottom of the incline before sounding the order to his own men to fall back.

Later that night they went round all the fallen. Wounded Granadan soldiers were taken to the village where Leonora, all attempts at maintaining her disguise now abandoned, helped by a handful of older men, all looking pale but determined, tended them as best they could. Wounded Spanish soldiers were also brought in. Those too badly hurt to walk were killed on the spot; those able to walk and with less severe wounds were also tended before being bound and tied together – with a little luck they would fetch good prices in the slave markets of Morocco. As he walked slowly past them all, Prince Ibrahim came to a sudden halt. Standing in the midst of a small group of Spaniards whose wounds were still being examined, one arm hanging by his side and his face covered in blood, was Santillana. Prince Ibrahim stopped in front of him.

'My lord Santillana, it grieves me to see you like this. I had thought of you before the battle started here this afternoon as being safely in Seville, preparing to march on Malaga.'

'We had thought to find this route unguarded,' said Santillana. 'Our scouts had reported that there were only a small handful of border guards at a small fort some twenty or thirty leagues beyond this point. It seems they were sadly mistaken. We have suffered heavy losses today. I fear for you, Prince, for your name will be all the more reviled at the Court of Spain after your victory here. It is a pity. You could have done so much better for Granada as a friend of Spain.'

'I am doing what I must, Santillana,' replied Prince Ibrahim softly. 'I believe you to be a man of honour. You would not have acted differently in my place.'

Santillana shook his head. 'I am not so sure. Your cause is doomed. Oh yes, you have stopped us today. We may even have to retreat. But the armies we have gathered will overwhelm Granada. You should not attempt to resist us.'

'You may be right, Santillana, even though I pray that Allah will otherwise. But even if you are right, for me it changes nothing. I fear that for tonight we have no option but to leave you bound with ropes with the other Castilian prisoners. This village was raided not long ago by Castilian marauders. All the villagers were either killed or carried off, and everything of value taken. There are many here looking for revenge. I will not ask you for a ransom, Santillana. As soon as this engagement is over, you will be free to go.'

'You are very generous, Prince.'

'Generous?' Prince Ibrahim shrugged. 'Treating you with honour, as a man whom I respect, gives me greater pleasure than any sum of money your ransom would bring me. But I fear that my generosity, as you term it, must be restricted to your person. Your companions were captured by my men and they expect their reward. Rightly so. Good night, Santillana. I will give orders that you should be made as comfortable as our conditions permit.'

Yakoub brought him word that up to two hundred and fifty enemy bodies had been counted. Granadan losses, by comparison, had been light with only fifteen killed and some forty wounded, most of them only slightly. The enemy had retreated to well beyond the two rock pillars. They had lit a number of fires and sentries had been posted. They would have to wait until daylight to form an opinion about their further intentions.

Prince Ibrahim slept fitfully that night. He and Leonora lay close together, their cloaks thrown lightly over them, alongside some twenty to thirty other Granadan soldiers. It had turned into a bright autumn night with the stars twinkling like diamantine fragments against a near perfect indigo backcloth. Although confident that there could be no further Spanish attack during the night, Prince Ibrahim had given instructions for sentries to be posted at the bottom of the incline. His mind was filled with thoughts of the day to come and trying to gauge the chances of continued successful resistance against the Spaniards, who remained much superior in numerical terms, were they to attempt to renew their advance.

He rose early, and asked Yakoub to make certain that all his men should be well fed. It had, he had learned, been a rule in the Ottoman armies and one whose value he had come to appreciate. It was while he was chatting with a small group of his officers that there was a long, but muted, blast on a trumpet. Almost immediately Leonora ran to him with the news that two Spaniards on horseback, carrying a white flag of truce, had come to the edge of the rock pillars. They had requested to speak with the commander of the Granadan forces.

Telling Yakoub to accompany him, Prince Ibrahim went down to meet the two Spaniards. Their mutual recognition was instantaneous.

'Prince Ibrahim,' said the Grand Inquisitor coldly as he drew near. 'I should have known it was you. You are indeed, in God's truth, spawn of the devil. I can only pity Granada that it has been cursed by your presence. Would that you had stayed in Istanbul!'

'I have not come here, Torquemada, to trade insults – murderer, torturer, vilifier though you are. You have come under a flag of truce and would do well to remember it. What is it that you ask?'

'Ask?' repeated the Grand Inquisitor. 'I ask nothing. But I suggest that it would be a matter of human decency and respect to bury our common dead. Our losses were substantial. We would like to take away the bodies of our fallen and give them a proper Christian burial. If you agree, I will send fifty unarmed men to carry out that task. The rest of my men will withdraw to a distance of two leagues.'

'I agree.'

'You have transgressed, Prince, and sinned to a point that is almost beyond redemption. But because of the many lives and souls that are at stake, I am prepared to hold out to you one last olive branch. You are an intelligent man. You cannot surely be blind to the overwhelming odds that are arraigned against you. You know the position of your own King, your liege lord and sovereign. Recognise the inevitable! Help us! Help me in the great enterprise of Granada! By acting in this way you can help to save Granada from misery and the risk of utter destruction. I will not offend you with offers of gold or titles, although clearly Spain would not fail to give recognition to an outstanding act of diplomacy on the part of one who has abducted a princess of the Royal House of Aragon. Think on it well, Prince Ibrahim.'

'Granada will not surrender, Torquemada. We cannot be simply subsumed into a totally alien state. Believe me, I do recognise the rising greatness of Spain. There is no doubt in my mind that your nation is about to be called to a great destiny. But the freedom of Granada is not for sale, however high the bid.'

'You are mistaken, Prince. I am sorry, for your refusal means that there may now well be a protracted war. But you are, I repeat, mistaken. Look well in the days to come for news from Malaga. It will, when you receive it, show you quite unmistakably how close we already are to the complete reunification of all Spain. For you, personally, there will be only a choice between death, dishonour or flight. There are no other paths open to you. If you will not consider your own position, then think at least of your men who are seemingly willing to die at your behest, and for nothing. Think too, for a moment, of Princess Leonora.

'But I can see that I speak in vain. I expect that we shall meet again, Prince, before this drama comes to its end. Until then, farewell.'

Prince Ibrahim watched in silence as the Grand Inquisitor and his companion turned and rode slowly away. It took no more than one day for the Spaniards to bury their dead. Prince Ibrahim had dispatched a messenger to the Grand Vizier in Granada to inform him of the repulse of the enemy force, and of the presence of the Grand Inquisitor as one of its joint commanders. He had let Santillana go free with mixed feelings. Magnanimity was a luxury that Granada could ill afford in its present predicament. Against this was the fact that it gave Granada – or to be more precise, and more honest, himself – a certain panache that brought a momentary lightening of the all-too-pervasive gloom.

Two days later, the Spaniards, their dead all buried in the forlorn wasteland of *Las Malistas*, withdrew. They went as they had come, riding for the most part in a long single file, their banners held aloft and with a demeanour as proud and determined as though they had been the victors in the battle of the pass of *Las Malistas*. It left Prince Ibrahim with an uneasy feeling that the Spaniards had perhaps not wholly failed in the objectives they had set themselves. He sent out patrols to observe their progress, but the reports they brought back all pointed to an apparently clear-cut decision by the enemy to abandon this particular line of approach. This being the case, there seemed little point in keeping his six hundred or so men in a macabre death-ridden village where the vultures still wheeled and circled silently overhead, their wings reflecting like ominous black shadows on the ground below. Prince Ibrahim decided to leave just a few scouts to be attached to the garrison of the *Torre Negra* and to return with the rest of his company to Zahara.

But even before they had begun to make their way back towards Zahara, the messenger he had dispatched to the Grand Vizier with the report of their victory in *Las Malistas* returned with news that destroyed any remaining wisps of elation. A large Spanish army, estimated at fifteen to twenty thousand men, had invested Malaga, while from the seaward side the post had been completely blockaded by a fleet of more than fifty ships anchored round it so tightly that not even a sprat could make its way through. King Boabdil had decided not to stay, but had left al-Taghri in command of the beleaguered city while he had returned to Granada with half of the army. However, Malaga was well provisioned and there was no immediate danger of its falling. It was hoped the Spaniards would soon tire of the siege of one of the mightiest fortresses of the whole Mediterranean area.

To Prince Ibrahim it all came as a devastating blow. Malaga, it seemed, reading between the lines, was to be left to its fate, and Boabdil had demonstrated, once again – and this time for all the world to see – his personal cowardice and total military incompetence. For Granada, Malaga was the all-important key. Through it pulsed its life-blood, its trade and commerce upon which the kingdom's wealth depended. Its only hope of succour now came from the Moorish kingdoms of Morocco. It was clear enough now what the Grand Inquisitor had meant when he had warned him to look for news from Malaga and described the odds stacked against Granada as overwhelming. Prince Ibrahim cursed volubly. How could it be that in the hour of its greatest need Allah could allow so contemptible a creature as Boabdil to sit upon the throne of Granada and connive at its own destruction? But what could he, with his small company, do now? For a few brief moments he considered abandoning it all and escaping with Leonora to a new life and a new world. He had good reason to believe that the Sultan would welcome him back. A high command in the Ottoman army would, in all likelihood, be his for the asking. It offered, too, a sweet taste of revenge for fortune and Allah was with the armies of Islam in the East. Leonora would be treated with respect as befitted her lineage and her status as his wife. He turned to her with admiration. She too had proved herself in the short campaign in *Las Malistas*. Her dedication, loyalty and powers of endurance and recuperation were of an altogether exceptional order. Their shared moments of intimacy had, perforce, been rare. Highly esteemed though he knew himself to be by the men under his command, Prince Ibrahim was not completely certain as to how they viewed his liaison with a renegade Spanish Princess.

After discussing the situation with Yakoub, Prince Ibrahim decided that he would return at once to Granada with Leonora and a small escort of six men. Yakoub was to stay in Zahara in command of the entire company and wait for further instructions. The news of the encirclement and siege of Malaga had inevitably had a depressing effect, and Prince Ibrahim was very concerned lest the morale of his men should suffer. It almost, for a moment, made him regret once again his generosity in letting Santillana go free without a ransom. Only gold, or the promise of gold, could stave off the gnawing effects of rampant depression. His men had won Granada's only victory to date and, by Allah, he would ensure that they were properly rewarded. He would address them all together before he set off for Granada. He instructed Yakoub to call all the men of the company to a meeting after their evening meal on the edge of the plateau where they had victoriously thrown back the Spanish invaders.

They foregathered quickly with a faintly swaggering buoyancy that brought a smile to Prince Ibrahim's lips. A dozen or so large logs had been rolled carefully together so that he was able to step on to them and be seen by all.

'By our victory here we have accomplished much,' he began in a deliberately undramatic tone. 'It was not a great pitched battle, nor were very large forces involved, but by standing firm and defeating the enemy, you destroyed the myth and aura of Spanish invincibility. If Granada fights as you fought here, then we need have no fear about the outcome of the war. Granada will survive.' There were cheers, and he could see a few smiles on some of the faces, but there was little sign of elation. 'You have heard the news from Malaga,' he continued. 'It shows how determined our enemies are and what forces they can put in the field against us. But I have no doubt that we shall repulse them there, as we have done here. We have done our duty proudly, victoriously, and can leave with our heads held high. I shall leave ahead of you at daybreak tomorrow to go to Granada, while you will make your way to Zahara and wait there until I rejoin you and send you further word. In Granada I shall inform our sovereign King Boabdil of what you have accomplished here. I am certain that he will wish to demonstrate his pleasure and his appreciation. In my own name I hereby promise two gold maravedis to each and every one of you. Test by fire brings men together and so it has been, I truly believe, with us. For those among you who were with me on the sea journey from Istanbul, our personal bargain has long been sealed. But for those of you who joined me here, it is a new covenant but one that is no less valid or heartwarming. May the blessings of Allah be upon you all.'

This time there was no mistaking the men's satisfaction. Many cheered and clapped or stamped their feet upon the ground in appreciation. But if there was indeed some jubilation, it still continued to fall well short of elation. These men were not fools and could read the menacing signs as well as he could himself. Nevertheless, Prince Ibrahim felt that the worst part of the chill of depression had been rubbed off and a better feeling of camaraderie and hopefulness restored.

For a while he strolled among the men of his company, chatting and laughing, hearing the occasional joke or banter, and nodding approvingly as the cooks restoked their fires and set to roast two oxen that one of the foraging parties had found.

After a while he was able to walk away unobserved with Leonora and go back to the rock pool where she had first come to him. She leaned against him as they stood and watched the water running down towards their pool.

He felt his body longing for her, the heat of his desire wetting his fingers with a moist clamminess so that he had to clench his teeth to refrain from a mad indulgence in his passion. It was fortunate that they could hear the bustle and occasional loud rumbustious noises of some of the men of his company at close quarters. Several times small groups came in their direction, nodding or giving them a friendly greeting, seemingly unaware of the sexual tumult in their breasts. Prince Ibrahim smiled wanly at his companion. Leonora did not speak but shook her head in mock despair. Slowly they sauntered back up the hill towards the small plateau where groups of men had begun to dance to the accompaniment of deep guttural chanting that swelled and contracted alternately in volume. There were some who were still singing when Prince Ibrahim lay down to sleep under the night sky with Leonora a short distance from him.

They left an hour after daybreak. Yakoub rode a short distance with them as Prince Ibrahim repeated his instructions to break camp and march back to Zahara and to wait there for further orders. Despite his profound concern for the future, the first part of their journey was pleasant enough. Both at the *Torre Negra* and in Zahara the news of the victory in *Las Malistas* had worked wonders. In Zahara small children rushed to touch his horse or his armour. Some of the older boys grabbed his hands to carry them to their lips. He reproached them gently, but their enthusiasm was overwhelming and contagious. But beyond Zahara, as they gradually began to draw near to Granada, there was an unmistakable change in atmosphere as joy gave way first, to depression, and then to fear, if not yet outright panic. The beautiful paradisiacal Granadan countryside was as enchanting as ever with its rich harmonies of colour and nature's exuberant and extravagant generosity; but through it all a mounting sense of fear was clearly perceptible. As they came close to Granada, Boabdil's irritation at his decision to go first to his sister's house on the occasion of his return from Istanbul came back to Prince Ibrahim's mind. He smiled grimly. King Boabdil could go to the devil. This time, as then, it was to Ayala that he would go first.

He found his sister in a state of distress. Ibn Zamnak's star was waning fast and his survival for much longer as Grand Vizier increasingly uncertain. Al-Zaqhal had returned empty-handed with nothing more than expressions of brotherly solicitude and vague references to an expeditionary corps that might be sent eventually by the Ottoman Sultan. Boabdil had become even more petulant and unpredictable than before.

'I see little hope for the future, Ibrahim,' she said, shaking her head melancholically. 'Boabdil sits every day in his council chamber, alone or with Sharif.'

'Sharif! Has he returned?'

'Yes. But only Boabdil knew the purpose of his mission, or its outcome. Ibn Zamnak has been told nothing. Nor has al-Zaqhal.'

They sat and talked in the peace of the inner courtyard of Ayala's house as they sipped through long straws from glasses where lime juice had been mixed with thin slices of orange and lemon and small cubes of ice. On a small table by their side, servants had placed wheat cakes dripping with honey and dried dates. Prince Ibrahim picked at them, almost absent-mindedly, licking the sweet honey from his fingers. It was as though Granada, or Boabdil its King, had a death wish, either unable or unwilling to summon up the energy to respond to the Spanish invasion. He could feel Leonora's eyes upon him; they had a poignant expression of solicitude, in which he could read the compassion she felt for the anguish in his mind and soul. He did not say anything to her but took and held her hand.

'We must try and talk to Boabdil,' he said at last. 'He must act. We cannot just sit here like oxen waiting for the butcher's knife.'

Ayala smiled bitterly. 'Do you think Ibn Zamnak has not tried?' she almost snapped. 'But Boabdil is the King.'

The words rang through his brain like a refrain as he lay that night in a deep voluptuous featherbed. Leonora lay naked beside him, whispering to him in the semidarkness as he kissed her breasts and willed his body to wait until their mutually mounting passion should make them forget reason and send their bodies into paroxysms of desire. These were the treasured moments of life, he now believed. In between their lovemaking he slept fitfully. Here, in Ayala's house, Leonora could reveal herself openly without any danger to herself, or to him. It was pleasant to dream of a world and a life where it could always be so, but these were dreams of whose insubstantiality he was only too aware. But while they lasted, these momentary glimpses of paradise constituted a precious joy.

He went quite early the next morning to the Alhambra Palace. The Grand Vizier greeted him warmly enough but, it seemed to Prince Ibrahim, with a tinge of despair in his voice. The man was visibly on edge, although whether his manifest unease was only his own, or on another's account, was not immediately evident.

'His Majesty is here,' said Ibn Zamnak after a few minutes of rather desultory conversation. 'We should perhaps seek an audience at once. It may help to put him in a better humour.'

Prince Ibrahim nodded his agreement. Ibn Zamnak went slowly out of the room, his shoulders stooped, leaving Prince Ibrahim to wait alone. Ibn Zamnak appeared to have changed much since their last meeting. On the table where he sat and worked, Prince Ibrahim could see several sheets of paper with closely-written words in serried ranks. He picked one of them up and gave a start of surprise. These were not dispatches or reports concerning the war, but lines of poetry expressing the anguish of a man at bay, facing condemnation and the extinction of hope. Prince Ibrahim paced up and down the room, his feet making no sound on the thick richly decorated eastern carpets. His mind was suddenly seething with ideas. That the situation facing Granada was black was clear enough, but even now it was not wholly, totally desperate. The situation called for a counter-stroke, of daring and imagination. His thoughts went back to *Las Malistas*, now free, in all probability, of Spanish troops. Just suppose for one moment that a small Granadan force, his own company with some reinforcement, were to march through *Las Malistas* and strike suddenly at either Seville or Cordoba. The effect could, with some luck, be fairly devastating. It was a gamble worth taking. Prince Ibrahim's enthusiasm grew as he turned his idea over in his mind. There were risks involved, but they seemed of no great moment. The worst that could happen would be the entire annihilation of the company in question, but it was not the loss of eight or nine hundred men that would determine the fate of Granada. That depended rather upon the injection of renewed hope into the Granadan high command. He continued to pace up and down the room, his hand grasping the hilt of his sword in his excitement.

But the excitement ebbed slowly as the hours went by and Ibn Zamnak did not reappear. Prince Ibrahim sat down once more at the Grand Vizier's desk and turned back to perusing his papers. The words were like chiselled marble, cold, brilliant and penetrating. He recalled Ayala's admiration of Ibn Zamnak's poetic skills. It was yet another of Granada's tragedies that he was not equally skilled in war. A servant came in at last with a tray of fruit which he placed softly by Prince Ibrahim's side. He ate slowly, his concern mounting at Ibn Zamnak's long absence, but forcing himself to curb and control his impatience.

It was not finally until late in the afternoon that Ibn Zamnak returned to summon him to an immediate council meeting. He looked bewildered and like a man in a trance, like a man who had been battered beyond his powers of endurance. He gave no indication of what had gone on before or of what had kept him so long, but only said in the briefest of words that the King required his immediate presence. It was, moreover, with an obvious effort that he preceded Prince Ibrahim into the audience chamber. It was, Prince Ibrahim observed, the same small assembly as before: the King, al-Zaghal, Sharif, the Grand Vizier and himself. Only al-Taghri was missing, and he was enmeshed in Malaga. King Boabdil scowled as he entered. Al-Zaghal, he noticed, was sitting with his shoulders hunched together and seemed to be trying to avoid looking at him. He suddenly appeared very old and vulnerable, and unbelievably distant from the bold, adventurous, daredevil prince of cavaliers whom he had met only a few months before on the road on his mission to the Court of the Spanish Kings. Sharif, on the other hand, had a slight sneer on his lips and was sitting immediately next to the King. His star, it seemed, was clearly in the ascendant. Boabdil wasted no time in expressions of welcome.

'It is my fate to be cursed with incompetents,' he shouted in a voice that nevertheless sounded thin and reedy, rather like that of a man seeking to play a part beyond his powers or wit. 'Incompetents,' he repeated, relishing the word as though it were a pastille that gave comfort to his throat. 'Incompetents,' he said for the third time, as he looked angrily first at al-Zaghal and then, but with noticeably less self-assurance, at Prince Ibrahim, who returned his stare unmoved. 'Where are the men from Fez or Marrakesh whom al-Zaghal was sent to bring to our assistance? Where? I will tell you where. They are still in the desert, riding their camels and with no intention of crossing the sea to meet the formidable might of Their Majesties of Spain. And you, Ibrahim, you and your futile skirmish in *Las Malistas* that has gained us nothing, save only Spanish fury at your ludicrous elopement with a dishonoured princess of Aragon and dictatorial demands from Spain for her restitution. Incompetents, I say again. And to crown it all, there is grim news from Malaga. Even al-Taghri, in whom I placed so much trust, is failing me.'

When Boabdil had finished speaking there was a momentary silence. Prince Ibrahim had clenched his fists. Sharif was smiling openly, sardonically. Al-Zaghal had made one quick movement with his right arm but had then sunk back into his hunchbacked position, both arms resting on the table in front of him. Ibn Zamnak sat white-faced and subdued, his eyebrows bulging and making Prince Ibrahim think fleetingly of him as a mesmerised frog. The blood, it seemed, had been drained out of the veins of the leaders of Granada. But, by Allah, he, Prince Ibrahim Ibn Sa'd, was not going to join this brigade of silent courtiers, browbeaten and tongue-tied by this King of straw, this simulacrum of a monarch. Boabdil, he noticed, was smirking now, believing no doubt that he had cowed them all.

'The situation is hopeless,' said al-Zaghal gloomily, raising his head. 'I had not believed the Spaniards could put so many men in the field, nor that they would have the fleets of Portugal and Navarre on their side to blockade our ports . . .'

'But you are the one who prattled so confidently about the help we would get from our brothers in Fez and Marrakesh,' Sharif broke in cuttingly. 'You old greybeard fool. Could you not foresee that the Spanish Kings would buy them off?'

King Boabdil nodded his approval with what looked like real jubilation at his uncle's humiliation. Prince Ibrahim shook his head in bewilderment. What sense did it make for the King to rejoice in his near kinsman's discomfiture when the cost to be paid for discord in their own ranks was so high?

'I believe, Your Majesty,' he said firmly, 'that you should reconsider your words.'

King Boabdil stared at him, his mouth half open as if in disbelief. His eyes flickered towards Sharif as if asking him to deal with this incident. Sharif needed no second invitation.

'When His Majesty wishes to hear your opinion, Prince, he will no doubt ask you for it. So far he has not done so. I would, in any case, as your friend and former secretary, advise you to conserve your energies to explain your abduction of a Spanish princess. It makes an accommodation with Their Spanish Majesties infinitely more difficult, and delicate.'

'An accommodation with the Spanish Kings,' repeated Prince Ibrahim slowly. 'Do I hear you correctly? You forget yourself, Sharif. I am no friend of yours, nor you of mine. Go back, cur, to your fawning and whining. It is what you are supremely fitted for. As for expressing my opinions, I am a prince of the Royal House of Granada and I shall say what I wish to say. You are wrong, Your Majesty, to accuse me of incompetence. For years men like al-Zaghal have warned you to strengthen Granada for a war that has become inevitable. You chose instead to joust and hunt or dally with your women. Now you speak of accommodation, of an understanding with our enemies when you know full well that they will only accept our virtually unconditional surrender. Our land, our gold, our faith, all these they will have and take away from us. Fight, King, and show yourself for once to be a man, if you can! Even at this late and terrible hour, a determined resistance could yet win us the day, or at least a reprieve. By the beard of Allah, I implore you, be a man worthy of your name, title and descent.'

Prince Ibrahim, who had half risen from his seat as he came to the end of his emotional appeal, sat down again and looked at al-Zaghal and Ibn Zamnak. Al-Zaghal was sitting bolt upright with his eyes glittering with a kind of feverish and yet contained excitement, while Ibn Zamnak had scarcely stirred. Across the table, Sharif's face was livid with anger, which he made no effort to conceal. His hand was on King Boabdil's arm, as if urging him to action.

'You . . .' hissed Boabdil, 'you presume to instruct me on kingship, on honour? You who so defiled your ambassadorial status by your lechery; you who have sorely jeopardised the possibility of an accommodation with Spain with your sordid copulation with a princess of Aragon. You great blundering fool! How is it possible that you can imagine that your small miserable little triumph has given you the right to insult your King? You have long been needing a lesson, and the time has come for you to be given it. You are under arrest, Prince Ibrahim, until such time as we have considered your position.'

Eight guards entered the chamber as King Boabdil finished speaking, leaving Prince Ibrahim no chance of escape. He looked at Boabdil with contempt. 'You are no King, Boabdil,' he said defiantly, 'but a sackful of wind and bombast. But be warned. The sheep that goes bleating to the tiger does not live long.'

'Take him away,' shouted Boabdil furiously to the guards. 'Strip him. Incarcerate him. Put him in the heaviest irons.'

They took him at once to the dungeons of the Alhambra Palace. The gaolers carried out the King's instructions to the letter, stripping him of all his clothes and leaving him only in his singlet before taking him to one of the lower dungeons and manacling his legs by the ankles so that he could only move a few paces, and that only with difficulty and in considerable pain. Nevertheless, they treated him with some regard. Even here, in this dark place, his fame and reputation were, it seemed, well-established. One of the gaolers brought him a flask of water and then, later on, some cold meats and dried fruit. A large lighted torch was placed above him in a bracket in the wall so that he had plenty of light. The dungeon itself was quite large, although well below ground level, and the walls were dry and the air reasonably fresh. There was a low wooden couch in one corner but it stood beyond his range of movement. There was also, however, a low wooden stool with a high back upon which he was able to sit. Next to it stood a small round iron table on which the gaolers had placed his flask of water and supply of food. As Prince Ibrahim struggled with feelings of despair he seemed to himself to be a helpless witness to Granada's agonising self strangulation.

*Chapter Nine*

# THE FALL OF GRANADA

They left him for two days in the dungeon. The gaolers came in frequently to see him, and it was from one of them that he learned that the King had given orders that he was to be released, but only on condition that he should be taken to his sister's house and stay there under house arrest. Failure to respect this restriction to his freedom of movement would be severely punished.

Leonora was waiting for him when he returned, under guard, from the Alhambra dungeon. The pain in both ankles made if difficult for him to walk normally, so that he was often compelled to hobble or shuffle by her side. But he refused the offer to have himself carried up to their room. Once there, she personally helped him undress and step into a bath of steaming hot water that had been placed there and gently rubbed the chafed and broken skin of his ankles with a soft balm that helped to still the pain.

'Leonora,' he whispered, 'Leonora. I had feared that I might not see you again.'

'We are not so easily parted, you and I,' she replied with a smile. 'Ibn Zamnak sent a message telling us of your imprisonment. He said he dared not risk coming in person lest Boabdil and Sharif should choose to take it as a sign of treasonable behaviour. I fear our Grand Vizier has become like putty in Boabdil's hands.'

Prince Ibrahim nodded. 'It is only too true. Perhaps he is too old, or perhaps he fears that he has too much to lose by opposing Boabdil's whims and wishes. But I was afraid lest Boabdil would have you seized and brought to him. He might well be tempted to see you as a possible bargaining counter in some of his dealings with Ferdinand and Isabella.'

'That only serves to show his total ignorance of our customs. For Ferdinand and Isabella I have become an untouchable, a creature so vile and loathsome that they would soil their eyes simply by looking at me. I have sunk too low for them even to be punished, for punishment could be seen as some form of recognition of a thing better left to putrefy and forgotten in the mire.'

'If not Ferdinand and Isabella, what then of the Grand Inquisitor?'

Leonora gave a small start of surprise. 'Torquemada! I had not really thought any more about him.' She paused for a moment. 'Perhaps. It is not impossible that he should still want to punish me.' She gave a sudden laugh. 'He may well see me as the voluptuous Eve who led his would-be Adam astray. He did, after all, have high hopes of you to help him with the conversion of the Moslems in Granada. Yes, I suppose Boabdil may have a chance of doing business there, although I suspect he is secretly in terror of Torquemada.'

Prince Ibrahim trembled despite himself. 'He is a more terrible foe than either Ferdinand or Isabella. Torquemada is not content with our lands, and they in fact matter little to him, but he does covet our souls and our minds. I fear that death would be the only sure way of escape from his clutches.'

'If that is indeed so, Ibrahim, then I shall not be afraid.'

He drew her to him. 'Nor I, Leonora, if it comes to that.'

They kissed tenderly and she drew him slowly to the couch in their room. She undressed quickly in front of him, revealing with pride the beauty of her body to the feasting eyes of her lover. Gently she lowered herself upon him, manoeuvring her body with a tantalising but loving slowness that enhanced and accentuated their pleasure.

The days that followed were at once an idyll and an incarceration. With Leonora, he dwelt in what seemed at times like a dream world, their present happiness masking a frightening uncertainty about the future. But if they feared it, they nevertheless fought jointly to banish it from their minds. Much of the time they were successful in their efforts to do so, although there were moments, usually at night as they lay close together listening to the silence all around them, when one or other would dare to peer with hushed words into that dark abyss. But mostly they drew back before they had done anything more than just lightly broach the subject.

For Ayala there were no dreams. Ibn Zamnak came very seldom now. When he did come, it was with a hesitant manner and the trembling ague of a man suddenly grown old. It was hard to see him now as the greatest poet of Granada's terminal years. If Ayala was heartbroken she did not show it. On the rare occasions that Ibn Zamnak did come, she was lively, buoyant and endearing. Only once did he stay the night and then left, almost like a thief, at the break of dawn without a further word to Prince Ibrahim or Leonora. At other times, Ayala often withdrew to her own quarters, busying herself with sewing or her needlework. When Prince Ibrahim raised the subject of Ibn Zamnak, she smiled wanly and begged him to change to another topic of conversation.

Prince Ibrahim made no attempt to leave the house. Ayala's servants had reported that at least a dozen guards had been posted round the house and that they were relieved at regular intervals. No instructions had come from the Alhambra Palace about Leonora, so that it seemed, for the time being at least, as though King Boabdil was content with the knowledge that she was within his reach should circumstances make her presence in Granada a useful negotiating counter.

The injuries to Prince Ibrahim's ankles healed very quickly. Anxious to maintain his physical and mental fitness, he sent for several fencing masters to come each day to his sister's house. With them he would fight with blunted swords or in protective armour for an hour at a stretch. He fought sometimes with curved scimitars but often, too, with the straight swords used by the Christians. He was a natural attacking swordsman with an elan and sheer natural ferocity that impressed even the best of Granada's fencing masters. He made a point also of meeting chess players. Not only did he find the games they played stimulating, but they helped to fend off more oppressive thoughts and, by reminding him of Samuel, stoked up the fires of his hatred of Torquemada and his accursed Inquisition.

It was on the following morning when he was busily engaged in one of his fencing bouts that Ibn Zamnak called unexpectedly and called out his name. Lowering his sword, Prince Ibrahim could see at once that one side of the Grand Vizier's face was twitching as though he had lost control of part of his facial muscles.

'What is it, Ibn Zamnak?' he asked solicitously.

'Malaga has capitulated.'

'Malaga!' Prince Ibrahim exclaimed in disbelief. 'Malaga has surrendered?'

'Two days ago. The blockade was so fierce and tight that the inhabitants were reduced very quickly to eating dogs, cats, rats and weasels. I understand their water supplies were being poisoned. The Spaniards gave al-Taghri a choice: "Capitulate and all your lives will be spared, or fight on until the end and anyone we capture will be hanged alive from the city walls." Even then, on Torquemada's orders, all the renegades they found in Malaga were put to death by having a sharp stake thrust through their anuses, and *Conversos* and Judaizers burnt at the stake. All the rest are being held for a ransom of ten thousand gold castellanos. Where such a sum is to be found, no one knows.'

'And al-Taghri himself?'

'A prisoner being held for ransom, like all the others.'

Prince Ibrahim waved his fencing partner away and sat down on the circular bench round the fountain in the inner courtyard. The fall of Malaga was indeed a devastating blow. While the theoretical possibility of the city's fall had been in his consciousness, he had never truly seen it as a serious possibility. The city had reportedly been well stocked and provisioned. It had had a large garrison and a proven commander of great ability and dependability. And yet Malaga had fallen after only a few brief weeks of siege. With it, the Spaniards had come into possession of Granada's main port, its main source of wealth, and its main line of communication with the world outside and the friendly Moslem kingdoms of Fez and Marrakesh in particular – as well as, he remembered as an afterthought, the fine Ottoman war-galley that had brought him back from Istanbul. It was indeed a devastating setback.

'How has the King reacted to the news?' he asked on a sudden whim.

'His Majesty has been in constant session with Sharif, whom he has made his Grand Chamberlain and Lord of Baza.'

'And not with you, his Grand Vizier,' said Prince Ibrahim in surprise.

'I am no longer much in his Majesty's confidence.' Ibn Zamnak hesitated for a moment before continuing. 'You should know that Sharif came back from the mission to Cordoba with a firm proposal. I do not know the precise contents, but I do know that King Boabdil seems little concerned about the war.'

'And al-Zaghal?'

'He has been a broken man since he returned empty-handed from Morocco. Broken like me, Ibrahim. Oh, you don't need to pretend otherwise. I know too much, and want too much. Boabdil has me by the throat.' He passed his hand over his eyes, wearily and sadly. 'Do not tell Ayala. I am man enough still to tell her myself. Only I have put off telling her until now. I could not bear to lose her esteem, and her love.'

'I will indeed leave it to you to tell her,' answered Prince Ibrahim coldly. 'I will not conceal the fact that I had hoped for more from you. Granada has indeed been unfortunate in the hour of its greatest need.'

Ibn Zamnak blushed violently under Prince Ibrahim's scornful glance. For a moment he made as though he was about to turn away, but then he changed his mind and stood his ground. 'I have not yet told you all. His Majesty requires your presence in the council chamber.'

'When?'

'Now. I am to return immediately to the Alhambra Palace. You are to accompany me.'

'You can go ahead on your own,' said Prince Ibrahim dismissively. 'I have to take my leave of Ayala and Leonora. You may inform the King that I shall wait upon him presently.'

'Then I shall wait for you.'

'No. I wish to go alone. Go, Ibn Zamnak, and carry back my message. You may rest assured that I shall not be long in coming.'

Prince Ibrahim went to his room, his thoughts in a turmoil. The loss of Malaga was a tremendous tragedy. Boabdil's motives and actions were hideously suspect. And why should he himself now, of all times, be summoned back to the council chamber?

He found Leonora studying the Koran. Somehow it seemed symbolic, although he could not immediately think of what. He kissed her lightly on the cheek and, in a few brief words, told her the gist of Ibn Zamnak's message. He dressed while she bombarded him with questions and surmises. Hers were unanswerable questions. What now? How much longer could Granada survive? What would become of them? He replied in monosyllables, while selecting his clothes with care. All in black, as befitted this solemn and mournful occasion, relieved only by his father's heavily embossed gold ring which he wore on a chain round his neck and his one remaining superb green jade dagger, a farewell present from Sultan Bayazet. Prince Ibrahim looked good, and he knew it. It was perhaps all a rather superficial addition to his confidence, but it nonetheless made him feel better for his forthcoming session with Boabdil. Leonora kissed him passionately on the lips as he left.

King Boabdil made little or no attempt to hide his irritation at Prince Ibrahim's late arrival. They were once more the customary participants except for al-Taghri, at the council meeting; but on this occasion Prince Ibrahim sat alone on one side of the council table while, across from him on the other side, King Boabdil was flanked by Sharif on his right, and the Grand Vizier and al-Zaghal on his left. It all had its underlying meaning and significance, no doubt – that indeed was clear enough – but Prince Ibrahim studiously ignored it all. If the King wanted his presence at this council meeting, there was certainly a reason for it; and that reason was certainly not of his seeking or asking.

'The Grand Vizier has told you the news of the fall of Malaga,' King Boabdil said in a low yet harsh-sounding tone of voice. 'It leaves the road to Granada open to the Spaniards. At this time of supreme peril we must all forget our former differences. We are prepared to overlook your past indiscipline, your lack of respect, your overweening pride. I have discussed the situation with al-Zaghal, as well as with my Grand Vizier and Grand Chamberlain. We are all agreed that there is only one man in whom our soldiers have faith enough to follow against the vastly superior forces with whom the Spaniards will now march on Granada. That man, Prince Ibrahim, we all acknowledge, is you. Al-Zaghal has been a great warrior in his day, but he has voluntarily stepped down from all his commands. We accordingly hereby appoint you as the new commander of the armies of Granada, from Jaen in the north to Malaga in the south. It is at once a great privilege and a great danger. You are, of course, free to refuse.'

'I thank Your Majesty for this remarkable royal expression of absolute confidence in my abilities,' said Prince Ibrahim dryly. 'It is, I fear, a chalice not devoid of poison. You may be certain that I accept the post of commander, but how many troops have we left, and how many do our enemies have? The odds are fearful. Have you considered well, Your Majesty, whether you still wish to fight?'

'It will be for you to fight, Prince,' said King Boabdil with a scowl. 'My decisions, as King of this country, are my own, and I am accountable to no man. Today, we have appointed you as commander of our armies. Tomorrow it may well be our pleasure to appoint another in your place if we lose faith in your abilities or come to have greater regard for those of another.'

'That is confidence indeed,' said Prince Ibrahim icily. 'But you have not answered my question. How many are our foes? How many are we now ourselves? What intelligence do we have about the enemy's intentions?'

'Very little, Prince,' said Sharif with a slight sneer. 'No doubt, now that you are to be in command, this gap will be speedily rectified. But, in very broad terms, we estimate the Spanish army that is moving up towards us from Malaga at close on seventy thousand men. The northern invaders, coming from Jaen, could well number fifty thousand.'

'And our strength?'

Sharif's sneer turned into a smile of near benevolence. 'Perhaps between ten and twelve thousand men.'

Prince Ibrahim looked at each one of them in turn, Ibn Zamnak, al-Zaghal, the King and Sharif. Al-Zaghal, his uncle and one-time supporter, sat with downcast eyes and said nothing. Ibn Zamnak sat as if in a trance with his eyes fixed on an unmoving spot on the ceiling of the council chamber. The King looked almost amused while Sharif had composed his features and adopted a studiously serious air.

'Ten to twelve thousand men.' Prince Ibrahim repeated slowly. 'Against one hundred and twenty thousand!'

'That does indeed appear to be the situation, commander,' repeated Sharif in a voice in which mirth seemed to be struggling with solemnity. 'It is a situation that will undoubtedly test your military skills to their limits. We are into the beginning of autumn. Winter is not far away. If we can hold up and delay the Spaniards until then we shall at least have a clear breathing space. To secure that, my lord Prince, is your task.'

'We shall hold a banquet tonight,' put in the King. 'We shall announce your appointment and you shall sit by my side.'

'I thank Your Majesty for this mark of distinction,' said Prince Ibrahim thickly, 'but if Your Majesty will forgive me, I shall immediately attend to my new duties. There is – but perhaps I do not need to remind you – much to be done and very little time in which to do it.' He bowed ceremoniously and, ignoring Sharif, took a brief leave of Ibn Zamnak and al-Zaghal, before turning and walking quickly out of the council chamber.

His thoughts, as he rode back to Ayala's house, were in a turmoil. Appointed commander-in-chief of the remnants of the Granadan army, he was expected, or so it seemed, to hold the immensely superior Spanish armies at bay for at least six weeks, and probably even longer. Only a miracle, or a series of miracles, could even begin to make that an achievable objective.

Although the doubts and suspicions fomented in his mind in the days that followed, Prince Ibrahim pushed them aside as resolutely as he could, choosing instead to concentrate on plans for the campaign that lay ahead. Reliable intelligence was his first and overriding requirement, and the scouts he sent out in large numbers soon brought back the news that, while little was stirring on the northern front on the road down from Jaen, preparations had indeed begun in earnest in Malaga for a march on Granada. There, large quantities of bombards, as well as gunpowder, bread, wine, cattle, salt and pigs had been brought together in readiness for a huge convoy of over three thousand carts and wagons. The Spaniards, it seemed, expected to have to put siege to Granada. Also being assembled were teams of carpenters and peons or peasants equipped with ladders, iron pikes, and long poles for ground levelling or scaling operations.

Prince Ibrahim had summoned his old company from Zahara and appointed Yakoub as his principal lieutenant. After consultation, they decided to send only a very small detachment of five hundred men to the northern borders with instructions to undertake regular daily patrols and minor raids with a view to making the enemy believe that there was a large Granadan force in their vicinity. That would leave almost the totality of what now remained of the Granadan army to hold the road from Malaga.

Leonora refused point-blank to leave him. Although her identity was now generally known, she was determined to remain in the page's costume that she had made her own. Prince Ibrahim made no further attempt to dissuade her. She was, after all, no more safe in Granada than riding by his side to the field of battle, for he felt more and more that he could not leave her unprotected in the same city as Sharif and Boabdil. Ayala, he believed, would be safe enough as long as Ibn Zamnak retained his by now largely honorary and nominal dignity of Grand Vizier. He had, in any case, little choice, for there was no way in which Ayala could have begun to endure the discomforts of military life. She had, furthermore, made it very clear that she intended to stay behind in Granada and pray for his success.

It was just three weeks after his appointment as commander-in-chief that Prince Ibrahim led an army of a little over eight thousand men, including some three thousand cavalry, south towards Malaga. King Boabdil watched them from the city walls as they went past, their right arms raised in a sign at once of respect and farewell. Prince Ibrahim had seen the King only once more in order to receive the official insignia of his command. Their meeting had been short and to the point, with no warmth, and of a very perfunctory cordiality. Sharif had also been present, but the two men had not exchanged any words. Prince Ibrahim felt a feeling of pride in his breast at the sight of his eight thousand men. They were good fighting-men. Almost all of them had had some experience of fighting against the Spaniards and seemed genuinely pleased to have him as their commander. He had made no secret of the very heavy odds against them, but had also urged them to remain loyal and true to their homeland. They had responded with loud cheers. Word had inevitably spread far of his sea-battle against the galley of the Hospitallers and of his victory at *Las Malistas* in the mountains. These exploits had given him an aureole of glory, the reputation of having Dame Fortune on his side, and of being a natural winner. As for the enemy, his army was still encamped on the outskirts of Malaga and had not yet commenced its march on Granada. But there were reliable indications that this would not be delayed much longer.

Prince Ibrahim and Yakoub had quickly concluded that their best chance of success lay in an early surprise attack on the Spanish encampment. It was highly likely that after their facile triumph at Malaga, and with the certain knowledge that little remained of the Granadan army, the Spaniards would be feeling supremely confident and perhaps, with luck, also a little careless. The scouts sent out to probe the enemy's intentions all came back with confirmatory reports that encouraged Prince Ibrahim to think in terms of an early and, indeed, immediate attack. He decided to use for this operation the company he regarded as his own personal and special troop that had served him so well in the brief campaign in *Las Malistas.*

His scouts had brought back the news that the main Spanish arsenal for the assault on Granada was close by the shore, not far from that part of the harbour where his old galley still lay at her moorings. While there had been some movement during the previous two or three days, there were no indications of an immediate Spanish initiative. King Ferdinand was reported to have left Malaga for Toledo, leaving Queen Isabella behind to organise and oversee at least the beginning of the march on Granada. The notion even flashed momentarily across Prince Ibrahim's mind that he might attempt to seize her as a hostage, but he quickly abandoned the idea as totally infeasible in the light of the sheer numbers of Spanish soldiers. A quick raid on the assembly camp for the march on Granada, on the other hand, seemed to hold out quite a reasonable chance of success.

He discussed the plan of attack at length with Yakoub and his other senior officers. They had quickly concluded that their only chance of success lay in a surprise attack with the use of firebombs as their principal weapon. It was decided to equip each and every man in their company of six hundred with a bundle of rushes dipped in oil to be lit immediately before they reached the compound where some two thousand wagons and carts with their intended cargoes of animals, gunpowder, sulphur, nitre, salt and wine had been assembled.

Prince Ibrahim decided to wait until well after nightfall before making his attack. The scouts brought back the news that the Spaniards had set only the most perfunctory of guards, seemingly convinced that with the fall of Malaga there were no hostile Granadan contingents left in the neighbourhood. There appeared to be an air of total confidence in the Spanish camp with a prevalent feeling that Granada's days were numbered and, with it, a highly pleasurable prospect of slaves and booty for all.

Despite the Spanish insouciance, Prince Ibrahim made his dispositions with the utmost care. He instructed five hundred and fifty of his men to cover the last three thousand paces that separated him from the enemy encampment on foot, leaving an élite contingent as rearguard with the responsibility of looking after their horses. Every man carried a large bundle of rushes that had been well soaked in oil with specific instructions to creep forward on hands and knees as far as possible towards the Spanish compound before lighting them and hurling them into the lines of carts, wagons and livestock.

During the afternoon, dark clouds had begun to roll up from the west until by nightfall they had come to cover much of the sky, blotting out the moon and stars and reducing visibility to just a very short distance. Prince Ibrahim prayed that it would not begin to rain. Rain, when it came, tended here to fall in torrents and could well oblige him to abandon his plan of attack. It was unlikely that there would be another occasion when the Spanish wagon train would be so easy and vulnerable a target. But rain or no rain, the time had come to try this particular throw of the dice, and to hope, or to pray.

Prince Ibrahim crept forward with infinite slowness. Leonora was immediately by his side. Far away to his left and right, five hundred and fifty other men were moving stealthily forward, with only the sound of the rushes they were carrying scraping the ground and giving any indication of their presence. As they drew nearer to the carts they could hear sentries laughing and joking, occasionally bullocks brayed or snorted, asses or donkeys neighed and grunted in a bizarre nocturnal cacophony. He felt his nerves grow taut as they came nearer and nearer. There were a number of camp fires round which they could now clearly perceive the Spanish sentries. Most of them were simply sitting on the ground, but every so often one or two would rise and stroll lazily round some of the nearest wagons.

An hour or more passed by before they had all come within easy reach of their targets. There had been no drops of rain and there were now even a few patches of cloudless sky with twinkling stars that gave them a faint glimpse of light where they were lying. Prince Ibrahim could distinguish up to some thirty men on either side of him, their faces like pale grey blobs just above ground level. He raised his head and peered ahead. The wagons and carts had been drawn up in what looked like four more or less parallel lines, at distances of perhaps fifteen paces between each row. Most of the animals that they could hear snorting and braying were tethered between the rows of carts. He could see one of the Spanish sentries stroking a horse's mane and occasionally putting his face against the animal's dark skin. He could hear the horse whinnying with pleasure. He felt a momentary pang of regret at the terror he was about to unleash on those poor beasts.

Groping in his pocket he pulled out his flints and, rubbing them gently together, blew on a small red flame till the bale of rushes by his side was well alight. Looking around him it was as if a long line of will-o'-the-wisps had suddenly appeared with a first tiny pinprick of light that quickly blazed up into huge torches. Prince Ibrahim gave a shout of command and, before the handful of Spanish sentries had had time to properly comprehend their fate, five hundred and fifty Granadans had leapt across the first line of carts and hurled their blazing torches in all directions. Tongues of fire began to leap up among them and, within seconds, there were loud explosions as several wagons laden with gunpowder went off like huge bombs that seemed to set the whole landscape on fire and lit up a gruesome scene of terror-stricken animals, blazing wagons and human figures with their clothes on fire screaming as they ran. Prince Ibrahim shuddered when he recognised some of these as being his own men.

The Spanish sentries were among the first to die. Dumbstruck and paralysed by the total unexpectedness of the attack, they mostly died where they stood or sat, although some of them also became victims of the serial explosions. The wagons carrying the gunpowder had been carefully spaced out. In the bright satanic glare of what had become a roaring conflagration, the remaining munitions wagons could be easily identified and destroyed, with the Granadans able to keep their distance or take shelter as they continued to hurl burning pieces of wood or debris at the enemy wagons.

In the midst of the conflagration Leonora, who had stayed close by him throughout, caught him by the arm and pointed in the direction of Malaga. They could hear the tocsin tolling. The alarm had been sounded and Spanish troops would soon be on their way. He smiled at her.

'Samuel would have been pleased,' she shouted above the din. 'I feel that this is his real funeral pyre!'

He nodded. The same thought had occurred to him. Yelling above the hubbub he shouted the order to withdraw. It was easier to return than it had been to come for the light of the burning wagons continued to throw a lurid red light over the land. They ran whenever they could, knowing it would not be long before the first of the Spanish soldiers appeared on the scene. But his own rearguard of fifty men with all their horses would also soon be there. He regretted having to abandon all thought of destroying the Ottoman galley at her moorings, but that was simply too foolhardy.

Fortune befriended them, and all his men were mounted before the first of the Spanish soldiers appeared. They were mostly foot-soldiers but a large body of horse could be dimly perceived assembling some little distance behind them. Prince Ibrahim sounded the order to withdraw. This was no time for futile and probably costly heroics; besides, his company had done enough for one day. For them too, it had been an expensive operation.

It was not until several hours later, in full daylight and after they had put some twelve leagues between them and Malaga, that Prince Ibrahim was able to ascertain the full extent of his own losses. Twenty-eight men were wounded, some of them with quite severe burns, but no less than another twenty-eight were missing, presumed killed or maimed beyond possibility of movement by the exploding gunpowder. It had most certainly not been a bloodless victory. But the mood of the company was nevertheless one of triumph, and a feeling that they had cocked a mighty snook at Their Majesties of Spain.

The Spanish troops made no real effort to pursue them and Prince Ibrahim and his men were able to conduct the greater part of their retreat back towards Granada at a leisurely pace. A messenger had been dispatched to the capital with the news of the successful raid on the enemy's wagon train and that there was now quite a good possibility that it would force a postponement of several weeks to their intended march on Granada. Morale in the company remained high. Prince Ibrahim, for his part, was buoyed up by a feeling of exultation, even if the thought of the totally unchanged massive numerical superiority of the Spanish army could not be eradicated from his mind. It gave him pleasure, too, to see Leonora's popularity with the men. Now that her sex and her true identity had become such a matter of common knowledge, it was as if she had become a kind of mascot, or talisman, vouchsafing them victory and good fortune. Leonora clearly revelled in her new role and would often spend hours chatting, laughing and joking, alternately in Spanish and in her hesitant Arabic, and looking happier in herself than he had ever known her to be.

It was Leonora, however, who was the first, as they approached Granada, to notice the absence of King Boabdil's royal standard on the tall flagstaff close by the Alhambra Palace. Prince Ibrahim grimaced. Could that wretched man have gone off hunting at such a time? But beneath that first suspicion he could already sense within himself a deeper doubt to which he scarcely dared to give expression. His eyes met Leonora's, and it was as if he could see reflected in them the confirmation of Boabdil's treachery. He spurred on his horse and, shouting to Leonora and Yakoub to follow him, galloped at full speed to the main gateway in the city walls. Ibn Zamnak was waiting for him there, and one look at his face was enough to tell Prince Ibrahim that his worst fears had proved only too true.

'His Majesty has gone,' stammered Ibn Zamnak, 'both he and Sharif. They left yesterday afternoon, and with only a handful of attendants, saying they were going to meet Queen Isabella. They have gone to negotiate a surrender.'

Prince Ibrahim looked dumbly at him. His limbs felt suddenly like so much lead.

'The people have begun to leave,' resumed Ibn Zamnak haltingly. 'Word has spread about the King's flight. Some people are fleeing eastwards towards Almeria on the coast, taking what they can. From there they hope they may still be able to obtain passage to Morocco.'

'Where is the rest of the army?' asked Prince Ibrahim woodenly.

'Most of them are still here in Granada, or camped a little way to the north. They are waiting for your return.'

Prince Ibrahim passed his hands wearily over his face. The taste of victory had indeed turned to ashes in his mouth.

'Where is al-Zaghal?'

'He has gone. He left no news, but rumour has it that he has left for Almeria.'

For a moment or two Prince Ibrahim stared at him in silence, unseeing, unable or unwilling to believe what he had heard. Then he turned to Yakoub.

'Make sure that our company is well received. They have just won a notable victory. I will not have that spoilt for them. I will go to my sister's house. We shall talk later.'

'Shall I call upon you there?'

Prince Ibrahim shook his head and a ghost of a smile flitted across his face. 'No. For so solemn a meeting as this, only the royal council chamber will do. We shall meet in the Alhambra Palace. Meet me there three hours from now.' He waited with Yakoub until the whole of his company had ridden through the city gate. Then he spoke again briefly with Ibn Zamnak before riding on with Leonora to Ayala's house.

It was a sombre reunion. Ayala's mood had become one of desperation. Ibn Zamnak, she said, had become a virtual anchorite in the palace, cloistered there more with his own dark moods than with the King or Sharif, even before their departure. He was an utterly broken man, broken by the smashing of his dreams and bemoaning the withering of his poetic inspiration. With Boabdil's surrender she could see no future for him, or for herself.

'I have no doubt Boabdil will negotiate good terms for himself. He probably did so already long ago. But for the rest of us here in Granada, what is there left for us?' She left the question unanswered, her words trailing in the wind like wizened strands. 'But what of you, Ibrahim?' she went on suddenly, her voice abrupt and to the point. 'Where will you go, and what is to become of Leonora?'

'The war is not yet over, Ayala. We shall see. I have no doubt but that there will be a Spanish ultimatum before long. Very soon indeed. Then we shall have to decide. Back to Istanbul perhaps. Who knows?'

'Why do you wait until then, Ibrahim? Why do you not leave now with Leonora? The road to Almeria is still clear. Once the Spaniards start their final march on Granada, who knows whether anyone will be able to escape.'

'I cannot leave now, Ayala. Of all the members of the royal House of Granada, I am, it would seem, the only survivor here in this city at the present time. Boabdil has betrayed us. Al-Zaghal has gone. Our dishonour is already deep enough.'

A smile began to play on Ayala's lips. 'I recognise the brother of old in you, Ibrahim. I only wish there were more men like you here. Promise me that you will never change. Never!'

'I swear it, Ayala. You need have no fear for me. I shall not easily abandon Granada to its fate.'

The feeling of uncertainty bordering on panic that pervaded Granada was palpable as Prince Ibrahim rode to the Alhambra Palace for his meeting there with the Grand Vizier and Yakoub. This time, in the absence of the King and his newly appointed Grand Chamberlain, Ibn Zamnak had summoned three of the leading citizens of the city of Granada. They were all three clearly deeply apprehensive. Ibn Zamnak acted as their spokesman.

'Our situation is hopeless. What can ten or eleven thousand men do against so many? If we attempt to resist any longer Granada will be utterly destroyed. We can only hope and pray that His Majesty will be able to negotiate fair conditions for us all.'

'The Spaniards will be content with nothing less than something close to total capitulation,' said Prince Ibrahim brutally. 'There is a not wholly unreasonable chance that we can defend the city until winter comes. With the losses we inflicted upon them in our attack on their camp near Malaga the Spaniards will find it hard to maintain an immediate siege for very long. They might then well withdraw and come back in the spring, or they might offer us more lenient terms. The harder and more costly for them the prospects of a protracted siege, the better your chances of securing at least a few minor concessions.'

'You are the commander now of Granada's army,' said one of the rich merchants brought into the meeting by Ibn Zamnak, 'but you are not the King. We do not want to see Granada destroyed. His Majesty has taken the prudent and only possible course.'

Prince Ibrahim shrugged. 'You are right, of course. I am not the King. But I am the commander of his army. If he orders me to surrender, then I shall have no option but to carry out his royal command. But, for the present at least, there is no such order. In these circumstances the best course – and in my view the only possible one – is to prepare to withstand a siege.'

'But if His Majesty proceeds with his negotiations you will not stand in his way?' inquired Ibn Zamnak.

'If His Majesty is prepared to agree and accept Spanish terms, then I will have no choice but to comply with his wishes.'

On this note the meeting ended. It seemed very clear that among the civilians, or at least the more well-to-do, there was little stomach left for fighting. Prince Ibrahim, accompanied by Yakoub, left the council chamber with a sinking feeling.

In the days and weeks that followed, he saw a great deal of Ayala. Both she and Leonora were indefatigable, accompanying him on visits, councils and meetings with the citizens of Granada. Prince Ibrahim continued to make his intentions very clear. A defenceless city could expect only a very short shift. It was in their own best interests to fortify the city as much as they could, to the best of their ability, to prepare for the eventuality of a long siege, and to evacuate, if necessary by force, all those who were too infirm or too old to assist in the defence of Granada.

It was between two such meetings that he and Leonora were married, in a mosque, with Moslem rites. A day later, a similar ceremony saw the wedding of Ayala and Ibn Zamnak. There were few guests, and few celebrations, but for Prince Ibrahim and Leonora, at least, it brought an inner glow of happiness and satisfaction. Throughout this period no word of any kind came from King Boabdil.

Despite the fear and trembling of many of the ordinary citizens of Granada, the work on the strengthening of the defences progressed well. Every day squads of up to five hundred men were sent on military exercises, while the rest of the army worked alongside the citizens of Granada on reinforcing the city. Within the walls large compounds were established for cows, bullocks, pigs and chickens, as well as specially constructed hangars for corn and maize. Prince Ibrahim decided to keep his three thousand horses until the last possible moment. If it came to it, they would help to supplement the city's meat supply. On his orders, large quantities of animal skins were dried and dressed and held in readiness to be soaked in water and hung over the structures of the animal compounds against the risk of firebombs and arrows.

Despite the lateness of the season it was not, however, until almost six weeks later that a Spanish advance guard appeared before the walls of Granada. Apart from a few light skirmishes there was no fighting. Prince Ibrahim had ordered his entire force of just under twelve thousand men to stay within the protection of the now quite formidable city walls. The sun that first day was of a coppery hue and it was a warm late autumn day. No real help could be expected from the weather for about another four weeks at least.

Two days later the Spaniards launched their first attack, followed soon after by a second, and then by yet another. They were all three beaten off with relative ease, but it was evident that these were little more than probes intended to test the strength and determination of Granada's defenders.

The next day a sudden violent thunderstorm broke early over the city so that the water poured in torrents through the narrow streets. Awesome thunderclaps echoed and re-echoed almost as though they were announcing the imminence of some catastrophe. It was as if nature, by some strange occult means, had become apprised of Spanish intentions for, as soon as the storm had abated, the defenders could hear the blast of trumpets from the direction of the enemy camp, followed soon after by the approach of a small cortège with a herald bearing the royal arms of Granada. Immediately behind him walked King Boabdil and Sharif

Prince Ibrahim watched them from the reinforced city walls as they drew nearer. Ibn Zamnak and Yakoub were by his side. In the streets below the people, informed about King Boabdil's approach, were gathering in groups, talking, shouting and gesticulating wildly.

Prince Ibrahim motioned to Ibn Zamnak to give orders to open the main city gate, but instructed Yakoub at the same time in a loud voice to have them closed immediately after the cortège's entry into the city and to be prepared for a surprise attack by Spanish troops. Then he walked down the steps to where Ibn Zamnak, who had preceded him, was already kneeling on the ground, pressing his head against King Boabdil's stirrups. Prince Ibrahim looked at him with distaste.

For a moment it seemed to Prince Ibrahim as though the King intended to ignore him completely, but then he appeared suddenly to change his mind.

'We are returned, Prince, to our city. In one hour's time the Grand Inquisitor and the Marquis de Santillana will come to join us at the palace. Make sure that they are adequately escorted. You are to come with them.' With that, he rode on without a backward glance, but turned to Sharif with a cold smile on his face. Prince Ibrahim could hear the occasional shouts of welcome for the

King, but for the most part the people of Granada were very reticent, at once hopeful and suspicious of his return.

The time passed slowly as Prince Ibrahim waited for the Grand Inquisitor and Santillana to come. It all boded ill for Granada. He spent the time back on the city walls looking searchingly in the direction of the enemy camp. It was possible to detect a great deal of movement with large bodies of men marshalling wagons and big wooden structures that looked like giant ballistae for hurling huge boulders against the city's defensive walls. It was clear that Their Spanish Majesties were not to be easily denied their prey.

His thoughts drifted from war to Leonora. Fate had not been kind to her. Born as a princess into one of the great royal houses of Europe, only to be taken by Tunisian corsairs, sold into slavery and prostitution, and finally linked to a man who would soon have no home and who could only hope, at best, to become a fugitive and a permanent exile. For him, Istanbul was the obvious place to go, but for Leonora it could hold only the horrors of the past. But where else was there for them to go? Possibly the Sultan might send him to one of the outer provinces of the Ottoman Empire, far from Istanbul, but on the cutting edge of Moslem expansionism where he would be able to take revenge for the conquest of Granada by the Christians.

He was shaken out of his reverie by the renewed sound of trumpets as a party of ten horsemen came cantering towards the gate. Their two leaders were unmistakable. The Grand Inquisitor and Santillana were both clad in full armour but riding with their vizors up. Their eight attendants were all similarly accoutred. Prince Ibrahim mounted his horse and gave orders for twenty of his men to wait for the Spaniards in order to escort them to the Alhambra Palace.

Torquemada greeted him with a tight-lipped smile. 'So, Prince Ibrahim, we meet yet again, albeit in somewhat different circumstances. You see, you would have done better to respond to my advances when you were at Their Majesties' Court in Cordoba. Even in *Las Malistas* I was prepared to give you another chance. Now I fear you will have to pay dearly for your foolish obstinacy. But lead on, His Majesty King Boabdil in expecting us in his palace, and we would not wish to keep His Majesty waiting.'

They rode on in silence, with Torquemada glancing inquiringly and arrogantly about him, while Santillana looked thoughtful and avoided looking Prince Ibrahim in the face. He, for his part, was reflecting on Torquemada's words. They held out little joy for him. For the first time he began to have a better inkling of the hatred that this man had for him. Small groups or clusters of

Granadans had gathered in the streets as they rode slowly past. For the most part they were silent with downcast or scowling faces. There were a few occasional shouts or screams in which fear and derision mingled. Torquemada ignored them.

When they came to the palace gates, King Boabdil was there in person to meet them. To Prince Ibrahim's disgust he appeared to cringe before Torquemada who treated him with the barest minimum of courtesy. Indeed, virtually ignoring the King, Torquemada and Santillana stalked into the palace and went straight to the great throne room. Torquemada took up a position to the right of the throne with Santillana a step or two below him. When King Boabdil made to take his place on the throne, Torquemada curtly instructed him to remain standing. On his orders a handful of other persons were admitted into the throne room. Besides Sharif and Ibn Zamnak, Prince Ibrahim recognised several of the leading merchants of Granada.

Torquemada unrolled a wide sheet of parchment and began to read. 'At the express command of Their Spanish Majesties, King Ferdinand of Aragon and Queen Isabella of Castile, I have come to sign, on their joint behalf, the terms of surrender of Granada and its annexation by the Spanish realm with immediate effect. The inhabitants of Granada, save only those exceptions to which I shall return, have the choice between leaving the country with such possessions as they can carry on their shoulders, or staying on condition that they openly denounce and forswear their present idolatrous beliefs and wholeheartedly embrace the one true Christian faith. All Jews must go and leave all their possessions behind. Renegades will be burnt at the stake.' Torquemada rolled up the parchment, looking round the room, and motioned for a table to be brought forward. Taking pens and ink from one of his attendants and the act of surrender and dispossession from another, he curtly ordered King Boabdil to sign before doing so himself. As soon as he had done so he fell on his knees and raised his hands in prayer to thank God for this great moment of Christian triumph. Prince Ibrahim waited with the rest until the Grand Inquisitor had risen.

'My lord Boabdil,' Torquemada resumed coldly, 'by this signature you have ceased to be King. In future you will no longer bear that title. You will be escorted tomorrow to your new estates in the Val de Purchena in the region of Alpajarras near Cartegena. Sharif will accompany you. You, Ibn Zamnak, are free to go. But,' he continued, turning to face Prince Ibrahim directly, 'there is one to whom we cannot be so merciful. With my lord Boabdil we had reached an accommodation that would have saved Spain the cost of this campaign. The jewel of Granada would not have been tarnished. Your example, Prince, had you but heeded our urging and advice, would have led and encouraged Granadans in their thousands to accept willingly our holy Christian faith. But you chose to spurn our offers, to elope with a princess of our Royal House of Aragon, and to slaughter our soldiers. In sentencing you to die, you may have the consolation of knowing that we see in your death a symbolic extinction of any further Granadan opposition. I hope, Prince Ibrahim, that that will at least satisfy your pride, for you have always been an arrogant man.'

Prince Ibrahim looked towards Boabdil but met with only feigned, or perhaps it really was unfeigned, indifference. Sharif was smiling, as he might have expected. Ibn Zamnak was in tears. In their different ways they had all abandoned him, relieved no doubt to see him made in some way a sacrificial goat to be slaughtered in a ritualistic affirmation of Spanish triumph and affirmation.

'Have you anything to say, Prince?' asked Torquemada coldly.

Prince Ibrahim drew himself up to his full height. His mind was in a whirl and the thought of death, now imminent, left him feeling dumb. But Torquemada had hit the right chord in accusing him of overweening pride. Yes, he was proud and would continue to be so right through to the bitter, galling, end.

'You have conquered, Torquemada,' he said in a low voice. 'Fortune has been on your side. But Islam is not so easily defeated and in the East it is our star that is in the ascendant. But if there is any room in your heart for feelings other than triumph and hatred, then be tolerant and merciful towards the people of Granada. Do not mistake me. I do not want your tolerance or mercy for myself, for I am your enemy and shall always be so. But the people here ask only to live. Spain has won a great prize. Do not tarnish it with bloodshed.'

Torquemada shook his head. 'You do not understand me, Prince. The fall of Granada is indeed a great triumph for Spanish arms. But the conversion of its infidel inhabitants is an even greater triumph that we offer humbly to our Saviour. For that no price is too high. As for your overweening pride, I will only add this to it before you die. You are the only man who could have saved Granada. Boabdil here is not fit to be called a man but rather a spineless continually vacillating scarecrow, and Sharif his contemptible little lapdog. Only you have the courage, skill and determination to challenge fate itself. It was well for us that the dice were already so heavily loaded against you when you returned from Istanbul.' He paused for a moment. 'But while high policy and punishment for your crimes require your death I have agreed to Santillana's pleas on your behalf that you should be allowed three days' freedom. Their Spanish Majesties, King Ferdinand and Queen Isabella, will make a triumphal entry into Granada in four days' time. You may spend the intervening time as you wish, but we shall require your presence here, in front of the Alhambra Palace, at daybreak on the fourth day from now. As for the Princess Leonora, her future will be for Their Majesties to decide. A nunnery in all probability.'

'How am I to die?'

Despite himself Torquemada threw Prince Ibrahim a brief look of admiration.

'That will be for Their Spanish Majesties to decide. It could be by fire, by hanging or decapitation. I shall recommend the last.'

Prince Ibrahim bowed. 'Then I will take my leave. For the present.'

'You will not forget. Daybreak on the fourth day from now.'

'I shall be there.'

Ibrahim walked slowly out of the great hall without a backward look. Three days of life were left to him. It was a gruesome message to take back to Leonora and Ayala. For a moment the thought of escape flitted across his mind. Alone it might perhaps be possible although even then, with Granada's surrender, it was at best an uncertain prospect. At the same time the consequences for those he would leave behind would, he knew only too well, be very painful. Torquemada was not a man to forgo his prey.

Leonora and Ayala were waiting for him. He embraced each of them in turn, searching for the right words for the news he had to tell them. 'I bring grim news,' he said, 'sad tidings for all of us.' He stopped for a moment as both women grasped him by the hand, their arms taut and their eyes clouded with tears.

'Tell us, Ibrahim,' whispered Leonora.

'Boabdil has surrendered to the Spaniards. All Moslems are free to leave, but taking only what they can carry, or to stay and accept conversion.'

'But where can we go?' asked Ayala. 'Who will accept so many refugees?'

'There is grimmer news than that,' added Prince Ibrahim quickly. 'All Jews are ordered to leave. Renegade *conversos* are to be burned alive. I am to be executed, publicly, on the fourth day from now.'

Ayala screamed and tore at her hair while Leonora threw her arms around him, sobbing quietly. 'I shall die with you,' she murmured. 'I cannot live without you now.'

Prince Ibrahim disengaged her hands. 'My darling, you must not die. You have a whole lifetime before you. Our love was starcrossed from the first, a Moslem prince and a Christian princess. From two countries at war and one now annexed by the other. Our poor human hearts cannot overcome obstacles such as these.'

Leonora smiled through her tears. 'Four days. Three days, two days and a half, is it a fragment of eternity. We shall drink in its beauty to the full, Ibrahim. Do not try to make me survive you. At best I would be left to pine and rot in a convent. At worst . . . who knows? I will not contemplate it. We have three days, Ibrahim, almost. We must not lose a single moment of them.'

Ayala had collapsed onto a pile of heavy brocade cushions. Although still sobbing loudly she was beginning to regain her composure.

'What of me, Ibrahim? Am I to die also?'

'No. Your life, like that of all the Moslem inhabitants of Granada is spared. You are free to leave with Ibn Zamnak, if that is your wish. You will be able to take all your jewels, all those you can carry.'

'But why cannot you?'

'I am to be made an example. Torquemada paid me the compliment that I embodied a potential Granadan resistance. By publicly executing me, they are destroying in the sight of all what they consider to be the only real threat to their future suzerainty over our kingdom.'

'But why kill you? Why not just drive you out, like the rest of us? As a refugee you could do little harm.'

'A refugee is still a living man. He can dream, plot, who knows, endeavour to preach or mobilise a Jihad. A dead man can do none of those things.'

'You could still save your life, Ibrahim, if you were to become a Christian,' said Leonora quietly, 'could you not? But I do not ask that of you, my dearest. You would not be the man I know you to be.'

Prince Ibrahim smiled at her. 'You are right, Leonora. There are even times when I think you know me better than I know myself. Ayala,' he went on, turning towards his sister, 'Ibn Zamnak is free to leave. Go to your husband and make your plans to depart as soon as you can. I do not believe that there is any real danger that the Spanish Kings will break their word, but any unforeseen incident could yet put everything at risk. Leonora and I will not stray from here.'

Leonora had spoken the truth, for the next three days were as if they had been transported to Paradise. But it was not in the heated passionate thrashings of their bodies that their happiness reached its apogee, but in their quieter moments as they lay or sat close together, naked or dressed, and found delight in each other's presence, words and laughter. All thoughts of the dreadful day to come had been eradicated, deliberately and ruthlessly, so that they lived only for the brief present which they were turning into their own version of eternity. Ayala and Ibn Zamnak came twice, their mood one of despair at the fraught uncertainty of the future, until they too came to draw some comfort and joy from the radiant happiness of two beings still more unfortunate than themselves. Once, too, there was an invitation, brought by a man of Boabdil's reduced entourage, to a reception in the Alhambra Palace which he had been permitted to give by Santillana, newly appointed as the Spanish governor-general of the province of Granada, as a sign of farewell to his former kingdom. Prince Ibrahim declined the invitation, addressing Boabdil sardonically as lapdog extraordinary and buffoon-in-waiting to Their Spanish Majesties.

On the morning of the fourth day they woke early. They had not spoken again of her future, but now it was Leonora who referred to it. Throwing off their thin coverlet, she raised herself above him, brushing his face with her breasts. 'Ibrahim,' she whispered, 'I am on fire for you. Love me once more. For the last time. Know in your passion, as I in mine, that I shall accompany you this morning to that other world. No, my darling,' she said, putting her fingers over his mouth as he attempted to speak, 'no, I have decided. You cannot stop me. You do not really want to stop me.'

He seized her and crushed her between his arms so that for a moment she cried out in mingled pain and pleasure. The thought of imminent death galvanised their bodies into a tempest of totally unrestricted physical madness that almost drove them out of consciousness. It left their bodies in a state of exhaustion, but with an inner contentment at the paroxysm of joy that they had known and experienced. The tiredness still clung to their limbs as they rose, washed and dressed for the great ordeal that was to come. He wore a heavy dagger, quite openly, at his side. She had slipped her green jade poniard inside the heavy bodice of her dress. It was well past dawn when they left Ayala's house. They had bidden her a sad farewell and Ayala had wailed loudly, but Prince Ibrahim and Leonora were still filled with a feeling of happiness and contentment that swept away all apprehension.

Despite the earliness of the hour, Torquemada and Santillana were there before them in the square in front of the Alhambra Palace.

'I see you are a man of your word, Prince, even at so solemn a moment as this,' said Torquemada, 'but I did not expect it to be any different. Princess,' he went on, turning to Leonora, 'I had not expected you. Your fate is less grim. His Majesty, King Ferdinand, has decided to send you to the Carmelite convent at Santiago de Compostella. But,' he shrugged his shoulders, 'if you wish to be a witness this morning, I see no reason to object. But I will put it to Their Majesties when they arrive.'

Torquemada dismounted and went to the mid-point of the square where soldiers were laboriously dragging a large granite block into an upright position. The executioner, a small but powerfully built man, clad in black and his face hooded so that only his eyes showed, stood slightly to one side, his axe at his feet. Twelve archers in the livery of Aragon were standing in a tight group. As soon as Torquemada was out of earshot Santillana had seized Prince Ibrahim by the hand.

'Prince, you can still save your life,' he said urgently. 'Throw yourself on the mercy of our Queen. In her joy at the re-conquest of Granada, she will grant you anything.'

'Forgive?' repeated Prince Ibrahim coldly. '*She* would forgive *me*? She, Santillana, she and all of you should seek forgiveness for the rape of Granada. But I could never forgive her, nor Spain.'

'You cannot roll back the inevitable,' said Santillana. 'I would see your life saved, but your obduracy will seal your death warrant. I hear the trumpets that announce the arrival of Their Majesties. Reflect, Prince, if you wish to live.' He left to make his way towards the royal cortège, leaving Prince Ibrahim and Leonora momentarily alone.

'They will not let me stay by you any longer, Ibrahim,' she said softly. 'I shall be required to sit with your judges and executioners. Be assured, my dearest, that the moment I see your hand seize your dagger, I shall be with you. We shall leave this life together. I swear it. I only hope that we shall be able to enter the next world hand in hand.' She kissed him lightly on the lips. 'Perhaps, Ibrahim, I carry your seed in my womb. If I do, then our child will die with us. It is better so. Farewell, my darling. My eyes will be glued to yours. I shall not fail you.'

He watched her go and wait until summoned to join the royal cortège. A makeshift stand had been quickly assembled and erected close to the executioner's block. The royal party climbed up gingerly, taking their places with care. King Ferdinand and Queen Isabella were joined by the Infantas, the Grand Masters of the Orders of Santiago and Calatrava, the Dukes of Medina-Sidonia and Cadiz, Nicolo Franco, the Papal Legate, and finally, Princess Leonora with Santillana by her side. Prince Ibrahim smiled bitterly. He could draw a macabre satisfaction from the high rank of the guests invited to be present at his death. Boabdil, it seemed, had not been invited to the spectacle, nor had Sharif. Perhaps the Spaniards held them too much in contempt. Theirs was a cruel code, but also an honourable one.

Torquemada came back to him with an escort of eight archers.

'It is time,' he said.

Prince Ibrahim did not hesitate but walked firmly to the centre of the square with its granite block. Once there he looked slowly all around him. Besides those on the royal stand there were perhaps some hundred spectators, mostly soldiers and archers in the livery of Aragon. High on the Alhambra Palace the sun had caught the fluttering banners of Aragon and Castile, fitting symbols of the downfall of Granada and the triumph of Spain.

Torquemada bowed in the direction of Kind Ferdinand and Queen Isabella. 'Your Majesties,' he cried in a loud voice, 'you in your great mercy have decreed that one man could expiate the misdeeds of all your Moslem subjects. This is the man. I do not need to recount the evil he has done, the damage he has caused, or his arrogant rejection of all our overtures. He has killed; he has dishonoured a member of our royal House; and he would raise Granada against us if he could. It is fitting that he should die.'

King Ferdinand rose, carefully, from his seat. 'Prince Ibrahim Ibn Sa'd of the formerly royal House of Granada, you have heard the Grand Inquisitor's words. As the woman you dishonoured is my kinswoman, you can expect no pity nor mercy from me. It is our sentence that you should die. But we will not deny a condemned man a right to speak. But be brief.'

With one quick bound Prince Ibrahim leapt up to the top of the granite boulder so that he towered above Torquemada and his troop of liveried archers.

'I have fought for Granada, the land of my dreams, a land of magical beauty, music, poetry and enchantment. Had she known of it, I think Scheherezade would have sung its praises in The Thousand and One Nights. Would that I had her magic carpet, woven wide and large, to bring reinforcements to our defence. Today, that all comes to an end, our culture ground to dust and rubble beneath your Spanish heels. Our mosques are to be desecrated, our religion defiled, our peoples impoverished if not enslaved, and others burnt at the stake or their intestines pierced with sharp reeds because of their religious flexibility. It is a world that I do not wish to see or know. You, Kings of Spain, gloating today in your conquest, have condemned me to be beheaded. What you do with my corpse is for you to decide, but I will die as I choose.'

Drawing his dagger and clutching it with both hands, his eyes sought Leonora. 'Now, my dearest, now!' he shouted, 'and may we go together into a Moslem Paradise.' As he thrust the dagger with all his strength into his chest, he staggered, falling to the ground below. His eyes, as he did so, were still fixed on Leonora, whose ornamented green jade poniard flashed in the sun as she rushed, unimpeded, to join him into their new odyssey, into an uncharted world.